Flights of Fancy

Books by Jen Turano

Gentleman of Her Dreams: A Ladies of Distinction Novella
from *With All My Heart Romance Collection*

A Change of Fortune

A Most Peculiar Circumstance

A Talent for Trouble

A Match of Wits

After a Fashion

In Good Company

Playing the Part

At Your Request: An Apart from the Crowd Novella from *All
For Love Romance Collection*

Behind the Scenes

Out of the Ordinary

Caught by Surprise

Flights of Fancy

Flights of Fancy

JEN TURANO

BETHANYHOUSE
a division of Baker Publishing Group
Minneapolis, Minnesota

Published by Bethany House Publishers
11400 Hampshire Avenue South
Bloomington, Minnesota 55438
www.bethanyhouse.com

Bethany House Publishers is a division of
Baker Publishing Group, Grand Rapids, Michigan

Printed in the United States of America

Library of Congress Cataloging-in-Publication Data
Names: Turano, Jen, author.
Title: Flights of fancy / Jen Turano.
Description: Minneapolis, Minnesota : Bethany House Publishers, a division of
    Baker Publishing Group, [2019] | Series: American heiresses series ; Book 1
Identifiers: LCCN 2018033954| ISBN 9780764231674 (trade paper) | ISBN
    9781493417339 (e-book) | ISBN 9780764233197 (cloth)
Subjects: | GSAFD: Christian fiction. | Love stories.
Classification: LCC PS3620.U7455 F58 2019 | DDC 813/.6--dc23
LC record available at https://lccn.loc.gov/2018033954

This is a work of historical reconstruction; the appearances of certain historical figures are therefore inevitable. All other characters, however, are products of the author's imagination, and any resemblance to actual persons, living or dead, is coincidental.

Scripture quotations are from the King James Version of the Bible.

Cover design by Dan Thornberg, Design Source Creative Services

Author is represented by Natasha Kern Literary Agency.

19 20 21 22 23 24 25   7 6 5 4 3 2 1

In memory of Dolores Turano
Love you always!
Jen

Chapter 1

"Wonderful news, darling. I have it on good authority from none other than Mr. Ward McAllister that the Duke of Montrose has taken a special interest in you."

With her brief respite from the frivolities transpiring at Mr. Theodore Davis's Newport cottage clearly at an end, Miss Isadora Delafield pulled her gaze from the sight of the moon casting its beams over the ocean. Turning, she discovered her mother, Hester Delafield, advancing toward her over the seashell path that meandered through the back courtyard.

Keeping her back ramrod straight, because doing anything less would bring on a certain lecture from her mother, she refused to sigh when she noticed Hester was bubbling with excitement as she stepped directly underneath a gas lamp.

"Isn't that the most *marvelous* news?" Hester all but gushed.

"I wouldn't go so far as to claim it's marvelous. Pleasant perhaps, but . . ."

"You've attracted the notice of a duke," Hester countered. "A circumstance that warrants the word *marvelous*, especially since

7

I learned of the duke's notice from, again, Mr. Ward McAllister, the social arbiter of our day."

Isadora tilted her head. "You may be putting too much stock in Mr. McAllister's assessment of the duke's interest in me. I only recently met the gentleman. It was not as if we spent more than a moment exchanging the expected pleasantries as I was presented to the duke in the receiving line."

Hester lowered herself onto the bench beside Isadora. "From what I understand, the duke lingered over your hand. *And*, according to my most trusted sources, he's been questioning everyone endlessly about you, which leaves me to believe the gentleman is well and truly smitten."

While there was no debating that the duke *had* lingered over her hand, Isadora was convinced that the lingering had merely been a ruse used by the duke to afford him the luxury of perusing the low neckline of her gown. His gaze had all but devoured her charms, making her so uncomfortable that she'd finally, and with a great deal of determined tugging on her part, retrieved her hand from his, earning a narrowing of the duke's eyes in the process.

Because she'd been instructed from a tender age that a lady was not to annoy a gentleman with lofty connections no matter the circumstances, she'd quickly summoned up her brightest smile, which seemed to have gone far in appeasing the duke's displeasure. He'd immediately returned the smile, shot another gaze to the neckline of her gown, and then, to her utmost disbelief, he'd had the audacity to send her what could only be described as a roguish wink.

His boldness, combined with the notion that he was apparently questioning everyone about her, left Isadora with the distinct impression that the man had traveled across the ocean to secure himself an heiress, as many aristocrats were doing these days. Regrettably, he'd apparently decided she was an heiress worthy of his consideration.

"I don't have the words to describe how delighted I am by this fortuitous turn of events," Hester continued. "I've always known your beauty and reputation for adhering to the proprieties would land you the cream of the crop, but a *duke*? Why, I'm all aflutter." She flipped open her fan and began applying it vigorously to her face, the furious fanning displacing strands of dark locks streaked with only a touch of gray that her lady's maid had spent hours arranging. "This is exactly why I've been so earnest with your upbringing. It's also why I insisted you wear that back brace for years, because it forced you to maintain a rigid posture, which draws attention to your lovely neck."

"I don't believe the duke is interested in me because I possess perfect posture."

Hester stopped fanning herself. "He's undoubtedly interested in your posture. He's a duke, and as such, he needs a wife who'll do justice to the title of duchess." She released a throaty laugh. "I don't imagine there are many slouching duchesses to be found over in Britain."

"I imagine you're right about that."

Hester released a satisfied sigh. "All the dance instructions, decorum lessons, fittings at Worth, and, well, I could go on and on, but allow me to simply say that you've been groomed from birth to make a most splendid match. All of my hopes and dreams for you are now coming to pass." She began waving her fan at a furious rate again. "When word of the duke's interest spreads, I do believe our standing in society will rival that of *the* Mrs. Astor."

Realizing matters were quickly getting away from her, Isadora rose from the bench, smoothing out a wrinkle from the fitted skirt of her ball gown. She summoned up a smile, even though she was fighting a curious urge to scowl. "Not that I care to disappoint you, Mother, but I must be perfectly candid before you begin picking out my trousseau. If it has escaped your notice, the Duke of Montrose is at least twice my age. I cannot in good conscience allow you to continue believing I would ever encourage him to pursue me."

Hester got to her feet and rapped Isadora's arm with her fan. "Don't be absurd. Of course you'll encourage him to pursue you. He's a duke, and there aren't many of those roaming around these days." She rapped her fan against Isadora's arm again. "And yes, he's older than you, but older gentlemen possess an air of sophistication that I've always found most appealing. There's been many a time I've wished I'd married an older man. Your father, as you know, is only two years older than I am. That right there could be to blame for why we're rarely in accord these days."

"You and Father are rarely in accord because he cannot abide society and you thrive in it."

"I suppose that is an excellent point. However, if he'd been older when we first met, I would have known straightaway that he didn't care for society. Not that you could be aware of this, but your father, at one time, adored attending balls, operas, and the frequent house parties. It wasn't until he reached his thirties that he grew bored with what he began calling 'ridiculous frivolities,' and that is when we began living separate lives."

"If you don't care to continue living separately from him, you could always join him on his yacht as he travels the world."

Hester shuddered. "And miss the New York season? I think not." Hester's gaze suddenly sharpened as she settled her attention on something behind them. "But enough about that. I shouldn't have broached the subject of your father because our talk has caused your cheeks to heat. You know I find blotchy skin most unattractive on you." She took hold of Isadora's arm and spun her around to face the ocean. "Let us hope the sea breeze remedies that situation because, don't look now, but the duke is heading our way. I imagine he's taken leave of the amusements inside the cottage because he longs to become better acquainted with you." Hester waved her fan, not in front of her own face, but in front of Isadora's. "Now, chin up, my dear, and for goodness' sake, smile. We mustn't allow the gentleman to get the impression you're a surly sort."

Fighting the impulse to bolt in the opposite direction, one that would take her straight off a cliff and into the sea, Isadora lifted her chin, forced a smile, and turned to greet the approaching duke. Her smile slipped, though, when she noticed that the duke had stopped a few feet away and appeared to be waiting for them to join *him*.

Before she could point out that breach of etiquette to her mother, Hester was off like a shot, stopping directly in front of the duke and dipping into a curtsy.

As the duke presented Hester with a bow, Isadora took a second to study the man, something she'd not bothered to do when she'd been presented to him in the receiving line, since she'd been more interested in getting away from him than taking note of his appearance.

Like all the gentlemen tonight, the duke was wearing a formal black jacket, matching trousers, and a brilliant white waistcoat and white tie. However, unlike the other gentlemen, he'd embellished his ensemble with a variety of jeweled pins and brooches, as well as added a good deal of lace to the cuffs of his jacket.

His blond hair, which could only be considered sparse, was combed over the top of his head, and his eyes appeared small in a face overly broad and somewhat flaccid, suggesting the duke was a man who enjoyed his food.

Shaking herself from her perusal when she realized the duke and her mother were watching her expectantly, Isadora forced feet that felt as if they'd been weighed down by chains into motion. Stopping in front of the duke, she reluctantly placed her hand in the hand he was holding out to her, finding herself oddly mesmerized by the large cuff link shaped like a snake that was attached to the lace at the edge of his sleeve.

"You've led me on a merry chase, Miss Delafield," the duke began. "I was beginning to fear I'd not be able to run you to ground before my most favorite of dances is to begin, that being the waltz. But here you are and looking just as lovely as I remembered."

He brought her hand to his lips and kissed her gloved fingers. Keeping a firm grip on her hand after he was finished, he sent her a smile that had revulsion crawling up her spine.

Why the mere sight of him smiling repulsed her she couldn't say with any certainty, although it might have something to do with the ominous air she felt swirling around him, an air that was dark and . . .

"Shall we return to the ball before we miss our opportunity to waltz?" he asked.

Pulling her hand from his, Isadora consulted the dance card attached to her wrist, lifting her head a second later as a large dose of relief swept through her. "I must beg your forgiveness, Your Grace, but I'm afraid the next waltz has been claimed by Mr. Arthur Langdon."

The duke's smile turned smug. "Mr. Langdon, you'll be happy to learn, has agreed to relinquish his waltz to me after I discovered he'd claimed that dance from you earlier. But there's no need to fret that he was uninterested in taking to the floor with you." He leaned closer. "It was only through my most fervent persuasion that I was able to convince him to grant me his spot on your dance card, a circumstance that proved that you, my dear, are in high demand."

Isadora glanced to her mother, finding Hester quirking a telling brow back at her. Knowing the look was her mother's way of encouraging her to say something of a witty nature in response to what the duke clearly thought had been a compliment, she managed a rather weak "Thank you."

That less-than-witty response had Hester stepping directly next to the duke. "I'm certain Mr. Langdon was honored to relinquish his dance to you, Your Grace," Hester said. "And while I know Isadora is honored to take to the floor with you, she seems overwhelmed by the privilege you've extended to her, which has rendered her almost speechless."

The duke inclined his head. "It is a privilege I'm more than willing to extend, Mrs. Delafield. From the moment I saw your lovely daughter in the receiving line, I knew she was a young lady deserving of my *particular* attention. Her beauty and charms—or rather, *charming* attitude—drew my notice at once. You'll be pleased to learn I've decided I desire nothing more than to become better acquainted with her as the evening unfolds."

"How delightful," Hester breathed.

"Indeed," the duke agreed. "And to expedite the process of becoming acquainted with your lovely daughter, I'm certain you'll want to repair to the ballroom, allowing me a few moments to converse with Miss Delafield without any disruptions."

Hester blinked. "You wish for me to return to the ballroom and leave you alone with Isadora?"

The duke beamed at Hester, showing a mouthful of sharp teeth. "I knew you were a lady possessed of keen insight, Mrs. Delafield. So—" he waved a hand toward the cottage—"we'll join you inside momentarily, but no need to fret that our being alone will be remarked upon. Being a duke, I'm afforded certain liberties, if you will, and those liberties include the luxury of not needing a chaperone to hover over me when a young lady has procured my fancy."

For the briefest of seconds, Hester hesitated, but then, to Isadora's disbelief, her mother dropped into a curtsy, straightened, and began walking across the courtyard without another word, leaving Isadora standing beside the dreadful duke with her mouth slightly agape.

CHAPTER 2

As her mother disappeared into the shadows, Isadora was left with the distinct impression that she might have miscalculated the extent of Hester's desire to see her only daughter married *extremely* well.

Her mother had *never* left her alone with a gentleman. That she'd done so now—and with a gentleman who seemed lacking when it came to matters of propriety—was clear cause for concern.

Hester had obviously made the decision sometime over the past few years that only an aristocrat would do for her daughter, which did explain, now that Isadora thought about it, why Hester had deemed so many of Isadora's previous suitors unacceptable.

They'd not possessed the one attribute Hester clearly wanted the most for her daughter—an illustrious title and the boost up the societal ladder that such a title would deliver.

An unexpected feeling began brewing in the pit of Isadora's stomach, something that felt very much like temper.

She was not a lady prone to fits of temper, having been told endlessly over the years that ladies possessed of questionable temperaments were relegated to the sidelines of society, never allowed to reach the pinnacle of societal success.

Now, however, when faced with the daunting dilemma of dealing with a mother who'd had no qualms about abandoning her only daughter to the dastardly Duke of Montrose, Isadora relished the temper now swirling through her, even feeling an unaccustomed desire to rebel.

She'd never been a rebellious sort, had always acquiesced to her mother's demands, but when confronted with the very real threat of being married off to . . .

A hand on her arm brought her immediately out of her thoughts.

"There's no need for you to look so troubled, my dear. As I told your mother, our being alone together will not be remarked upon. And even if it is, those remarks will only be flattering toward you for drawing my attention." His lips twisted into what she assumed was supposed to be a charming smile, even though it came across as patronizing, before he tucked her hand into the crook of his arm.

"And while I do enjoy a lady who embraces a demure attitude, and I know you've had little opportunity, if any, to converse with a duke before," he continued, "our time out here will be for naught if you remain mute. With that said, allow me to move our conversation forward with a few questions."

When the duke rubbed a hand down her arm, Isadora couldn't contain a shudder, an action that wasn't lost on the duke, whose eyes began gleaming in a most disturbing fashion. Thankfully, the wind took that moment to swirl around them, lending Isadora the perfect excuse to draw their most inappropriate interlude to an end.

"I'm more than willing to answer your questions, Your Grace," she began, "but I'm afraid this wind is chilling me to the bone. I really must insist you escort me back to the ball before both of us catch a cold and our teeth begin chattering."

"Nonsense," he countered as he smiled wider than ever, revealing teeth that she only then noticed were somewhat yellow. "That's a balmy breeze if I've ever felt one and feels refreshing after suffering the closeness of the ballroom."

Isadora forced a smile of her own, although she couldn't be

certain it was a pleasant one. "Perhaps I'm coming down with more than a simple chill and have already caught a cold. If that is the case, I'll understand if you'd rather not waltz with me to spare you the chance of procuring an illness."

The duke waved that aside before he pulled her into motion and began moving at a snail's pace toward the cottage. "All three of my previous wives were constantly plagued with one illness after another, but I'll have you know I never once suffered the annoyance of catching any of their many and varied illnesses."

"You've had *three* wives?"

"Indeed."

"What happened to them?"

"They're . . . no longer with us. Died far before their time. Terribly tragic for me, of course."

"I am sorry for your losses. I imagine your children must have suffered somewhat dreadfully when their mothers died."

"Not one of my wives was capable of bearing children," he said in an offhanded manner before he stopped walking and turned his full attention to Isadora. "I'm now in desperate need of an heir and a spare, which is why I've decided to look for my next wife in America. From what I've been told, Americans are a hardy breed, and—" his gaze traveled the length of her person—"fertile."

Wishing she'd misheard him but knowing he'd spoken the word *fertile* out loud, Isadora struggled to think of something to say to that, breathing a sigh of relief when the duke opened his mouth again, apparently having more to say, although she did hope it wasn't about fertility.

"From what I've been able to gather, you're known to be quite the accomplished young lady, and I heard tell you attended Miss Gibbons' School for Girls."

"How flattering to discover you've been making inquiries about me," Isadora murmured.

"I've always believed flattery is the fastest way to impress a young lady." The duke chuckled, sending his two chins jiggling. "Flattery aside, though, allow us to return to Miss Gibbons'

School for Girls. Should I assume you received a thorough education there?"

"As thorough as one would expect from a school that educates girls, although I wouldn't claim my education rivaled that of my brothers."

"And thank goodness for that," the duke said with a bob of his head. "We gentlemen do not want our ladies to be too intelligent. All we truly want is for our ladies to possess a beautiful face and figure."

His gaze sharpened as it traveled over her person, leaving her distinctly uncomfortable, before he lifted his head and settled his attention on her face. "Your bone structure is truly remarkable, and I don't believe I've ever seen eyes that particular color of blue." He leaned closer and peered into her eyes. "Sapphire, I would say is the color, although they might appear such a dark blue because of the darkness of your hair, and then there's your . . ." He drew back, and his gaze dropped to the neckline of her gown, where it stayed as he seemed to lose his train of thought.

Not caring to be looked over as if she'd turned into a piece of prime horseflesh, Isadora cleared her throat. "I'm sure there must be attributes gentlemen appreciate in ladies other than mere physical appearance."

The duke dragged his gaze away from her neckline and shrugged. "I suppose that does have merit because I've long thought a lady's allure is increased when she possesses skill in the feminine arts such as painting and flower arranging. I also imagine most gentlemen expect ladies to be accomplished with musical instruments while having the ability to sing a pretty song without setting the dogs to howling." He patted her arm. "May I dare hope you're a lady possessed of great talent with *all* the feminine arts?"

"I've never set dogs to howling, although—"

"How lovely," the duke interrupted before she could admit that her singing had been known to send dogs scurrying out of the room. "And what of poetry? I must admit I find it enjoyable to discuss poetry with the ladies."

"I prefer discussing novels over poetry."

The duke arched a sandy-colored brow. "My dear girl, you must abandon reading novels posthaste. Novels are only suitable for the simpleminded, and you would not care for anyone to believe you're simpleminded, would you?"

Even though she'd been instructed by numerous decorum instructors to maintain an attitude of agreeableness whenever she was in the company of men, Isadora found herself incapable of agreeing with that nonsense. "I don't believe anyone could claim that novels such as *The Scarlet Letter* or *Moby Dick* are meant for the simpleminded. They're literary masterpieces, and as such, they expand the mind, not simplify it, and are two of my most treasured reads." She conjured up a smile when she realized she might be grimacing. "I also enjoy all the works of Jane Austen, finding her books to be very well written, as well as entertaining."

The duke gave a wave of a lace-embellished sleeve. "You're far too young to comprehend the dangers novels pose to the feminine mind. But take it from someone older and far wiser, you must discontinue such reading at once."

Drawing herself up to her full height, a height she just then noticed was superior to the duke's, Isadora opened her mouth, only to be denied a response when the duke continued speaking.

"May I dare hope that, unacceptable reading habits aside, you're competent on the back of a horse?"

She swallowed the argument she'd been about to make regarding novels and nodded. "I've been told I have a good seat, Your Grace. I was taught how to ride by my father, an expert horseman."

"Your instruction came from your father, not a trained riding instructor?"

"My father, Frederick Delafield, is considered an expert horseman, so there was no need to hire on an instructor."

"That does pose a problem since American men aren't known to sit a horse properly," the duke said, more to himself than to Isadora. "But no matter. I have plenty of competent instructors at my beck and call. They will certainly be able to bring your riding skills up to snuff if I come to the decision you're suitable for what I need in a . . . well, no need to get ahead of ourselves quite yet."

Her cheeks suddenly felt overly warm, even with the breeze still blowing in off the ocean. "American gentlemen are not lacking in their riding skills, sir," she replied, astonished that she couldn't seem to stop herself from arguing with the man, no matter that she knew she was courting disaster by doing so. "Nor are they inferior to any Englishman, as can be seen by their ingenuity in creating vast fortunes through the sweat of their brow and by their unrivaled thirst for advancing their many and varied business interests."

The duke patted her arm again. "My dear girl, because of my *noble* birth, I possess a superior intellect over *most* men, not simply Americans. Despite that indisputable fact, though, allow me to simply say that American men prove their *inferiority* by the mere idea they've had to use the sweat of their brows to garner their fortunes. We Englishmen, especially those of us of the aristocratic set, never stoop to manual labor."

"My goodness, but it does seem to me as if the two of you are getting on famously," Hester suddenly exclaimed, appearing from out of nowhere, as if she'd been lurking in the shadows and realized a timely reappearance was needed. "And forgive me for interrupting, but we wouldn't want the duke to miss his waltz, now, would we?" she asked, narrowing her eyes ever so slightly at Isadora before she turned back to the duke and smiled. "May I dare hope you've been able to become better acquainted with my daughter?"

"Indeed." The duke returned Hester's smile. "She's a delightful young lady, and I'm so relieved to learn she *did* attend Miss Gibbons' School for Girls—a school I've heard is quite exclusive, although not as exclusive as the schools in England."

For the briefest of seconds, Hester's smile dimmed, but then she hitched it back into place. "You'll find that my Isadora has received a most impressive education, Your Grace. And add in

19

the notion that she's perfectly capable of presiding over the most elaborate society . . ."

As Hester launched into what amounted to nothing less than a long list of accomplishments, Isadora couldn't help but feel as if she really *had* turned into a prized piece of horseflesh being brought up for auction. It was not a feeling she cared for in the least and another bout of temper clawed its way through her, temper that was apparently responsible for what she heard spill through her lips before she could stop herself.

"Shall I open my mouth so the two of you may inspect my teeth?"

Hester stopped talking and her lips thinned, but then she let out a titter and rapped Isadora with her fan, although it wasn't a loving rap and might very well have left a bruise.

"What a wonderful sense of humor you have, darling, but do know that you might want to allow the duke more time to become better acquainted with you before you bring out that humor again. We wouldn't want him to conclude you have a *sarcastic* side, would we?"

Not allowing Isadora a second to answer that absurd question, Hester took hold of the duke's other arm and, in a blink of an eye, steered them through the French doors and into the ballroom of the grand cottage.

The duke paused directly inside the doorway, waiting there as if he wanted to ascertain if all the guests would take note of their appearance, which, of course, they did.

Silence settled over the ballroom as practically everyone gazed their way, reminding Isadora of brightly colored birds of prey that had just found their next meal.

Glittering tiaras sparkled under the light cast from the numerous chandeliers, and then gloved hands were raised as the silence disappeared and excited whispers began running rampant through the ballroom.

"Your Grace," someone exclaimed, rushing up to join them. That someone turned out to be none other than Mrs. Stuyvesant

Fish, one of the worst gossips society had ever known. "I was hoping you'd reappear soon. I convinced Mr. Davis to hold off having the orchestra begin the waltz, but I must say—" she leaned closer—"the guests were beginning to grow restless, and Mr. Davis does so long to create an amusing night here at his new cottage." She straightened and gestured to the room at large, drawing even more attention their way.

She nodded to their host for the evening, Mr. Davis, a thin gentleman who was standing a few feet away from them. "His Grace has now reappeared, and with our lovely Miss Delafield in tow, so if you'll instruct the orchestra to pick up their instruments, Mr. Davis, we'll get the waltz underway without further delay."

Knowing there was no choice but to take to the floor, since doing otherwise would guarantee tongues would continue to wag, and not in a favorable fashion, Isadora soon found herself being escorted by the duke across the ballroom floor.

It took a great deal of effort to keep a smile on her face, especially when the duke kept inclining his head in a regal manner to every guest they passed, exactly as if those guests were his loyal subjects and he, being a magnanimous sort, was bestowing favor upon them.

Once they reached the very center of the ballroom, he released his hold on her and presented her with a bow, smiling in clear approval when she dipped into a perfect curtsy, then straightened.

"Lovely," he murmured right as the first note sounded. He then took hold of her hand and swept her into motion, treading on her foot in the process.

Resisting a wince, she soon found herself participating in one of the most unusual conversations she'd ever shared with a dance partner, the topic of that conversation being the proficiency of the duke's waltzing abilities.

"You're most fortunate in being given the opportunity of taking to the floor with me," he said as he stepped on her foot again. "That's twice you've put a foot out of place, my dear, but do know that I'm an expert at making my partners appear flawless with their steps, no matter their inadequacies." With that, he twirled her around with a flourish, almost knocking her into a couple that quickly darted out of their way.

Vowing then and there that she was never going to take to the floor with the duke again, Isadora wobbled for a second until she regained her balance. Lifting her head, she discovered the duke watching her with a condescending smile, as if it had been her fault she'd lost her balance in the first place.

"Shall we continue—and with a bit less theatrics, if you please?" he asked, taking a firm grip of her hand and twirling her around without allowing her the courtesy of a response.

"It's encouraging to discover you're a lady who seems to possess a most vigorous attitude," the duke all but panted after he finished twirling her around again and they were facing each other. "I cannot recall a time when a lady has managed to keep up with me, but that vigor you embrace is exactly what I've been searching for in a young lady. Pair that with your lovely hips, ones I haven't neglected to notice should be well suited for childbearing, and I'm sure you'll be delighted to learn my interest in you is increasing by the second."

Never having had a gentleman remark on her hips before, nor been in the company of a man who was so pompous and full of himself that he seemed incapable of realizing he'd crossed a boundary line that was never supposed to be crossed, Isadora could only pray the waltz would come to a swift end. Before that hoped-for event could occur, though, she suddenly felt his finger glance over the very top of her neckline.

"Ah, lovely indeed," he rasped.

Without allowing herself a moment to reconsider, she placed her foot directly in the path his foot was about to take. As he stumbled over it, his arms went flailing about, which had the immediate result of him releasing his hold on her. Without bothering to see what happened next, Isadora abandoned the etiquette rules she always adhered to, spun on her heel, and stalked off the ballroom floor, leaving the duke and his infuriating attitude behind.

CHAPTER 3

"Forgive me for being blunt, Izzie, but you've apparently gone completely mad."

Isadora tilted her parasol and settled her attention on Miss Beatrix Waterbury, her very best friend and the only person to ever call her Izzie. That Beatrix was currently scowling as she manned the oars of the rowboat they'd rented at Central Park spoke volumes since Beatrix was a lady normally possessed of a sunny disposition.

"I've not taken leave of my wits, Beatrix. I'm simply trying to avoid marriage to the Duke of Montrose, a gentleman I find utterly repulsive."

Beatrix stopped rowing. "Do you not think fleeing from New York in what I can only believe is a flight of fancy might be taking matters a bit too far?"

"Have I ever struck you as a lady inclined to flights of fancy?"

"Well, no, which takes me back to my earlier statement regarding the soundness of your mind."

Isadora set aside her parasol, leaned forward, then took hold of the oars Beatrix had now completely abandoned. Giving them a tug, which only succeeded in moving the rowboat forward a few inches, she frowned. "This rowing is far more difficult than I imagined. How is it that you're so adept at it?"

Beatrix shoved aside a red curl that had escaped its pins, blowing out a breath of clear exasperation. "Do not think you can distract me so easily from the matter at hand. But to answer your question, I've been rowing for years. My brothers taught me when I was all of five years old, and we would take our small boats out on the Hudson while visiting our country estate in Tarrytown."

"You never invited me to go rowing with you in our youth, and our country estate is but a mile away from yours."

Beatrix rolled her green eyes. "Do you honestly believe your mother would have allowed you to go off on the Hudson alone with me?"

"Probably not," Isadora admitted before she smiled. "Unless I brought a brigade of servants with me to man the boat and make certain we stuck to the shoreline."

"Which would have been no fun at all. So, moving back to your flight of fancy . . ."

"It's *not* a flight of fancy. It's a desperate attempt on my part to escape a marriage my mother is determined to see take place."

"Your mother has always been difficult, but she's not a completely unreasonable woman. I'm certain if the two of you were to sit down and discuss this situation rationally, she'd eventually conclude that this duke is not the gentleman you're meant to wed."

Isadora tugged on one of the oars, which sent the boat turning to the right. "Mother is not presently in a rational frame of mind. She actually banished me from Newport three days ago, insisting I return to the city until I agree to pen a pretty letter of apology to the duke, begging his forgiveness for giving him what amounted to the cut direct." She shuddered. "I cannot imagine the gossip that must be swirling around Newport. You know everyone will have taken note that I'm no longer there, which will then have their tongues wagging most assiduously."

Beatrix's nose wrinkled. "Your mother does loathe having even a whiff of gossip about your family."

"Exactly, but she should have known that banishing me from the summer social season would have the gossips coming out in droves. That right there proves my point about her not being in a rational frame of mind. That's one of the reasons why I'm fleeing from New York until word can reach my father that I need his assistance."

"Isn't your father traveling around the world again on his yacht?"

"He is."

"He could be gone for months."

"Possibly, but I have high hopes he'll return to enjoy the hunting season come fall. And my brothers are gallivanting around Europe, so they can't help me either."

"You cannot go off on holiday by yourself until the fall. It's only July." Beatrix looked out over the water for a long moment before she suddenly nodded. "I'll have to come with you."

"Absolutely not."

Beatrix waved the protest aside. "It's the only solution, even *if* that decision will certainly leave me at sixes and sevens with my mother." Her eyes began to twinkle. "Did I tell you that my mother is still incredibly put out with me because I disguised myself as a jockey and took my filly around the track at Jerome Park a few times?"

"You neglected to mention anything about a jaunt to Jerome Park."

"Well, I'm mentioning it now." Beatrix released a dramatic sigh. "Mother is convinced I've finally stepped beyond the boundaries of proper decorum. That's why *I* was deprived of a summer season in Newport this year and had my credit pulled from all the department stores." Beatrix grinned. "I have to admit that racing my pony down the track at breakneck speeds was well worth missing out on the tried-and-true summer frivolities."

"You've never enjoyed society's frivolities, so I'm certain being deprived of a summer in Newport is not bothering you overly much, although . . ." Isadora tilted her head. "You do enjoy your shopping."

"Which is why it's fortunate I've saved my pin money over the years for a rainy day."

Isadora nodded. "I've saved my pin money as well, and good thing I have since I'm going to need my rainy-day funds to see me through the next month or so, but *you* won't be able to come with me."

"Of course I'm coming with you. You're not prepared to take off on a holiday on your own."

Isadora turned and glanced over her shoulder, finding that while she'd been conversing with Beatrix, a gathering of gentlemen had assembled on the banks of the small lake. As soon as they seemed to notice her watching them, they immediately began waving, calling out invitations for her and Beatrix to join them.

Sending the gentlemen a halfhearted wave in return, while wishing there might come a day when she stepped outside the family mansion and wasn't recognized as one of the great American heiresses, she turned around again and tightened her grip on the oars. Drawing in a breath, she began applying herself to the task of rowing the boat as fast as she could, wanting to put sufficient distance between her and the men so she'd be free to speak with Beatrix without being interrupted. Lifting her head a full minute later when she heard what sounded like sputtering, she found Beatrix looking remarkably soggy, the reason for that evidently being all the water her rowing was sending into the boat.

Isadora stopped rowing right as Beatrix leaned forward and held out her hands. Not wanting to argue with her friend, especially since Beatrix was looking more bedraggled than usual, which was saying something because Beatrix was not a lady who was ever overly concerned with her appearance, Isadora handed over the oars.

Not that she would admit it to Beatrix, but she was rather relieved to abandon the difficult chore of rowing. She was quite certain she'd pulled a muscle, and her arms were trembling like mad.

"I have no idea how you've convinced yourself you're capable of striking out on your own on some type of holiday," Beatrix said as she began rowing them smoothly across the lake, quickly putting distance between them and the gentlemen lingering on the shore.

"I'm not going on holiday."

"So you've said, but surely you must realize that traveling around the country for a month or two is considered a holiday, especially if you decide to travel to some of the lovely resorts we've visited in the past—resorts I truly wouldn't mind visiting again."

Isadora picked up her parasol and angled it just so to keep the sun from her face. "Perhaps if I were to explain in some detail what I have planned, even though Mr. Godkin and Mr. Hatfield thought it best to leave you in the dark for your own good, you'd understand why it's impossible for you to accompany me."

"Am I to understand you haven't been completely forthcoming?" Beatrix demanded as she released her hold on the oars. "I thought we were best friends."

"We *are* best friends, and as such, you must know that when my mother discovers I've gone missing, you'll be the first one she interrogates. Mr. Godkin and Mr. Hatfield convinced me it would be for the best to leave you out of most of this mess. In fact, I don't think they'd approve of my disclosing the little bit to you I already have."

Beatrix narrowed her eyes. "How in the world did your family butler, Mr. Godkin, and my family butler, Mr. Hatfield, get involved in what I'm going to assume is some type of outlandish plan?"

Glancing around to ascertain there were no other boats nearby, especially boats filled with the members of the press who were always trailing her around the city, Isadora breathed a sigh of relief when she discovered they were well away from everyone and turned her attention back to Beatrix.

"After Mother sent me packing from Newport, and in the company of the dour Miss Carr to chaperone me no less, I immediately sought out the counsel of Mr. Godkin. He may be our family butler, but he's always been willing to lend me advice whenever I've been in need. He, after hearing my sad tale about the Duke of Montrose, sent for your butler, Mr. Hatfield, hoping Mr. Hatfield would have information about the duke since your butler used to live in London."

"And did Mr. Hatfield have information about the duke?"

"I'm afraid so, and none of it encouraging." Isadora leaned forward. "From what Mr. Hatfield disclosed, the duke is not an honorable man, and he's also not a man used to being rejected. Because I delivered him a most grievous insult by abandoning him in the middle of the dance floor, Mr. Hatfield believes the duke will now want to seek out some manner of retribution."

Beatrix frowned. "Surely you don't believe a duke would stoop to that level, do you? I've always thought that aristocrats were a most snobbish sort. I would believe your insult of abandoning him on the dance floor would have been seen by him as a mortifying setdown, one he wouldn't want to chance experiencing again."

"I would have thought that as well, but according to Mr. Hatfield, the duke is a most self-centered man, one who can't comprehend that a lady might not enjoy his company. Mr. Hatfield now fears the duke sees me as a challenge, one he's determined to win."

"He can't win a challenge if you're unwilling to participate in it."

"He can if he somehow manages to set me up in a compromising situation, which would then force me into marriage."

Beatrix's mouth dropped open. "Mr. Hatfield believes the duke capable of that type of duplicity?"

"He does." Isadora shook her head. "I also got the distinct impression that Mr. Hatfield was holding something back about the duke, something he was reluctant to disclose, but something that compelled him to encourage me to leave the city as soon as possible. That something is also what I think is behind the plan he and Mr. Godkin want to put into play—a plan that will not work if you accompany me."

Crossing her arms over her chest, Beatrix pinned Isadora with a steely gaze. "Out with it. What is this plan?"

"All I feel comfortable telling you is that it's a plan that will see me safely removed from the duke's intentions while also keeping me well away from my mother's demand that I accept the duke's suit."

"You must know that when your mother discovers you've left the city, she'll hire on the Pinkertons to track you down."

"I'm hoping that the letter I've already composed for her will dissuade her from doing that. She won't want anyone to learn that I've fled because of her demands. And I also wrote in that letter that I won't be returning to the city until after Father returns from his trip. He, I'm pleased to say, is not fond of the latest fashion of acquiring titles, so he'll set my mother straight in a trice. I simply need to stay hidden until that happens."

"How in the world do you think you'll be able to remain hidden? You're known as one of the greatest beauties of the day, your photograph graces the papers on an almost weekly basis, and you draw attention wherever you go—not that you do that on purpose, mind you, but that is what happens. You've also been, forgive me, remarkably sheltered your entire life, which means you're ill equipped to take care of yourself."

"I'm not completely helpless."

Beatrix quirked a brow. "You've never dressed yourself."

"True, but I'm sure I'll be able to figure that out. In all truthfulness, I'm looking at this as a grand adventure, a chance to strike out on my own and leave all the attention I always receive behind me."

"But it's not acceptable for a young lady to travel unaccompanied."

"It is if I'm not traveling as a society lady."

Beatrix's gaze sharpened on Isadora's face. "You will explain that remark—and in depth, if you please."

Relieved when a duck chose that moment to take flight, Isadora watched it glide across the water and land on a grassy hill that was devoid of people, save one lone man who, she was surprised to note, was waving her way in a manner that could only be described as enthusiastic. Setting aside her parasol, she leaned forward.

"Not that I'm trying to avoid answering you, Beatrix, but does that look like Mr. Hatfield over there?"

"Why would Mr. Hatfield be in Central Park?" Beatrix asked even as she turned her attention to the man Isadora was watching. "That *is* Mr. Hatfield, but what could he possibly be doing here?"

"Perhaps you should row us over there so we can ask him."

Nodding, Beatrix soon had them skimming over the water, but for some reason, she suddenly stopped rowing before they reached the shore.

"I'll take us all the way in after you finish explaining that statement you made about not traveling as a society lady," Beatrix said.

"But what if Mr. Hatfield tracked us down to Central Park because he has a matter of great urgency to discuss with us?"

"Then I suggest you spit out your story quickly."

"You're not going to let this go, are you?"

"You've known me practically all of our twenty-two years. Do you really think I'll let it go?"

Isadora blew out a breath. "Fine, I'll tell you, but not in detail. In fact, all I really think you need to know is that I'm truly not going on a flight of fancy or a holiday, but instead, I'm going, ah, undercover, so to speak, and . . . in disguise."

"Disguised as what, pray tell?"

Isadora winced. "Now, don't overreact, but I, along with Mr. Godkin and Mr. Hatfield, have decided I'll be most successful with staying hidden if I disguise myself as a servant and obtain some type of . . . employment."

For the briefest of seconds, Beatrix didn't say a single thing, but then she was suddenly rising to her feet, quite as if she'd forgotten she was in a boat. "You *have* lost your mind because—"

Before Beatrix could finish what was certain to be a tirade, she suddenly lost her balance, and with flailing arms and a rustle of expensive fabric, she tumbled out of the boat, Isadora following a second later when the boat capsized.

CHAPTER 4

Floundering as her feet touched the bottom of the lake, Isadora regained her balance, relieved to discover the water only came up to her waist. As she glanced around for Beatrix, laughter bubbled up her throat when she discovered her friend thrashing about, water dripping from her now hatless head. Beatrix stopped thrashing as her gaze settled on Isadora.

"How in the world is it possible that you didn't become completely submerged after you fell out of the boat?"

"I'm sure I have no idea, although luck might have been in play."

"I doubt that, but do know that it's highly disconcerting to discover that even when you're thrust into a mishap, you always seem to manage to retain your composure." Beatrix shoved aside hair that was plastered to her face before she looked past Isadora and frowned. "There's no need for you to come in after us, Mr. Hatfield," she called out. "Izzie and I are fine and will join you momentarily."

With Beatrix by her side, Isadora began slogging her way to shore, noticing as she did that Mr. Hatfield was in the process of rolling down the legs of his trousers, apparently having rolled them up when he'd been considering plunging into the lake to rescue them.

Reaching the shore, she took the hand Mr. Hatfield extended to her and moved to drier land. Turning, she frowned at Beatrix, who was still in the water, scanning the surface of the lake.

"Miss Beatrix," Mr. Hatfield said, releasing Isadora's hand. "What are you doing?"

"Thinking about going after my hat. I'm currently on a limited budget, and I don't have as many disposable funds as I normally do to replace a hat I found most charming."

Mr. Hatfield shook his head. "There's no time for that, and besides, your hat is most likely ruined. We must get you and Miss Isadora into the carriage, and with all due haste."

Beatrix turned from the lake and frowned. "It's not as if we're in danger of catching a cold, Mr. Hatfield. It's a balmy day."

"I'm not worried about you catching cold, Miss Beatrix." Mr. Hatfield gestured to the right. "I'm worried about all those gentlemen—along with a few reporters, if I'm not mistaken—being given enough time to intercept us."

Isadora swiveled her head and found a crowd rushing around the edge of the lake, all of whom were evidently intent on assisting her and Beatrix.

"We should go," she said, earning a nod from Beatrix in return. Picking up the sodden folds of her skirt, Isadora hurried into step behind Mr. Hatfield.

"While I have no idea why you stood up in a rowboat, Miss Beatrix," Mr. Hatfield called over his shoulder, "your mishap may have given us the perfect excuse to whisk both of you from Central Park." He increased his pace even as he raised a hand, which had a carriage moving their way. "I was concerned tracking the two of you to Central Park would raise some questions, but we've now been provided with a reasonable explanation as to why you'll be departing from the park so rapidly."

"Why would you worry about having an excuse to explain our departure from Central Park, and why are you even here?" Beatrix asked, huffing just a touch as she practically ran beside Isadora.

"There's no time to explain just yet," Mr. Hatfield said as the carriage stopped beside them. He grabbed hold of the door and pulled it open. "In you go."

Before Isadora had a chance to properly take her seat, Mr. Hatfield was slamming the door shut behind him. The carriage lurched into motion, and then they were careening over the grass toward one of the gravel paths that meandered through Central Park.

Mr. Hatfield leaned forward and pulled two blankets from under the carriage seat, handing one to Beatrix and the other to Isadora. Sitting back on the seat, he removed his hat, then ran a hand through his hair.

Beatrix began wringing water from her skirt. "Is now a good time to ask what you're doing here, Mr. Hatfield?"

"It's difficult to know where to begin."

"Does it have something to do with the ridiculous plan Izzie was just getting around to telling me—the one where she's considering going off on her own to obtain some manner of employment?"

Mr. Hatfield settled a stern eye on Isadora. "You were not supposed to tell Miss Beatrix anything about our plan."

"She was insisting on accompanying me when I told her I was going to leave the city. I really had no choice but to explain a bit about the plan so she'd understand why she couldn't come."

Mr. Hatfield turned his attention to Beatrix. "It's imperative that you speak nothing about what I'm going to disclose after you quit this carriage, because I fear Miss Isadora's very life is in danger now."

A trickle of fear traveled down Isadora's spine. "My life is in danger?"

Mr. Hatfield gave a bob of his head. "Mr. Godkin recently sent me a most urgent message, telling me that the Duke of Montrose has arrived in the city, and . . . he's currently at your residence on Fifth Avenue."

Isadora's brows drew together. "My mother had the audacity to bring the duke back to New York with her?"

"Your mother is still in Newport, which speaks volumes about the duke's true intentions. He's also accompanied by men Mr. Godkin described as intimidating, and because of that, we have no choice but to get you immediately out of the city."

"That seems a bit drastic," Beatrix said. "I've yet to be convinced this Duke of Montrose poses such a great threat to Izzie. He's a duke. One would think he'd adhere to the strictest sense of decorum, not put his very reputation in jeopardy by participating in shenanigans."

"He's not a normal aristocrat," Mr. Hatfield began as he caught Isadora's eye. "And Mr. Godkin and I were not completely forthcoming regarding the extent of the danger the duke poses to you."

"You told me he might try to put me in some manner of compromising situation," Isadora said slowly.

"And I still believe he'll do exactly that, but there's something I need to disclose to convince you that you have more to fear from the duke than merely marriage."

"I can't imagine there'd be *anything* more fearful than marriage to that vile man."

"There is, which is why Mr. Godkin and I came up with the idea of you hiding yourself in some obscure household as a servant." Mr. Hatfield shook his head. "We know it's completely ludicrous to even contemplate sending a sheltered heiress out on her own in the world, and we were actually considering revising the plan and having you take off in the company of a companion to visit the West."

"Which would be a far more practical solution," Beatrix pointed out.

"Indeed, if we were dealing with a merely determined gentleman, not a diabolical one," Mr. Hatfield returned. "But allow me a moment to explain the duke more sufficiently. That will allow both of you to understand the urgency of the situation, as well as understand why it's imperative Miss Isadora goes deep into hiding."

He settled back against the seat. "It is not well known, but I was once employed by the duke. I soon realized after accepting employment in the duke's household that he was a most disagreeable man. He treated his wife at the time in a deplorable fashion and was never satisfied by any of the services his staff performed for him. He was always in the company of intimidating men, who were tasked with the job of spying on the duke's staff. I decided it was not an atmosphere I was comfortable working in. But because the duke was known to be vindictive if someone left his employ, I was forced to put an entire ocean between us to be certain I would be able to find new employment after I left his service."

"You had to leave your country behind because you were once employed by the duke?" Beatrix asked.

"Indeed, especially after I was accused of unbecoming behavior by the duke's men, even though I'd done nothing to warrant those nasty accusations."

"That's horrible."

Mr. Hatfield nodded. "I thought so as well at the time. But then after I became employed by your family, Miss Beatrix, I realized I'd been granted a blessing instead of a punishment by having to move to America. I have more friends in this country than I ever had in England, Mr. Godkin being one of them. He's well aware of my past, which is why he called on me after you arrived from Newport, Miss Isadora. He was most distraught about what had happened to you with the Duke of Montrose and wanted to get my opinion of the man." Mr. Hatfield's lips thinned. "I'm afraid I had nothing good to say about the duke, which made Mr. Godkin realize every effort needed to be made to help you escape from the insanity that always seems to surround the duke."

Isadora wrapped her blanket a little more snugly around her. "The Duke of Montrose is insane?"

"Or evil. It's rather difficult to know for certain." Mr. Hatfield consulted his pocket watch, then lifted his head. "Mr. Godkin and I agreed to disclose to you that we felt the duke might try to force you into marriage with him, but we also agreed that there was no need to frighten you to death by disclosing the duke's foulest of secrets. With him arriving so unexpectedly in the city, though, and without being in the company of your mother, I'm afraid there's no choice but to divulge all the nastiness to convince you of the danger you're in. It will also explain why you'll have to go through with our original plan, but far sooner than we expected."

Mr. Hatfield shifted on the seat. "There's no easy way to disclose this, so I'll simply be blunt. There's always been talk that the duke did away with his previous three wives."

Silence settled over the carriage until Beatrix cleared her throat. "Forgive me if I misunderstood, but it almost sounded to me as if you said there's a chance the duke might have murdered all of his previous wives."

"You didn't misunderstand, Miss Beatrix. Whispers have been traveling through England for years about the duke and his unfortunate wives, but no one has ever been able to prove he purposely did away with them. They were apparently sickly women, incapable of bearing children, but when I was in the duke's employ, there were tales of poison being bandied about. The authorities never looked into the matter, though, since he *is* a duke and any suspicions that were brought to their attention were done so by mere members of the serving class."

Isadora swallowed. "But this isn't England, it's America. Surely our authorities would be able to stop the man from his dishonorable intentions toward me if they were told about his past."

"I'm sure they would, if they could intervene in time." Mr. Hatfield leaned forward. "What you must understand, Miss Isadora, is this: the Duke of Montrose is a crafty soul, and he's apparently determined to acquire you. If he places you in a compromising situation, you'll be ruined unless you marry him. And then, if you displease him once you're married, well . . . that's an outcome I'm certain you want to avoid."

A trace of alarm flickered through Beatrix's eyes. "But surely we can come up with a better plan than sending Izzie out to seek employment somewhere."

"There's no time to devise another plan," Mr. Hatfield countered. "Besides, even though the plan is outlandish, that's exactly

36

why it'll work. No one in their right mind would think to look for Miss Isadora in the wilds of Pennsylvania."

"She's going to the wilds of Pennsylvania?" Beatrix asked.

Mr. Hatfield's eyes grew wide. "I should *not* have told you that."

Beatrix fished a soggy handkerchief out of the reticule that was still attached to her wrist and began wiping it over her face. "But you did, so you might as well tell me all of it, and you can start by telling me where we're going since I know the carriage is not heading for Fifth Avenue."

"We're going to Grand Central Depot, but then, after I see Miss Isadora off, I'll be taking you home."

"Shouldn't you take me back to Central Park so I can fetch my buggy?"

"I've already sent the groom who accompanied me to Central Park to fetch your buggy. And while I originally did that because I wanted you to drive to Ladies' Mile, where you would have spent the rest of the afternoon perusing the shops to give you a credible alibi, that plan all but disappeared the moment you landed in the water."

He released a breath. "I'm not certain how we're going to explain Miss Isadora's disappearance now. I also don't know how we're going to convince anyone that you, Miss Beatrix, don't possess information regarding her whereabouts since I've just realized everyone chasing after you would have taken note that both of you left the park in the Waterbury carriage."

Isadora tapped a soggy-gloved finger against her chin. "What if you say that you came to fetch Miss Beatrix home because she had a pressing appointment she'd forgotten about, and you then offered me a ride because I'd gotten drenched in the lake and did not want anyone to see me in such a disheveled state?"

"Everyone knows I'm always forgetting appointments," Beatrix said, her lips beginning to curve. "And everyone knows that you never appear in public in a disheveled state, so clearly you'd want to be taken directly home. But what about Miss Carr? Your chaperone is certain to know you never arrived back at your house."

Isadora smiled. "She's not presently at home. She was most put out when you arrived to fetch me in your two-seated phaeton because there was no room for her. And because she promised my mother she would keep an eagle eye on me, I know for a fact that she'd already sent for a carriage to be readied for her so that she could follow us to Ladies' Mile, the destination I told her I was visiting today."

"You told Miss Carr we were off to the Ladies' Mile?"

"Shocking, I know, since it wasn't exactly truthful, but ever since I returned from Newport, I've been finding myself behaving quite out of character."

"The duke will know you never arrived home," Mr. Hatfield pointed out.

"Not if you tell anyone who comes asking that I had the driver let me off at the service entrance because of my sorry state."

"That could work," Mr. Hatfield said. "But we really must get down to the instructions I need to give you, Miss Isadora, before we reach the depot." He picked up a leather satchel that was lying beside him on the seat. "First, know that later on this evening—and by that I mean as late as we can manage—Mrs. Peck, your cook, will stumble upon the letter you wrote to your mother. She'll then be encouraged by Mr. Godkin to send a telegram to Newport, but by the time your mother can manage to travel back to the city, you should be safely away."

He nodded to the satchel. "After you procure yourself a train ticket, I suggest you spend your time on the train looking over the numerous advertisements I collected for you from the newspapers I found in Mr. Waterbury's study." He glanced to Beatrix. "It's fortunate your father has business interests throughout the country. He subscribes to papers from many different cities, which aided in my search for positions outside of New York. Pennsylvania papers had many positions advertised, so that is why we decided that state would be the best place for Isadora to hide."

"It is an obscure place, to be sure," Beatrix muttered as Mr. Hatfield caught Isadora's eye.

"I've numbered and circled the positions I feel are most appropriate for you, while also including letters of reference I personally penned. Those letters will hopefully aid you in securing a position."

Before Isadora could think of anything to ask because her mind seemed to have gone curiously numb, Beatrix let out a snort.

"The major flaw I see with this plan is that there's little chance Izzie will be able to pass herself off as a servant. She's never so much as touched a mop or dustcloth in her life."

Mr. Hatfield inclined his head. "That's why Mr. Godkin and I decided the position of housekeeper would be more appropriate for Miss Isadora over that of a maid."

Beatrix opened her mouth, an argument obviously on the tip of her tongue, but then she closed her mouth and frowned. "But what type of reference letter could you have penned for her? She's never worked a day in her life."

"True, but Miss Isadora does have a wonderful ability for organization, which was clearly seen at the charitable luncheon she organized a few months back." He sent Isadora a smile. "And while I may have taken a few liberties with your letter of reference, I was rather vague about your actual employment history. I never stated you'd been employed by the Waterbury family, only that you possess skill with organizing staff and households."

Isadora ignored the fact that Beatrix's eyes were now as wide as dinner plates. "I'm certain I will be more than proficient at organizing some obscure country estate. My family does employ numerous housekeepers at our various residences. From what I've observed, they seem to be mostly tasked with organizing the staff and keeping the house running smoothly."

"You've never been responsible for organizing a household staff," Beatrix pointed out.

"True, but I have conferred with our many housekeepers when my mother is unavailable."

"Conferring with a housekeeper about what flowers should be brought in from the hothouse or what meals should be added to the weekly menu is not the same as organizing an entire staff." Beatrix nodded to Mr. Hatfield. "And not that I want to point out the obvious, but there is a chance some of these potential employers will check up on that reference letter you've penned for Izzie. When that happens, you could very well find yourself unemployed if my parents get wind of what amounts to fraudulent claims on your part."

Mr. Hatfield shook his head. "It's highly doubtful your parents will learn about anyone checking up on the references since I specifically left instructions that any questions were to be directed to me." He held up a hand when Beatrix opened her mouth. "I know the risks, Miss Beatrix, and I'm willing to lose my position if the end result is keeping Miss Isadora from marrying the Duke of Montrose."

"But Izzie has never been an adventurous sort," Beatrix argued. "What's been planned for her seems to me to be an adventure of impressive proportions."

Mr. Hatfield nodded to Isadora. "Do you believe you're capable of experiencing this type of adventure?"

Isadora considered the question for a moment before her shoulders sagged ever so slightly. "Beatrix is right. I'm not an adventurous sort. I don't know if I can successfully obtain employment, let alone stay employed for long if someone offers me a position."

Leaning across the space that separated them, Mr. Hatfield unexpectedly placed his hand on top of Isadora's. "My dear, it has been my experience that God occasionally throws obstacles our way so that we're forced to grow into the people He wants us to be. You are far stronger than you think. I imagine, even with what must seem like insurmountable mountains placed in your path, you'll soon discover strengths you never knew you had."

He looked out the window and frowned. "We're almost to the depot, but if you truly believe this plan is too much for you, I'll not have the driver stop. We'll simply have to come up with something else."

Isadora glanced out the window as well, taking in the sight of carriages rumbling to and from Grand Central Depot. "You truly believe the duke has dastardly intentions toward me?"

"I do."

"And you also believe that he might have poisoned one or all three of his previous wives?"

"I'm afraid I believe that as well."

She turned from the window. "Then I really have no choice but to go through with this plan. As everyone knows, society overlooks members of the serving class, so while the plan is more than peculiar, it might very well work."

Mr. Hatfield nodded. "Very well then, let us return to the advertisements we've selected for you to answer. The best of the bunch is on top of the pile and that position is located in . . ." He trailed off and turned to Beatrix. "Perhaps you could cover your ears?"

"Not a chance, but if you're concerned someone will coerce any information you're about to disclose out of me, do know that they'll have to kill me first."

The very corners of Mr. Hatfield's lips twitched. "A bit dramatic, even for you, Miss Beatrix." He nodded to Isadora. "You'll be going to Canonsburg first, to an estate by the name of Glory Manor. We would have normally sent out an inquiry to ascertain that the position is still available since it was posted in a newspaper from a few weeks ago. However, we don't have the luxury of sending out queries, so simply travel to Glory Manor and present yourself. Then, if the position is filled, move on to the next advertisement. They're numbered for you."

Apprehension shot through Isadora. "Where is Canonsburg?"

"It is a small town outside of Pittsburgh, where no one would think to search for you. When you arrive, you'll need to ask for directions to Glory Manor, and you'll also need to hire a wagon or whatever they have available in town to take you there." Mr. Hatfield fished a black reticule out of his jacket pocket and handed it to Isadora.

"Mr. Godkin and I thought this bag might be more appropriate for a woman interested in securing a housekeeping position because your reticules are a little too . . ."

"Fashionable?" Isadora finished for him.

"Exactly," Mr. Hatfield returned. "It's filled with money Mr. Godkin retrieved from wherever it is you stash your spare funds, and there is additional money hidden in the lining of your trunk."

"I have a trunk?"

"Mr. Godkin took it upon himself to ready a trunk for you after deciding you needed to get out of town posthaste. He told me to tell you he's fairly certain he remembered to include everything a woman of service needs, raiding the wardrobes your family keeps for the members of your staff. He also wanted me to tell you he begs your pardon if he missed something, since, as a confirmed bachelor, he is not overly familiar with everything a woman needs to prepare herself for the day."

"I hope Mr. Godkin packed the plainest clothes he could find," Beatrix said. "Although I'm not certain even plain clothes will be enough to disguise the fact that Izzie's only twenty-two, far younger than any housekeeper I've ever met."

"I almost forgot," Mr. Hatfield said in response to that, reaching into a bag beside him and pulling out a pair of the ugliest spectacles Isadora had ever seen. "These have clear glass so they won't distort your vision, but I suggest you wear them at all times, and make certain your hair is always pulled tightly into a—I think women call them *buns*—on the back of your head. That will give you an unassuming appearance, although you could always consider powdering your hair to make you appear older, but I imagine there's little hope Mr. Godkin would have remembered to include powder in your trunk."

"And there's always the chance I'd forget to powder my hair some morning, which would draw unwanted questions," Isadora said.

"True, but speaking of forgetting, you must remember this at all costs—you're no longer going to be Isadora Delafield, but Izzie

Delmont, or rather Mrs. Delmont." He held out the spectacles, then smiled as Isadora slid them over her nose. "Much better." He patted the bag. "Mr. Godkin packed a change of clothing for you, which you're going to need to change into because, while the walking dress you're currently wearing is certainly charming, it's also certain to draw unwanted attention your way. And, well, it is rather wet."

"Shouldn't she go by a name that's not remotely close to her actual name?" Beatrix asked as Isadora took the bag Mr. Hatfield passed to her.

"It'll be easier for her to cover up a mistake if her alias is similar to her real name," Mr. Hatfield argued. "Besides, you're the only one to ever call her Izzie." He turned back to Isadora. "You will need to send me telegrams, keeping me informed about where you are so we'll be able to come fetch you the moment the situation with the duke is resolved, or if your father returns early to handle that man."

Isadora nodded. "I will, and you'll make certain Mrs. Peck gets that note to my mother?"

"I will," Mr. Hatfield said as the carriage slowed and pulled into Grand Central Depot. "Before we say good-bye, do you have any other questions?"

"It's not a question so much as a concern," Isadora began, lifting her head. "I'm afraid I might have a bit of difficulty changing my clothing because this walking gown buttons up the back, and . . ."

She pretended she didn't see the telling look Beatrix sent Mr. Hatfield before her friend yanked the curtains shut that covered the windows of the carriage.

"We'll join you outside, Mr. Hatfield, after I help Isadora change."

Mr. Hatfield reached for the door. "*You* will stay in the carriage, Miss Beatrix, and on that, I'll hear no argument."

Ten minutes later and dressed in a plain white blouse and gray skirt, with her hair pulled into a severe knot on the back of her head, compliments of Beatrix, Isadora found herself standing in front of a train bound for Pittsburgh.

"I'm not certain this is actually a good plan now that it's time to see you off," Mr. Hatfield muttered.

"I have a few doubts as well," Isadora admitted. "Who knew it was so difficult to purchase a train ticket, or that the station clerk would get so surly simply because I accidently asked for a ticket to Cincinnati instead of Canonsburg? I'm still a little confused why I have to travel to Pittsburgh and change to a different train there."

"Because that's how train lines work," Mr. Hatfield said, his voice holding a touch of what could only be described as panic. "Perhaps we should consider trying to hide you with friends instead of sending you out of the state on your own."

For the merest of moments, Isadora considered that. When faced with the reality of taking off on her own, the unwelcome truth of how unsuited she truly was to living in the real world could no longer be denied. Before she could voice her misgivings, though, an image of the Duke of Montrose sprang to mind. That image had her straightening her spine.

"It's a brilliant plan, Mr. Hatfield, and one I should at least try." She reached out and touched his arm. "I'll be fine. Besides, it's not as if ladies don't go off on their own all the time to seek out employment."

"True, but most of those ladies have not experienced life quite as you have."

"Which means I have something to prove—if only to myself." She smiled. "I'll send a telegram as soon as I'm able, so now all that's left to do is say our good-byes."

After giving Mr. Hatfield a kiss on the cheek, one he'd certainly not been expecting, Isadora climbed the few steps leading into the train car, took a seat, and then watched steam roll past her window as the train began to move out of the depot. Opening the satchel Mr. Hatfield had given her, she pulled out the newspaper on the top of the pile. Circled in the very middle of the newsprint was the advertisement Mr. Hatfield felt was best suited for her.

WANTED: HOUSEKEEPER
INTERESTED APPLICANTS APPLY TO
GLORY MANOR
MAIN STREET SOUTH—PAST BLACK BROTHERS FARM
1 GLORY LANE
CANONSBURG, PENNSYLVANIA

Lifting her head, she felt a bit of her anxiety fade away. Canonsburg was surely the picture of rural America, filled with lazy summer nights and fields fragrant with wildflowers. And while the small town would afford her the perfect place to hide, it would also give her a wonderful opportunity to enjoy a bit of relaxation in the country on what she was certain, given the name *Glory Manor*, was a most lovely estate.

CHAPTER 5

CANONSBURG, PENNSYLVANIA

Mr. Ian MacKenzie was a gentleman who'd acquired the reputation of being a savvy man of business. That savviness had earned him the respect of industrialists throughout the region, as well as earned him a substantial fortune before he reached the age of thirty. His ability to negotiate the most difficult of contracts meant he was always in high demand within the iron and steel industries. And he was not a man accustomed to taking no for an answer or having to resort to pleading to secure his way in the end.

However, the sight of Mrs. Gladstone, the housekeeper who'd only been employed at Glory Manor for a mere three weeks, standing in the entranceway to his aunt and uncle's farmhouse with her packed bag by her feet, had him considering falling to his knees and begging the woman to reconsider her decision to abandon her position.

"I'm certain my uncle didn't mean to frighten you with that chicken," he began, earning a huff of disbelief from Mrs. Gladstone in the process.

"It wasn't the chicken that frightened me, Mr. MacKenzie, although I wasn't expecting your uncle to arrive in the kitchen with a chicken that was very much alive after I asked him to fetch me a chicken in the first place. I was *expecting* your uncle to fetch me a chicken from the ice shed, one that was not still breathing. But, being new to the ways of living on a farm, I assumed your uncle was looking for my approval as pertained to the chicken he'd fetched." She drew in a shaky breath. "Imagine my horror when after saying that the chicken looked pleasantly plump and would make a lovely meal for supper, I then found myself the victim of uncalled-for accusations, your uncle calling me nothing less than a would-be chicken murderer."

Ian ignored the throbbing that was beginning to take up residence in his head. "I do believe I told you about my uncle's fondness for his farm animals."

Mrs. Gladstone's nostrils flared. "You neglected to tell me your uncle has an aversion to eating any of the animals on this farm, which, if you want my humble opinion, is beyond peculiar. I've never known farmers to be squeamish about such matters, although that does explain why Glory Manor receives a weekly delivery from Henderson's Meat and Poultry Company."

Because he knew there was no logical explanation for his uncle's unusual affection toward his animals, as it was simply a curious quirk the man had adopted years before, Ian settled for a shrug and a smile. "Uncle Amos has always been a man some might consider a bit eccentric. Still, it was not well done of him to rail at you. Do know that I intend to speak with him about the matter just as soon as you and I resolve the business of you vacating your position."

"There's nothing left to resolve, Mr. MacKenzie, except for you to accept my tendered resignation and to pay me the wages I'm due. I'm only thankful you received the urgent telegram I sent you in Pittsburgh yesterday and realized matters had turned nasty on your uncle's farm. Because you're now here, I feel free to take my leave from a farm where lunacy seems to be the order of the day."

"Uncle Amos is not a lunatic. He simply suffers occasional memory lapses. Those lapses, I'm all but convinced, are responsible for his behaving in unexpected ways at times."

Mrs. Gladstone jabbed a finger toward a window that faced

the front yard. "If it has escaped your notice, sir, your uncle is currently trying to walk a chicken he's attached to some type of tether about the yard."

Leaning around Mrs. Gladstone, Ian caught sight of Uncle Amos holding fast to a piece of rope that did appear to be wrapped around a chicken, one that was squawking up a storm in protest. "That's probably just another attempt on my uncle's part to see how best to keep the chickens from escaping from the chicken coop."

"Did you notice your uncle seems to have lost his trousers and is outside in his drawers?"

Ian returned his gaze to the window, squinting at his uncle, who'd now abandoned the piece of rope and was being chased across the yard by the chicken he'd tried to tether.

"He's not in his drawers. Those are pants cut off at the knee that my uncle wears to swim in, an activity he tries to do at least once a day."

"A man his age should not be wearing short pants, no matter if it's for swimming or not," Mrs. Gladstone said with a sniff. "And not that this is my business, but I've known people with memory lapses. The best treatment for those people is to have them committed to an asylum where they're kept away from normal folk and can't offend innocent bystanders by calling them chicken murderers."

Annoyance was swift.

Uncle Amos, along with his wife, Bertha, although she only answered to the name Birdie, believing Bertha didn't suit her in the least, had raised him from the age of seven, having plucked him out of his father's house, where he'd suffered immeasurable abuse. They'd given him a home at Glory Manor, fed him whenever he was hungry, and enrolled him in the local school, providing him with the education that had allowed him to crawl his way out of abject poverty and amass a fortune that would ensure he never lacked for the creature comforts in life again.

The gratitude and affection he held for them, even though they weren't related to him by blood, meant he would do whatever was in his power to keep his uncle out of an asylum, even if his uncle *did* begin abandoning his trousers and took to roaming the hills and valleys of Glory Manor stark naked.

"Suffering infrequent bouts of confusion does not warrant a stay in an asylum," he said shortly, earning a pursing of the lips from Mrs. Gladstone in response. "But because it can be a trial to deal with a person who embraces an eccentric attitude, and I understand how my uncle calling you a . . . ah . . . chicken murderer might have frightened you, allow me to present you with what I'm sure you'll see as a lucrative offer. If you agree to continue as housekeeper at Glory Manor, I'll agree to substantially increase your wages."

"How substantial?"

"I'll take your salary from twenty-five dollars a month to . . . shall we say . . . thirty dollars?"

"I think not."

"Thirty-five?"

She glanced out the window and smiled, the smile having Ian turning his attention to the scene in the front yard, a scene that came complete with his uncle galloping across the grass, apparently trying to herd what seemed like every chicken they owned back to the chicken coop.

Forcing his attention back to Mrs. Gladstone, he found her watching him with one of her bushy brows arched, a far too telling look in her brown eyes.

He had to force the next words out of his mouth. "Forty dollars."

Just as Mrs. Gladstone's lips began to twitch into what might have been a smile of acceptance, a loud ruckus came from the vicinity of the kitchen. As what could only be numerous pans falling to the floor sounded around them, Mrs. Gladstone's other bushy brow arched to join the first one even as her lips spread into a satisfied smile.

Realizing he might be dealing with a woman who possessed a

touch of talent for the art of negotiation as well but unwilling to allow her to completely best him in a business transaction, Ian abandoned all sense of pride and decided it was time to revert to charm.

Summoning up the smile he'd been told by numerous ladies was worth its weight in gold, especially since it apparently showed his dimple to advantage, Ian turned to Mrs. Gladstone. Taking hold of a hand she immediately tried to tug away from him, he lowered his voice to what he considered his most soothing of tones, used to seal many a deal over the years.

"Mrs. Gladstone, please, I'm *begging* you to accept my last offer of forty dollars a month. I'm in *desperate* need of retaining your services since I have numerous business meetings scheduled in Pittsburgh over the next month. I won't be able to leave Glory Manor if you don't stay since my aunt is still recovering from the accident she suffered last month. And while she's adamant that she can look after matters here without much help, that simply isn't the case."

Mrs. Gladstone pulled her hand from his and crossed her arms over her ample chest. "Of course she can't take care of matters without much help, not since those four children arrived here two days ago. Granted, Birdie does a wonderful job of looking after those children, odd as they are, but she's not capable of doing all the laundry that comes with adding four members to a household." She narrowed her eyes at Ian. "I did not sign up to tend house *and* four children."

"If you will recall, there weren't any children at Glory Manor when you first came to work here, nor did I have the slightest inkling children coming to live here was a possibility. Their arrival two days ago was completely unexpected and only happened because there was nowhere else for the children to go. I fully intend to hire on someone to look after them, especially since my aunt informed me only an hour ago when I arrived from Pittsburgh that she believes we need to offer the children a permanent home at Glory Manor."

Mrs. Gladstone considered him for a long, uncomfortable moment. "I might consider staying for fifty dollars a month *and* your word that you will hire on someone to look after the children as soon as possible." Her gaze turned shrewd. "I'd also like your word that after you complete that fancy house I've heard you're building outside Pittsburgh, you'll transfer me there to take up the role of your housekeeper, since I've discovered after coming to Glory Manor that I'm not fond of country living."

Feeling as if the negotiation had gotten completely away from him, Ian shoved a hand through his hair, knowing Mrs. Gladstone had backed him straight into a corner.

His demanding schedule required him to return to Pittsburgh within the next few days, but the very thought of giving in to the woman's unreasonable conditions left a sour taste in his mouth.

"I cannot promise you a position of housekeeper in Shadyside, Mrs. Gladstone, because I have no idea when I'll find the time to set the house up with furnishings. As it stands now, my new house consists of numerous empty rooms, so I have no need of a house-keeper, since there's currently nothing in my house to keep." He summoned up a smile, hoping it might melt a bit of the frost that had entered Mrs. Gladstone's eyes. "But I will increase your wage to fifty dollars a month and give you an extra day off a month if you'll agree to remain in your position here."

For a second, he thought Mrs. Gladstone was going to refuse, but then she gave a quick bob of her head. "I suppose that is a fair offer, but I'll need an extra day off every week, not simply one extra day a month."

"You already get Sundays off, and a half day off every week."

"True, but I believe I need that extra full day to help me keep a cheerful disposition."

If Ian wasn't of the belief Mrs. Gladstone did seem to think her disposition was cheerful, he would have laughed. But since he did have important matters waiting for him in Pittsburgh, and he couldn't very well attend to those matters if she abandoned her post, he refrained from laughing and forced another smile.

"I certainly wouldn't want you to lose your sense of cheer, and because you did come with a most impressive letter of reference, I'll agree to—"

Before he could get any additional words out of his mouth, even if those words did seem to be sticking in his throat since Mrs. Gladstone's terms for continued employment were nothing short of robbery, another ruckus sounded from the kitchen right before complete and utter disaster appeared in the form of a cow.

It wasn't just any cow, but Buttercup, his aunt's favorite cow and one that, for some unknown reason, was meandering ever so slowly through the kitchen door, chewing something Ian was afraid might have been the pie Mrs. Gladstone had mentioned she'd baked for after supper. As Mrs. Gladstone began sputtering, Buttercup then began ambling down the hallway, swinging her large head back and forth until she spotted a vase of fresh flowers. Stopping at those flowers, she took a moment to sniff them right before she knocked the vase over, sending water splashing over a floor he knew Mrs. Gladstone had recently mopped.

As he turned back to Mrs. Gladstone, apprehension stole through him when he found that lady shaking her head as she glared at Buttercup.

"No, I'm sorry, Mr. MacKenzie, but even fifty dollars a month and an extra day off is not enough for me to participate in the madness that's clearly descended on this place. In the interest of preserving my sanity, I believe it'll be for the best if I search out employment where I won't have to tolerate cows strolling through the house. If you'll excuse me, I'm off to see if one of the men in the barn will give me a ride into town."

Snatching up her bag, Mrs. Gladstone turned on a sensible heel and marched through the door, leaving Ian with a cow that was slowly munching on what had only recently been a charming display of wildflowers.

CHAPTER 6

Striding back into the farmhouse five hours later and feeling remarkably weary, although given the day he'd been having, that wasn't unexpected, Ian stopped directly past the threshold when he noticed that Buttercup was once again standing in the hallway.

"I hope you're happy with yourself, Buttercup. Because of your antics, I was forced to drive Mrs. Gladstone into town since no one else was willing to take on that daunting task. And then, after I dropped her at the train station, I was forced to give noncommittal replies time after time to the local townsfolk who kept tossing names of potential housekeeping candidates at me after they realized my housekeeper had fled from Canonsburg."

Buttercup let out a moo around the mouthful of flowers she was chewing, salvaged from under the table, if he wasn't mistaken.

"What are you even doing in the house? Don't you have a perfectly good barn to use?"

"She's been keeping me company, Ian, and good thing she has since I'm beginning to believe Mrs. Gladstone might have been responsible for discouraging all of my friends from coming to Glory Manor to visit. If you ask me, Buttercup did us a favor by ridding us of a most unpleasant woman."

Turning toward the voice, Ian found his Aunt Birdie wheeling herself down the narrow hallway in the wheeled chair he'd brought her from Pittsburgh. Her white hair was pulled into a stern bun without a strand out of place, but the housedress she was wearing hung on her frame, suggesting her appetite had yet to recover after she'd suffered an accident over a month before.

Leaning down when she rolled to a stop beside him, Ian kissed the wrinkled cheek Aunt Birdie presented him.

"Unpleasant or not," Ian said as he straightened, "Mrs. Gladstone was an extra pair of hands around here. You're still recovering after being tossed from that plow, and"—he continued when she opened her mouth, an argument evidently on the very tip of her tongue—"do not try to convince me you're completely healed. You're using your wheeled chair, something you only resort to when you're overly tired."

Annoyance flickered through her eyes. "I'm only using the chair because I can move at a remarkably fast clip. It has nothing to do with how tired I may or may not be. I'm not ancient, you know, only seventy."

"You're seventy-nine, almost eighty, and you suffered an accident that would have seen a woman half your age take to their bed for a month."

"I'm *tougher* than women half my age."

"Clearly, but I won't have you running yourself ragged around the farmhouse. I intend to hire another housekeeper as soon as possible."

"We don't need another housekeeper. I'm perfectly capable of managing matters on my own."

"You just offered four children shelter here—perhaps permanently—although what you were thinking when you did that, and at your age, I truly have no idea."

She immediately turned ornery. "I may be seventy-nine, dear, but age is merely a number. I've always thought of myself as being twenty-eight, which is younger than your thirty-three, and I'm more than capable of seeing after four children."

"Mrs. Gladstone said they're odd children."

"Of course they're odd. They've been uprooted from everything they've ever known."

"How did they end up here?"

Aunt Birdie's lips thinned. "From what I was told, the Duffy children were left to fend for themselves after their father went to work one morning and never returned home. The eldest child, Primrose, mentioned that her father occasionally stopped at a tavern after work and sometimes didn't return to them for a day or two. A few weeks ago, though, Mr. Duffy never came home, that sad state of affairs only coming to light when the rent came due. Apparently, when Mr. Duffy could not be found, the landlord called the authorities. The children were then hauled off to an orphanage, but once there, it was discovered there was not enough room to keep all of them." She caught his eye. "That's when someone connected with the orphanage recalled that I'd offered shelter to orphans in the past."

"And they sent you a letter of inquiry to see if you'd be willing to help?"

"No, the woman from the orphanage simply showed up here with the children—a brilliant strategy, if you ask me, because I only had to take one look at those four frightened little faces and knew it was my God-given duty to offer them a place to stay."

"But it was originally supposed to be a *temporary* place to stay?"

"It was, but I changed my mind about that after the children had been here for about an hour." She smiled at him. "You would have done the same if someone had come knocking on your door, needing a place for four wee ones."

"I doubt anyone would knock on my door since I am a bachelor. But it bothers me that someone from the orphanage asked for your assistance. Did the woman who came out here with the children not notice your slightly advanced years or that you're recovering from an accident?"

"I wasn't in my wheeled chair when she came, nor was I using my cane."

"She didn't notice the fading bruises on your arms?"

"She might have, but I also told her that with the help of Mrs. Gladstone, we'd be more than capable of looking after the children, which is why I think the woman made the decision to leave them here."

"But Mrs. Gladstone is no longer here, which means you will need to be cooperative and agree that we have no choice but to hire another housekeeper."

"I don't like you spending your money on such frivolous matters," Aunt Birdie said, spinning her chair around and wheeling it down the hallway.

Ian followed her, stopping in front of the screen door that led to the front porch. "I have more than enough money to cover the cost of a *full* staff for you here, as you very well know. But because I know you'll balk at that, we can compromise and agree I'll only hire on a new housekeeper, as well as a governess to see after the children."

"We don't need to hire on a governess. The children will attend the local school come September."

"Isn't one of the children too young to attend school?"

"Well, yes, Daisy is only three, but I'm more than capable of seeing after one little girl while the other children are at school."

"Humor me and agree to the governess."

Aunt Birdie quirked a white brow. "And if I don't care to humor you?"

"Then you'll have no choice but to eventually move in with me at my new residence outside of Pittsburgh because you're certain to become overwhelmed with the daily tasks at some point."

"Amos would go into a full decline if I took him away from Glory Manor."

"Then you'll need to agree to outside help because you must know I'll not have another good night's sleep if I'm constantly worrying about your welfare."

"You're going to resort to guilt now?"

Ian inclined his head. "I didn't get where I am today by always playing fair. If appealing to that tender heart you so efficiently hide behind your bossy nature is what it takes to get you to agree to my little request, I'm not above using that tactic."

"I'm not bossy."

"You are, and you're also the most stubborn woman I know. Your stubbornness is exactly why you didn't send me a telegram last month letting me know that Uncle Amos was no longer capable of using the plow."

"If I'd sent you a telegram, you'd have been on the first train home, taking on the mundane task of plowing up a few rows of soil to plant beans we don't even need, but beans Amos was fretting about not planting."

"True, but then you wouldn't have been on the plow. I would have."

"And then you might have been injured instead of me when the plow broke, which would have left you unable to return to Pittsburgh to attend to all those business matters of yours."

From the stubborn set of her jaw, Ian knew this particular argument was one he wasn't going to win. "What say we agree that your days of operating farm equipment are now firmly behind you."

"Fine."

"Wonderful. And you'll be cooperative about hiring on additional help?"

"I suppose that wouldn't kill me, but . . ." Aunt Birdie stopped speaking as her eyes suddenly lit up. "Did I mention that Mrs. Rogers's niece, Miss Olive Perkins, has recently moved to Canonsburg?"

A sigh escaped him. "I don't believe you did."

"Rumor has it she's a *delightful* young woman, and if memory serves me correctly, Olive might have recently held a position that had something to do with the care of children."

"Is your memory really serving you correctly, or is this another one of your attempts at matchmaking?"

Aunt Birdie looked a touch guilty. "Perhaps Olive might have been more along the lines of a lady's maid, but everyone knows some of those ladies are somewhat childlike with all the demands they make of their staff."

Ian swallowed a laugh. "You're incorrigible, but I don't need you to find me a wife."

"You haven't appeared to experience much success with the young ladies in Pittsburgh."

"I do well enough with the ladies. I simply haven't found a lady in possession of all the qualities I've decided I need in a wife."

Aunt Birdie rolled her chair an inch forward, rolling over his foot in the process. "Are you still determined to marry a lady from a society family, one who comes with a father possessed of connections that will further increase your stature in Pittsburgh business circles as well as societal ones?"

Moving well away from her chair, Ian bent over, rubbed his foot, then looked up. "It's a logical choice, Aunt Birdie, and will ensure that any children I might eventually have won't be harmed by my unfortunate ancestry. I want my future children to benefit from my fortune and enjoy all the advantages it will bring them. That means I must marry well, which means I eventually need to set my sights on a Pittsburgh society lady."

Aunt Birdie immediately took to *tsk*ing. "From what little I know of the ladies roaming the society events in Pittsburgh, they're very proper and may not be the type of women to keep you warm at night."

"Then I suppose it's fortuitous that I've equipped my new home with forced heat."

Aunt Birdie's lips twitched before she turned her attention out the screen door, leaning close to the screen. "Is it my imagination or is Amos trying to round up his chickens again?"

Ian looked out the screen, reaching for the doorknob a second later. "I'm afraid it's not your imagination, although how the chickens got out of their pen for a second time today is beyond me. If you'll excuse me, I think Uncle Amos may need some assistance."

Striding through the door and then down the porch steps, Ian reached his uncle's side, and after listening to his uncle rant about how someone was up to some skullduggery and kept releasing the chickens, Ian began herding the chickens back to the coop, a difficult task if there ever was one. Before he could get even one chicken put away, a childish shriek of delight distracted him.

Looking in the direction of the shriek, he saw a little girl of no more than three race into view and across the front yard, her chubby little legs pumping as fast as they could. Smiling at the sight, he watched her run, his smile fading when he realized she was heading directly for the duck pond. Remembering exactly how much appeal that pond had held for him as a child, Ian broke into a run and raced after her.

"Stop!" he yelled, but instead of stopping, the little girl's legs pumped faster than ever. Before Ian could catch up with her, she threw herself straight into the pond.

Not bothering to kick off his shoes, he dove into the murky water, panic flowing freely when he couldn't see so much as an inch in front of him. Fighting through algae that seemed to be attacking him, his head split the surface of the water and . . . he found himself staring at a small face, the only part of the little girl visible as she bobbed in the water, grinning as if she were having a most marvelous time of it.

Grabbing hold of her, he pulled her close. "Thank goodness you know how to float, but you're not allowed to swim in the duck pond ever again without an adult with you."

"Swim!" she all but shrieked, patting her hands against the water and sending water up his nose.

Sputtering, Ian kept a firm grip on the squirming child and began hauling her back to shore, earning himself a glare from the imp he was holding when he reached the shore and began climbing from the pond.

"Swim!" she demanded again.

"No more swimming." He set her down, brushing wet hair from her face and uncovering green eyes that were shooting sparks his way. He resisted a smile. "After we get you into dry clothes, I bet Uncle Amos would love to have you join him in the game he's playing with the chickens—a game I'm going to call 'fetch and return to the coop.'"

"Chickens!" she roared, and then, before he could remind her about the dry clothing, she was off like a shot across the yard in the direction of Uncle Amos, who'd just rounded the corner of the house, the flock of chickens now chasing him.

"Daisy didn't mean no harm, sir. She just likes them ducks that swim in the pond, but I'll be telling her she shouldn't be jumpin' in to swim with them. She's real good about mindin' me and my sisters."

Turning, Ian found a thin boy with an untidy shock of bright red hair watching him warily, his green eyes filled with worry.

"Little girls can be incredibly tricky to keep track of. That was Daisy?"

The boy nodded.

"Daisy seems especially precocious."

"What does that mean, *precocious*?"

"Trouble," Ian said with a grin. "But no time to explain the intricacies of girls just now, we've got some chickens to catch. Before we do that, though, I'm Ian MacKenzie."

"I'm Henry, sir. Henry Duffy."

Ian held out his hand, drawing it back when the boy took a step away from him. "It's nice to meet you, Henry."

Henry tilted his head. "Why isn't your last name Alderson, like Uncle Amos and Aunt Birdie?"

"Because they're not my real aunt and uncle, although they're the only family I know, since they took me in when I was just around your age."

Henry dug a bare foot into the dirt. "You were an orphan?"

It would have been easy to simply nod and leave it at that, but something told Ian that the boy standing in front of him needed to hear the full truth.

Squatting down to look Henry in the eye, Ian shook his head. "I wasn't an orphan, Henry. My mother died when I was really young, but my father was alive at the time I came to live at Glory Manor—he simply didn't want to take care of me any longer."

"My pa left me and my sisters all alone, like he done forgot about us," Henry whispered.

"I'm sorry, Henry. I imagine there's a reason your father never came back to you and your sisters, but I'm sure that doesn't lessen the hurt you're feeling."

Henry's eyes turned suspiciously bright. Dragging a ragged sleeve over his eyes, he looked away, then took a single step forward. "There's a wagon comin' down the lane. It looks like the ice wagon that was here yesterday."

Remembering how it felt to be abandoned by a father, as well as remembering how he'd not cared to discuss that event either, Ian pushed aside the questions he longed to ask Henry. Straightening, he squinted in the direction the boy was now pointing. "That is the wagon from Mummel's Ice House, but I wonder what it's doing back here already if ice was just delivered yesterday. Shall we go investigate?"

Henry nodded, and together they began walking toward the incoming wagon, their progress coming to a halt when moos of clear distress suddenly sounded from the vicinity of the front porch.

"Looks like Buttercup's stuck again," Henry said, nodding toward the porch. "She must have figured out how to open the front door, but she don't like steps. I'll go walk her through the house and out the back door." With that, Henry bolted away, calling over his shoulder that he'd be right back after he rescued Buttercup.

As Henry reached the porch, Uncle Amos rounded the house again, chickens still in pursuit, with Daisy now chasing after the chickens, flapping her little arms and giggling madly. When she caught sight of Ian, she made a beeline straight for him, lifting up her arms when she was a few feet away.

Unable to resist the child, he caught her up into his arms, then lifted her up on his shoulders, her shrieks of laughter having him laugh in return. Looking up, he frowned as the wagon that had been trundling down the lane suddenly turned around and headed back toward town, leaving a woman standing in the dust the wagon wheels had created.

She was dressed in a plain skirt and blouse, had an unassuming hat on her head, and was wearing what appeared to be spectacles on her nose. She was also, curiously enough, standing next to a large traveling trunk and clutching what seemed to be a newspaper.

"Pretty," Daisy yelled, pulling his hair with surprisingly strong fingers as she apparently caught sight of the lady as well.

"She might very well be at that, although it's difficult to say from this distance. Shall we go see why she's here?"

"Go!" Daisy yelled, giving his hair another yank.

Deciding that was excellent advice, and trying not to wince even though it felt as if Daisy had pulled out half of his hair, Ian started forward, making it all of three feet before Uncle Amos suddenly rushed into view.

That Uncle Amos was carrying his rifle was less than an encouraging sign, even with the knowledge that Aunt Birdie had hidden any ammunition to the rifle months before. Before he could intervene, though, Uncle Amos stopped, lifted the rifle, and aimed it directly at the woman.

It came as no surprise when the woman took one look at the rifle now pointed her way, let out a hair-raising shriek, spun on her heel, and dashed straight back down the lane.

CHAPTER 7

Being chased by an elderly, gun-toting man, one who was wearing short pants and shouting something about her trying to steal his chickens, was not what she'd been expecting when the helpful delivery man from the ice shop in Canonsburg had dropped her off at Glory Manor.

She'd also not been expecting to find herself deposited on what seemed to be some type of farm, complete with chickens running amok and a cow standing on the front porch.

Glancing over her shoulder, Isadora was horrified to discover that the elderly man, instead of being left in her dust, was gaining on her. Lifting up the hem of her skirt another inch, while realizing that the corset she'd fought to put on that morning at the delightful inn where she'd spent the night seemed to be coming unhooked, she increased her pace, trying to ignore that her lungs felt as if they were on fire.

Darting off the dirt lane, she headed for the forest to her right, the curious thought springing to mind that when faced with the very real threat of being shot by an obviously demented man, the idea of marriage to the Duke of Montrose wasn't looking nearly as unappealing as it once had been, even if there were rumors regarding the man and his many deceased wives.

"Uncle Amos! Stop chasing that poor woman, and for heaven's sake, put the rifle down before someone loses an eye."

Not waiting to see if Uncle Amos, apparently the name of the man chasing her, did as asked, or even bothering to see who had yelled those slightly encouraging words, Isadora jumped over a fallen log. Stumbling when she reached the other side, she regained her balance, then plowed forward into the forest, fighting through leafy branches that seemed intent on delaying her flight.

Pushing aside a springy branch, she blinked as it came flying back at her, knocking her straight off her feet and ripping her hat off her head.

Tumbling to the ground, she winced right before she found herself rolling down a steep embankment directly past the tree that had attacked her. The only saving grace she could see was that the embankment was covered in leafy green plants, ones that, thankfully, cushioned her fall when she finally reached the bottom and landed face-first in a large bunch of them.

Pushing herself up to her elbows, while wishing she'd not abandoned her gloves on the wagon ride to Glory Manor because her hands were resting in what was clearly mud, she stilled when small pebbles began rolling her way. As she lifted her head, the reason behind the rolling pebbles became apparent when a pair of muddy boots came sliding into sight, although that sight was somewhat blurry because her spectacles were now splattered with mud.

Since those boots were attached to legs that seemed far too muscular to belong to the elderly man, she didn't feel the need to flee, not that she was certain she could anyway because every inch of her body seemed to be protesting the tumble it had just taken.

When the boots stopped a few feet away from her, she tipped her spectacles down her nose and found a man frowning at her—a man who fit the word *manly* to perfection.

He was well over six feet and his shoulders were incredibly broad, their breadth shown to advantage because the shirt he was wearing was soaking wet and clinging to him. His jaw was strong, and stubborn if she wasn't much mistaken, and his lips were firm and unsmiling, but she didn't allow herself to dwell on that as she continued her perusal. His nose looked as if it had been broken at some point in time, what with the slight bump right in the middle, and his eyes were the greenest green she'd ever seen. His hair seemed to be a brownish color, but since it was also wet and plastered to his head, it was hard to say with any certainty, although . . .

"I don't mean to alarm you, but there's a large snake right beside you. It's not poisonous, and I'll take care of it, but we've got a more serious situation than the snake, because . . ."

Whatever else the man said, Isadora didn't hear because the moment he said *snake*, she turned her head. Sure enough, looking back at her out of eyes that clearly had murderous intent lurking in their depths was the most enormous snake she'd ever seen, one that was hissing and clearly preparing itself to strike.

Screaming so loudly she hurt her own ears, she jumped to her feet, turned, and rushed forward, tripping over another branch, which had her plummeting toward the ground again, landing right in the center of additional cushy green plants. Breathing in the earthy scent, she rolled from her stomach to her back and simply stayed there, praying she wasn't soon going to be consumed by a snake that could only be described as monstrous in size.

A shadow drifted over her, right before the man with the compelling eyes came into view.

Feeling at a distinct disadvantage since she was spread out on the forest floor, she stuck her hands through the plants to push up from the ground, stopping when the man moved closer.

"Don't move," he ordered in a voice that was so commanding she froze on the spot, even though she'd never in her life had a man speak to her in such a fashion.

"Is it the snake?" she whispered.

He stepped gingerly to her. "You scared it away when you screamed."

"Then why can't I move?"

"Because you're lying in the middle of poison ivy. I need you to stay still so I can get you out of there without getting more of the poison on you than you already have."

"Poison ivy?"

"It's a nasty plant that should be avoided at all costs, but since you've landed in it twice now and rolled down an embankment filled with it, it's cause for alarm."

Before she could ask additional questions about a plant that did sound rather horrid, Isadora was scooped straight up into the man's arms and brought close to a chest that was as muscular as it looked. Then, without saying a word, the man turned and began running with her up the embankment, reaching the top an impressively short time later. Instead of setting her on her feet, though, he began running through the forest, not slowing his pace even when they left the forest behind.

The next sight to catch her eye was the farmhouse she'd seen upon arrival, but instead of heading toward that house, the man made a sharp right and continued running, not stopping until they reached the banks of a pond. Before she could utter a word of protest, the man plunged straight into the water, taking her with him.

The second she hit the water, she let out a scream, which came to a rapid end when the man dropped her underneath the water, effectively stopping any additional screaming she might have been contemplating.

He then began swishing her around in the water, quite like she imagined a person might do when they washed laundry, before he finally pulled her back to the surface again just when she was certain she was running out of breath.

"What in the world do you think you're about?" she demanded. "Unhand me at once, or . . ."

The rest of what she knew would have been a scorching tirade ended when the man disappeared under the water, rose out of that water a mere blink of an eye later, and then began slapping mud he'd retrieved from the bottom of the pond over her face.

"Stop that," she all but sputtered as he continued slathering mud on her, his attention now centered on the small bit of exposed skin on her neck that the high collar of her blouse wasn't covering.

"Hold still, I'm trying to help you."

"Help me from what?"

Smearing mud down her wrist and then onto her hand, he frowned. "I'm hoping that the mud will get rid of some of the poison, but poison ivy is tricky, and there's no telling if this will work." He looked her up and down. "Not that I want to alarm you, but the poison may very well have seeped through your gown, which means you might want to remove it and really give yourself a good scrub."

She lifted her chin. "As delightful as *giving myself a good scrub* sounds, I believe I'll keep my clothing intact, thank you very much."

"I wasn't planning on staying in the pond with you while you had that scrub."

"How reassuring." With that, she turned toward the bank, preparing to make what would certainly amount to a grand exit, but she slipped in the mud and plunged underneath the water again, sputtering her way to the surface after she finally found her footing, thankful at least that her plunge had washed the mud from her spectacles.

The first sight to greet her was that of the elderly man who'd been chasing her. He'd apparently joined them in the pond while she'd been submerged, but instead of glaring at her, he was smiling broadly, his brown eyes twinkling.

"What a lovely day to take another dip in the pond," he said as he paddled up to the man who'd been slathering her in mud. "Invigorating, isn't it, Ian?" He stopped paddling and stood up next to the man apparently named Ian. "I must say it's *wonderful* that you've decided to visit us at Glory Manor. But when did you arrive, and . . ." The man turned to Isadora, his eyes crinkling at the corners. "Goodness, you've got a lady in the pond with you, one you're covering in mud, which is somewhat odd. Shall I help?"

Before Isadora could voice her objection, the man disappeared underneath the water, returning a second later with a hand filled with mud that he immediately dumped over Isadora's head.

Having no idea what to do or what to say to the elderly man who was now disappearing underneath the water again, Isadora lifted her mud-covered face to the man named Ian and discovered him smiling back at her.

"This is not amusing," she began right as the elderly man resurfaced, both of his hands filled with mud.

Unwilling to be the target of that mud, she took a step backward, losing her balance in the process and finding herself underwater yet again.

As Isadora wondered if she should simply swim away from the curious encounter she was experiencing, strong arms lifted her up, and then a steadying hand was placed at the small of her back.

"Are you all right, Miss . . . ?" Ian asked.

She pushed the spectacles that were sliding down her nose firmly back into place. "It's Mrs. . . . Mrs. Dela . . . er Del . . ." She pressed her lips together, trying to recall who exactly she was supposed to be. Thankfully, the name popped to mind a second later. "Delmont. I'm Mrs. Delmont," she said right before she was distracted by the troubling notion that her feet seemed to be sinking straight down into the muck of the pond.

"And isn't that just a shame," the elderly man said with a shake of his head. "I thought you were Ian's new wife, but since you just claimed to be a Mrs. Delmont, well, I must have been mistaken." He smiled and held out a hand filled with mud. "I'm Amos Alderson, dear, but you must call me Uncle Amos. Everyone does."

Before she knew it, Isadora found her hand being taken by Uncle Amos, mud squishing between her fingers as he gave her hand a good squeeze. He then thrust their joined hands underneath the water, swishing them around a few times until he got distracted by a duck swimming past them.

"I must see if I can beat that duck to the other side of the pond," he said, and off he went, swimming with a surprisingly graceful stroke through the water.

Returning her attention to Ian, Isadora found him watching Uncle Amos with a fond expression on what she realized was a very handsome face.

Shoving that thought aside because now was hardly the time to descend into fanciful thinking since she was standing fully dressed in the middle of a body of water, something that was becoming a frequent occurrence since she'd only yesterday been standing in a lake in Central Park, Isadora realized that while she'd been admiring Ian, he'd turned from his uncle and was watching her.

"I fear I've neglected any semblance of manners," he began, holding out his hand. "I'm Ian MacKenzie, Mrs. Delmont. I'm also really sorry for what you must see as a most peculiar welcome."

Placing her dripping hand into his, Isadora nodded. "It was somewhat unusual, and not exactly what I expected when I decided to apply for that position advertised in the Pittsburgh paper."

"Huh, imagine that. I placed that advertisement weeks ago. I wouldn't have thought there were still any newspapers carrying the posted position."

Isadora withdrew her hand from his. "I saw it in an older newspaper, Mr. MacKenzie, but thought I'd take a chance and present myself at Glory Manor in the hopes that the position was yet to be filled. From what I was told by the helpful ticket man at the Canonsburg train station, I have reason to hope that you may very well still need a housekeeper considering a Mrs. Gladstone, your recent housekeeper from what I heard, left on a train earlier today."

"And the ticket man at the train station encouraged you to travel out here and put in your application?"

"He did, as did all the gentlemen who seemed to be passing the time by sitting in rocking chairs at the train station, keeping the ticket man company."

Ian ran a hand through his hair. "I sometimes forget how word travels in small towns, but those men were right. We do need another housekeeper here at Glory Manor, and—"

Before he could finish his sentence, Uncle Amos suddenly popped up from underneath the water directly beside her, shaking his head and sending water flying from his white hair.

"Did I hear you say something about a position?" Uncle Amos asked as he pulled a water lily off his jacket and placed it in the water.

"Mrs. Delmont has come to see about a position I posted in the *Pittsburgh Gazette* a few weeks back," Ian said.

Uncle Amos watched the water lily drift away, then smiled as he returned his attention to Ian. "That must have been what Birdie was going on about the other day." His smile widened before he clapped Ian on the shoulder. "It's about time you've decided to find yourself a wife, especially since your children could certainly use a motherly influence. And how clever of you to find that wife by placing an advertisement for a mail-order bride."

CHAPTER 8

Feeling as if she'd been dropped into the middle of one of the madcap comedies she enjoyed on Broadway, Isadora turned to Ian after Uncle Amos dropped underneath the water again and found him pinching the bridge of his nose, quite as if he might be developing a headache.

"Just to be clear," he finally said when he apparently noticed she was watching him, "I did *not* post an advertisement for a mail-order bride."

"I wouldn't imagine you'd need to advertise to find a bride."

As soon as those words left her lips, Isadora couldn't help but hope the silt that was sucking her feet deeper into the pond would simply hurry up and swallow her whole. It was not like her to speak so forwardly to a man she'd only just met. She was known throughout society as a lady possessed of a distant and reserved nature, but there was simply something that was causing her to behave in a very un-Isadora-like fashion lately, and . . .

Her train of thought came to a rapid end when he flashed a grin her way. The sight of that grin stole the breath right out of her chest, robbing her of anything remotely sophisticated she might have wanted to say to him and leaving her feeling nothing like the cultured society lady she'd always prided herself on being.

"Why do I get the distinct feeling you didn't intend to voice that particular statement?"

Knowing she had nothing remotely witty at her disposal with which to respond to that, Isadora settled for readjusting spectacles that now seemed to be stuck to her hair, realizing as she did so that she'd lost her hat when she'd fled into the forest.

"You wouldn't have happened to have seen where I lost my hat, did you?" she asked, grateful to have something to say to redirect the conversation.

"It must have fallen off in the forest, but no need to fret. I'll go search for it after we get out of the water." He leaned closer to her. "I'm sorry about what happened before with Uncle Amos. He's been suffering from bouts of confusion of late. And, for some reason, he's taken to believing everyone is out to steal his chickens and cows."

"*Has* someone been stealing his chickens and cows?" Isadora asked.

"That's highly doubtful since this isn't what anyone would consider a true working farm these days. We're down to only a dozen cows, and I know for a fact none of those have gone missing. As for the chickens, they're not a creature that often gets stolen. I've just not been very successful with convincing Uncle Amos of that."

Isadora frowned. "Does Uncle Amos make it a habit to chase people around with his rifle when he decides they're out to steal his animals?"

"Will you think poorly of him if I say yes?"

Isadora smiled. "Since he's clearly suffering from an ailment probably brought about by his advanced years, no. Although I do think you might want to consider relieving him of his rifle so that someone doesn't accidentally end up dead when he's in a confused state of mind."

"My aunt has already taken the precaution of hiding all the bullets."

"Thank goodness for that." She tried to lift a foot and realized she was well and truly stuck. "I do hate to be a bother, but would it be possible for you to help me out of the pond? I can't seem to move."

In the blink of an eye, Ian was right beside her, and then, in the blink of another eye, she was plucked out of the muck and into his arms again, her breath leaving her the moment she was brought up against his muscled chest.

Calling herself every sort of ninny for apparently being susceptible to a finely muscled chest, she cleared her throat, struggling for something to distract herself from her unusual reaction to the man.

"What happened to your previous housekeeper, the one who caught a train earlier today?" was all she could come up with to say as Ian sloshed his way through the water.

"She decided to flee . . . ah . . . I mean *investigate* other employment opportunities."

"Why?"

"I could be wrong about this, but after being called a would-be chicken murderer by my uncle, and then encountering a cow moseying through the house, I believe Mrs. Gladstone realized she wasn't cut out for life at Glory Manor."

"Your uncle called her a would-be chicken murderer?"

"I'm afraid so."

"And then she encountered a cow moseying through the house?"

One side of Ian's mouth quirked. "She did, which was unfortunate because I'd *almost* convinced Mrs. Gladstone to stay on in her position."

"But the cow changed her mind about that?"

"I believe so, especially after Buttercup ate the pie Mrs. Gladstone made for supper, and then went about eating a flower arrangement I'm fairly certain Mrs. Gladstone assembled herself."

Isadora frowned. "Did your uncle also chase this Mrs. Gladstone around with his rifle?"

"Oddly enough, no."

"May I assume it's uncommon for cows to stroll through a house and then help themselves to pie?"

"I would hope so." Ian grinned. "Buttercup, though, is a most unusual cow, and she's apparently been invited into the house by my aunt, who seems to enjoy her company while she recovers from an unfortunate accident."

"Perhaps you should consider getting your aunt a dog. I imagine any housekeeper would be more accepting of having one of those in the house over a cow."

"My aunt and uncle had a dog until recently," Ian said, reaching the shore and heading up the slight bank of the pond. "Sparky disappeared a month or so ago." He stopped once he reached a grassy spot and set her on her feet. "Uncle Amos is convinced someone stole him, which is why I believe he's become so fixated on the idea that someone is out to steal all his animals."

"Do *you* believe someone might have stolen this dog?"

Ian shook his head. "Sparky was an ordinary dog, which makes it rather unbelievable that someone would want to steal him. It's more likely he suffered from an accident while he was ambling around the farm. I've yet to find any proof of that, though, since this farm encompasses many acres and Sparky's remains could be anywhere."

"That's a morbid thought."

"Indeed." He smiled. "And since it's hardly good form to discuss morbid topics with a woman I've only just met, allow me to broach a different subject. As I mentioned, the housekeeping position is available once again, and since you went through the bother of traveling out to Glory Manor, I'd be more than happy to discuss that position with you further, after I see your references, of course."

Taking a second to scratch at an arm that had begun to itch, Isadora frowned. "When you were talking about Buttercup, you mentioned she'd eaten a pie that Mrs. Gladstone made. Did she make that pie because she loves to bake, or is baking a skill you expect from a housekeeper?"

Ian returned the frown. "You do know how to cook, don't you?"

"Would it ruin my chances of having you offer me employment if I admit I don't?"

"How can a housekeeper not know how to cook?"

"Have you employed many housekeepers here at Glory Manor?"

"Well, no."

She smiled. "That explains it, then. You see, most houses that have the wherewithal to employ housekeepers also have the wherewithal to employ cooks. That is why I've never been required, or even asked, to cook for a family before."

"I have the wherewithal to employ a cook, but it took every negotiating skill I possess to get my aunt to even agree to bring on a housekeeper."

Isadora began squeezing water out of a skirt that was most assuredly ruined. "I didn't mean to suggest you were incapable of paying a cook, Mr. MacKenzie. I was simply trying to explain why I've never been required to cook. The houses I'm accustomed to organizing have all had large staffs, something I assumed would be the case at a country estate named Glory Manor."

"What's your idea of a large staff?"

"The usual, I expect—a butler, housekeeper, a wide assortment of maids, numerous footmen, and then grooms and stable masters to look after the horses."

"Besides the housekeeping position, we only employ a few men to help with the animals."

She tilted her head. "Which does explain why you'd want a housekeeper comfortable with fixing meals."

"And you're not comfortable with that?"

"I'm not what anyone would call proficient in the kitchen, and that's not false modesty on my part." She swiped her sleeve over her spectacles, smearing a touch of mud over the glass in the process. Lowering her hand, she peered through the now-murky lenses, finding Ian watching her closely. "Should I assume you've already decided I'm not right for the job?"

To her surprise, Ian shook his head. "You may not be fully qualified for the type of housekeeping position we need here, but I do have another position available, one that does not involve cooking but merely taking care of a few children—four, to be exact."

"You have four children?"

He shook his head. "They're not mine and have only recently come to live at Glory Manor, much to my surprise."

"How is it possible you were surprised to find four children living at your home?"

"This is my aunt and uncle's home."

"But you live here?"

"Occasionally, although I mostly only visit these—"

"Swim!"

"Oh no, not again," Ian exclaimed right as a little girl with red hair plaited in two messy braids ran into view, her chubby little legs carrying her toward the opposite side of the pond, her clothing apparently having been abandoned somewhere along the way since she was completely naked.

"Daisy, no!" Ian shouted as he turned and raced back into the pond, diving through the water and then swimming for the other side, his strong strokes no match for the determined child now racing for the water. The little girl darted to the right, then to the left before she launched herself into the air, hitting the water a second later with a gleeful shriek right before she disappeared under the water.

Without hesitating, Isadora dove into the water as well, knowing there was little chance Ian would have seen where the child had entered the water since he'd been swimming furiously toward a spot the child was no longer near. She made it all of ten strokes before realizing she'd made a very grave mistake.

The heaviness of her clothing was beginning to suck her underneath the water, and her skirt was tangling around her legs, making it next to impossible to kick herself back up to the surface.

Before she knew it, she was dropping through the water like a stone, descending foot after foot with alarming speed.

When she finally reached the bottom of the pond, she was almost out of air, so planting her feet as firmly as she could on the squishy pond floor, she pushed off from the floor with every bit of strength she had left, her efforts all for naught when she jolted to an abrupt stop.

The reason for the stop became immediately clear.

Her skirt was caught on something she couldn't see through the murky water, and no matter how hard she tugged, she couldn't get free.

As her lungs continued to protest their lack of air, panic swept over her when the thought sprang to mind that she was not going to be able to free herself in time.

Stars began to form behind her eyes, but then a hand suddenly wrapped around her arm and began tugging her upward, that hand disappearing when she didn't move more than a few inches.

As darkness began to take hold, Isadora felt something sharp against her hip and then she felt a lovely sense of weightlessness that allowed her to begin moving upward.

Wondering if she'd be greeted by her grandparents when she reached heaven's gate, a place she was convinced she was about to enter, her wondering came to a rapid end when bright light almost blinded her, and then . . . she drifted back into lovely darkness . . . until . . .

Air was suddenly pushing into her lungs, the source of that air coming from something placed over her lips, something that felt surprisingly supple and . . .

"Come on, Mrs. Delmont, you can do this. Breathe."

Additional air filled her lungs as Isadora realized that air was coming directly out of someone's mouth but . . . that couldn't be right . . . unless . . .

Further contemplation was abruptly pushed aside when water that was swishing around inside her began rising up her throat. Jerking her head to the right, which effectively left behind the lips she thought might have been attached to hers, she coughed up what felt like half the pond, gasping for breath.

"I thought she was a goner for certain."

"She was underwater for a really long time."

"Was you kissing her, Mr. Ian, because you thought she was dead and you were sayin' good-bye to her, but now that she's not dead and you were kissing her, you're gonna marry her?"

"I wasn't kissing her, Henry," Isadora heard Ian say. "I was trying to get her to breathe, and there's no need to call me Mr. Ian. Ian will do just fine."

"It sure did look like kissing to me," another voice chimed in, this one belonging to a girl. "And my mama used to always tell me that if you kissed a boy, you was gonna have to marry that boy, so you'd better be sure you liked him. Do you think that lady likes you, mister?"

"His name's Ian," the boy named Henry said. "And his last name isn't Alderson like Aunt Birdie or Uncle Amos, it's Mac-Kenzie, *and* he lived here from when he was my age until he done grew up."

"Aunt Birdie says she's gonna see about having us live here until we grow up too," the girl said. "And since you was just kissing that lady, Ian, I bet she'll come live with us here after the two of you get married and all."

Isadora's eyes flew open, and she discovered numerous faces peering down at her, four of those faces belonging to children, one of whom, she was relieved to discover, was the small girl who'd jumped into the pond.

"We're not getting married," she finally rasped as she coughed again and grimaced at the brackish taste in her mouth. "Although I am curious as to why you were kissing me."

Ian frowned even as he pulled open one of her eyes, peered into it, then did the same with her other eye. "I wasn't kissing you, Mrs. Delmont, I was trying to revive you. I once saw a man trying to bring around another man by breathing for him. And after I got you back to shore and noticed you weren't breathing, that's the first thing to spring to mind, and thankfully, it worked."

Ignoring the fact that her lips were tingling, assuredly so because his lips had only recently been pressed against them, Isadora pushed herself to a sitting position. "And did that man recover as well?"

"I do believe he did." He lifted his head and smiled at the children. "Why don't all of you take Daisy to the water pump, get her cleaned up a bit, and then perhaps see if she remembers where she abandoned her clothes?"

"Daisy don't like the water from the water pump," the boy said, crossing his arms over his chest.

"Perhaps a bath would be more inviting," Isadora said, her suggestion having the curious effect of the children looking at her in what could only be described as horror right before they bolted away, leaving her and Ian alone.

Isadora frowned. "That wasn't the reaction I was expecting."

Ian frowned as well as he considered the retreating children before he looked back to her. "Indeed, but since I'm not overly familiar with these children, I'm afraid I have no ready explanation regarding their unexpected flight."

"Perhaps we should go after them to discern what it was I said that apparently offended them."

"An excellent suggestion to be sure, and one that suggests you're more familiar with children than I am."

Before she could contradict that, Uncle Amos came splashing out of the pond, holding a dripping piece of fabric in his hand.

"Thought you might like to be reunited with this," he said, holding out the piece of fabric. "I think it's part of your skirt."

Glancing down, she felt heat flood her face when her gaze settled on legs that were barely covered by her petticoats and the ragged remains of what had once been a rather drab skirt.

"Sorry about that," Ian said with a nod to her legs. "Your skirt was snagged on a branch at the bottom of the pond." He pulled a wicked-looking knife from the waistband of his trousers. "Lucky I had this on me to cut you free, but I'm afraid your skirt is probably beyond repair."

"I have other skirts in my trunk, and if someone could fetch that trunk for me, I'd appreciate it. I'm hardly making a good impression dressed in my petticoats."

Ian sent her a rueful smile. "Since I'm the one responsible for your current predicament, I don't think you have to worry about the type of impression you're making."

His smile sent additional heat traveling to her cheeks, but she was suddenly distracted from his smile when she caught a glimpse of her hand and noticed what seemed to be red bumps on it.

"How peculiar," she said, turning her hand from side to side as she looked it over.

Kneeling beside her, Ian took hold of her hand, studying it for a brief moment before he lifted his head. "I was hoping you'd be spared this after we got you washed off."

"What do you mean?"

"Unfortunately, you seem to be unusually susceptible to poison ivy and are already showing some symptoms from your encounter with the plant." His eyes widened as he peered at her face.

"What is it?" she whispered.

"We'd best get you up to the house" was all he said to that.

She soon found herself in his arms again, held against a chest she couldn't appreciate as much this time, the reason for the lack of appreciation all due to the unfortunate reality that she was beginning to itch . . . quite dreadfully.

CHAPTER 9

THREE DAYS LATER

"I'm beginning to think arming Mrs. Delmont with a cowbell might not have been the most brilliant of ideas," Ian said, pausing in the doorway of the kitchen as the clang of the cowbell echoed through the ceiling directly above his head.

Aunt Birdie looked up from where she'd been sorting through cookie cutters at the kitchen table. "She does seem to enjoy ringing the bell, but since my hearing isn't what it used to be, it doesn't bother me in the least. And because I don't want to suffer another lecture from you about overexerting myself, I've become quite adept at ignoring the clanging instead of going upstairs to see what Mrs. Delmont needs."

Knowing his aunt grew overly tired whenever she tried to climb stairs, while also knowing she *wasn't* bothered by any of the many lectures he'd given her since her accident, Ian settled for sending her a smile as he glanced at the ceiling again. "Don't you find it curious that a woman intent on procuring a housekeeping position seems to have little reluctance in making so many demands?"

"There's something curious about Mrs. Delmont, there's no question about that," Aunt Birdie said. "Not that I've had much contact with her, but she's surprisingly refined for a woman in service. I would imagine there's an intriguing story there, but what that story is, I couldn't hazard a guess."

"She's not mentioned anything to me about what she was doing before she arrived at Glory Manor."

"Have you asked her any questions about that?"

Ian smiled. "Well, no. I haven't had the heart to interrogate her, not with how pathetic she looks covered in a rash that was oozing somewhat dreadfully yesterday."

"I imagine the oozing is what's keeping her confined to her room."

"Then let us hope it has run its course. Perhaps then she'll feel comfortable leaving her room, which should have the ringing of the cowbell coming to an end."

Aunt Birdie set aside a cookie cutter. "You have no one to blame but yourself for the cowbell situation. You did give the bell to her, but with the best of intentions, of course, after you realized her voice was going raspy from calling out so often for assistance. Frankly, you can also shoulder some of the blame for her demanding ways."

"How do you figure that one?"

Aunt Birdie arched a brow. "Have you not taken it upon yourself to read to her every night?"

Knowing his aunt would read far too much into his decision to spend time reading to Mrs. Delmont in the evenings if he allowed her to think on it too much, Ian shrugged. "You must realize that I've only done so to try and distract her from her itching."

"Or you've done so because you find her intriguing."

"Or I find myself finally having an excuse to delve into a Jane Austen novel," he countered, which earned him a smile from his aunt.

"Jane did pen some lovely stories, but I fear your good intentions of trying to distract Mrs. Delmont are allowing a familiarity to grow between you. I'm sure she's not been employed in a household before that would encourage that type of familiarity, and that might be exactly why she seems to have no qualms about making demands."

The bell took that moment to clang again, but before Ian could even think about seeing what Mrs. Delmont needed now, he glanced out the screen door, frowning when he noticed Buttercup, along with three other cows, ambling across the lawn toward the farmhouse. "Looks like you're about to get some visitors, but how do you imagine all those cows got out of the barn?"

Aunt Birdie craned her neck. "Buttercup is a most intelligent cow. I would guess she somehow managed to open the gate and the other three cows followed her." She suddenly looked a touch guilty. "Buttercup must have let them know that I always keep a bucket of apples by the back door to hand out as treats."

"It's little wonder all the animals on the farm have been making so many escapes, what with you giving them treats." Ian bit back a grin when his aunt looked guiltier than ever. "You do realize that Uncle Amos believes someone keeps letting all his animals free on purpose, don't you?"

Aunt Birdie frowned. "I've not given a single treat to any other animal except Buttercup."

"Good to know." He turned back to the door when the cows began mooing in a rather anticipatory manner. "Because I know you'll get up from your chair the moment I leave the kitchen to dole out some treats, I'll do it for you this time. But you're going to have to stop with the treats before utter chaos descends upon the farm."

Aunt Birdie muttered something noncommittal under her breath that left him grinning as he picked up the bucket of apples and headed out the door. He was greeted with additional moos from Buttercup, Minnie, Esmeralda, and a cow he thought Uncle Amos might have named Thomasina. "This is not going to become a habit," he told them, handing out apples all around before he strode back into the house, ignoring the mournful moos that followed him inside.

Setting the bucket on the counter directly beside the basket of eggs he'd recently collected from the henhouse, he glanced to the ceiling again as fresh clangs of the cowbell rang out.

"Aren't you going to see what Mrs. Delmont wants?" Aunt Birdie asked after he, instead of leaving the kitchen, washed his hands in the sink, then wet a towel and wiped from his face some of the grime that he'd acquired while he'd been working on the farm.

"I'll look in on her in a moment, although I can't imagine what she could possibly need now. I've already taken her a lunch tray, changed the linens on her bed, and given her an entire box of Arm and Hammer soda so she could make new paste to slather over her rash."

Hanging the towel on a rack beside the sink, Ian walked across the kitchen and sat down next to his aunt. "I haven't told her this, but she's looking somewhat frightful today, what with the way the paste cracks when it dries. She keeps demanding a mirror, but that's one demand I'm not going to appease."

"Maybe you *should* give Mrs. Delmont a mirror so she can take stock of the damage."

Ian shuddered. "The first night she was here, she descended into a state of hysterics after she caught a glimpse of herself. It took me almost an hour to convince her she wasn't going to be permanently disfigured."

Aunt Birdie picked up a cookie cutter shaped like a sheep, moving it to a pile she'd begun assembling to her right. "From what little I saw of her when you carried her into the house when she first arrived, I got the impression she might be a very beautiful woman. In my experience, beautiful women always find it most distressing when their beauty goes missing."

"Given her dreadful spectacles, I'm not certain Mrs. Delmont is one of those women who puts much stock in beauty. The ladies I mingle with in Pittsburgh society wouldn't be caught dead wearing spectacles, let alone ones that are less than fashionable." He plucked an apple from the basket sitting in the middle of the table. Picking up a knife, he began cutting the apple into slices. "But speaking of Pittsburgh, I will need to attend to some business matters there soon. I've been considering officially offering Mrs. Delmont a position, although I've also been considering placing another advertisement in the papers and starting from scratch."

"For what it's worth, I think you might want to wait until Mrs. Delmont is up and about before you make any decisions. Once she's out of her room, you'll be able to judge for yourself whether she's qualified for taking on the responsibilities needed here at the farm. Although I'm still not convinced we truly need the services of a housekeeper."

"If you want to offer the children a permanent home, a housekeeper is nonnegotiable."

Aunt Birdie waved that aside. "We'll see, but tell me this, how are matters with the farm hands?"

Since there was little point in continuing with a conversation his aunt had no desire to continue, Ian took a bite of his apple, then washed it down with a glass of milk his aunt had poured for him from the pitcher on the table. "I told you that Uncle Amos chased off three men yesterday, accusing them of being responsible for letting the chickens free the other day. That leaves only Hank to help with the animals. But there's no need to fret that we'll be short-handed for long. I rode into town early this morning and managed to hire on two new hands. They'll be here tomorrow."

Aunt Birdie opened her mouth but was interrupted from whatever she'd been about to say when another bout of clanging rang out, this time more insistent than the last bout.

"Perhaps you *should* check on her," Aunt Birdie said once the clanging stopped. "The children were keeping her company this morning, but they ran outside about thirty minutes ago, saying something about going off to name some chickens. They've been very attentive to Mrs. Delmont's bell ringing, which means they might abandon the fun of naming chickens if they think she needs them. That would be a shame because I don't believe the children have experienced much fun in their short lives."

Ian pushed back his chair and rose to his feet. "I'm ashamed to admit I've not found much time to spend with the children yet. Uncle Amos has had me riding along the fence line checking for damage. It took me hours yesterday and a few more today to repair some damage we did find. Even so, I well recall how it feels to land in a foreign world, and it's not well done of me to neglect the children simply because I'm buried in work."

"The children have been fine without your attention, dear. They've been spending the past few days getting to know me, as well as exploring the house and barns. They've also been spending quite a bit of time with Mrs. Delmont, whom they've taken to addressing as Izzie." Aunt Birdie's eyes softened. "Poor little Daisy was having a hard time saying 'Mrs. Delmont.' And even with me finding something peculiar about the woman who has barricaded herself upstairs, I must say that it speaks well of her that she was so quick to offer the children the use of her first name."

"Do you think it wise for the children to spend time with Mrs. Delmont since it's yet to be decided if she'll be remaining here after her poison ivy clears up? I would hate for them to become too attached to her and then have her abandon them."

"I fear they've already become attached to her, at least the girls. Primrose is especially drawn to her."

"Primrose is the eldest child?"

Aunt Birdie nodded. "Primrose is nine, but I must say she's old for her years. Then there's Henry at seven, and I do believe he is a bit of a scamp. Violet is five, but she's not warmed up to me yet and barely speaks. And then there's Daisy, who is three and seems to have adjusted to Glory Manor better than any of her siblings."

Ian raked a hand through his hair. "I didn't even think to ask if the children have everything they need, such as clothing or toys."

"I was intending to propose a shopping trip with you at some point. But Reverend Davis was with the children and the woman from the orphanage when they first traveled to Glory Manor. He later sent around numerous articles of clothing for the little ones. And while the clothing was from the donation box at the church, it'll do until we can get the children to the store, which I hope can happen soon."

"I'll make a note of it and find time to take them or have whomever I might hire as our new housekeeper take them," he said as yet another clang rang out, which had Aunt Birdie sending him a pointed look.

He held up his hands. "I'm going, I'm going, although Mrs. Delmont probably only wants a cup of tea or . . ."

A shrill shriek suddenly interrupted him, followed by a thump, which had him immediately abandoning the kitchen and racing for the stairs.

CHAPTER 10

Chickens, Isadora was convinced, were horrid creatures, especially the one that had just tried to attack her. That was why she was currently standing on top of a chair, wielding a book as a weapon in one hand, while ringing the cowbell every other minute because the clanging seemed to be holding the chicken at bay.

Being careful to keep her lips pressed together because the chicken had a tendency to rush forward whenever anything resembling a shriek passed Isadora's lips, she eyed the distance to the door, wondering if she was fast enough to get to it without suffering a chicken attack in the process.

Tightening her grip on the bell while considering if she should try throwing a book at the chicken to distract it, even though the first book she'd thrown hadn't distracted it in the least, she couldn't help but question how her life had turned so peculiar.

If anyone had told her two weeks prior that she'd be trundling off to the wilds of Pennsylvania because of a deranged duke, or that she'd have to run for her life from an elderly man sporting a rifle with no bullets, she would have thought they'd gone mad. Add in the additional troubling events of tumbling into more than one poison ivy patch, being dumped unceremoniously into a pond by a man who was by far the most attractive man she'd ever met, and almost drowning in that very pond after attempting to rescue an adorable imp, it did seem as if her life was never going to return to normal again.

It certainly wasn't normal that her daydreams had turned from dwelling on heroes found on the pages of her favorite novels to dreams of one Ian MacKenzie. Frankly, her life of late seemed to be turning into an honest-to-goodness plot twist found in some of the romances she enjoyed, a plot complete with the hero pressing his lips to the heroine's after only a few pages had passed.

It wasn't that she'd never felt a man's lips on hers before, but the chaste kisses she'd received in the past had always been followed by fervent apologies and requests to speak to her father . . . although Ian hadn't actually kissed her but had merely been pressing his lips against hers in a desperate attempt to breathe life back into her lifeless, breathless body.

Isadora used the edge of the book to scratch an itch on her nose right as a perfectly reasonable explanation regarding why she'd taken to dreaming about Ian sprang to mind.

He was the first person to ever rush in and save her from the jaws of death. That meant it was completely normal for him to occupy her dreams, although she did need to nip those dreams in the bud before she took to mooning over a man she barely—

The door to her bedchamber suddenly burst open as the object of her dreams rushed into the room, which had the chicken letting out a fierce squawk as it took to ruffling its feathers.

"What's wrong?" Ian demanded, his gaze jumping from her to the chicken and then back to her.

For the briefest of moments, she found herself unable to speak because her mouth had gone remarkably dry at the mere sight of the man, and her knees went all sorts of wobbly, although that might have been because she was standing on a less-than-sturdy chair.

Her reaction to the man was troubling because she couldn't pinpoint what it was about him that intrigued her. He certainly wasn't dressed in a manner that usually appealed to her, considering he was wearing a shirt that had a large tear running down the front of it, as if he'd gotten caught on something while he'd been doing whatever it was that farmers did. That he'd not bothered to change his shirt suggested he was a man not overly concerned by his appearance. That idea was further proven when she glanced at his trousers and found them smudged with dirt.

Lifting her gaze, she settled it on his hair, frowning when she realized that he didn't have merely brown hair as she'd first thought, but more along the lines of a brown mixed with auburn. That hair was currently tousled and curling over the collar of his torn shirt, looking quite as if he'd forgotten to comb it after he'd gotten up that day. He also was in desperate need of a shave, although the lack of a shave did seem to lend him a rather rakish air, and . . .

"Mrs. Delmont. You're going to have to tell me what's wrong if I'm to know how to assist you. You might also want to explain why you have a chicken in your room."

Wondering who Mrs. Delmont was until she suddenly recalled *she* was supposed to be Mrs. Delmont, Isadora wobbled a bit on the chair, giving the cowbell a wave a second later when the wobbling set the chicken into a frenzy.

To her dismay, the cowbell did nothing to stop the frenzy since the chicken was now darting back and forth through the rungs of her chair, squawking louder than ever. A second later, it jumped on the chair she was standing on, and a second after that, it was underneath her dress, pecking at her legs and beating at them with its wings.

Forgetting that the chicken didn't seem to be fond of shrieking, Isadora opened her mouth and began screaming at the top of her lungs, her screams coming to a rapid end when she suddenly found herself scooped straight off the chair and into Ian's strong arms.

Turning, he strode with her toward the door, leaving the chicken behind.

Finding herself held yet again in his well-muscled arms, Isadora found it rather difficult to breathe, a troubling circumstance if there ever was one. Knowing a distraction from those well-muscled arms was in order if she wanted air to return to her lungs, she struggled for something else to think about—that something turning into a contemplation of the man carrying her.

He had an easy stride that brought to mind memories of the magnificent cats she'd seen on one of her trips around the world. Those large cats were captivatingly graceful when they were at their ease, but when they moved into motion, there was no denying the power they possessed—a power that suggested they were dangerous in the extreme.

Ian MacKenzie possessed that same sense of power, and if she wasn't much mistaken, he was a man who could turn dangerous in a split second. She'd never been around such a dangerous man before, but for some reason, she wasn't bothered by the danger that fairly radiated from him and found it rather . . .

"This is going to be a slightly tight squeeze up the stairs, Mrs. Delmont, but I think, given the fright you just suffered, it might be for the best if we put an entire floor between you and the chicken."

Shaking aside all thoughts of dangerous men and how attractive she apparently found them, even though she'd never considered herself a lady drawn to men who possessed such an air, Isadora finally noticed that Ian was carrying her up a very steep flight of stairs. Having no idea where those stairs led, and only then remembering that it was hardly acceptable to be carried off to some remote part of the house in the arms of a gentleman, she opened her mouth to protest but found that protest dying on her tongue when he reached the top of the stairs.

As he set her on her feet, all thoughts of adhering to the strict proprieties she'd always embraced disappeared in a trice as a sense of anticipation flowed through her.

CHAPTER 11

"It's a library," Isadora exclaimed, her gaze traveling around a room that had floor-to-ceiling bookshelves stuffed to the gills with books.

"I imagine you weren't expecting to find a library in the attic," Ian said with a grin, which caused a dimple to pop out on his cheek, one that . . .

Forcing her attention away from Ian and his evidently far-too-intriguing dimple, Isadora strode over to one of the shelves. "I must admit I wasn't, at least not such an extensive library." She dipped her head so she wouldn't bump into the sloping attic ceiling, reaching out to touch the spine of a tattered copy of *The Taming of the Shrew*. Turning, she smiled at Ian, who'd moved up to join her. "This is the one book by Shakespeare I never cared for."

"Because you fear you share some of Katherina's traits?"

For a second, Isadora found herself impressed that he could recall the heroine's name in the story until she realized what he'd said. "What do you mean by that?"

Ian smiled a charming smile, which did absolutely nothing to defray the bit of temper that was causing heat to settle on her cheeks. "Surely you must know that you're a slightly demanding woman, quite like Katherina."

Her temper edged up a notch. "You find me demanding?"

"When you use that particular tone of voice, certainly, and you have been applying yourself rather diligently to the cowbell."

An argument immediately rose to the tip of her tongue, one she swallowed when she realized Ian might have just made a sound argument. Walking across the attic because his nearness made it difficult to think, she stopped in front of an open window that was allowing a warm breeze to flow into the room. Shifting aside the curtain, she looked out over the farm, trying to collect her thoughts.

No one in her entire life had ever had the audacity to call her demanding, but . . . she could not avoid the truth of Ian's statement, and, in all honesty, she probably did possess a few traits that were very similar to Katherina in *The Taming of the Shrew.*

She'd grown up in the lap of luxury, spoiled by her parents and raised with the expectation that her every whim would be met by people paid to see to her creature comforts. She'd never once considered that her demands cast her in a less-than-pleasant light, but now, after having that brought to her attention, and rather matter-of-factly at that, she really had no choice but to agree that she, Isadora Delafield, *was* a demanding woman, which then suggested that she might not be very . . . likeable.

Something unpleasant settled in her stomach.

She didn't *want* to be unlikeable, nor did she, for a reason she wouldn't allow herself to contemplate too closely, want Ian MacKenzie to conclude she was nothing more than a demanding shrew.

"Forgive me, Mrs. Delmont. I fear I've just delivered you a crushing insult when I simply meant to be amusing."

Drawing in a breath, Isadora turned from the window. "There's no need for you to apologize, Mr. MacKenzie, for you've spoken nothing less than the truth. I *have* been demanding and have abused your hospitality most egregiously by being far too liberal with the cowbell. I owe you an apology, not the other way around."

Ian surprised her when he merely smiled. "Apology accepted. And in your defense, you've been laid low because of poison ivy and were, at least a short time ago, only being overly diligent with ringing the cowbell because you apparently had some type of altercation with a chicken."

"I'm afraid Elmer was the clear winner in our altercation."

"Elmer?"

Isadora grimaced. "The chicken. He took an intense dislike of me from the moment the girls left him in my room, mistakenly believing I'd enjoy Elmer's company while they went off to name more chickens, and . . ." She frowned. "Perhaps Elmer is a very astute chicken, and after concluding I'm a demanding sort, he decided to put me in my place."

"I'm fairly certain that was not the case since chickens aren't known for being all that intelligent, which might make it difficult for a chicken to reason out that a person possesses a demanding nature." He caught her eye as his lips began to curve. "Tell me this, though, why are you calling the chicken *Elmer*?"

"The girls thought it would be a treat for me if I got to name it." She shuddered. "Uncle Amos apparently realized that not all of his chickens had names, and he enlisted the help of the children to rectify that situation." She shuddered again. "Elmer began stalking me the second the children left the room. And not that I'm trying to excuse my excessive ringing of the cowbell, but it *was* the only thing that seemed to hold off Elmer's advances."

"You could have merely run from the room," Ian pointed out.

"And risk the chance of spreading my poison ivy around the house where anyone might catch it? I think not."

"Is that why you've confined yourself to your room and the spare bathing chamber?"

Isadora gave a bob of her head. "Certainly. But why did you think I'd confined myself to my room?"

"It might be for the best if that question remains unanswered," Ian muttered before he was once again smiling his charming smile at her.

"Do not tell me that you thought I was staying in my room because I was being difficult, did you?"

Ian winced. "Will you be overly annoyed with me if I admit I thought you'd barricaded yourself in your room because you were embarrassed by the state of your face?"

"I haven't seen the state of my face in over two days."

"And for good reason since the last time you saw your face, well, there's no need for us to revisit that disturbing scene."

"Am I to understand that my face looks no better than it did when it was swollen and oozing unpleasantly?"

"Hard to say with any certainty since you have soda paste smeared all over you, some of which has gotten on your spectacles, which has to make it somewhat difficult to see." Ian took a step closer to her, reached out, placed his hand on her chin, and tilted it up, looking at her closely. "From what little I can tell through the paste, though, I would imagine your rash is drying up nicely."

"Comforting words indeed, but again, I wasn't staying in my room because I was self-conscious about my appearance."

"My apologies, then, Mrs. Delmont. It appears I was mistaken regarding your actions, and it was very commendable of you to maintain your distance from everyone, even if it was unnecessary because poison ivy isn't contagious."

"What?"

"It's not passed from person to person. You have to touch the plant to get it."

She moved to a ratty-looking chair and plopped down. "It's little wonder you found me demanding, and that explains why, when you apparently heard me ringing the cowbell so diligently a short time ago, you didn't bother to rush up to investigate why I was ringing the bell in the first place."

Ian sat down in a chair facing her. "I thought you might have been ringing the bell to tell me you wanted me to fetch you a mirror or a cup of tea. But if I'd known you were being stalked by a chicken, I would have come sooner." He smiled. "I'm still interested in hearing how you came to choose Elmer for that chicken's name."

"I thought he looked like an Elmer at first because he was somewhat adorable when he was in Primrose's arms. But then, after the girls left and I got a glimpse of his true personality, I think I misnamed him. He's much more along the lines of a Nigel, or perhaps even a Percival, names I've always believed aptly portray somewhat shifty sorts."

"I have friends named Percival and Nigel, and they're not shifty in the least."

"My apologies to your friends. Perhaps I should leave the honor of renaming the dastardly creature to you to avoid further insults to additional friends of yours."

Ian smiled. "I would not care to deprive you of naming your first chicken. But you might get Elmer to stop chasing you if you were to choose a more feminine name, such as Elmerita, perhaps."

"Why would I want to name him Elmerita?"

"Because Elmer is no he. She's a she."

"Surely not?"

Ian settled into the chair. "You don't know much about farms—or chickens for that matter, do you?"

"I know about chickens, although I'm only familiar with the many dishes they're served up in, and I especially enjoy chicken simmered in a delightful cream sauce with cranberries for garnish."

"Don't let Elmer hear you say that. She'll really have an issue with you if she thinks you're considering serving her up in a sauce."

Isadora resisted the unusual urge to roll her eyes. "I'm hoping to never encounter Elmer again, but I am curious to know how you can tell she's a she instead of a he."

Ian suddenly coughed, but it almost sounded as if he was trying to disguise a laugh. "I don't believe that's a conversation anyone would consider proper. None of the etiquette books I've read have ever suggested that broaching topics regarding how to know different genders of chickens when in mixed company is acceptable. With that said, all you really need to know is that Elmer is a hen, which is female. Roosters are male, and you can tell roosters a mile away because they often possess surly attitudes."

"Then Elmer should be a rooster because he, or rather she, is definitely surly, but . . ." Isadora leaned forward. "You read books on etiquette?"

He gestured to one of the bookshelves. "There's an entire shelf over there dedicated to etiquette books. My favorite is *The Gentlemen's Book of Etiquette and Manual of Politeness* by Cecil B. Hartley. It's proven itself invaluable with allowing me to study expected manners gentlemen need to know as they go out into the civilized world."

"My mother insisted I read *The Ladies' Book of Etiquette and Manual of Politeness* by Florence Hartley when I was ten. But I'm surprised you'd take it upon yourself to study what I always found to be a less-than-stimulating topic. I would have thought you'd prefer studying books on crop rotation or what truly makes a chicken a female as opposed to a male."

"*If* I spent my time as a farmer, I'm sure I *would* devote myself to books on farming, but as I mentioned when we first met, I no longer live on this farm."

A trace of trepidation tickled the back of her neck. "If you're not a farmer, what do you do?"

For a second, she didn't think he was going to answer her, but then he shrugged. "I'm a man of business, doing most of that business in Pittsburgh."

"What type of business?"

"I wouldn't want to bore you with the details."

"Didn't you care for farming?" she pressed.

"I've always believed farming is a noble occupation since without it, well, everyone would starve." He crossed a leg over his knee. "But after I came to live with Aunt Birdie and Uncle Amos when I was seven, my aunt realized rather quickly that I wasn't meant to live my life on a farm because I was drawn to more mental tasks than physical ones."

Isadora glanced at his chest. "It seems to me like you spend a great deal of time doing physical activities be—" She snapped her mouth shut, wondering not for the first time why she was suddenly allowing all sorts of nonsense past her lips.

"Perhaps I didn't phrase that properly," he said, clear amusement in his eyes. "I've never balked at doing manual labor, which is how I achieved my size. But after I began working for men involved with the iron and steel industry, I realized that my size worked to my advantage, which is why I took up boxing." He smiled. "Getting into a ring a few times a week does seem to allow me to maintain my size."

"Clearly," Isadora muttered before she frowned. "Are you one of those men who work with the labor unions?"

"In a manner of speaking. But getting back to why I'm not a farmer"—he gestured around the room—"when Aunt Birdie introduced me to books and realized I was completely smitten with the written word, she encouraged me to pursue an education instead of farming, and she helped me assemble this library over the years."

He rose to his feet, moved to a bookshelf, and plucked one of the books from it. Holding it up, he smiled. "Aunt Birdie used to take eggs and sell them to our neighbors in Canonsburg, and after I came to live with her, she always set aside some of her egg money to purchase books for our library." He nodded to the book in his hand, one that was well worn and missing a chunk of the cover. "From the moment Aunt Birdie and I read *Frankenstein*, I was enthralled with books. I realized that reading opened up an entirely new world to me, allowing me to experience adventures I never thought I could."

Warmth immediately flowed through her.

She'd never met a man who admitted to being enthralled, let alone smitten, with the written word. Most men in her social circle looked on reading novels as a frivolous pursuit and certainly never broached the topic of novels in conversation with her. That Ian was not only comfortable discussing his favorite works of the day, but also seemed comfortable discussing what sounded like an early life without many advantages, gave her a new respect for the man as well as left her feeling somewhat unbalanced.

He was clearly a successful man, although she didn't understand why he seemed so hesitant to discuss his business. Most gentlemen of her acquaintance were eager to share their business successes with her, always trying to impress her with their achievements. That she knew they were also eager to garner her affections because of her father's large fortune was a given, which made her wonder whether Ian's behavior would change toward her if he knew the truth about . . .

"But enough about me, Mrs. Delmont. Tell me something about you. How did you become a housekeeper?"

"I think before I answer that, I should ask you, after my inappropriately demanding actions, if you're still interested in offering me a position here."

He considered her for a long moment. "I will if you have the proper qualifications."

Disappointment slid through her even as an image of the dastardly Duke of Montrose flashed to mind. She was still in desperate need of a refuge from that horrid man, but she had no proper qualifications to share with Ian, something he would quickly realize since he was obviously an intelligent man, and . . .

Her thoughts were suddenly interrupted when Elmer came squawking into the room, flapping her feathers and charging directly Isadora's way.

She was up on top of a chair in a flash.

"I told you Elmer has it out for me," she said, not amused when Ian began laughing even as he intercepted Elmer, scooped the chicken into his arms, and headed for the door.

"If you'll excuse me, I think it's past time I returned this little mischief-maker to the chicken coop."

"If you ask me, she's got murder on her mind, not mischief."

Smiling when Ian seemed to release a bit of a snort to that remark, Isadora stayed on top of the chair as Ian and Elmer disappeared through the door.

Waiting until she was certain they'd reached the bottom of the steps, Isadora climbed from the chair, shaking out the folds of the housedress she'd borrowed from Aunt Birdie. It was three sizes too big but was far more comfortable than the night rail she'd found in her trunk, one she'd never seen before and couldn't imagine where Mr. Godkin had found it.

She made her way to the window, and pushing aside the curtain, she smiled when Ian strode into view, her smile widening when she noticed he was talking to Elmer.

There was something inherently charming about him, even though she was convinced that lurking underneath that charm was a formidable and dangerous man. But even with the danger, she, for some reason, felt safe with him, as if she instinctively knew he was a gentleman who'd protect those around him.

What felt exactly like a shot of lightning suddenly surged through her as an undeniable truth took that moment to settle into her very soul:

Ian MacKenzie was more than capable of taking on the Duke of Montrose.

She'd been told the duke was a dangerous man, but she had the sneaking suspicion he would be no match for Ian.

Ian would never allow a man of the duke's reprehensible character to get the better of him, nor would he allow the duke to achieve his desire of marrying her if she were under Ian's protection.

Unfortunately, she'd made a horrible impression on the one man who truly could keep her safe. She also didn't have an impressive letter of reference, rather more of a vague one. That meant there was little hope Ian would find her worthy of a position at Glory Manor unless she could somehow convince him she was an exceptional housekeeper and could keep Glory Manor running in fine form.

How she was to manage that daunting feat was beyond her, but she was going to have to figure that out if she wanted to remain in the safest place possible until the situation with the duke was resolved.

Lifting her chin, she squared her shoulders. From the time she'd been a small child, she'd been told that a lady's appearance could make all the difference in the world. That meant her first order of business would be to wash the soda from her person and set herself to rights.

Then, and only after she'd dressed herself in a manner befitting a woman of service, she'd turn her attention to figuring out how to convince Ian she was not merely a ridiculous woman who'd named a female chicken Elmer but rather a capable woman worthy of employment.

CHAPTER 12

After returning Elmer to the chicken coop, Ian headed across the yard, smiling over the rather curious encounter he'd just had with Izzie Delmont.

She was one of the most unusual women he'd ever met, and he was quickly coming to the belief he might have misjudged her.

Even though there was no questioning whether she possessed a demanding nature—because she did—he hadn't neglected to realize that she'd been completely oblivious to that undesirable trait. Her reaction when he'd pointed out her demanding ways had been quite telling, and if he wasn't mistaken, now that she'd been made aware of how others perceived her, she might very well take steps to rectify her behavior in the future.

That she shared a love for the written word was a certain mark in her favor. He'd always found well-read ladies to be incredibly appealing, and even though it was strange to be intrigued by a woman who was oozing and slathered in . . . He suddenly came to a dead stop in the middle of the lawn, shaking his head as if that would dispel the curious thoughts now rumbling around his mind.

He had no business considering how appealing Izzie Delmont was. He'd sworn at a relatively young age he'd only set his sights on a woman possessed of a certain social status, and a housekeeper, through no fault of her own, didn't exactly have the . . .

"I hate to bother you, Mr. MacKenzie, but you're gonna have to have a talk with your uncle."

Shoving aside his disturbing thoughts, Ian found Hank, their only remaining hired hand, stomping his way.

"What happened?" Ian asked.

"Amos accused me of stealing a chicken, but before he could pull out that ever-handy rifle of his, I spotted you taking the missing chicken back to the coop." Hank raked a hand through sweaty sandy-colored hair. "Now, I like working at Glory Manor, sir, but I ain't gonna be here much longer if I keep gettin' abused by your uncle."

Looking past Hank, Ian saw Uncle Amos wandering in the direction of the chicken coop, his unloaded rifle slung over his shoulder. "I'll go have a word with him."

"I'd appreciate that. Work ain't easy to come by, but a man can't continue being threatened with a rifle when he's just trying to milk some cows. Tends to make a person a little jumpy."

"Perfectly understandable." Ian rubbed his chin. "How about you take the rest of the day off—with pay, of course? That might help you get that jumpiness under control, as well as give you some relief from my uncle."

Hank dipped his head. "That's right kind of you, sir. Like I said, I enjoy the work here and would hate to lose the position."

"And I'd hate to lose you. I know it's been difficult on the farm lately, what with Uncle Amos not being himself and seeing skullduggery around every corner." Ian blew out a breath. "I'm hoping that since Aunt Birdie is beginning to feel more like her old self again, he'll calm down and life on the farm will return to normal."

"You ever think about selling the farm, taking your aunt and uncle off to Pittsburgh with you? Seems to me Glory Manor's getting too much for them."

"Aunt Birdie will hear nothing about moving to Pittsburgh. She's convinced Uncle Amos will only be content if he's left to live out his life here. Because of that, I don't have the heart to try and convince her to sell."

"There's been many farmers around these parts thinking about selling their land," Hank said, stepping closer and lowering his voice. "A man showed up here a few months back, interested in buying this place. Your Aunt Birdie sent him packing before he could even tell her how much he was willing to offer for the farm."

"She never mentioned a thing about a man inquiring about purchasing Glory Manor." Ian frowned. "You wouldn't happen to know more about this man or why he wanted to buy Glory Manor?"

Hank inched closer to Ian. "Now, this is just hearsay, mind you, but apparently this man was an agent for some wealthy investors interested in acquiring land to mine for coal . . . or maybe it was oil." Hank lowered his voice to barely a whisper. "Not that I want to be givin' you advice, sir, but what with the way your Uncle Amos seems to be losing his wits, you might want to look into finding that agent and seeing what he has to offer."

"There's little point in my speaking with that agent, Hank. I gave my word to Aunt Birdie that she and Uncle Amos could stay here forever. I have every intention of honoring that word, no matter if I have to hire a hundred people to help them look after the place."

"Don't you think it's a waste of money to hire on more help when there's not enough animals left here to consider this a proper farm? Amos don't even grow many crops these days."

"It's not about the money. Aunt Birdie and Uncle Amos were kind enough to take me in and look after me from the time I was seven. It's my turn to look after them."

"Right honorable of you, sir, but again, it might not hurt to look up that agent. Your aunt and uncle aren't getting any younger, and they're not going to be around forever."

Ian winced. "Don't let Aunt Birdie hear you talking like that. I doubt she'd appreciate hearing you think she's at her last prayers."

A ghost of a smile flickered across Hank's face. "I won't bring it up again. And with that said, I think I'll take you up on your offer of an afternoon off with pay. You sure you're up for takin' care of all the chores still left to do without me?"

"I'll be fine, thank you." Ian smiled. "And no need to worry that your afternoon off will have you doing more than your fair share of jobs tomorrow. I've hired on two new hands to work around the farm. They'll be here come morning."

"How did you find men willing to work here? Everyone in town knows that Amos has turned difficult. I wouldn't think there'd be many men willing to face a rifle for the slightest infraction, no matter that it's well known you pay a fair wage."

"Mrs. Rogers at the general store was manning the cash register when I stopped by to pick up more Arm and Hammer soda for Mrs. Delmont. She knew of some men looking for positions. She also told me she'll be spreading the word that I'm looking for more help, which means we'll soon have this farm filled with enough hands to handle all the work."

"Seems like me and you have been handling that work just fine."

Realizing he might have injured Hank's pride by implying the work wasn't getting done to satisfaction, Ian inclined his head. "You've been doing a wonderful job, Hank. There's not a man around who works harder than you, but I'm not going to be here all the time. I have pressing business that needs to be attended to in Pittsburgh."

"I'll be happy to oversee the new men, sir, after you return to Pittsburgh, but what about the house? Who is gonna be responsible for that or for looking after all them children?"

"I haven't quite figured that out yet, although Mrs. Rogers did say she knows of more than one young woman who'd be happy to accept employment here."

"Rumor in town has it that the young women in Canonsburg are looking for more than employment from you." Hank gave a bob of his head. "Thought you should know that so you'll be careful. Wouldn't want to see you get tricked into anything. And on that happy note, I'll bid you a good afternoon and see you in the morning."

As Hank loped away, Uncle Amos suddenly strolled into view. Knowing there was little reason to delay having a chat with him about frightening off help they were in desperate need of retaining, Ian strode over to join his uncle.

"Ah, Ian, I didn't know you were planning on visiting Glory Manor today," Uncle Amos said, smiling as he caught sight of Ian.

Seeing little point in explaining he'd been at Glory Manor for days, Ian fell into step beside his uncle. "I hear you were recently missing a chicken."

"I was, but it turned back up in the chicken coop, so I was worried for nothing." He frowned and stopped walking. "Who told you it was missing?"

"Hank, who also told me you accused him of stealing it while directing your rifle at his face."

Uncle Amos's eyes clouded with confusion. "I don't remember threatening Hank. I might have asked him if he knew the whereabouts of the chicken, but I wouldn't have threatened him or accused him of stealing it."

"I'm afraid you did, and Hank had nothing to do with the missing chicken. The children simply took it up to Mrs. Delmont's room so she could name it."

"I'm not certain why you're addressing dear Izzie as Mrs. Delmont. You are soon to be married to the woman, so it's perfectly acceptable for you to use her given name."

"Who told you I was going to marry Mrs., er, Izzie?"

Uncle Amos tilted his head. "It might have been the children, or maybe it was Hank." He frowned. "I think Hank might have also told me to keep an eye on Izzie because she likes to steal chickens."

A sigh escaped him. His uncle was clearly confused again, which lent a certain urgency to finding additional help for the farm.

"Whoever told you I'm going to marry Izzie was mistaken. She's merely a candidate for a housekeeper position we need to fill. As for chickens, she doesn't seem to care for them, so I don't believe you need to worry she'll try and filch one of them."

"She doesn't like chickens?"

106

"Not at all. Frankly, I think she would be perfectly content to never encounter another chicken again, especially after Elmer—that's the chicken she named and the one that was missing—took an immediate dislike to her and chased her around her room."

"Elmer's an odd name to choose for a hen."

"She thought it was a he, not a she."

"Ah well, that explains much." Uncle Amos clapped him on the back again. "And it's just as well you're not intending to marry her. A woman who doesn't like chickens isn't to be trusted."

Swallowing a laugh, Ian began walking again, promising Uncle Amos he'd go fishing with him just as soon as he got caught up with all the chores he had left to do. As Uncle Amos agreed that would be a splendid way to spend the afternoon, their progress toward the house was interrupted when Henry suddenly dashed into view, waving a piece of paper.

"This just came for you," he yelled to Ian, running up to join him. "The man who delivered it said it's one of them telegrams." He thrust the telegram at Ian. "I never seen a real telegram before. I bet it says somethin' important."

Knowing there was little doubt that the contents of the telegram were indeed important, Ian opened it up and frowned. "Looks like I'm needed in Pittsburgh as soon as possible, which is a bit of a problem."

Uncle Amos shook his head, his eyes now bright and devoid of even a hint of confusion. "There's no reason for you to think you need to stay here and mind the farm. I've been minding Glory Manor for over fifty years."

"True, but you've now got four children to mind as well, and Aunt Birdie is still recovering from her accident."

"But what about Izzie? I thought you told me she'd come here to apply for a housekeeping position. Don't see why you shouldn't just give it to her. That way, you'll be able to go to Pittsburgh and not have to worry about us."

Finding it more than curious that his uncle could be completely out of his mind one moment and then completely rational the next,

Ian folded up the telegram and shoved it into his pocket. "Perhaps I should speak with Izzie, even though I have some doubts about her qualifications."

"You could always offer her a temporary position," Uncle Amos suggested, taking Ian aback by the soundness of that suggestion. "That would fill the void for the moment, and that would give you an opportunity to check out her letters of reference, if she came with any, that is."

"That is some excellent advice, Uncle Amos, and certainly worthy of consideration." He sent his uncle and Henry a smile. "If you'll excuse me, I'm off to have a chat with Mrs. Delmont."

As he strode away, he refused to wince when he heard Uncle Amos question Henry about who Mrs. Delmont was and why Ian was off to have a chat with her.

Taking a detour toward the water pump, wanting to wash up after being near the chicken coop, he slowed his pace when he spotted Primrose, Violet, and little Daisy standing a foot away from the pump, eyeing it warily.

"It doesn't bite," he said, drawing their attention and immediately finding the wariness in their eyes increasing as they watched him approach.

Remembering all too vividly how it felt to be uprooted from everything known and thrust into a world that was completely foreign, he continued forward, smiling at the girls once he reached the water pump. "I hear all of you have been spending some time naming the chickens."

Not one of the girls returned his smile, their gazes on the water pump he'd begun to prime. The second water came pouring out the spout, the girls jumped backward, little Violet stumbling into Primrose, who grabbed hold of her, steadied her on her feet, then sent a glare to Ian, as if it had been his fault they'd almost suffered a tumble to the ground.

"Aunt Birdie told us we couldn't help her make cookies until after we wash up," Primrose said. "We couldn't figure out how to use that pump, but now you're here and the pump seems to be workin' just fine." She scowled. "That means we can't tell Aunt Birdie the pump is broken."

"Which, oddly enough, does explain why you're glaring at me," Ian said before he stuck his hands under the running water. "All of you do realize, even with it becoming remarkably obvious that you dislike bathing, that washing your hands isn't the same as taking a bath, don't you? As you can clearly see, there's not nearly as much water involved."

"Aunt Birdie said we was to wash our faces too," Violet said, taking a step toward him. "And she even said we wasn't to forget our necks."

"That's almost like taking a bath," Primrose added before she caught Ian's eye. "Mrs. Lyman—she's the woman that Pa paid to watch us every now and again before he went missing—told us our mama died because she liked to take so many baths and those baths done gave her a chill and killed her."

Ian completely forgot about keeping the water running as temper crawled through him. His father had often told him bathing was harmful, had done so merely to spare himself the bother of making certain his one and only child was clean. Ian had the sneaking suspicion that this Mrs. Lyman might have used the same tactics with the Duffy children to save herself some work.

The children's father had evidently not been diligent with making certain the woman tasked to look after his children *every now and again* was qualified for the work she'd been paid to do, which spoke volumes about the man's suitableness as a parent.

With disgust for Mr. Duffy mixing with the temper, Ian drew in a breath and slowly released it, knowing he couldn't very well voice that disgust to the children. Their father might have abandoned them, but he was still their father. Even though his own father had sorely abused him from the moment his mother had died until he'd come to live at Glory Manor, there was a part of Ian, albeit a small part, that loved the man. He'd always held out hope that his father would one day want to come and take him home, or at least track him down and apologize for all the abuse he'd given his only son. That day had never come, nor would it since his father had died years before, and . . .

"Maybe that pump is broken now, Prim, and Ian is lookin' so mad cuz he don't know why there's no more water comin' out of it."

Forcing down the temper that was flowing through him, caused by thoughts and memories that were hardly productive, Ian summoned up a smile, unsurprised when it did not have the wariness in the girls' eyes dissipating.

"I'm not angry about the water pump, which isn't broken by the way. And I'm not angry with any of you, if that's your next question." A sigh escaped him. "I'm angry at the circumstances you've been forced to face, and I'm sorry to hear about your mother. It must have been horrible to lose her."

Primrose began inspecting the end of a red braid, one tied with a bit of string. "She died a few months after Daisy was born. Me and Henry remember Mama, but Violet doesn't, and Daisy never even knew her."

"I'm sure your mother didn't want to leave you, Primrose, just as I'm sure she didn't die from taking a bath," Ian began quietly. "She must have suffered from an unexpected illness."

"It was the bathing. Mrs. Lyman said so." Primrose hugged her arms around her thin body. "That's why we decided we weren't takin' no more baths. If one of us gets sick, we'll get separated for sure since everyone knows people don't like to keep children who are sickly."

Ian frowned. "Aunt Birdie is even now making plans to offer you a permanent home at Glory Manor, which means there's no need for you to worry you and your siblings are going to be separated."

Primrose gave a jerk of her head. "And we appreciate that offer, but Aunt Birdie might not be around to see all of us grown and out of the house, which means this isn't a permanent home for us, and we could be separated."

He'd forgotten how matter of fact children could be about their circumstances, forced to become that way because the future was always so questionable for children who were born into abject poverty and then suffered the loss of one or both of their parents. He'd been much the same way in his youth.

Unfortunately, he'd not found the time to truly consider the children's circumstances, which meant, since he'd never been one to make promises he wasn't certain he could keep, he had nothing of worth to say to the girls, at least not yet.

"Even though I realize there's much to discuss about your future," he finally said, earning a slight widening of the eyes from Primrose, as if she hadn't been expecting him to address their future, "this isn't really the moment for that because I've not had the time to consider the matter properly, and . . . Aunt Birdie is evidently waiting for all of you to bake cookies." He grinned. "I've enjoyed many an afternoon making cookies with Aunt Birdie. Allow me to simply say that you haven't lived until you've been given the very great pleasure of licking a spoon filled with the most delicious icing you've ever tasted."

"Aunt Birdie puts icing on her cookies?" Primrose asked, moving an entire inch toward him as Violet and Daisy did the same.

"Oh, Aunt Birdie won't be putting the icing on her cookies. All of you will be doing that, but only if you agree to wash up."

The sisters exchanged looks, and then, to Ian's surprise, little Daisy toddled forward and beamed a gap-toothed smile at him. "I want icing." She held out her arms. "Wash up, pweez?"

Smiling at the dirty little girl with the messy red braids and not wanting to waste a prime opportunity, Ian took her hand and situated her beside the water pump. He gave the handle a few pumps, then resisted a laugh when Daisy immediately began shrieking as cold water splashed over her. Helping her rid herself of at least one layer of dirt, and then using the cloth he'd dried his hands on to attack her neck, he finished up a few minutes later, nodding at the clean and remarkably pink face looking back at him.

"Beautiful," he exclaimed, right before Daisy suddenly threw herself at him. She planted a wet kiss against his cheek when he lifted her up, completely stealing his heart in the process.

When he turned to Primrose and Violet, he found the sisters once again watching him warily, apparently not convinced that washing was not going to leave them with a deadly cold. Setting Daisy down, he showed Primrose how to operate the pump, explaining that the water would come out slower if she didn't pump it rapidly. Then, after telling Violet to try and get as clean as she could because Aunt Birdie would notice if she wasn't clean, he sent the sisters a smile and headed into the house, touching his cheek where Daisy had kissed him.

"The girls decide to wash up?" Aunt Birdie asked as she walked across the kitchen, carrying a bag of flour.

Striding to her side, he took the flour from her, helped her into a chair, and set the flour on the table. After sending her a shaking of his head, which she ignored, he smiled. "Daisy's somewhat clean, but Primrose and Violet are still a little hesitant about getting wet."

"I imagine their father, exactly like your father, convinced them bathing is harmful to a person."

"Curiously enough, it wasn't their father. It was a woman hired to look after them when their father wasn't around, a Mrs. Lyman, I believe."

Aunt Birdie's eyes flashed. "I hate to speak ill of a woman I've never met, but it seems to me Mrs. Lyman wasn't what I'd call a loyal woman. She clearly abandoned those children when Mr. Duffy went missing." She shook her head. "I'm afraid our world is a most troubling one at times, what with how often people forget to show kindness to those most vulnerable. I imagine it must pain God no small amount when He witnesses us ignoring those in need."

"I imagine it does, but I also imagine He takes pleasure in watching people like you and Uncle Amos," Ian countered. "You didn't ignore the plight of the children, which means their future is looking much brighter."

"Amos and I won't be around forever, dear." She looked up from the bag of flour she'd just opened. "Someone will need to take over for us—and that's you, if it was in question."

"You want me to take over the running of Glory Manor?"

"No, I want your word that you'll see after the children when Amos and I are no longer here."

Even though Ian had only very recently begun considering the children and their futures and had, on some level, known this conversation was coming, he wasn't prepared for it. "You know that a bachelor isn't exactly the best person to raise four children, don't you?"

"Which is why I also expect you to promise me that you'll devote a great deal of effort to finding yourself a bride."

"You could live for years," Ian pointed out, hearing a hint of desperation in his tone.

"Or I could be dead tomorrow," she countered. "And if that were to come about, I'm sure I'd enjoy a more peaceful transition to the hereafter if I knew the welfare of the children was settled and that your future was settled as well."

"I'm not currently interested in a specific woman, so a wedding probably won't take place anytime soon."

Aunt Birdie released a bit of a humph. "I heard you were kissing Izzie down by the pond. If you ask me, that implies you have a bit of interest in her."

Ian shot a look to the back door, where the faces of three little girls were pressed up against the screen until they seemed to realize he was watching them. In a fit of what almost sounded like giggles, they turned and ran away. Refusing a smile because that would only have his aunt thinking up all sorts of different scenarios, he returned his attention to her.

"Contrary to the chatter of children, I was not kissing Izzie. I was trying to force the breath back into her lifeless body."

Aunt Birdie's eyes widened. "You saved her life?"

"I'm not certain I'd go that far because there was the chance she'd begin breathing on her own again, but . . ."

"You're connected to her forever now, which means, at the very least, you'll have to offer her the housekeeping position."

Ian's brows drew together. "Your thought process, Aunt Birdie, is downright terrifying. I will admit, however, that I'm going to consider offering her employment but only because we need help around here, not because I'm connected to her for life." He caught her eye. "However, connections aside, if I need remind you, I thought we agreed you were going to discontinue your attempts at matchmaking."

Aunt Birdie gave a breezy wave of a hand. "You wouldn't care to deprive an old lady of a spot of fun, would you?"

"You told me just the other day that you don't think of yourself as elderly."

"Shouldn't you seek Izzie out and begin interrogating her on her housekeeper skills?"

"I wasn't intending to interrogate her but merely ask her to tell me about her past work experience. Then, if I find that satisfactory, I'll have her show me how she'd go about doing a few household chores."

"I'm so relieved to learn I won't have to go through an interrogation process. And I'm sure *you're* relieved to learn that I've now abandoned my room and that I'm here to present myself as your next potential housekeeper."

Turning toward the door, Ian found Izzie standing there, the sight of her leaving him feeling as if someone had punched him in the gut.

Gone was the soda paste that had been practically covering her from head to toe the past few days, revealing one of the most beautiful faces he'd ever seen, even with a bit of a lingering red rash and those hideous spectacles perched on the bridge of her nose.

His gaze drifted from her face, taking in the practical white blouse paired with a black skirt and the white apron she'd put on over the blouse. Gone were the housedresses she'd borrowed from Aunt Birdie, revealing a figure that was trim yet possessed of delightful feminine curves.

Dragging his attention away from those curves when he realized it was less than acceptable to be gawking in the first place, he settled his attention on her face again, finding her watching him closely.

Clearing his throat, he summoned up a smile. "You took a bath."

"And discovered my rash has greatly improved in the process." She lifted her chin. "That means I'm ready to roll up my sleeves and get right to work." She smiled even as she reached into her apron pocket, pulling out a sheet of paper. "As you'll see from this reference letter penned by Mr. Hatfield, head butler to the esteemed New York Waterbury family, I'm very proficient with organization, and I have . . . ah . . . a wonderful work ethic."

He wasn't certain, but it almost seemed as if she'd grimaced after she'd gotten that last part out of her mouth. Before he could question her about that, she was smiling again.

"Having said that and having had the wonderful opportunity to spend the last few days at Glory Manor, I'm convinced this farm is exactly where I'm meant to take up employment. All that's left to do now is discover when you'd like me to start, but do know that I'm available immediately."

CHAPTER 13

"And the last stop on our tour is the laundry room," Ian said three hours later, gesturing around the room they were standing in. "I'm sure nothing in here needs explaining, although I can't be certain about that since you did seem to have quite a few questions about the ice shed."

Isadora dredged up a smile, ignoring what seemed to be apprehension in Ian's eyes. There was no debating that she'd asked numerous questions about the ice shed, but in her defense, she'd found it odd that a farm would have cuts of beef and chicken delivered weekly instead of making use of the livestock she assumed was readily available in the barn. However, after Ian had explained Uncle Amos's curious reluctance to consume the animals he apparently thought of as friends, she'd been rather relieved, especially when she realized she'd never be served a dish that had Elmer as the main course.

Not that she was overly fond of Elmer, but she didn't despise the little beast so much that she'd want to see it served in a butter sauce, or . . .

"You're not saying much, Mrs. Delmont. Should I assume that's because you're composing numerous questions about laundry, a task I've always thought was rather straightforward? But given

116

your descent into muteness, it might not be as straightforward as I originally believed."

Shoving aside all thoughts of Elmer being served up on a plate, Isadora could only pray that the horror now chugging through her veins would not decide to settle on her face. Looking horrified would hardly encourage Ian to believe her claim of being a competent housekeeper, but in her honest opinion, there was nothing straightforward about the room she was in.

Piles of clothing and linens were stacked on the floor, and there was the oddest contraption sitting against the wall, one that resembled a large barrel with curious cranks and handles attached to it.

She kept her smile firmly in place. "While laundry is, as you said, straightforward, I'm afraid I'm not familiar with . . ." She waved at the contraption that had captured her attention.

"It's a washing machine."

"Is it really?" she breathed, stepping closer to the machine and giving it a good look. Lifting her head, she frowned. "I've never seen one quite like this before."

To her relief, Ian didn't look taken aback by her admission but smiled instead. "I'm not surprised. I only recently acquired that from a friend of mine who'd purchased a newer washing machine he thought was an improvement over that model." Ian shook his head. "I think my friend is feeling a bit remorseful, however, because this beauty works like a charm, whereas the new one my friend bought has all sorts of problems. That one over there was invented by a woman named Margaret Colvin. She introduced it to the world at the Centennial International Exhibition in 1876 in Philadelphia, which is how my friend came to learn of it."

"How educational. But tell me this, how does it work like a charm?"

For a moment, Ian didn't respond, but then he stepped closer to her. "You have operated a washing machine, haven't you?"

"*Operate* is such a vague term."

"Do not tell me you've never done laundry before."

The truth was . . . of course she'd never done laundry before, nor had she ever seen a washing machine in her life. But because she'd decided the safest place for her was at Glory Manor, and the only way she was going to be able to stay was if she could convince Ian she had some sort of value, Isadora decided to throw herself on whatever mercy he might have in that far-too-masculine body of his.

"I must admit I've not had much experience with laundry, but I'm a fast learner. If you could merely show me the basics of how to operate that machine, I'm certain I'll be more than proficient with laundry after I complete all of"—she gestured to the piles littering the floor—"that."

Unfortunately, he did not seem to be in much of a merciful frame of mind.

"What say you and I put our tour on hold until I take a closer look at that reference letter you gave me. I'm getting the distinct impression you may not have the basic experience needed for filling the position."

"As you pointed out after you read my reference letter the first time, my expertise is centered around organization, not the execution of actual labor. Regardless, even though I clearly lack some of the skills that are apparently required for a housekeeper here at Glory Manor, you are, if I need remind you, in a bit of a pickle. You don't have any other candidates lining up to take on the position, so why don't we simply agree that I have much to learn and get on with the lesson of how to operate a washing machine?"

Ian's brows drew together. "It's unfortunate women aren't readily accepted into the world of law because, honestly, you'd make a fine attorney. That was some remarkably quick thinking on your part, and you make a compelling argument."

Warmth flowed through her. "No one has ever complimented me on my quick wit before."

"Probably because you're a beautiful woman and people tend to believe beautiful women only want to hear compliments about their beauty, although . . ." He winced. "I probably shouldn't have said that."

Isadora grinned. "I think I can forgive you that lapse. It's also reassuring to know that my face has not been permanently disfigured, because I doubt you'd proclaim me beautiful if I was still looking the way I did when I first came down with poison ivy."

"Does this mean I should expect you to ask for a mirror now?"

She glanced at the washing machine. "I have far too much to learn to concern myself with my appearance right now. Besides . . ." She raised a hand and touched the still-bumpy skin on her face. "I think I should wait a few more days to take a look at my face since this is not the smooth skin I'm used to."

"It's not as bad as you think."

"Which is a reassuring turn of phrase to be sure. But let's return to what we were discussing before. What can you tell me about the basics of laundry?"

Ian, annoyingly enough, crossed his arms over his chest. "We were more recently discussing your reference letter."

"I thought we put that discussion to bed."

"No, we didn't, although I must give you credit for being rather adept at distraction. However, I would like to peruse your reference letter one more time, so I'm now going to encourage you to trot right up to your room and fetch it for me."

She smoothed back hair that was coming undone from the knot she'd managed to make on the back of her neck. "Trotting, as I'm sure you're aware, can be exhausting. If you've forgotten, I've only recently emerged from my sickroom. With that said, I'm sure you're in perfect agreement that I should conserve my strength so that I'll be able to tackle the daunting, or rather, exhilarating task of learning how to operate a washing machine."

Not wanting to allow him time to compose an argument, Isadora marched across the room, stopping in front of a machine that looked quite unlike anything she'd ever seen before. Considering it, she leaned closer to what seemed to be some type of barrel. "This is where the laundry goes, doesn't it?"

She wasn't certain, but it almost sounded as if Ian snorted before he joined her beside the machine. Sending her an exasperated look, he lifted the lid on the barrel. "Since we're already here, it won't hurt to continue our lesson, but do know that I *will* see that reference letter again before we begin talking about the terms of employment."

"There are terms to my employment?"

"You'll want to be paid a salary, won't you?"

Isadora blinked. "I imagine so."

"Then we'll need to discuss terms and decide what type of salary your experience warrants, which is another reason why I'll need to see your reference letter again." He frowned. "And upon further reflection, I'm curious as to why you took that letter away from me, since employers usually keep those letters after a potential employee hands them over."

She peered into the barrel. "I have limited reference letters with me. Since you didn't actually offer me a position after you read my reference letter, I thought it best to take it back so I won't take the chance of running out of reference letters if I'm forced to travel from one posted position to another." She straightened. "There's something in there."

"That would be the laundry."

"Ah, so it is." She stuck her hand in the barrel and gave the laundry a poke. "It's wet."

"Because I put it through the wash cycle before I got distracted answering your many summons and then rescuing you from a rogue chicken."

She turned to him and frowned. "If you'll recall, I did apologize for my demanding ways. I thought you'd accepted my apology and moved on. I'm not certain about that now, though, since you've broached the topic again."

"That's another impressive argument, but before we get distracted with what will certainly be a riveting debate, should we simply get to the business of teaching you how to operate this washing machine?"

Her lips quirked at the corners. "Sorry, go on."

She thought his lips might have quirked as well, but before

she could tell for certain, he'd turned his attention back to the machine. "Because the washing part of these clothes has been done, I can't show you how to wash the clothing, but I will explain the process. First, you fill the tub with water, which you get by attaching the black hose to the spigot on the sink over there." He nodded to the sink in question. "Because the hot water is temperamental at times, and if you're washing whites—which need to be washed in hot water, if you didn't know—it's for the best if you heat water on the stove and then bring that water in here and dump it into the tub along with colder water you get from the sink."

"I need to lug hot water all the way from the kitchen to this room?"

"Unless you have a better idea of how to get hot water in here, yes."

"Perhaps I should start taking notes."

She wasn't certain, but it sounded as if Ian snorted again right before he strode across the laundry room and through the door.

Not having the least little idea if he planned on returning or why he'd left the room in the first place, she turned her attention to the washing machine, hoping that she might somehow understand how it was meant to be used. Frankly, she had no idea why there were numerous cylinder-shaped tubes attached to the side of the tub or what those tubes were meant to do.

"I've found you a pad of paper."

Taking the paper, along with the pencil he gave her, Isadora nodded. "Excellent. Carry on."

"Has anyone ever told you that housekeepers aren't usually so bossy with their potential employers?"

"Fill the tub with water," she said instead of answering his question, writing that down before she looked up again. "And then?"

"You wrote down filling the tub with water?"

"I told you I needed to take notes, and I don't want to forget anything."

Shaking his head, Ian launched into a lecture about how to go about washing the laundry, explaining how much soap she was to add to the tub after she'd filled it with water and then showing her how to turn a crank that moved the contents of the tub around, cleaning the clothes in the process.

"You'll know you're finished with the cranking when your arm feels about ready to fall off, and then you'll need to move on to the wringer."

"The wringer? That sounds like something you'd find in a torture chamber."

"I'm certain there are many people in this country, mostly women, who do believe the laundry room is a torture chamber. But as for the wringer, it merely wrings the water out of the clothing after that clothing has been rinsed with clean water, something I've just remembered we'll need to do to the clothing currently in the washing machine."

"Rinse the clothing," she said, writing that out on the page.

"Before you can rinse the clothing, though, you'll need to drain the water out of the tub, then replace it with fresh water."

The next few minutes passed with Ian showing her how to drain the tub, then how to attach the hose to the sink to refill the tub with clean water. He then stepped away from the machine, allowing her a chance to use the crank. She found that chore far more difficult than she'd imagined since it took quite a bit of effort, as well as a bit of perspiration, to get the laundry swishing around. By the time Ian decided the laundry was sufficiently rinsed, she was perspiring more than she'd ever perspired in her life and her arms were shaking like jelly.

"So now, after we drain the tub again, we'll be able to move on to the wringer process, but before we do that . . ." He nodded to a pile of linens. "It's always best to have a look at what laundry is going into the tub next."

Isadora moved to where she'd left her notes and glanced over the page. "And because those are whites, we'll have to boil water to add to the tub."

"Very good. Why don't you see about getting the water boiling while I empty the water from the tub so we'll then be able to get on with the wringing?"

Even though she had no idea how to boil water, Isadora nodded and headed for the door, praying that boiling water merely sounded like a daunting task but would, in reality, turn out to be a mundane sort of chore that wouldn't be daunting at all.

CHAPTER 14

"I've clearly lost my mind."

Ian, realizing he'd spoken that telling statement out loud, pressed his lips together and returned to the laundry, wondering what he could have been thinking to even consider the possibility of offering Izzie Delmont a position of employment.

She was completely lacking when it came to anything concerning basic housekeeping skills. And he should have nipped the idea of employing her in the bud the moment he'd taken a look at her letter of reference.

The only thing impressive about that letter was that it was written on a very expensive piece of vellum in a very fine hand. But even with that, the letter a Mr. Hatfield, butler to the Waterbury family, had penned was vague in the extreme, and nowhere had there been any mention of an actual position Izzie had held.

That should have been reason enough to rethink offering her employment, although before he'd been able to scan the letter again, or broach what he felt were obvious deficiencies with the contents of the reference, she'd plucked it right out of his hand. She'd then said something like "That's that," sent him a smile that could only be described as charming, and quit the room, reappearing a few moments later after she'd apparently packed her letter away.

Even with her ridiculous explanation regarding why she'd taken her reference letter back, a reason that was peculiar since she could have merely asked for the reference letter back if he *didn't* extend her an offer of employment, he'd still found himself giving in to her instead of demanding she fetch the letter straightaway.

It was quite unlike him, this wishy-washy attitude, especially because this was a clear matter of business, and he'd never been wishy-washy about business matters in his life.

Reinserting the plug after he'd drained the water from the tub, he straightened and leaned a hip against the washing machine, his thoughts returning to his concerning behavior of late. There had to be a reasonable explanation as to why he was continuing to demonstrate tasks such as laundry to a woman who was not remotely qualified for the position he needed to fill, especially when it made more sense to ride into town and look into hiring . . .

Ian froze on the spot when an explanation did come to him, one that left him reeling ever so slightly.

He, Ian MacKenzie, a no-nonsense gentleman if there ever was one, was fascinated with Izzie Delmont—even with her demanding ways, bossy nature, and ineptitude when it came to anything involving household matters.

That fascination, he was almost afraid to admit, was exactly why he'd continued with what was certain madness, even though doing so was, well, mad.

He was known for being a tough negotiator, making certain he was always getting the best contracts when it came to labor disputes. He was also known for encouraging the labor leaders to hire only the most qualified of candidates, and yet . . . it was a complete stretch to think Izzie was in any way qualified to run Glory Manor.

Pushing away from the washing machine, he squared his shoulders, knowing it was past time to reenter reality. That meant he needed to saddle up his horse and ride to Canonsburg, hoping Mrs.

Rogers would be able to point him in the direction of a competent housekeeper, one who was hopefully over the age of fifty and one he wouldn't find fascinating, or worse yet . . . intriguing.

Moving for the door, he paused when he realized that Izzie would be more than disappointed to learn he was not going to offer her the position. Consoling himself a second later when he remembered he did still need to hire someone to look after the children, and the children did seem to like Izzie, he strode from the room. When he walked through the kitchen a moment later, his arrival was greeted by a moo from Buttercup as she peered into the kitchen through the screen door.

"I see Buttercup's come for another visit," he said, smiling at Aunt Birdie, who was sitting at the kitchen table with the children, all of them involved in various stages of cutting out cookies. Izzie was standing in front of the stove, looking, for some curious reason, rather grumpy as she peered into a pot of what he was going to assume was water.

"Buttercup's sad because she wants some apples," Henry said. "But Aunt Birdie told me if I feed Buttercup apples, I have to wash up *again*, and . . ." He shuddered.

"Maybe you could feed her the apples, Ian," Violet said, looking up from the dough rolled out in front of her. "You don't seem to mind washin' up."

"That sounds like an excellent idea," he returned, earning a shy smile from Violet in response. "I'm curious, though, why no one suggested Mrs. Delmont feed Buttercup a few treats, since I'm sure Buttercup's been more than vocal with her begging."

Aunt Birdie's head shot up. She met his gaze, and then she shook her head just the slightest bit before she slid a glance to Izzie. She might have, he wasn't exactly certain, winced. "Izzie's waiting for the water to boil. It's tricky business, boiling water, and she shouldn't be distracted. Since I'm sure you agree with that, it would be best if you give Buttercup her treat." She looked Izzie's way again and definitely winced. "This is her second attempt, but she does seem determined to get it right this time."

Having no idea what could have gone wrong with Izzie's first attempt to boil water, but knowing better than to ask since Aunt Birdie was now sending him a pointed look, Ian walked across the kitchen. His eyes widened when he got a closer look at Izzie and noticed that her blouse and apron were soaking wet. Refusing a smile, he picked up the bucket of apples and headed out the door.

After giving Buttercup a few apple chunks, Ian ignored the mournful moos she immediately began to make when he told her that was all she was getting. Taking a moment to wash his hands under the water pump, he made his way back into the house, joining everyone at the kitchen table.

"Are some of these new cookie cutters?" he asked, considering the metal shapes spread over the table

Henry nodded and held up the cookie cutter he was using. "Uncle Amos just made them. It's a chicken, and he wants us to make enough cookies so every chicken in his coop is . . ." He wrinkled his nose. "I don't remember the word he used."

"*Represented*," Primrose told him. "Even the roosters."

Henry pointed to his cookie. "See, that blob is supposed to be the rooster's crown."

Ian grinned. "Very nice."

"Mine's Elmer," Violet said, showing him hers. "I'm gonna put pink icing on it and give it to Izzie 'cuz Elmer's her chicken now."

Glancing toward Izzie, Ian fought a laugh when she sent Violet a weak smile before she returned her attention to the pot on the stove.

"We never had sugar cookies before," Primrose said. "But Aunt Birdie told us we could lick the bowls *and* have two cookies once they're done."

"Cookies!" Daisy bellowed, her recently clean face smeared with cookie batter, suggesting she, unlike her siblings, had already done her fair share of licking the bowl.

Remembering the wonder of having his first encounter with cookies while sitting in this very same kitchen, as well as remembering how quickly he'd come to feel a sense of safety he'd never

127

known until he came to live at Glory Manor, Ian's heart gave an unexpected lurch. Summoning up a smile, he picked up one of the prepared trays.

"Shall I get this into the oven so you won't have to wait long to taste your first sugar cookies?"

With all the children agreeing that was a good idea, Ian moved to the oven as Izzie stepped out of the way. Sliding the tray into the oven, he straightened, then frowned when Izzie stepped right back in front of the oven again, staring at the pot. "Have you ever heard the expression that a watched pot never boils?"

"I can't say that I have, but would it boil faster if I stop watching it?"

He had the sneaking suspicion her question was completely serious, which spoke volumes about her experience, or lack thereof, in the kitchen.

"Probably not, but if you were to put a lid over that pot, that would have it boiling faster."

"Why will putting a lid on top of the pot make it boil faster?"

"Because it captures the heat."

Her eyes widened. "Why, that's brilliant. I would have never thought of that." Sending him a smile that, concerning enough, seemed to steal the very breath from him, she hurried across the kitchen, returning a moment later with a lid that didn't quite fit the pot, but one she used nevertheless. "What a clever recommendation. Should we time it now and see how long it takes for the water to boil with the lid on?"

He immediately found himself pulling out his pocket watch, a frisson of something curious shooting through him when she reached out and touched his hand with hers, bending closer to look at the dials on the watch.

"Ian, come help Violet roll out her dough," Primrose called. "She's havin' trouble."

Thankful to have a reason to press his pocket watch into Izzie's hand and then put some distance between them as he went to sit beside Violet, he took the rolling pin Violet handed him and immediately turned his attention to rolling out cookie dough. He was soon swept up in the excitement of making the cookies with the children, their enthusiasm for such a simple activity contagious.

Ten minutes later, and after he'd taken the first tray of cookies out of the oven and put another one in, the water on the stove was boiling merrily away, something Izzie had neglected to notice because she'd gotten distracted with a bowl of icing Aunt Birdie asked her to stir.

"I believe the water is boiling."

Abandoning the icing, Izzie consulted the pocket watch. "Ah, eleven minutes. I'll need to add that to my notes." She looked around. "I wonder where I left them?"

"They're in the laundry room."

"Which is where I need to return now that the water is boiling."

When she went to reach for the handle, he caught hold of her hand. "You can't pick that up without a mitt. You'll burn yourself. And because you've obviously had some difficulties with the water already, allow me to take this back to the laundry room for you."

"I can do it."

"I'm sure you can, but since I am a gentleman, humor me and let me play the gallant."

"You do remember I'm trying to impress you with my proficiency regarding household chores, don't you?"

"I don't think I'll ever be able to forget that."

Ignoring the way her nose was wrinkling, Ian grabbed an oven mitt, told everyone he'd be right back to fetch the next batch of cookies from the oven, picked the pot up from the stove, turned, then paused when he noticed Aunt Birdie waving his way.

"There's no need for you to hurry back. Primrose seems to have an affinity for working in a kitchen. Because of that, I'm willing to hand over the responsibility of taking the cookies out of the oven. I imagine she'll do a more than competent job with that task."

"She's only nine," Ian pointed out, earning a glare from Primrose in the process.

"I've been using a stove since I was six."

Ian inclined his head, realizing that the child now glaring his way had obviously been given responsibilities from a very young age, quite like he'd been given before he came to Glory Manor. "My apologies, Primrose. I didn't mean to insult you."

For a second, she continued glaring at him, but then she inclined her head in return. "I know how to cook *and* take a tray from the oven."

Aunt Birdie clapped her hands. "How delightful, my dear. You have no idea how I've longed to have someone to work with in the kitchen. I imagine you and I are going to have all sorts of fun trying out new recipes." She smiled at Primrose's siblings. "And all of you are going to be the tasters of those recipes."

Leaving the children asking Aunt Birdie what recipes they should have Primrose try first, Ian fell into step beside Izzie, being careful not to spill the hot water as they walked.

"Your aunt has a way with managing children," Izzie said.

"That she does, but speaking of Aunt Birdie's managing ways, I should probably mention that she might try her hand at managing you as well."

"Since I'm clearly in need of direction with managing this house, I'll welcome her managing ways."

Ian winced. "I wasn't referring to her trying to help you manage the house."

Izzie stepped into the laundry room. "What were you referring to, then?"

Taking a second to set the pot on top of a scarred table, Ian turned and found Izzie directly behind him. She was tilting her head and considering him closely through the lenses of her hideous spectacles.

"How long have you been wearing spectacles?" he asked instead of answering her question.

"For what feels like forever," she said, pushing the spectacles in question back up her nose. "But returning to your aunt—how might she try to manage me?"

"It's not so much managing you as manipulating you," he admitted, wincing when she blinked somewhat owlishly back at him.

"Aunt Birdie hasn't struck me as the manipulating sort," she said slowly. "But how do you think she'll try and do that?"

"I imagine she'll begin by pointing out what she feels are my greatest strengths, such as loyalty or charm or, well, whatever else she decides will impress you. She'll then try to ferret out what your feelings for me might be, and then . . ."

He stopped speaking when Izzie suddenly began to laugh.

"This is not an amusing matter" was all he could think to say as she took off her spectacles, swiping her eyes with her sleeve.

She shoved the spectacles back up the bridge of her nose, gave a last hiccup of amusement, then caught his eye. "This doesn't sound like manipulation to me. It sounds like matchmaking."

"Which, in my humble opinion, is worse than manipulation."

She gave another hiccup of amusement.

"It's not funny." He blew out a breath. "Aunt Birdie wants to see me happily married before she leaves this earth. And I'm afraid that with Uncle Amos's declining state of health as of late, it's made her somewhat . . . determined."

"How delightful."

Of anything he'd been expecting Izzie to say, *How delightful* hadn't crossed his mind. "She's an incredibly wily woman when she sets her mind to it, and I want you to be prepared for a direct attack from her, especially if I'm in Pittsburgh. She's already tried to convince me that the encounter you and I had by the pond, the one where I tried to assist you with breathing, has left us connected for life in some curious manner."

Izzie waved that aside. "There's no need for you to worry about me even *if* Aunt Birdie has her heart set on a bit of matchmaking. Marriage is not high on my list of priorities these days, so I assure you, I'll not set my cap for you, no matter how determined she turns."

"Is that because of Mr. Delmont?"

"Who?"

"Your *husband*?"

For a second, Izzie looked rather confused, but then, to *his* confusion, she mumbled something that sounded like "I knew that was going to be an issue" before she gave an airy wave of her hand. "Ah yes, quite right, Mr. Delmont." A small smile played around the corners of her mouth. "All I'm comfortable saying about him is this: Have you ever met a housekeeper who went by the title of *Miss*?"

"Is that an actual question or some type of puzzle?"

"You seem to be an intelligent man, Mr. MacKenzie. I'm certain you'll figure it out eventually."

Ian considered her for a moment. "Are you implying there is no Mr. Delmont?"

She considered him right back before she shrugged. "I'll leave that for you to determine, but returning to the laundry situation, if you've forgotten, I'm attempting to impress you, so . . . to the washing machine."

Giving his arm a surprising pat, she turned on her heel and walked away, leaving him feeling oddly relieved that she might never have been married, but also disgruntled since she'd blithely admitted she wouldn't be tempted to set her cap for him.

CHAPTER 15

As Izzie considered her notes, Ian couldn't seem to tear his gaze from her or banish the disgruntlement that was still chugging through his veins.

He was considered one of the most eligible bachelors in Pittsburgh, and yet Izzie didn't seem remotely interested in him. In fact, she apparently found the idea of Aunt Birdie playing matchmaker rather amusing.

She had to have concluded that he was a man of some means, and he knew she found him somewhat attractive since she'd said, right after making his acquaintance, that she wouldn't imagine he needed to advertise for a bride. She also knew they shared an interest in reading, which he found to be quite compelling. But even with all that, she didn't seem overly impressed with him.

That right there explained exactly why he was standing perfectly still in the laundry room, staring at her in what was clearly a mesmerized state.

From the time he'd begun amassing a fortune, women had shown a great deal of interest in him. Those women were from all walks of life—some belonging to the wealthiest families in Pittsburgh and some not possessing much money at all. Their interest had turned him cynical over the years, especially when he'd finally realized that most of the women were more interested in his fortune than the man who'd made it.

Izzie Delmont apparently wasn't interested in him at all, or she was, but only as a potential employer, which meant . . .

"I still have no idea what all those cranks and handles do."

Blinking out of his thoughts, Ian found that while he'd been pondering ideas best left unpondered, Izzie had moved from her notes and was now contemplating the washing machine.

"Here, I'll show you," he said, forcing aside any disgruntlement he was still feeling because he certainly didn't want her to decide he was a churlish sort, although why he didn't want her to come to that conclusion was beyond him.

Taking a moment to explain how the cylinders worked and how a person had to reach into the tub and pull out a piece of laundry before they could begin the wringing process, something he thought would be self-explanatory but turned out to be anything but, he stepped aside.

"So, now you're ready to begin wringing, and then after the clothing has been wrung out—"

"We'll be done with the laundry for the day?"

His brows drew together. "No. We'll only be halfway done. It has to be hung out to dry, and then, now don't faint dead away, but it'll need to be ironed."

"Ironed?"

"To get the wrinkles out."

"How, pray tell, does one go about ironing out wrinkles?"

"One usually uses an iron, an object that's triangular and is heated by placing it on top of the stove."

Izzie's face fell. "I have to use the stove again?"

Suddenly remembering he'd decided *before* the boiling water debacle that he was *not* going to hire Izzie to manage Glory Manor because she truly was not experienced enough to take on the role, he opened his mouth, but then closed it almost immediately when she suddenly squared her shoulders and nodded.

"I'm certain ironing must be easier than boiling water, so no need to fret I won't be able to handle the job."

Seeing little point in abandoning their lesson now, especially when faced with a woman who clearly was beginning to realize she was out of her depth and yet had not given up, Ian smiled. "How about we concentrate on the wringer right now? We won't need to use the iron until later today, after all of these clothes are dry."

She shoved a hand in her apron pocket, pulled out what looked to be a hairpin, pushed back a strand of hair that had escaped what he only then noticed seemed to be a good twenty pins, and stuck the new pin into her hair, adding it to the rest. He refused to laugh when another curl immediately sprang free, falling in front of her face—a curl she ignored.

"I'm definitely never taking clean clothes for granted again," he thought he heard her say as she reached into the washing machine and retrieved one of his shirts.

"What was that?"

"Nothing. I'm simply all aflutter with anticipation over learning what using the wringer entails."

"You don't look all aflutter. You look more along the lines of astonished, probably due to the notion you had no idea how much work was involved to produce clean laundry."

"I never look astonished. My mother always said astonishment is unbecoming in a . . ." She stopped talking, shook out the shirt she was holding, then thrust it his way. "Perhaps you should demonstrate first before I give it a try."

Taking the shirt from her, he moved to the wringer, stuck the collar of the shirt into the wringer, then turned the crank that was attached to cylinders, pulling the shirt through those cylinders and squeezing the water from it as it pulled. Holding the shirt up once it made it through the wringer, Ian smiled. "See? It's not nearly as wet." He placed it in an empty basket, then nodded to her. "You try."

Reaching into the tub, Izzie tugged another shirt out, stuck a piece of it into the wringer, then gave the crank a few turns. She lifted her head and smiled. "Would you look at that. I'm wringing."

"You've really *never* done laundry before, have you?"

"Will you think poorly of me if I admit I may not have what anyone could consider practical experience?"

Ian tilted his head. "Why would you apply for a position you're clearly not qualified for?"

She gave the wringer another crank. "I thought Glory Manor, given the name, was a country estate, not a farm. I assure you, I'm more than qualified to manage staff on a country estate."

"How can you manage the task of making certain laundry is completed to satisfaction if you have no idea how to perform that task yourself?"

"Because if laundry is clean and properly put away, I know the task was well performed, and if it's not, well, the person in charge of the laundry needs to try again."

"How is it possible you didn't know that putting a lid on a pot makes the water boil faster?"

"I didn't know because, again, I'm used to grand estates, and I was never required to perform any specific tasks in the kitchens. That's what people hire cooks to do."

"Which makes it confusing why you've suddenly decided you'll be a proficient housekeeper at Glory Manor. You don't appear to have the experience needed to take on this position."

She abandoned the shirt still halfway through the wringer. "That almost sounds as if you're having second thoughts about hiring me."

"Truth be told, I've passed second thoughts and moved on to around the fifth thoughts."

She returned to the wringer, giving the handle a decidedly determined crank. "Haven't you ever wanted to prove something—something that might seem downright impossible but will mean the world to you if you can succeed in the end?"

The offer he'd been about to make to her regarding looking after the children died on his tongue. He'd set about proving his worth from almost the time he'd arrived at Glory Manor. He'd been able to do just that because Aunt Birdie and Uncle Amos had had faith in him and given him a chance. Without that chance, there was every likelihood he'd be laboring in the mills, earning a meager salary, and living in the same derelict neighborhood he'd grown up in.

"I've never been challenged," Izzie continued, sending the shirt the rest of the way through the wringer and then picking it up and tossing it into the basket and retrieving another piece of laundry, which she stuffed into place before she looked at him. "I can do this, Ian, or I mean, Mr. MacKenzie. I know I can. Besides, you're needed back in Pittsburgh. I doubt you're going to be able to find a suitable housekeeper simply strolling around the streets of Canonsburg anytime soon."

"One never knows."

She narrowed her eyes. "I realize I'm not what anyone would call the best candidate for the position, but one cannot underestimate the power of enthusiasm, something I guarantee you I've acquired for this particular position."

She gave the crank to the wringer a turn, smiling when the pair of trousers began rolling through the cylinders. "See, I told you I'm a fast learner."

"And while I appreciate that, along with your clear sense of enthusiasm," he began, bracing himself for the reaction he knew his next words would bring about, "as a man of business, I've always demanded a certain level of competency from the people I work with. I'm afraid to say, from what I've seen today, that no matter how much enthusiasm you have for this . . ."

The rest of his words died a rapid death when Izzie suddenly let out a yelp right as a loud ripping noise sounded, and then . . . she was standing remarkably close to the wringer, missing the front half of her blouse, along with her apron, those two articles of clothing having been sucked right up into the cylinders.

"It won't let me go," she breathed, giving her blouse a tug even as she gave the handle another turn, effectively pulling her even closer to the wringer.

"Stop cranking it. You're making it worse. And I don't want to alarm you, but I think your chemise is being sucked up as well, and . . ."

Stripping his shirt off, Ian moved directly beside her. He yanked his shirt over her head, having to wrestle it down her body when she seemed to be fighting him.

"Quit moving. You're not helping matters."

A second later, she was standing still as a statue, her eyes wide when she turned her head and settled her gaze not on his face but on his chest.

"Goodness," she breathed. "You're, ah . . . practically naked."

"I am not, I'm merely without a shirt, something I do believe you should appreciate since my shirt is now offering you a semblance of modesty."

"Oh right, but . . . goodness."

Stepping back, he shook his head. "Your reaction does seem to lend credence to the fact that there truly is no Mr. Delmont. But should I also assume you're not in possession of any brothers?"

"I have three, but they're not, well . . ." She took a second to look him up and down before her eyes widened and her gaze seemed to linger on his chest.

Even though he'd received his fair share of admiration from the ladies over the years, there was something remarkably satisfying in knowing Izzie, no matter that she'd proclaimed herself uninterested in setting her cap for him, seemed to be slightly fascinated by the sight of his bare skin.

That fascination went far in soothing his pride, and . . .

"Perhaps we should try to figure out how to get my shirt out of the wringer," she said, pushing all thoughts of soothing his wounded pride aside.

"Good idea," he said, leaning forward to inspect the wringer. He straightened. "I'm afraid your apron and your blouse are ruined, so it might be faster to simply have you remove the blouse. If you'll just shrug out of the sleeves, I think it'll come right off you, since there's not much left to it."

"That's not something I was expecting to hear today," she muttered before she shrugged out of the sleeves of her blouse. She then began fighting with his shirt to get her arms into those sleeves, twisting and turning until she slid on some water that had splashed on the floor, letting out another yelp as her feet swept out from under her.

Catching her before she could hit the floor, Ian brought her up against his chest, pulling her close.

Regret was immediate because the feel of her hands pressed against his skin sent his senses reeling and a bolt of lightning traveling from where her hands were touching him all the way down to his toes.

He also felt the most unusual urge to tilt her head back and kiss her, an urge he knew he shouldn't give in to, but it was an urge he couldn't—

"Primrose is gonna be sad she missed you kissin' Izzie again, Ian," a voice suddenly said from somewhere in the laundry room. "She and Aunt Birdie keep talkin' about how nice a weddin' is. Can I be the one to tell them one's gonna be happenin' now?"

Sanity returned in a split second. Placing his arms on Izzie's shoulders, he took a step away from her, made certain she'd found her balance, then almost forgot someone else was in the room with them when he caught her gaze and saw a most curious look in her eyes, or perhaps that was . . .

"Ah . . . Ian? You want me to come back later?"

Forcing his attention away from Izzie, Ian turned and found Henry standing just inside the doorway, holding a telegram in his hand and grinning.

"I wasn't kissing Izzie, or ah, Mrs. Delmont, Henry," he managed to say. "She got her shirt stuck in the wringer, and then . . . well, no need to go into all the particulars. What's that you have there?"

"Another telegram. And the man who delivered it said he was gettin' annoyed over havin' to travel out here so often."

Striding across the room, Ian took the telegram from Henry,

who was still grinning. Opening it, he read the contents, blowing out a breath as he lifted his head.

"It appears matters have turned dire in Pittsburgh. I'm being met at the train station tomorrow morning by one of my business associates."

"Which is why it's fortunate you have me to step in and oversee Glory Manor while you're away." Izzie walked to join him, then laid a hand on his arm, snatching that hand away a second later, quite as if she'd somehow forgotten he was missing a shirt. "I can do the job. You simply need to give me a chance."

"You just got yourself stuck to a washing machine."

"I'm sure that happens all the time."

"I've never heard of such a thing before."

"Only because the people who've gotten stuck have obviously been too mortified to admit it to anyone."

"Which is an excellent point, but you and I both know you're woefully deficient with basic housekeeping skills."

"*Woefully deficient* might be a bit harsh." She sighed, drew in another breath, then narrowed her eyes a second later, quite as if she'd come up with yet another argument. "You're a man of business."

"Was that a question or a statement?"

She ignored that as she took to tapping a finger against her chin. "I know men of business, and it seems to me they're always looking for the best deal."

"I won't argue with that, although successful men of business are also always looking for the most competent people, ones worthy of the salary they're going to be paid."

"Exactly," Izzie agreed. "I'm going to offer you a deal."

"A . . . deal?"

"One you won't be able to refuse." She nodded. "If you'll offer me the position of housekeeper at Glory Manor, I'll work for no salary for . . . shall we say two weeks?"

"You really don't understand how business deals are supposed to work, do you?"

140

She ignored the question. "If after that two weeks, you still find me *woefully deficient*, I'll leave Glory Manor on my own accord and won't even make you feel guilty about sending me away."

"But what if you burn down the house?"

"I assure you, I am not so inadequate that I would burn down the house." Her eyes flashed. "Why, I have to imagine that when you return from Pittsburgh, you'll be so impressed with my proficiency that you'll be begging my pardon for insulting my abilities and offering me a tidy wage to continue working for you."

Glancing at the telegram he was still holding, and realizing that he really didn't have many options, Ian looked up and caught her eye. "You promise me you won't burn down the house?"

"You have my word."

He shot a look to Henry, who was nodding back at him, evidently adding his approval to a plan that was sheer madness. Looking back to Izzie, he frowned.

"You'll work as a housekeeper with no salary for two weeks, but more importantly, you're giving me your word this house will still be standing when I return in a few days?"

She smiled. "I am, and you won't be sorry. I have every confidence you'll not be disappointed with my efforts, especially when you find this house not only still standing but running in a very organized and efficient fashion."

CHAPTER 16

Catching the biscuits on fire was most assuredly not the best way of honoring her promise to keep the house from burning to the ground.

Beating the now-flaming biscuits with a towel she'd grabbed from the sink, Isadora coughed and gave a bit of a wheeze as a plume of black smoke rose from the disaster on the baking sheet.

A large torrent of water suddenly flew past her, and with a hiss and a sizzle, the flames went out, leaving only a smoldering mass of charred biscuits behind.

Waving away the smoke that was obscuring her vision, Isadora lifted watering eyes and discovered Primrose standing beside her, holding an empty bucket.

"That was close," Primrose said, setting aside the bucket. "Are you all right, Izzie?"

Izzie found the simple question a bit perplexing.

Was she all right? It was truly difficult to say.

The chore of watching over the biscuits had been a simple one. And yet, because she'd become absorbed with an image that kept springing to mind of Ian not sporting a shirt and displaying muscles that should come with a warning attached to them, she'd failed—miserably.

She was not a lady disposed to fanciful thinking about any gentleman, and yet, for the life of her, she couldn't stop thinking about Mr. Ian MacKenzie, thoughts that had seen her almost catching the house on fire.

It was beyond peculiar, this fascination she seemed to have for the man. But that fascination, instead of fading the moment he left Glory Manor that morning at the unheard-of hour of six, seemed to be growing. Thoughts of Ian were coming to mind every other second, even as she'd been trying to complete a few of the tasks he'd left written for her on a *very* long list.

Those thoughts had left her with some interesting conclusions, the most important of those being this—he was an intriguing man.

He was kind, charming, undoubtedly handsome, *and* he was a man of compassion. His sense of compassion was exactly why she'd known that bringing up her desire to prove herself and rise to the challenge of taking on the role of housekeeper would have him changing his mind and offering her the position.

It had not been her finest moment, especially when she'd hardly risen to that challenge by neglecting the biscuits and allowing them to burn to a crisp.

Shoving that less-than-comfortable thought aside, she poked a finger in the charred mass of dough, her thoughts, annoyingly enough, immediately returning to Ian.

He was far more intelligent than she'd first assumed, a trait she'd always been drawn to, although the few intelligent gentlemen who'd struck her fancy over the years had been quickly dismissed by her mother as unsuitable. Hester's loftiest goal apparently centered around acquiring a title for Isadora, no matter if Isadora wanted it or not.

Her lips began to curve at the thought of her mother's reaction if she learned that her only daughter was a tad intrigued by a man who'd grown up on a farm and gave an entirely new meaning to the term *masculine*, and . . .

"Izzie, come quick! The goats are eating the laundry."

Even though goats eating laundry was not something she'd imagined anyone ever bringing to her attention, Isadora couldn't claim it came as any surprise, not with how her day was shaping up.

Bolting for the door with Primrose at her side, she rushed into the backyard, skidding to a stop at the chaos transpiring before her.

Goats, creatures she was not familiar with in the least, were frolicking through the laundry, kicking up their heels and bleating up a storm as they snatched one piece of laundry after another from the clotheslines.

To her disbelief, they were then eating that laundry as they continued racing through the remaining wash that was snapping merrily away in the breeze. In all honesty, they were acting like they'd not eaten in months because as soon as they finished a piece, they snatched fresh laundry from the line, as if they wanted to sample everything she'd hung out to dry.

For a second, all Isadora could do was watch the horror unfolding in front of her, thinking of all the hours it had taken to wash the laundry being eaten or scattered willy-nilly. As her gaze drifted from one naughty goat to another, she suddenly realized that it was going to be up to her to stop the madness before every piece of laundry was soiled or consumed. Surging into motion, she dashed through the lines of laundry, annoyed when her efforts only had the goats scattering to all corners of the yard, taking laundry with them.

Setting her sights on a goat that was racing around with a frilly apron trailing out of its mouth, she ran after it and got it cornered by the side of the house, but when she lunged to grab it, it feinted to the right and Izzie landed in the dirt, clear sounds of amusement coming out of the goat's mouth as it pranced away from her.

"Get back here," she yelled, pushing herself to a sitting position as the goat bolted across the yard.

"Goats can be highly unpredictable."

Shielding her eyes with a hand that was no longer what anyone would consider clean, Isadora found a man standing a few feet away from her, shaking his head as his gaze traveled over the destruction the goats had left in their wake.

"I didn't know Glory Manor had a flock of goats," she said, accepting the man's outstretched hand when he moved to stand in front of her and offered her a hand up.

"Goats don't travel in flocks. They travel in herds."

"Something I never thought I'd have a reason to learn," she said. "You must be Hank."

He nodded, released her hand, then raked his hand through straw-colored hair. "I am, and you're Mrs. Delmont." He nodded again to the goats running amok. "I'm sorry about the goats. I was busy showing the new hires around the farm and didn't realize Amos must have forgotten to shut the gate where the goats were grazing." He scratched his chin. "I'd best get them collected before Amos returns from fishing. Wouldn't want him to decide someone is now trying to steal the goats along with the cows and chickens."

Wiping her hands on her apron, Isadora frowned. "Does Uncle Amos forget to close the gate often?"

Hank shrugged. "He won't admit to that, but it has been a recurring problem."

"Then you don't believe someone is trying to steal the animals?"

"Glory Manor doesn't have many animals to speak of, not compared to the other farms in the area. Doesn't make much sense that someone would want to steal the few on this farm." He suddenly looked worried. "Best not to mention that to Amos, though. He's a little peculiar these days, so I've found it's better to let him believe all the conspiracy theories he's come up with of late than argue with him."

"Wouldn't it be better to let him know he's just been forgetful when it comes to closing the gate?"

"He's sensitive about his memory. The slightest thing can set him off, so it's easier all around if I just agree with him." His gaze returned to the laundry scattered around. "I'll help you clean up this mess after I collect the goats. As I said, it won't do to have Amos find them out here. He'll think some type of skullduggery is taking place."

"We wouldn't want that, but . . ." Isadora stopped talking when her gaze landed on Violet clasping a muddy frock in one hand while dashing what looked to be tears from her face. "Excuse me," she said to Hank as she hurried over to Violet.

Kneeling beside the child, Isadora touched her shoulder. "Violet, what's wrong?"

A small sob was Violet's only answer as she held up the small dress, then wiped her nose with a dirty hand.

"The goats ate our clothes," Primrose said, coming up to join them, holding another dress that had a large hole in it in one hand, while holding Daisy's hand in the other. She nodded to Henry, who was running after a goat that had a pair of trousers in its mouth. "We only had a few changes of clothing, and now I think we might be down to the ones we're wearing and the one other change of clothing that's up in our rooms."

Isadora frowned. "Were you not given an opportunity to pack up your belongings before you came to Glory Manor?"

Primrose returned the frown. "We didn't have any belongings that the woman from the orphanage thought were . . . I think she said *worthy* of being packed. We came here with just the clothes we was wearing."

"You didn't bring *anything* with you?"

Primrose shrugged. "There wasn't much we would have wanted to bring. Pa got rid of Mama's things after she died, and it wasn't like any of us had any treasures that were real important." She pushed aside a strand of red hair that had escaped a messy braid. "But Reverend Davis, he's the minister in town, sent a basket of clothes he said was ours to keep, and that's what we've been wearing this past week."

Violet rubbed the small dress she was holding against her face. "This . . . was the . . . most bea . . . ut . . . iful dress I ever seen." Her eyes brimmed with tears as she held the dress out for Isadora to see. "It's purple, just like violets are purple." She drew in a ragged breath. "Mama named me Violet because they was one of her favorite flowers." With that, she hugged the ruined dress to her tiny frame and released another sob.

The sight of Violet in such obvious distress sent a wave of something peculiar crashing over Isadora as an unpleasant realization took that moment to settle in her very soul.

She'd always considered herself a sophisticated lady, educated by numerous governesses over the years, and then sent to a prestigious school for young ladies. She'd traveled around the world and spoke more than one language, but her sophistication was nothing but a ruse because, clearly, the world she thought she knew so well was nothing like the world the children standing right beside her inhabited.

She'd been sheltered and catered to her entire life and had certainly never wanted for anything, not that she'd taken even a moment to be grateful for the luxurious and pampered life she'd led.

Her slightest desires were always met by the army of paid employees her family kept at their disposal, paid to indulge Isadora's slightest whim, no matter what it was or the inconvenience it might cause the Delafield staff.

Her vast collections of the latest fashions were displayed in special rooms in the many houses her family owned. She'd always assumed that numerous changes of clothing a day were normal, but now, when faced with four children who were evidently brokenhearted that their hand-me-down clothing had been all but destroyed by goats, she was quickly beginning to realize that the world she thought was normal was nothing of the sort.

It was becoming obvious that the world was not a kind place for many of its inhabitants and had certainly not been kind to the children standing before her.

That idea left her reeling and caused the blinders she'd apparently been wearing for her entire life to fall.

Straightening, she reached out and took the ruined dress

from Violet, determined to make matters right with the Duffy children.

"I need to speak with Aunt Birdie, children. I'll be back directly."

"Do you want us to clean up this mess out here?" Primrose asked.

Isadora glanced around the yard and squared her shoulders. "It's my fault the laundry got ruined, Primrose. I'll clean up the mess after I speak with Aunt Birdie, but if you'd be so kind as to make sure the goats don't eat more laundry while I'm gone, I'd appreciate it."

"We can do that," Henry said, charging with Daisy through what little laundry was left hanging, a goat giving chase a second later, which had Henry and Daisy letting out shrieks as they scattered in opposite directions.

"You couldn't have known the goats would get out," Primrose said quietly, moving to take Violet's hand before she caught Isadora's eye.

"True, but I promised Ian I'd look after all of you, and I've done an abysmal job. Do know that I intend to do much better from this point forward."

Pretending she didn't see the clear skepticism in Primrose's eyes, Isadora turned on her heel and headed for the farmhouse.

Edging past Buttercup, Isadora slipped through the screen door, turning to look through the screen when Buttercup emitted a mournful moo. "You can't come inside."

Another moo was Buttercup's response to that.

A smile tugged at Isadora's lips. "How about if I promise to bring you some apples after I speak with Aunt Birdie?"

To Isadora's surprise, Buttercup's tail began to swish back and forth, and taking that as a sign the cow's obviously tender feelings were no longer hurt, Isadora turned and stepped farther into the kitchen.

Her gaze immediately settled on Aunt Birdie, who was leaning on a cane directly in front of the oven, her forehead furrowed as she surveyed the mess Isadora had left behind when she'd gone to attend to the goat situation.

"I'm sure you've got a few questions about how all that happened" was all Isadora could think to say.

When she swiveled around, Aunt Birdie's lips, surprisingly, curved into a smile. "No truer words were ever spoken, child, but . . ." She gestured to Isadora. "Why are you covered in dirt?"

Isadora set Violet's ruined dress on the kitchen table. "There was an unfortunate incident with the goats. And while I'd dearly love to say I handled it, I'm afraid the goats got the better of me, and we now have laundry strewn about the yard—at least the parts of the laundry the goats haven't eaten yet."

"What in the world were the goats doing running around the yard?"

"Hank seems to believe Uncle Amos forgot to shut the gate before he left to go fishing."

Aunt Birdie frowned. "That does seem to be occurring often of late, but it's quite unlike Amos to be so careless, even with his failing memory. He's always taken great pride in caring for his animals."

"The goats don't seem to have come to any harm, if that makes you feel better," Isadora began. "Although I wouldn't be surprised if they came down with stomachaches since laundry can hardly be good for a goat's digestion."

Aunt Birdie waved that aside before she slowly walked over to join Isadora at the table. After leaning her cane against the table, and then nodding to an adjoining chair, she sat down, waited for Isadora to do the same, then smiled. "Goats rarely suffer from stomach ailments. They've even been known to eat tin at times. But what happened to the biscuits?"

Isadora rubbed a hand over her face. "I'm afraid I was careless with watching the oven, and before I knew it, they were on fire." She glanced to the biscuits and fought a wince. "But not to worry. After I finish cleaning up the mess in the yard, I'm determined to set the kitchen to rights, and then I'll whip up a new batch of biscuits."

With her eyes widening in what appeared to be horror, Aunt Birdie glanced to the oven, then turned back to Isadora, reaching out to place a hand on Isadora's arm. "My dear, it's always been my belief that God gives all of us certain gifts. You, I'm confident in saying, have not been given a gift as pertains to anything involving a stove. And with that said, and because I do think you may have promised Ian you'll keep the house from burning to the ground, we should agree that cooking, baking, and even boiling water should be left to me."

Swallowing the argument that was on the very tip of her tongue because she knew with every essence of her being that Aunt Birdie had just voiced a suggestion that could very well keep the house from being burned to a crisp like the biscuits, Isadora fished out the list Ian had penned for her from her apron pocket. Laying it on the table, she drew her finger down the list and shook her head. "Ian's hardly likely to agree to keep me on permanently when he discovers I'm unable to complete five of the twenty or so chores he left for me to finish. Those five chores, I'm sad to say, all involve cooking, baking, boiling water, and"—she lifted her head—"I'm not sure what he meant by *putting up jam*, but I'm going to assume that has something to do with the kitchen."

She wasn't certain, but Isadora thought Aunt Birdie might have shuddered before she gave Isadora's arm a good pat.

"Putting up jam, which involves boiling berries, straining them, and cooking them, while also boiling jars over the stove before putting the jam into them, is not going to be an ideal task for you to try and accomplish," Aunt Birdie said. "As I mentioned, I believe God gives all His children certain gifts. And while I don't think your gift is in the kitchen, I'm sure you're possessed of a gift, most likely several. All that's left for you to do now is determine what that gift, or gifts, may be."

Isadora tried to think of something she was overly proficient with, but nothing of consequence sprang to mind, at least nothing that could be considered important, such as competently feeding a family with edible food.

Her only skills as far as she knew were being able to speak on topics that gentlemen found interesting, such as the weather, maintaining perfect posture, and painting charming pictures, although she wasn't actually certain she was good at painting, no matter that everyone always claimed she possessed clear talent.

Unwilling to admit to Aunt Birdie that she couldn't think of a single gift God might have bestowed on her, not that she'd ever really contemplated the subject of God and His gifts before, preferring to keep thoughts of God to the hours she spent in church on Sundays, and the occasional Wednesday evening service, Isadora summoned up a smile.

"What gifts do you believe God has given to *you*?" she finally settled on asking.

Aunt Birdie returned the smile. "I'm not certain I'd call this a gift, more along the lines of a life purpose, but I was given the opportunity to raise Ian and provide him with the education he needed to achieve the success he so longed for." Her eyes crinkled at the corners. "I'm sure if God had not put Ian in my path, or whispered in my ear that day so long ago that I needed to give him a proper home, he'd not be where he is today. He'd be eking out a living working in the mills instead of—" She suddenly stopped talking, sent Isadora a look that had guilt written all over it, then picked up the list Isadora had left on the table and began taking an unusually marked interest in it.

"Instead of what?" Isadora pressed.

Aunt Birdie lifted her head. "Has Ian mentioned anything at all to you about what he does?"

"He said he was a man of business, but he didn't elaborate."

"I can't claim I'm surprised." Aunt Birdie suddenly began considering Isadora with a rather interesting look in her eyes. "I do find it encouraging that he'd admit he's a businessman to you, even with him not elaborating. He's always reluctant to discuss matters of business with anyone outside of his Pittsburgh associates or social circle. That he'd broach the matter with you, well, I certainly see that as progress."

A tingle of apprehension began creeping up Isadora's spine. "Ian's involved with Pittsburgh society?"

"I'm afraid so, even though I've been trying to convince him that gaining entrance to that society, and then continually climbing the proverbial society ladder until he reaches the very top, should not be his life's ambition."

"His life's ambition is to reach the top of Pittsburgh's social ladder?"

"It is."

Isadora tilted her head. "Why would he then warn me that you may have matchmaking on your mind, that matchmaking certain to fail because he obviously wants to marry a society lady to improve his social standing?"

Aunt Birdie blinked. "He told you I have matchmaking on my mind that he believes involves you?"

With a nod, Isadora smiled. "He did, but don't worry that I've set my cap for him or am disappointed that I don't possess lofty enough connections for him to consider me a suitable candidate for marriage. The last thing I want is a husband."

"Is that because of something that happened with Mr. Delmont?"

Isadora felt heat settle into her cheeks. She'd never been a lady comfortable with spreading false tales, not that she'd ever had a reason to since she'd always been one to follow the rules. Now, however, the tales she'd woven about her identity were becoming more and more difficult to keep, but she wasn't comfortable with lying to the woman sitting beside her.

Aunt Birdie was obviously a strong woman, having lived her life on a farm. But she was also a compassionate woman and had taken children into her home because they'd had nowhere else to go.

That meant she was a woman who demanded respect, and she was a woman who demanded the truth, if only in part.

"I'm afraid there isn't a Mr. Delmont."

Aunt Birdie sat back in the chair and pinned Isadora with a stern eye. "So you *are* here under false pretenses, aren't you?"

"Are you going to send me packing if I admit that I am? Although I must tell you that I only assumed the title of missus because no one will hire an unmarried lady in any position except for the lowest of maids."

Aunt Birdie pursed her lips and stared at Isadora for an uncomfortable moment before she suddenly nodded. "A logical explanation, to be sure. I might have done the same if I'd been forced to seek out employment in my youth."

"So you're not going to ask me to leave?"

"Not today, but know that I'm well aware there's something curious about you. However, having said that, I don't get the impression you're a malicious sort. You're also a hard worker—some might even say an overly enthusiastic one—but you somehow managed to convince Ian you were worth hiring, so for now, you may stay."

"What if I told you Ian only hired me because I presented him with a business proposition he couldn't refuse? And by that, I mean I agreed to work for the next two weeks without drawing a wage."

Aunt Birdie's mouth made an O of surprise. "Good heavens, child, you understand him."

"You're obviously reading far too much into the proposition I broached to Ian. I don't understand him at all."

"Nonsense. You knew he wouldn't be able to refuse an offer where he's getting a housekeeper, even a rather questionable one, for such a bargain." Aunt Birdie's gaze sharpened on Isadora. "No one has ever understood my Ian, but that you do, and in such a short period of time . . . well, it's telling."

"Telling?"

"You've obviously been sent here for a reason, and that reason must have something to do with Ian."

Isadora's mind went curiously blank for all of a second until alarm bells suddenly began clanging in her head.

Ian had warned her that his aunt was wily and intent on matchmaking, but Isadora certainly hadn't expected the tactic Aunt Birdie seemed to be using now.

"As I mentioned before, I'm not looking for a husband," she said slowly.

Aunt Birdie arched a brow. "Perhaps not, but if I'm right about this, and I do believe I am, a higher power is at play here, my dear."

"You think *God* led me here?"

"But of course, and He might very well have done so to help you discover something about yourself or to discover your true purpose in life, which might involve my Ian."

Uncomfortable with the direction the conversation seemed to be heading because she was not used to discussing matters of God and men over the kitchen table, Isadora picked up Violet's dress and held it up. "I think my only purpose right now is to figure out if this can be salvaged."

"A clever way to change the subject, my dear. But do know that we'll continue this discussion after you and I become better acquainted." Aunt Birdie sat back in the chair. "Once that happens, I expect you to disclose the secrets you're obviously keeping, but I won't press you just yet."

"How . . . reassuring."

"Indeed. Now, with that settled, let me see the worst of that dress."

Spreading the dress out on the table, Isadora sighed when she noticed the many holes and rips in it. "I'm not certain it's salvageable."

"I'm afraid you're right."

Isadora frowned. "Is there a store in town that might sell ready-made garments for children?"

"The general store does have a selection of ready-made clothes. If you're comfortable driving the wagon into town, you could see if there's anything available that would fit the children. If there isn't, you could purchase some fabric, and I could sew the children some new clothes." She smiled. "I'll send you with a note penned to Mrs. Rogers, who runs the store, and she'll see to it that you're allowed to put the purchases on our account."

"I'm not charging anything to your account," Isadora argued.

"It's my fault the children lost their clothing, so I'll pay to replace that clothing."

Aunt Birdie immediately took to *tsk*ing. "You'll do no such thing. Ian set up that account for me, and he's a more-than-generous man and would never balk at any charges made, especially not when you're purchasing much-needed items for the children. He was planning on shopping for the children before he got called back to Pittsburgh anyway."

"But it was my fault their clothing was destroyed."

"It was hardly your fault the goats got loose, and I'll not hear another word on the matter."

Isadora shook her head. "I'm perfectly capable of paying for the items of clothing that were damaged under my watch."

"What part of *I'll not hear another word on the matter* did you not understand? And forgive me for reminding you of this, but you're not going to be paid for two weeks' worth of work, unless . . ." Aunt Birdie's gaze sharpened. "Do you need a position because you're in need of funds, or . . . something else?"

An image of the Duke of Montrose's leering eyes and roving hands flashed to mind. "Something else," she heard slip out of her mouth.

"And is this something else because you're running from the law?"

"Do I look like a woman who'd have a reason to run from the law?"

"You could be a master of disguise. Do you need those spectacles?"

Unable to help but wonder how she'd apparently been coerced into revealing almost all of her secrets—and to an elderly woman who went by the name of Aunt Birdie, a name that should have belonged to a dear, dotty woman, not an overly astute and crafty one—Isadora felt her shoulders sink into an honest-to-goodness sag.

"I don't need them," she finally admitted.

"What do you need? The truth, if you please."

Her shoulders sank another inch. "I need a place of refuge to hide from a man who wants to marry me."

Aunt Birdie folded her arms over her chest. "Now, that wasn't so hard to divulge, was it?" She nodded. "Thank you for being honest, and your secret is safe with me. I've never been fond of men who can't respect a woman's wishes, so you'll have the refuge you need at Glory Manor. Do know, though, that Ian is a man who is fiercely protective of anyone in his care. You should tell *him* your secrets. I assure you, he'll go above and beyond what is needed to keep you safe if you take him into your confidence."

Even though Isadora knew divulging her true identity to Ian MacKenzie was a logical solution to her problem, there was a part of her that wasn't ready to resume being Isadora Delafield.

She was woefully inept when it came to living in the real world and had made a complete and utter mess of the few tasks she'd sworn to Ian she'd be able to complete with proficiency.

She knew she needed to truly prove, if only to herself, that she was capable of more than simply being a wealthy lady of high societal standing. And perhaps, just perhaps, she'd find that purpose in life that Aunt Birdie seemed so convinced God meant for her to find—a purpose that would be more fulfilling than buying new wardrobes every season or attending balls that all seemed to be the same after a while.

Rising from the chair, she smiled. "I will consider that, Aunt Birdie, but I would appreciate it if we could keep my secret, for the moment, between the two of us."

Aunt Birdie inclined her head. "Then that's what we'll do, dear. And now, with that settled, let us return to the list Ian left for you to complete. Your secret will be easier to keep if you're able to convince Ian you're worthy of permanent employment, but you might need some help with learning how to do all the tasks he's left for you."

Isadora picked up the list, reading down the items, lingering on one that caught her eye. Lifting her head, she smiled. "While I know this is not a task he left for me, I'm very proficient with shopping. Shopping is an experience in and of itself, which means . . ." Her smile widened. "The appeal of shopping for new clothing may very well give the children the incentive to allow me to complete one almost impossible task Ian left for me—getting them into a bath."

CHAPTER 17

PITTSBURGH

"Are you confident you'll be able to convince the labor that it's in their best interest to accept the decrease in wages we're proposing?"

Rising from his chair, Ian nodded to Victor Laughlin, a man who had a large fortune wrapped up in the iron and steel industries. Victor was one of the few industrialists Ian considered more friend than business associate. He'd also become a mentor of sorts after Ian made his acquaintance while he'd been a student at the Western University of Pennsylvania. Victor had come to speak on the opportunities available within the iron and steel industries. Ian, more than impressed with the man, had sought him out after the lecture. From that point forward, Victor had taken a personal interest in him.

He'd introduced Ian to influential Pittsburgh businessmen, and then had gone out of his way to direct Ian into lucrative investment opportunities once Ian had begun to draw a steady wage and had a few dollars to invest. Those few dollars had quickly multiplied, as had his esteem for Victor Laughlin. That was why, when Victor sent him the telegrams asking him to return to Pittsburgh to handle some delicate negotiations with the men from the

Amalgamated Association of Iron and Steel Workers of America, Ian hadn't hesitated.

He'd been more than a little wary about leaving Izzie to manage Glory Manor. But after Aunt Birdie had reassured him that she was feeling almost like her old self again and would be able to guide Izzie through any situation that might arise while he was gone, he'd been put somewhat at ease.

"The union men aren't unreasonable, Victor," Ian began. "They know their members need to work to put food on their tables and provide shelter for their families. And they're also used to being asked for concessions based on the supply and demand for their products." He nodded to the other men gathered around the table in the office building not far from the Pennsylvania Railroad depot. "As I mentioned earlier, we may need to ask for an eight percent decrease in wages as opposed to twelve percent. We might also need to consider shortening the average work day from twelve hours to ten and abandoning the double shifts many of the mills are requiring their laborers to work."

Murmurs of dissent were immediate.

Mr. Benjamin Jones, chairman of Jones and Laughlin Limited, banged his fist against the table. "Have you gone mad, MacKenzie? We can't cut hours. Production will suffer, as will profitability."

Ian shook his head. "Profitability will suffer more if the workers go on strike, effectively shutting down the mills. It will be more beneficial for everyone involved if we modify our demands of cutting wages while giving the workers some manner of compensation for cutting the wages to begin with."

"They'll not be making as much money if we cut their hours," Mr. John Collingwood pointed out, taking a puff of his cigar and then blowing out the smoke in Ian's direction.

Ian waved the smoke aside. "They won't be taking as big of a financial blow if we put them on a set weekly wage instead of an hourly one. I'm of the belief they won't balk as much at having their wages decreased if they find themselves with a few extra hours to spend outside the mill atmosphere."

"They'll just spend those few hours drinking in one of the many taverns in town," Mr. Harry Paul pointed out, his ruddy complexion suggesting he spent many an hour in those very same taverns.

"Which is their choice," Ian said. "If I need remind you, gentlemen, we're not in the business of dictating what the workers do with the few scant hours they have when they're not working. We're in the business of industry, and occasionally, it does require compromise."

"Seems to me you might not be the man for this job after all, MacKenzie."

Looking toward the man who'd just spoken, Ian found Mr. Nigel Flaherty watching him out of narrowed eyes through the smoke of the cigar he was chomping on.

Of all the men gathered in the room, each one of them men of industry and fortune, Nigel Flaherty was the most ruthless, immoral, and unpleasant of the bunch. Not only was he heavily invested in iron and steel, but he also held interests in numerous railroads, bridges, oil, and just recently, coal. He was driven to become the wealthiest man in the nation, and because of that it was always difficult to reason with him, especially when it came down to matters of profitability.

Ian inclined his head in Nigel's direction. "If you will recall, Nigel, I was chosen for these negotiations because I have a proven reputation for succeeding with delicate contract matters where others have failed. However, if you and everyone else in this room have concluded I'm not the right man for the job, by all means, find someone else. There are other attorneys in this country—many, I'm certain, with degrees obtained from one of the esteemed law schools America offers these days. I, as I'm sure everyone knows, earned my law degree through an apprenticeship. And while I fully understand the laws of the land, I also understand that some in this very room would be more comfortable having their interests looked after by a Harvard or Yale man. Because of that, feel free to bring on someone else. I have more than enough work to keep me occupied and would actually be relieved to have these negotiations taken off my plate."

Nigel leaned forward, taking the cigar from his mouth. "Your skills at negotiation are well known, MacKenzie, but it's been my observation over the last few years that you tend to sympathize with the laborers a little too much for my liking—a direct result of your once being one of them, and a result of your being a son of an immigrant."

Ian arched a brow. "I haven't worked in the mills as a laborer since I was seven years old, and the only reason I was working then was because I was large for my age and my father lied about how old I was. As for my being the son of an immigrant, if my memory serves me correctly, your own father arrived on these shores from Ireland years ago with nothing to his name but the clothes on his back."

Nigel's dark eyes narrowed. "True, but unlike your father, mine set himself up in trade from the moment his foot hit American soil. Your father took a menial job at the mills. From what I understand, he never left those mills, whereas my father enjoyed great success with building up the Flaherty empire."

"My father died over ten years ago, and we hadn't spoken for over ten years before that, which makes it somewhat confusing why you believe my interaction with the laborers would be colored by my relationship, or lack thereof, with my father." Ian tilted his head. "It's also confusing why you seem to have taken a great deal of time to ferret out information regarding my history."

Nigel waved aside a plume of smoke. "I always make it a point to learn as much as I can about my . . . *contemporaries.*"

Ian strove to maintain his temper. Clearly, Nigel didn't view Ian as his contemporary, no matter that Ian had built up a considerable fortune of his own. It was an attitude he'd experienced often while climbing his way out of the world he'd been expected to embrace. However, it was an attitude he'd experienced less and less over the past few years, his reputation as a savvy man of business and a man capable of successfully negotiating with the many different unions going far to prove he was not a man easily dismissed.

"Why don't we wait and see what Ian can do with the union men before we decide to bring anyone else into the negotiating process?" Victor said, rising to his feet and moving to stand beside Ian. "I believe I speak for the majority in this room when I say we have every confidence you'll be able to navigate your way successfully through all the demands the unions are certain to broach. And, on that note, we should let you get on with matters."

Before Ian could do more than nod to the table at large, Victor had hold of his arm and was walking with him across the room, down a long hallway, and then out into the smoky air of a Pittsburgh early afternoon.

"You shouldn't put much stock in anything Nigel said" were the first words out of Victor's mouth as they moved farther into the never-ending smog that blanketed Pittsburgh at all hours of the day or night, making it difficult to judge the current time without the benefit of a pocket watch. "He's being difficult because he's set his sights on Miss Lillian Moore, who everyone knows has set her sights on you."

"Nigel is a good twenty years older than Miss Moore, and besides that, I have not given Miss Moore any reason to believe her interest in me is returned."

"She's one of the most eligible young ladies in Pittsburgh, and it would not hurt your social or business standing if you were to align yourself with her and her family. Mr. Richard Moore is worth millions, and his wife has set herself up as one of the leading society matrons in the city."

"They don't live in the city, Victor. They live in Shadyside, right up the road from me, and only four houses removed from you."

"Which could prove convenient if you'd settle your attention on Miss Moore." Victor shook his head. "How many times have I told you that the key to great success lies more with whom you know and your connections than the talent you have with making prudent business investments and deals?"

Ian smiled. "You've been quite vocal in sharing advice with me that will see my standing in the Pittsburgh social and business community grow. And while it's obvious your marriage to Dorothy Clemson provided you with invaluable contacts, she's also a lovely woman, possessed of a charming nature. Miss Moore, on the other hand, has what I can only describe as a questionable disposition. She's spoiled, willful, and incredibly demanding."

"That's merely because she's an only child and has parents who indulge her every whim."

"Whims she would expect me to indulge if I pursued a courtship with her."

Victor smiled. "Well, there is that. But what of Miss Florence Howe or her sister, Miss Ella Howe? They're both lovely girls and well connected. I would think you'd find the idea of marriage to either of the Howe sisters intriguing."

"The *idea* of marriage to a well-connected young lady is certainly intriguing," Ian admitted before he shook his head. "But I've yet to find a young lady ensconced in Pittsburgh society who intrigues *me*. I find conversation with the Howe sisters to be rather difficult. They only seem interested in speaking of the weather or the fashions that can be found in the Pittsburgh department stores. When I've tried to engage in more stimulating conversation, such as inquiring about what books they enjoy reading, Miss Florence and Miss Ella always look completely horrified, as if reading books is something to be avoided at all costs."

"Gentlemen such as yourself, ones who have social ambitions that rival their business ambitions, cannot have it all, Ian. Young ladies from the best families are raised to believe that intelligence is not a desirable trait in women and is a sure way to end up a spinster, thus the reasoning behind their limited conversational abilities."

"That seems like a somewhat antiquated notion, especially given the strides the suffrage movement has made of late."

Victor clapped him on the back. "I'm sure that society ladies in more established places, such as New York City, are more progressive. But this is Pittsburgh, and we've only just begun establishing our social presence. Because of that, our young ladies are encouraged to maintain a demure and, need I say, dull attitude." He smiled. "But if you find that attitude not to your liking, perhaps you should travel to New York to discover if there's a more progressive young miss just longing to abandon life in that bustling city and join you here in Pittsburgh." He gestured to the clouds of black smoke swirling in the sky, smoke so dense it obliterated any sign of the sun. "I'm sure a New York socialite would love having an opportunity to enjoy all that Pittsburgh has to offer, notwithstanding the smog that does occasionally make actions like drawing in breaths of air hard to accomplish at times."

Ian grinned. "Yes, I can see where our soot-drenched skies would be a compelling reason for a lady to abandon one of the greatest cities in the country. But from what I've been told, and I got this from none other than Andrew Carnegie, New York socialites are being swept up in the rage of procuring titles from across the ocean. I don't believe my lack of a pedigree or the fact that I didn't go to an illustrious university like Harvard is going to look all that impressive to ladies intent on securing themselves an aristocrat."

"It's only a matter of time before our university in Pittsburgh rivals Harvard, Yale, or even Columbia. As for your lack of a pedigree, I would have to imagine many a young lady would overlook that since, according to my wife, young ladies find you to be rather handsome, and they are apparently susceptible to"—he waved a hand at Ian's chest—"all that."

"I'm not certain my *all that* is enough to impress a New York society lady."

Victor laughed. "Perhaps not, although it does give you an edge over other eligible gentlemen, at least here in Pittsburgh. Add that with the fact that you've amassed quite an impressive fortune over the last few years with all the prudent investments you've made, and I have to believe you'll enjoy success with whatever young lady you set your sights on to marry." His smile faded. "You should make that decision sooner than later, though. There are many who still believe a man is more settled once he marries, and if you were to marry, I know your standing within society would benefit tremendously."

Ian blew out a breath. "I know you're right, but it all seems somewhat depressing, choosing a woman simply because she can elevate my social and business standing in the world."

Victor stopped walking. "Don't tell me there's a heart of a romantic lingering under that broad chest of yours, because I have to admit that I've never taken you for a romantic sort."

Ian stopped walking as well, as a truth he'd never once contemplated rose up inside him, leaving him feeling distinctly unsettled.

He'd decided years before that he'd need to marry a well-connected woman to ensure any children he might have would not suffer the slights he had in his youth because of his Scottish heritage, his abusive and alcoholic father, and the poverty he'd experienced until Aunt Birdie and Uncle Amos had taken him in.

But even having made that decision, and even though he'd been presented to more than a few young ladies who'd let it subtly be known they'd be eager to accept his suit, he'd yet to settle his attention on any specific lady.

Was his reluctance in the matter of choosing a wife merely because he was being overly particular or . . . could it stem from the idea that Victor was right and that he wanted more from a relationship with a lady than merely a means to achieve all the goals he'd set out for himself?

Could he, perhaps, be dragging his feet with acquiring a wife because he was actually looking for romance, or . . . love from a potential spouse?

Ian shook that thought straight out of his head because his main goal in life had always been to pursue business opportunities and increase his fortune with every new pursuit, which meant he had no room in his life for romance. He summoned up a smile. "Don't be ridiculous. Of course I don't have a romantic heart. I'm much too practical for that nasty business."

Victor arched a brow. "That's quite the elegant argument from an attorney and, in all honesty, lacks the conviction I've come to expect from you." He pulled out his pocket watch and took note of the time. "However, now is hardly the moment to delve into the subject more thoroughly. It's a little early for lunch, but would you have time to join me before you meet with the union men?"

Taking out his own pocket watch, Ian peered through the gloom at the dial. "If we make it a quick meal I can, which is good because I've just now realized I'm famished. I was late getting away from Glory Manor, and only had time to eat a few pieces of toast Aunt Birdie gave me for breakfast as I headed out the door."

"Then we'll make it quick because you always think best when you're not hungry."

Exchanging a smile, the two men began making their way down the street, stepping over abandoned railroad ties as they walked toward the many taverns in the area. Stopping in front of one that had a sign with *Norma's* painted over the doorway, Ian turned to Victor.

"Do you mind if we eat at Norma's? I've been woefully neglectful with my patronage of this tavern, and Norma gets a little worried if I don't show up every few weeks." He smiled. "She's been feeding me ever since I stumbled into her tavern when I was a student, starving and exhausted from working at the telegraph station and studying for some exam or another." His smile widened. "She served me up steak, potatoes, vegetables, and pie and made me promise to take better care of myself or else she'd take to bringing me lunch during class. Since I wasn't keen to take on the ribbing I'd get from my fellow students if Miss Norma started showing up at the university, I agreed to eat here at least three times a week while I was a student, and even though she's a businesswoman at heart, she gave me those meals practically for free, refusing to allow me to pay the prices stated on the menu."

"And that right there is why it's a mystery to me that you've yet to marry. Women of all ages seem to want to take care of you. I have little understanding why you'd let Miss Norma look after you, but not a young lady who could make your life more comfortable as well as make that house you're building a real home."

Ian moved to the door leading into Norma's. "You do realize that your interest in getting me married off almost puts you in the category of matchmaker, don't you?"

"A frightening notion to be sure, but one I feel might be necessary to see you well settled." Victor smiled. "Apparently, it's not only women who want to take care of you. And on that note, allow us to get on with our lunch, even if I have to admit that Miss Norma scares me half to death whenever we eat here." His smile turned into a grin. "However, since I'm eating with you, and you have a reputation for holding your own if there happens to be a brawl"—he gestured to the door Ian had yet to open—"lead the way."

Pulling open the door, Ian frowned at Victor. "Miss Norma's not scary. She's merely a no-nonsense sort who was forced to make a living for herself and her three children after her husband died years ago in a mill accident."

"She's taller and broader than I am and carries two pistols on her belt," Victor countered as he walked with Ian into the tavern. "She also carries a very sharp-looking knife in the pocket of the apron she always wears."

"Which is very practical considering she spends hour after hour serving surly men who have enormous appetites, few manners, and a tendency to swing first and ask questions after they've knocked out whoever they think has offended them."

"Which makes me wonder why you always insist on eating here when you're in this part of the city," Victor muttered as they stepped farther into Norma's and were immediately shown to a table by one of Norma's now fully grown sons.

Taking a seat, Ian glanced around, smiling at the sight of all the men from the various mills wolfing down their meals, their boisterous voices mixed with the clatter of silverware.

That Miss Norma didn't put on any fancy airs, limiting the silverware offered to her guests to one fork and one knife, and a spoon only if a person ordered soup, was exactly why Ian preferred eating at her tavern when he was visiting the mills.

He never needed to worry that he'd pick up the wrong utensil, forget to wipe his mouth after every bite, or neglect to place his napkin on his lap. There'd been many a dinner he'd attended in Pittsburgh where he'd spent the entire meal walking on eggshells, uncertain he was remembering all the rules that went with polite society and knowing full well that someone would take note if he used the wrong knife or, heaven forbid, allowed any peas to tumble from his fork as he tried to raise them to his mouth.

"Ah, Ian, my dear boy, I'd begun to worry about you."

Turning to the voice, Ian rose to his feet and kissed the cheek Miss Norma, as she preferred to be called, presented him.

Waving him back into his chair, Miss Norma plunked her hands on her hips. "You've not paid me a visit for more than a month."

"I'm afraid work has kept me busy of late, Miss Norma, and I had to return to Glory Manor to take care of a few issues that developed on the farm."

"Your Aunt Birdie recovered from her accident?"

Ian frowned. "How did you know about that?"

Norma frowned right back at him. "I would imagine you told me or . . . no, now that I think on it, I heard the news from Mrs. Gorman."

"Mrs. Gorman?"

"She's a woman involved with the United Presbyterian Orphan Home."

"How did she learn about Aunt Birdie's accident?"

Miss Norma smoothed back a section of brown hair streaked with gray that had escaped the bun she always wore at the back of her neck. "Let me take your order first, dear. We'll catch up after you've been fed." She stopped her son, who was walking by, took a few menus from him, then handed those menus to Ian and Victor. "We got a special today on fried chicken. It comes with potatoes and carrots."

An image of Izzie standing on a chair while Elmer fluttered

her wings and then burrowed underneath Izzie's dress flashed to mind. Blinking to disperse that image because Izzie Delmont was occupying far too many of his thoughts today, he opened the menu and began looking it over. "I've had a few unfortunate situations with chickens lately, Miss Norma. I think I'll stick with the steak."

Miss Norma frowned. "You've been eating chicken that hasn't been prepared properly?"

"It's the still-living chickens that have been causing me problems. I lost a housekeeper because she thought the chicken Uncle Amos brought in from the chicken coop was meant to be used for dinner. Uncle Amos then accused Mrs. Gladstone of being a chicken murderer, and after that, well, there was little hope she'd agree to stay on."

"Amos has always been a little peculiar when it comes to his animals," Miss Norma said before she nodded to Victor. "What'll you have today, sir?"

"I'll have the chicken because I've not had any issues with chickens lately—or ever, for that matter," Victor said with a smile, handing his menu to Miss Norma, who then hurried away to place their orders.

"She never remembers my name," Victor said with a shake of his head. "One would think, given how often I come here with you, that she'd try a little harder."

"Miss Norma is horrible with names. Don't take it personally."

"It doesn't seem as if she's ever had a problem remembering your name."

"Because she evidently decided to make me an unofficial member of her tavern family." Ian smiled. "And I also might have, a few years back, helped her out with an issue she was having with a man who tried to force her into selling her tavern to him."

Victor's brows drew together. "You really can be a dangerous man when crossed."

"And in a daunting atmosphere like Pittsburgh, that's come in handy at times."

"I suppose it does, what with how often you deal with . . ." Victor gave a wave of a hand to the rough customers eating at Norma's. He turned back to Ian. "But speaking of daunting, if you've lost your housekeeper, who is minding the farm while you're here?"

"I've already hired another housekeeper."

Victor frowned. "How did you manage that?"

"She showed up at the farm the same day Mrs. Gladstone left, clutching the newspaper I'd posted the position in."

"And she was a qualified candidate?"

An image of Izzie stuck to the washing machine flickered to mind. Unwilling to admit his concerns about Izzie to a man who certainly wouldn't understand, Ian found himself nodding. "She was in possession of an impressive résumé, one that came from the house of Mr. Arthur Waterbury in New York."

Victor sat forward. "Arthur Waterbury? Why, I've met the man, and if your new housekeeper worked for his family, I'd say she's probably overqualified for the position at Glory Manor."

"You know Arthur Waterbury?"

"Indeed. He's an incredibly wealthy man. Made the bulk of his fortune in mining, then moved on to oil. I met him in New York City about a year ago because he was interested in investing in one of our steel mills." Victor tapped a finger against his chin. "If memory serves me correctly, he has an unmarried daughter, and . . ." His eyes widened. "Unless that situation has changed, and I haven't heard any rumors suggesting otherwise, this daughter was rapidly approaching spinsterhood, which means . . ."

"What?" Ian pressed when Victor suddenly stopped talking and got a most unusual look on his face.

"I would think that's obvious, but since you're not following what I'm saying, allow me to spell it out for you. Miss Waterbury is an American heiress who, for some unknown reason, has yet to marry. And you're a handsome industrialist who could benefit from marrying a New York socialite." Victor leaned farther over the table and lowered his voice. "You could schedule a meeting with

Arthur Waterbury using your new housekeeper as an excuse—saying something to the effect that you were checking up on the reference, and then . . . if you play your cards right, you may very well find yourself in a position to court an honest-to-goodness American heiress."

CHAPTER 18

Rubbing a hand over his face, Ian frowned. "How did we end up talking about American heiresses when only a moment ago we were speaking of chickens?"

"Because you've hired on a housekeeper who was once employed by one of the great American families." Victor beamed. "If you were to marry the Waterbury heiress, men like Nigel Flaherty would stop behaving as if your every decision needed to be questioned, and as if you weren't their equal in every way, business or social."

Ian's lips quirked as an odd thought suddenly struck. "Do you know that Izzie, or rather, Mrs. Delmont, wanted to rename a cantankerous chicken named Elmer to Nigel after she decided it was a shifty sort. I discouraged her from doing that because I know men named Nigel who aren't shifty in the least, but I apparently forgot about Nigel Flaherty."

Victor's gaze turned shrewd. "Who is this Mrs. Delmont, or rather Izzie, as you called her?"

"She's the new housekeeper."

"And you address her by her given name?"

Ian's collar suddenly felt rather tight. "Well, no, not to her face. That would be inappropriate."

"As is thinking of her by her given name." Victor leaned forward. "How old is she, and could she possibly be an attractive woman?"

Ian shifted on the chair, quite as if he'd suddenly turned into a naughty lad being taken to task by his teacher. "I suppose she is attractive, although for most of the time we've been acquainted she's been covered in a most hideous rash."

"Why do I get the distinct impression your housekeeper is more than merely attractive?" Victor asked, his question causing Ian to tug at a collar that now seemed intent on strangling him.

"I'm sure I have no idea."

"Is she an older woman?"

"Well, ah . . ." Relief shot through him when Miss Norma took that moment to reappear by their table, carrying two dishes in her hands that she quickly set down in front of them. Taking a seat next to Ian, she smiled.

"Now, where were we?"

Glad to be given an opportunity to change the topic of conversation away from Izzie, especially because Victor seemed to be heading in a direction Ian wasn't comfortable going, he returned Miss Norma's smile. "You were about to tell me how a Mrs. Gorman became aware of Aunt Birdie's accident."

"Ah yes, so I was." She leaned forward. "Mrs. Gorman, as I mentioned, works with the United Presbyterian Orphan Home. She, bless her heart, has had a hard time of it lately finding places for all the children needing good homes. She often stops in to see if I know of any families willing to take a few children in when the orphanage is out of room. I must say I was stumped at first when she told me there were four children needing to be placed in a home. But then I remembered how Birdie and Amos had taken you in all those years ago, so I directed Mrs. Gorman to Glory Manor."

Ian lowered the knife he'd been using to cut up his steak. "Did Mrs. Gorman expand on what the children had been through?"

Miss Norma gave a sad shake of her head. "From what I understand, they lost their mother a while ago, right around the time the youngest was born. Their father, Roy Duffy, seemingly tried to take care of them, but he eventually, as so many widowed men do, brought the children to the orphanage."

"I thought Aunt Birdie told me that the children were abandoned."

Miss Norma nodded. "Well, yes, they were, the second time. The first time they arrived at the orphanage, their father agreed to pay the orphanage fifty cents a week per child, which would ensure that the children got to stay at the orphanage together. However, according to Mrs. Gorman, he stopped paying the money at some point. The orphanage was then forced to track him down, and they found him working the night shift at one of the mills."

"So he *was* working?" Ian asked.

"Indeed, and after learning the orphanage couldn't guarantee the children would stay together without him paying their fee, he apparently told them his wages had been cut, which was why he was delinquent. But even knowing that, the orphanage still wouldn't promise him the children wouldn't be separated, so he fetched the children and brought them home with him."

Ian frowned. "It doesn't sound as if he is a horrible father. Simply fell on hard times when his wages were cut."

"It's a problem throughout the city, dear. Men who've lost their wives are often forced to use the orphanages to watch over their children while they work. But then, if the mills reduce wages, as they're often known to do when productivity slows, the men are unable to pay the weekly orphanage fees and are either forced to see their children shipped out of the city, adopted by other families, or put to work as nothing more than indentured servants." She sighed. "Many of these men fetch their children home but are forced to leave them to fend for themselves for hours on end when they go off to work their long shifts in the mills."

Something unpleasant settled in Ian's stomach, and it wasn't the steak. He was currently in the middle of negotiations with the labor unions, tasked with the job of getting the unions to accept a decrease in wages until demand rose again for the iron and steel they produced in the mills. He'd never once considered how that reduction would affect children, but now that he knew, it gave him an entirely different perspective on the matter.

Taking another bite of steak, even though it was now tasting like leather, Ian followed it up with a drink of ale, frowning as he considered Miss Norma. "Do you know how it came to be that Mr. Duffy ended up abandoning his children?"

"Mrs. Gorman thought Mr. Duffy tried to take care of his children for a while since he apparently hired on a woman to look in on them when he was working. But then, what with the long shifts at the mill and the appeal of drinking when he wasn't working, he apparently forgot he had children at some point and neglected to return home to check on them, leaving the children on their own. The rent on their rooms came due, and when that rent wasn't paid, the landlord contacted the police, who then contacted the orphanage. Mrs. Gorman then came to see me because the orphanage didn't have the space to take in four new children."

Ian frowned. "And then I suppose that's when my aunt agreed to take the children. She's decided she'll provide them with a permanent home."

Miss Norma's brows drew together. "Birdie's a little old to be raising four children, Ian, especially since you told me Amos has been having difficulties with his memory. I would never have suggested Mrs. Gorman pay her a visit if I thought she'd do more than offer them a temporary home until other plans could be made, or if I'd known about her accident before Mrs. Gorman returned and told me about it."

Ian touched Miss Norma's arm. "There's no need to worry you've caused Aunt Birdie a hardship. She loves having children in the house again, and I can assure you I'll be hiring on help to look after them."

"Or you could take them in and raise them here in Pittsburgh," Miss Norma suggested.

"I'm hardly in a position to take on a fatherly role."

"You could if you found yourself a wife."

"What is it with everyone trying to get me married off today?" he muttered to no one in particular, earning a smile from Miss Norma as she rose from the chair and exchanged looks with Victor.

"You keep on him about finding a wife, Mr. Laughlin. Ian's not getting any younger, and it seems a shame he's living all alone in that big house he's building in Shadyside." With that, she took a step away from the table, faltering when Nigel Flaherty suddenly edged around her and stopped directly beside Ian.

How long he'd been in the tavern, Ian couldn't say, but he had the most curious feeling Nigel had been eavesdropping on his conversation, a suspicion proven true mere seconds later.

"No wonder you said you had more than enough work these days if you're taking in orphans," Nigel said, sitting down in the chair Miss Norma had only recently vacated.

"*I* haven't taken in any orphans, Nigel," Ian said shortly. "My aunt has. A commendable act of compassion, wouldn't you agree?"

"Or yet more proof that you and yours are far too sympathetic to the very people who seem to think they deserve better compensation at the risk of digging into our profits."

Ian's jaw clenched. "Whatever sympathies I may hold for the laborer have never affected my negotiation abilities, nor do I expect them to today."

"Then I suggest you get to negotiating, MacKenzie, because from what I understand, those laborers are close to going on strike. Do know that I, along with many others, will hold you personally responsible if that does indeed come to pass."

Rising from the chair, Nigel headed out of the tavern.

"Such a pleasant man," Victor said as Ian returned to his steak, realizing that it was almost time for his meeting and yet he'd barely made it halfway through his meal.

Finishing a short time later, Ian paid the bill, leaving a large tip for Miss Norma, who'd stopped by the table once again to give him and Victor brown bags with large slices of pie in them.

"You make sure to come back sooner this time," Miss Norma said after Ian kissed her cheek, leaving her pink and smiling back at him.

"I promise. And now, if you'll excuse me, I have a meeting with the union men. We're in the midst of negotiating contracts."

Miss Norma's smile faded. "You remember where you came from, my boy, when you're in that meeting. Remember that you could very well have been one of those workers if God didn't have grander plans for you, plans aided by your aunt and uncle."

Wondering if he'd soon be unable to breathe, what with the way his collar kept feeling tighter and tighter, Ian kissed Miss Norma's cheek again, electing not to make any promises he might not be able to keep.

Even though he'd always been driven, determined to amass a fortune that would never see him hungry again, he realized that there'd been a price required to achieve his current level of success—that price being setting aside what he knew to be right in order to obtain the success his business associates expected of him.

Making his way out of the tavern, he shook Victor's hand, pausing when Victor gave him a reassuring pat on the shoulder.

"You'll do fine, Ian, and I expect you to fill me in on all the details soon." He tilted his head. "Are you planning on traveling back to Glory Manor after your meeting?"

"I'm afraid not. I have another matter to take care of for John Collingwood. He's having difficulty with some transportation issues surrounding a shipment of ore. Something to do with the railroads trying to increase their fares. After I look into that situation, I have more meetings with other union men from the steel mills, and then after that, if nothing catastrophic develops, I'll return to Glory Manor, hopefully within the week."

Wishing him good luck, Victor walked away as Ian turned and strode in the opposite direction.

He soon found himself walking with men making their way toward the many factories that were located next to the river, soot and smog swirling around them as they walked.

They were rough men, built like bulls from the manual labor they performed. But even though they were rough, and most of them uneducated, they were men he could relate to, and men he enjoyed speaking with whenever he had an opportunity to do so.

Exchanging nods with a few of the men, Ian felt a trace of remorse run over him at the thought that he was off to negotiate contracts that would see money taken out of the pockets of possibly every man who walked near him.

Men exactly like the ones surrounding him had always looked out for him after his father forced him to work in the mills as a child. And yet, after he'd risen far higher than he ever imagined he would within the iron and steel industries, instead of looking after these men as they'd looked after him, he was championing the industrialists—the wealthy few who earned vast sums of money—himself included in that list these days.

After taking a moment to ask if anyone knew a Mr. Roy Duffy, which no one did, Ian watched the men walk toward a shift that was fraught with stifling heat and dangerous conditions. As he watched them, he couldn't help but wonder if Nigel had the right measure of him after all.

He *was* sympathetic toward the laborers, knowing what it took for them to return to the mills day after day where they faced long hours of backbreaking work and understanding exactly why they were considering going on strike—even if it meant they'd have no income until the strike was resolved.

They were being asked once again to accept a decrease in their wage, while still being required to do the same amount of work. They were also undoubtedly aware that the investors and owners were still adding to their coffers, even with reduced orders for iron and steel.

It was a business where supply and demand often saw profitability suffer, but because industry was alive and well in the country, profits were always reestablished at some point. That was exactly why he felt compromise was in order, but there was no telling whether the union men would agree to the compromises he was about to propose, or if the investors and owners of the mills would agree to those compromises if Ian was successful in his deliberations.

He couldn't help but wonder whether Aunt Birdie and her questions regarding whether he was truly following God's purpose for his life held more merit than he'd considered. And if so . . . what was he supposed to do next?

Reminding himself that he wasn't representing the laborers at the meeting that was about to take place, but rather the investors and owners who'd entrusted him to see after their best interests, no matter the methods those interests might force Ian to take, he squared his shoulders, hoping he'd be able to end the day without losing a bit of his soul in the process.

CHAPTER 19

Taking the reins in a practiced hand, even though Clyde, the work-horse pulling the wagon, didn't seem to need much guidance as he plodded down the dirt road, Isadora glanced over her shoulder.

The sight that met her gaze had her lips curling into a smile. Three mutinous little faces were staring back at her, those faces remarkably dirt-free and rather pink from the scrubbing they'd recently experienced.

"Isn't this a lovely day for a drive?" she asked, earning an immediate nod from Daisy, who was sitting directly beside her. That nod was accompanied by a grin as the little girl scooted closer to Isadora on the wagon bench, pressing her tiny body against Isadora's side and melting Isadora's heart in the process.

Out of the four children, Daisy had been the easiest to get into the bath. She'd put up a fuss at first, screaming so loudly Isadora was certain her hearing would never be the same. But unwilling to admit defeat before she'd gotten even one child clean, she'd plucked a squirming Daisy straight off the floor, stripped off her frock, then plopped her into the steaming bath, getting completely soaked in the process.

Thankfully, it had taken only a minute for Daisy to realize she wasn't going to suffer a horrible death from being in the bath, and before three minutes had passed, the little girl had made the monumental decision that baths were fun.

After scrubbing the child with a lemon-scented soap Aunt Birdie had provided, she'd had every hope the three older children, after seeing how much fun Daisy had in the bath, would be more cooperative. Sadly, that had not been the case.

Violet had cried throughout most of her bath, stating in between sobs that she could feel herself coming down with a cold. Primrose had chosen to remain mute during her time in the water, while sending Isadora glares as she'd scrubbed herself clean, and Henry, well, he'd been the most difficult of the bunch.

Refusing to strip down in front of Isadora because he didn't want her to see his "boy parts," as he'd called them, he'd shut himself in the bathing room, and after a lot of splashing and loud muttering, he'd finally opened the door, revealing a clean face and hands. Upon closer inspection, though, Isadora had found his neck still filthy, and when she peered down the back of his shirt, she'd realized that he'd not bathed at all, merely washed off the areas he thought would show.

It had taken him three more trips into the bathing chamber, as well as the threat that she would assist him if he came out dirty again, before he'd finally taken a bath, his howls of outrage practically rattling the closed door as he went about what he'd evidently thought was torture.

Now, over two hours later, and faced with three children who were still decidedly put out with her, Isadora felt as if she'd accomplished a feat worthy of praise. That she could finally cross off one of the items from Ian's list also left her feeling relieved. And because she could say she'd completed the task of getting the children to bathe in a somewhat competent fashion, she was not feeling quite as useless as she had after she'd caught the biscuits on fire and allowed the goats to eat half the laundry.

"Bird!" Daisy yelled, pointing to the sky as a red bird flew by.

"It *is* a bird. A cardinal," Isadora explained.

Daisy tilted her head. "Card-in-al."

"Yes, cardinal. Very good." Isadora smiled. "You're a very curious little girl, Daisy, and incredibly bright as well."

"The ladies at the orphanage thought she was slow-witted because she doesn't know many words."

Isadora turned on the seat and directed her attention to Primrose. "How do you know this?"

Primrose shrugged. "The women at the orphanage used to say that about Daisy all the time. They also said that even though she's young, her red hair would make it difficult to find her a permanent home, as well as for the rest of us, since we all have red hair."

Temper was swift. "There is nothing wrong with having red hair. One of my best friends has red hair, and she's absolutely delightful." Isadora drew in a breath and slowly released it. "As for those women saying that about Daisy, they were clearly mistaken. They were also horribly wrong for speaking such a thing with you anywhere near them."

Primrose wrinkled her nose. "Grown-ups never notice when children are around."

Since her own mother had rarely noticed Isadora throughout her youth, except when she'd had whatever governess had been employed at the time bring Isadora into the library at the end of the day to hear a progress report, Isadora couldn't argue that point.

"Even so," she settled on saying, "it was not well done of these people to say such falsehoods about darling Daisy." She put the reins in one hand, then reached out and patted Daisy's arm. "Simply because Daisy doesn't speak much doesn't mean she's slow-witted. My friend with the red hair, Beatrix, didn't speak a single word until she was Daisy's age but is now possessed of a most impressive vocabulary." She smiled at Daisy, who was watching her with eyes as round as saucers. "You are a very smart girl, Daisy, and do not ever allow anyone to tell you differently."

Turning her attention back to the road, she squinted at what appeared to be a collection of buildings in the distance, a sure sign they were getting closer to the town of Canonsburg. Before

182

she could point that out to the children, though, something Primrose had previously said distracted her. Turning around again, she frowned.

"I thought there wasn't room for you to stay in the orphanage, which makes it curious as to how those women were able to make such an absurd judgment about Daisy so quickly."

"There wasn't room for us at the orphanage the second time," Primrose said. "We spent a lot of months there the first time."

Isadora pulled the horse to a stop, turning around fully on the seat. "You were sent to the orphanage twice, and one of those times you stayed there for months?"

"Pa tried to take care of us for as long as he could after Mama died," Henry said, rubbing a finger over his nose. "But it got too much for him because he had to work all the time."

"He took us to the orphanage so that we'd all get to stay together," Primrose added. "He had to pay money every week to make sure that happened, but then . . ." Her forehead puckered. "He ran on some hard times, and that's when he couldn't pay the fees no more."

"What happens when the orphanage doesn't get their fees?" Isadora asked.

"They split brothers and sisters up, send them to different orphanages that have room. They even send children out to work as indent something or other."

All the air seemed to get stuck in Isadora's lungs. "Indentured servants?"

"That's it." Primrose nodded. "I was lucky not to get sent away as a servant, but that's only because one of the women who worked at the orphanage decided to try and run Pa down before they could send us away. She found him at the mill and he came lickety-split to fetch us."

"And were you happy to be able to go home?"

Primrose exchanged a look with Violet and Henry before she looked back at Isadora. "We were happy to see Pa again. He's not a bad man, no matter what anyone says about him."

"And would you want to go home to your father again, if that was a possibility?" Isadora asked.

Primrose hesitated for just a second. "We want to see Pa again, but we love staying at Glory Manor. Pa's just not real good with looking after us. That's why we didn't find it so awful bad to be sent off to the orphanage that first time. We got to take lessons with a real teacher and—"

"They fed us," Violet said softly, then pressed her lips together as if she'd said too much.

Isadora's brow furrowed. "You didn't always have enough to eat when you lived with your father?"

Primrose shook her head. "Pa tried his best, he really did. But he works all the time, and . . . he likes to drink when he says life gets too hard. We was used to him disappearing for a few days at a time. But then, a few weeks ago, he didn't come back." Her lip trembled ever so slightly. "He must not have remembered that the rent needed paid and that he'd left us with no money or that Mrs. Lyman wouldn't check in on us no more once she wasn't gettin' paid."

"The man who collects the rent called the police when we told him we didn't know where Pa was," Henry said, his pale cheeks suddenly sporting two bright spots of color. "And then the police took us to the orphanage again, but it was full up."

Violet leaned forward. "But then Aunt Birdie wanted us. And we love it at Glory Manor. There's food and animals, and Aunt Birdie said we was going to get to go to school come fall." She smiled shyly. "I like school, and I'm hopin' to learn how to read better this time."

Something uncomfortable began bubbling through Isadora. "Have you not been to school often?"

Primrose shook her head. "After Mama died, Pa needed me and Henry to mind Violet and Daisy. There wasn't time for schooling. But we did get some learning in the first time at the orphanage, like I said. I'm just hopin' that the other children won't make fun of us because we don't know all that much."

The very idea that the children were fretting about being made fun of at school had Isadora squaring her shoulders. "There's plenty of time before school starts in the fall to bring all of you up to snuff, or at least improve your reading and writing skills. And while I know that I've not made much of an impression with my abilities around the house, I'm more than capable of tutoring you in the basics. Perhaps the general store will have a few books we can put to good use as early as this evening after I finish my chores. Although I have to imagine Ian's library also has some books we can use." With that, she turned front and center, gave a flick of the reins, and they were off again.

"So, you're really takin' us to shop in a *store*?" Henry asked, appearing directly behind her shoulder.

"I didn't realize that was in question. Why do you think I insisted all of you take a bath and comb your hair if we weren't heading out to shop in a store?"

"We thought you were just using the treat of getting some new clothes to get us into the tub," Henry said. "Me and my sisters thought that you were really just gonna take us over to the church in town and see if Reverend Davis had some more clothing in the poor box he'd give us to wear."

"While I'm certain this Reverend Davis would be more than willing to share any clothing that might have been donated, we're not going to the church. We're off to purchase *new* clothing—as in never-worn-by-anyone-else-before clothing."

"They got clothing you can buy and walk out of the store with?" Primrose asked, joining her brother.

"That's what Aunt Birdie told me. I'm not certain how large the selection will be, though. But if we don't find much, Aunt Birdie told me to purchase some fabric and she'll sew some clothing for you."

"We've never had new clothes before," Primrose said. "But that does explain why you were so determined to get us into the bath."

"Shopping for new clothing is meant to be an experience, one not to be undertaken lightly or . . . while dirty. However, even though I did want you to be well scrubbed for this occasion, I also promised Ian I'd do my best to get all of you to bathe, so I might have used the lure of shopping to convince you to get into the tub."

Primrose tilted her head. "You know you're not supposed to tell children your tricks, don't you?"

Isadora's lips curved. "I'm certain it will come as no surprise that I know next to nothing about children."

"You didn't tell Ian that, did you?"

Returning her attention to the road as the wagon crested a hill and the town of Canonsburg spread out in front of them, Isadora shrugged. "I don't believe he was under the impression I have much experience with children."

"But what if he decides you're not what he needs in a housekeeper and then decides since you don't know much about children, he'll need to bring in someone new to watch Daisy when the rest of us go off to school come fall?" Primrose asked.

Knowing there was little likelihood that she'd still be at Glory Manor come fall, but not wanting to disappoint children who'd suffered far too much disappointment in their young lives, Isadora summoned up a smile. "I imagine there are far more competent women out there who'd be much better suited to looking after Daisy than me."

"But Daisy likes you," Primrose argued as Daisy nodded her head in clear agreement. "And you don't have to worry that me, Henry, or Violet will be much trouble."

Henry grinned. "We'll be good because we like you and want you to stay on at the farm."

"You didn't like me so much an hour ago."

Henry stuck his head over the seat. "That was before we got to know you. You're a nice housekeeper, and you don't talk to us like other grown-ups do. You just act like we're people."

"You are people," Isadora said. "But perhaps I'm not supposed to talk to you like I talk to grown-ups, which could very well be exactly why I'm not qualified to watch over you." She smiled. "I could do irreparable harm and not even realize I'm doing it."

"I imagine you talk to us like you do because you weren't treated like a baby when you was young," Primrose said, the crooked braids Isadora had attempted bouncing as she nodded her head.

Isadora considered Primrose's words. The truth of the matter was that she'd *not* been treated like a child by her many governesses and nannies because she'd been raised to believe she was superior to anyone working for her family. Frankly, she had to imagine all her governesses had found her to be incredibly willful, spoiled, and a somewhat unlikeable child.

Most of the children she'd grown up with, except for Beatrix, of course, were possessed of the same willful natures, but now, when faced with children who seemed genuinely delighted with the slight bit of attention and notice she'd given them, she couldn't help but feel ashamed of her younger self and the self-importance she'd worn like a cloak of honor.

Looking up at the blue sky, she questioned whether Aunt Birdie had the right of things and that she might have, possibly, landed at Glory Manor because she needed to find her purpose in life. Or, at the very least, discover some painful truths about herself, which could, hopefully, lead her to live a more meaningful life, not that she had the slightest idea what that might entail, but it was an interesting . . .

"That man's trying to get your attention."

Blinking out of her thoughts, Isadora looked to where Henry was now pointing and found a man hurrying down the steps of a building that had *Feed Store* painted on a sign. He was waving his hands and shouting something to her, but all she could think of was that she was a woman alone, responsible for four children, and didn't have so much as a stick to defend them against anyone interested in . . .

"Ma'am, slow down. Your—"

Giving the reins a determined flick because her father had warned her time and time again that kidnapping was a real threat to someone of their station, Isadora kept a firm grip on those reins as well as a firm grip on Daisy.

"Sit down, children," she called as Clyde picked up his pace, leaving the man who was still yelling behind her in a cloud of dust.

"Stop, you're about to lose—"

With a thud, the wagon tilted to the left, and a second later, a wagon wheel rolled by.

Before Isadora could do more than gape at the wheel, the wagon lurched forward, and then she was flying through the air.

Grabbing hold of Daisy, she held the little girl tightly as the ground rose up to greet her.

CHAPTER 20

Little hands touching her face sent a wave of relief through Isadora as she opened her eyes, finding Daisy peering back at her.

"We fly!" were the first words out of Daisy's mouth. "Like card-nal."

Drawing in a painful breath since she'd evidently knocked the wind out of herself as she hit the ground, Isadora smiled. "We did fly, but thank goodness you're all right." She looked around for the rest of the children. "Is anyone hurt?"

"We're fine," Primrose called. "Bit dusty, but not dirty enough to take another bath today."

Isadora's lips began to curve. "Duly noted, although do know that baths are going to be a recurring occasion from this point forward, at least two times a week."

As the three older children immediately took to grumbling, Isadora shifted Daisy from where she'd been sitting on top of her to the ground, discovering that a large crowd had gathered around them. Pushing herself to a sitting position, she found a hand held out to her a second later.

"You all right, ma'am?" the owner of that hand asked as she accepted the help up.

Brushing dirt from her skirt, Isadora raised her head and found the same man who'd been yelling at her standing beside her.

"I'm fine. Shaken, of course, but I don't believe I injured anything when I fell."

"I tried to warn you that your wheel was wobbling, but you must not have heard me."

"I apologize for that, sir," Isadora began. "I originally thought you meant to harm us."

"Who would try to harm a woman and four children when they were just riding down the road?"

"When you put it that way, it does sound rather ridiculous, but . . ."

"You ain't from around here, are you?" the man pressed.

"She's clearly that new housekeeper who recently took on the position out at Glory Manor. And of course she's not from around here, Stanley. Talk has it she's from one of the big cities, which would explain why she felt she was about to be accosted."

Looking to the right, Isadora frowned at the woman who'd just spoken. "How is there any talk about me?"

The woman smiled and stepped closer. "That's the beauty of small towns—nothing goes unremarked upon. But I'm forgetting my manners. I'm Mrs. John Gillespie, but you can call me Anna. And you . . ." She smiled. "You must be Izzie."

"You know my name?"

Anna nodded. "Hank has kept everyone apprised of what's been happening lately at Glory Manor whenever he's stopped by town." She smiled at the children. "You're the Duffy children. I've been hoping to meet you."

When Primrose, Violet, Daisy, and Henry simply stared back at Anna with wide eyes, Isadora moved to stand beside them, taking a moment to perform introductions.

"What beautiful names you have, girls," Anna exclaimed. "I imagine your mother must have loved flowers."

A ghost of a smile flickered over Primrose's face. "She did, ma'am, and even wanted Henry to be named *Hawthorne*, but Pa was having none of that."

Henry muttered something about telling tales under his breath as he kept his head lowered.

"Henry is a fine name and suits you admirably, young man," Anna said.

"And Henry has been very helpful around the farm," Isadora added, sending Henry a wink when he lifted his head. "As have all the children, even Daisy, who seems to have a great affinity for the ducks."

"Ducks!" Daisy yelled with a grin.

Returning the grin, Isadora took a moment to look the children over, brushing dirt from their clothing. "Are you sure none of you were hurt when you got tossed out of the wagon?"

"Me and Primrose landed on our feet," Henry said.

"But I felled and hurt my elbow," Violet said, speaking up in a voice that was no louder than a whisper right as her little lip started trembling.

As a single tear trailed down Violet's cheek, Isadora knelt beside the child. "I'm sorry." She leaned forward and kissed the elbow, taken by complete surprise when Violet suddenly threw her thin arms around Isadora's neck and clung to her. Gathering the child into her arms, she rose to her feet, blinking away tears that took her by surprise.

"The children certainly do seem to have taken to you," Anna said. "Which explains why Ian hired you on." She shook her head. "None of us in town thought there was even a remote chance he'd replace that Mrs. Gladstone with you, but here you are, which I say is a step in the right direction for Ian."

Isadora shifted Violet on her hip. "I'm not certain what you mean by that, and how does everyone know I went to Glory Manor to apply for the housekeeping position?"

Waving that aside, Anna smiled. "The station master mentioned at the church supper the other evening that he'd told you he knew the housekeeping position had become available again after Mrs. Gladstone showed up in town, anxious to get on the first train out of here. And then Mr. Mummel remarked at that same supper that

191

he'd offered you a ride to Glory Manor." She gave Isadora's arm a pat. "And before you ask me how I knew you were from a big city, folks around these parts don't have fancy steamer trunks like the one Mr. Mummel said you brought with you."

"I suppose my trunk is fancy," Isadora said before she turned and looked at the wagon, wincing at the sight of the missing wheel. "I can't imagine how that wheel came off." She drew in a sharp breath. "Goodness, is Clyde unharmed?"

"He's fine," the man named Stanley said, moving from where he'd been standing beside Clyde. He walked to the rear of the wagon, shaking his head. "I'm surprised the wheel broke right off like that, though." He leaned closer, fiddled with the axle, then pulled out what looked to be some type of metal rod. "Looks like the pin broke straight in two." He handed the pin to another man who'd joined him, who then handed it to another man, and the pin soon passed down a long line of men, all of them considering it closely.

"I'm afraid Glory Manor has suffered a few unfortunate events lately," Isadora said, her heart melting when Violet laid her head against her shoulder. "I was told the plow broke as Aunt Birdie was using it, an accident responsible for her not being able to get around easily over the past few weeks."

Anna exchanged a look with Stanley, returning her attention to Isadora a second later. "There's been a rash of accidents on quite a few local farms lately. I recently learned that all the chickens on Black Brothers Farm took ill, many of them dying, and then Brody Fine over at Harvest House found something had attacked one of his raspberry fields, wiping out a good deal of his profits in the process." She shook her head. "His wife puts up the most incredible raspberry jam, but I suppose she won't be worrying about that anymore, not when talk has it the Fines are thinking about selling the farm." She leveled an eye on Isadora. "Do be sure to tell Birdie that. She's friends with Opal Fine, and I imagine she'll want to say a proper good-bye if the Fines go ahead and sell."

"I'll be sure to tell her," Isadora said.

"I appreciate that." Anna took a step closer. "How are those new hired hands adjusting to life at Glory Manor?"

Since Isadora wasn't comfortable sharing what Hank had whispered to her about those hires before she'd left for town—that they didn't seem to be taking very well to the animals—she settled for a shrug. "I've not really had an opportunity to speak with those men yet."

Anna smiled. "I imagine your new position is keeping you busy, but speaking of that, how are *you* adjusting to life at Glory Manor?"

"It's been a little hectic of late."

"We had a fire in the kitchen this morning," Primrose said, speaking up. "It burnt the biscuits to a crisp."

"And don't forget about the goats eating our clothes," Henry added. "That sure was unexpected."

"And Izzie got sucked right into the wringer," Violet said, lifting her head from Isadora's shoulder, her eyes wide. "Good thing the wringer didn't suck her all the way in 'cuz we like Izzie, even if she made us take a bath."

Anna raised a hand to her throat. "Goodness, it does seem as if you're having a time of it out there." She looked at Henry. "Did goats really eat your clothes?"

Henry nodded. "That's why we're here. We was goin' to get us some new ones at the general store."

"We're *still* going to get you clothes," Isadora said. "I just have to figure out how to get the wheel fixed first so we can get back to Glory Manor after we're done with our shopping."

"There's no need for you to worry about that," Stanley said, nodding to the other men who'd joined them. "We'll get the wheel fixed for you, and then we'll bring the wagon to the general store when we're finished."

"I wouldn't want to put you out."

"It's no bother at all." Stanley waved toward a building up the street. "You go on to the store and do that shopping. The wagon won't take us long, and we'll look after Clyde, give him some oats and water."

"This is very kind of all of you," Isadora began, earning nods from the men. "And do know that I'll be happy to compensate you for your troubles if you'll provide me with a bill after you're done."

Stanley shook his head. "There's no need for that, and we'll hear no arguing from you."

"Amen to that," Anna said, stepping closer to Isadora. "And now that that's settled, how about I show you to the general store?"

Realizing the matter was settled whether she wanted it to be or not, while also feeling rather bemused by the idea that complete strangers were evidently perfectly content to step in and assist her, Isadora thanked the men again, and then followed Anna down the street. Settling Violet more comfortably against her, she reached out and took hold of Daisy's hand, smiling at Henry and Primrose, who'd stepped directly behind her.

"You'll find Canonsburg to be a most welcoming town," Anna said before she began pointing out different shops, slowing to a stop as she gestured to a building in the distance.

"That's our church where Reverend Davis gives a most uplifting sermon on any given Sunday." Anna caught Isadora's eye. "Can I assume that you'll be bringing the children to the service this Sunday?"

Isadora lowered Violet to her feet, taking hold of the little girl's hand. "Ian didn't put taking the children to church on the list he left for me before he went off to Pittsburgh."

"Attending church isn't something normally found on a list, dear," Anna said, tilting her head. "Did you not attend church regularly where you used to live?"

"My family and I attended church every Sunday when we were in the city, but I fear I haven't even considered attending church since I reached Canonsburg."

Anna nodded. "I'm sure it's been quite the adjustment getting settled. But you'll feel much more at home once you begin to meet all the good folk in Canonsburg. There's nothing like the sense of community you'll experience after you become introduced to everyone, something I know Reverend Davis will make certain happens come Sunday after the service."

Isadora leaned closer to Anna and lowered her voice. "I should tell you that I've only been hired on a temporary basis, which means I might very well find myself leaving Canonsburg in the not-too-distant future."

Anna's eyes narrowed. "Ian hired you on a temporary basis?"

Isadora smiled. "I'm afraid so, but in his defense, I'm not exactly qualified for the position because my experience with running a household is rather limited, and I've never even been on a farm before." Her smile turned into a grin. "In all honesty, Ian only hired me because he needed to attend to some pressing business in Pittsburgh and I was his only option."

Anna pursed her lips. "Everyone lacks experience when they first start out in life, my dear. I would think it'll take no time at all for you to adjust to your new position. Once you do that, Ian will be more than happy to offer you a permanent role at Glory Manor."

"I'm not sure how competent I'll be, especially not after I almost burned the house down this morning and then allowed the goats to eat the laundry."

"Hmm . . ." was all Anna had to say about that before she began walking again, stopping in front of a large building a moment later. Gesturing to the building that had a large sign with the words *General Store* painted on it, she smiled. "I'm sure you'll be able to find the children some clothing here. Although . . ." Her smile faded. "You won't find as much variety as you would in a store such as Joseph Horne Company in downtown Pittsburgh, but one can't really expect to find that level of shopping in a small town like Canonsburg."

"I've never heard of Joseph Horne Company."

"It's a marvelous store—seven stories high, mind you—and they have fashions that a person would only expect to find in New York City." Anna beamed. "I bought a lovely shawl there last year, and me and the husband always go down to Pittsburgh around Christmas to shop, although the prices are rather dear, so we don't come home with much."

"Perhaps I'll need to speak with Ian and convince him a trip to Pittsburgh might be in order to add to the children's wardrobes before they go off to school."

"That would be a treat for the children," Anna said, walking to the door of the general store and holding it open. "For now, though, we can hope you'll find a few items here that will suffice." She turned to the children. "Ready for an adventure, children?"

As the children immediately began nodding, Anna ushered them into the store, Isadora following a second later, finding herself beyond curious to see what a general store actually looked like inside and if it could, in any way, compare to the sophisticated stores she'd shopped in around the world.

CHAPTER 21

Stopping directly inside the store, Isadora found herself in a most charming space, taken aback by the extent of the inventory surrounding her.

Shelves running from the floor to the ceiling were stocked with tins and small boxes carrying a range of products from soap to cakes of yeast, while jars that were filled with a variety of candies sat on the glass cases. Pots and baskets were hanging from hooks on the ceiling, and large bags of what appeared to be flour were stacked on the floor.

Turning, Isadora discovered all four children staring with wide eyes at the jars of candy.

"I believe we should start our shopping adventure with candy before we begin looking at the clothing," she said.

Henry's mouth dropped open. "You're gonna buy us a piece of candy?"

Isadora's heart gave a lurch. "You have had candy before, haven't you?"

Primrose nodded even as she took a step toward the candy counter. "Mama used to get us a piece for Christmas when she was living, but we haven't had any since she died."

Blinking away tears that threatened to blind her, Isadora summoned up a smile. "You may each choose a few pieces, but only eat two of them now. I don't want any of you to come down with a stomachache."

That was all it took for the children to rush to the candy counter, peering at every jar as they went about what was obviously the daunting task of trying to decide what candy would be the most delicious.

"Ah, I see I have some customers," a woman exclaimed, bustling through a door at the back of the store, her arms filled with bolts of fabric. Depositing the fabric on top of a counter, she smoothed a hand over her brown hair and smiled at Isadora. "You must be Izzie, and I want to say your last name is Delmont, but I'm not certain about that."

Before Isadora could respond, Anna spoke up. "It *is* Delmont, Maggie. She's Mrs. Delmont, but everyone calls her Izzie. Hank told me." Anna nodded to Isadora. "This is Maggie Rogers, Izzie. She and her husband run the general store, and she's just the person to help you find some clothing for the children."

Maggie's eyes began to gleam. "You're here to buy clothing? How wonderful. We've only recently gotten in a nice selection of dresses for girls, since it's time to stock up for the coming school year." She took a step toward Isadora. "May I dare hope that Ian has given you a nice budget to clothe the little darlings who've come to live at Glory Manor?"

"He wasn't actually home to give me a budget, but Aunt Birdie told me to put the purchases on his account. She gave me a note so you'll know I'm not up to anything shady."

Maggie's eyes gleamed brighter than ever. "Well then, since Ian is known to be a most generous man, I'm going to assume he'll want the children to have quite a few new outfits." She eyed Isadora up and down. "We've got some lovely calico dresses as well, dear. Some of the colors would look lovely on you."

Without allowing Isadora a second to protest, Maggie hurried over to the children and introduced herself. She began putting their candy selections in brown paper sacks, taking out a pad of paper from her pocket on which she then began compiling a tally of prices.

"You've just made Maggie's day a whole light brighter," Anna said, right as the door to the general store opened and an entire swarm of women hurried in. "I was wondering when everyone would arrive to meet you." She smiled and waved the women over. "Word must have already gotten out you've come to town."

Before she knew it, Isadora was being introduced to all the women, finding herself slightly overwhelmed with the crowd continually streaming into the store. After meeting an Alice, Cora, Maribeth, three women named Betty, and then a Wilda, Isadora finally made it to the last woman waiting to meet her, a Miss Olive Perkins, who'd only recently returned to town.

"I believe that's everyone," Anna said, smiling at all the women now watching Isadora closely. "I've already told Izzie that she would receive a warm welcome after church on Sunday, but how lovely that she'll now have friendly faces to greet her, which will make it so much easier for her to attend the service."

Having no idea whether she'd be going to church on Sunday, not with how life on the farm had been shaping up, Isadora merely smiled in response, relieved when Violet stole up beside her and took hold of her hand. Looking down, she found the little girl clutching a sack of candy.

"We was wonderin' if we can eat that candy now," Violet all but whispered.

"Of course you may, but remember, only two pieces."

Running back to her siblings, Violet opened her bag, as did the other children. Isadora watched as they popped what looked to be pieces of peppermint candy in their mouths, all four children grinning in sheer delight the second the candy hit their tongues.

Surprisingly enough, after they'd enjoyed exactly two pieces of candy, they closed the sacks Maggie had given them, seemingly content to mind her suggestion of having only two pieces in the store.

"Done already?" Maggie asked.

"Izzie said we was only to eat two pieces right now," Henry said. "But that sure was some tasty candy."

Maggie smiled. "I'm delighted you enjoyed it. Now, shall we see about finding all of you some new clothes?"

Taking hold of Daisy's hand when the little girl immediately scampered to her side, Isadora followed Maggie and the rest of the children through the store, leaving the crowd of women behind. Walking into another room, she stopped directly over the threshold, impressed by the amount of merchandise stocked around her. A second later, a young woman stepped forward, a bright smile on her face.

"On my word, but Hank wasn't jesting. You really are a lovely woman, and you're certainly far younger than any of us expected Ian's housekeeper to be."

"Thank you?" was all Isadora could think to respond as she took the hand the woman was extending to her.

"I'm Miss Susan Rogers," the woman began. "And do forgive me for staring, but again, you're remarkably young, and as I said, lovely, and . . ."

"I'm not who anyone expected Ian to hire?" Isadora finished for her with a grin.

Susan returned the grin. "Not even close." She released Isadora's hand and nodded to the racks of clothing around the room. "My parents own this store, but I'm responsible for buying the goods in here. Dare I hope you're here to do a bit of shopping?"

"We are, and we'll take whatever you have available for the children in their sizes."

"Did I mention how *delighted* I am to meet you?" Susan exclaimed before she hurried over to the children, and before Isadora knew it, the girls were being directed to a dressing room behind a curtain, their arms filled with dresses.

Susan turned her attention to Henry next, eyeing him for a moment before she looked to Isadora. "Are we going with trousers, short pants, and shirts today, or should I also see if we have a few jackets that might fit him?"

"He'll probably need jackets for when he goes to school, won't he?" Isadora asked.

Susan shook her head. "Not all the boys wear jackets, especially not when school first starts and they're working in the fields before they go to class." She pulled out a few pairs of trousers from a rack. "But it won't hurt to have him try on a jacket or . . . three."

Handing her choices to Henry, who wasn't looking exactly pleased about having to try everything on, Susan showed him to a room that seemed to be a storage room, closing the door firmly behind him and telling him he'd need to show them the clothes once he changed.

"I see you've done this before," Isadora said, remembering her recent experience with trying to get Henry to bathe and him being less than cooperative.

"The girls are always easy," Susan said. "But the boys, well, I imagine they'd rather be anywhere else than in a store shopping for clothing." She moved to stand beside Isadora. "If we can't find clothes to fit them, do know that we carry the latest Montgomery Ward catalog. We can always order you items from it."

"I've never heard of a Montgomery Ward catalog. You can order clothing from them and they deliver to you?"

Susan's brows drew together. "I thought everyone knew about Montgomery Ward and their catalog. My friends and I buy a lot of our clothing through them when we can't get the latest styles in the store."

Unwilling to tell Susan that she purchased most of her clothing in designer salons in Paris, Isadora walked to a rack of dresses, looking them over until she spotted one that caught her eye. Pulling it from the rack, she held it up. "This looks to be about Aunt Birdie's size. Do you think she'd like it?"

"Yes, she'd adore it. Pink would be a lovely color on Aunt Birdie." Her eyes sparkling, Susan took the dress from Isadora and hurried away to wrap it in paper, stepping past another woman who walked right up beside Isadora.

"I'm Olive Perkins, if you've forgotten," Olive began. "And I'm quite certain you're feeling like a bit of an oddity, what with everyone clamoring to meet you."

"It is a little curious," Isadora admitted. "And I'm not certain why everyone is doing that clamoring."

"Because you're the woman no one ever expected Ian to hire." Olive shook her head. "He's a bit of a hometown hero, what with how successful he's become. But he's turned a little peculiar since he went off to Pittsburgh, a circumstance that has had all of us worried about him for years."

"Peculiar how?"

Olive smiled. "He's apparently decided that everyone under the age of thirty is out to try and marry him, but he's been more than vocal about wanting to marry a woman a little more sophisticated than what can be found in Canonsburg."

Isadora frowned. "Why are you smiling about that? Seems rather insulting, if you ask me."

Olive waved that away. "Ian's always been driven, so his wanting to marry up is no surprise. What he doesn't know, though, is even with most women finding themselves swooning ever so slightly over his lovely face and . . . well, all those muscles of his, none of us in town have the slightest desire to marry him." She gave a bit of a shudder. "Who in their right mind would want to enter into a society atmosphere, what with all the rules involved?" She sent Isadora an expectant look.

"Who indeed?" Isadora said somewhat weakly.

"Exactly. But when Hank came to town the other day and told us about you staying on the farm, it allowed the people of this town, all of whom adore Ian, to finally have hope that their favored son was realizing there's more to life than merely amassing a fortune and climbing up a social ladder."

"And they realized this because . . . ?"

"He hired you."

"Perhaps he was impressed with my housekeeping abilities."

"You told me you're not gifted with housekeeping skills," Anna said, bustling into the room with Maggie Rogers by her side, all the other ladies squeezing into the room after them. "That's why we've decided to intervene."

Apprehension was swift. "Intervene?"

"But of course, dear, it's what we do. But first, we will need you to convince Birdie that there's no need for her to be embarrassed about us coming out to the farm to lend our assistance."

"Why would you think Aunt Birdie would be embarrassed about that? She doesn't strike me as the type to embarrass easily."

Anna and Maggie exchanged looks before Maggie caught Isadora's eye. "That's what we always thought, but then Hank told us that Birdie was merely using Mrs. Gladstone's surly nature as an excuse to keep us away. She's always been an independent sort, so we concluded that she was uncomfortable not being her normal independent self, what with trying to recover from her accident and all."

Something began niggling at the back of her neck. "Hank certainly does seem to spread a lot of gossip around, doesn't he?"

"He is a talker," Anna agreed, shaking her head. "But he's also a reliable sort, helping out where he's needed and taking on additional work at all the farms around here when someone needs a helping hand."

"And he's a local Canonsburg man?" Isadora asked.

Maggie looked to all the women gathered in the back room. "How long has Hank been here?"

"At least six months, if not longer," said a woman Isadora thought might be Wilda.

The niggling increased, but before she could ask any additional questions about Hank, Anna cleared her throat. "Since you seem to believe Birdie won't be upset if all of us descend on Glory Manor, you may tell her to expect us tomorrow bright and early."

"Bright and early to do what?" Isadora asked.

"Help you get Glory Manor back into shape." Anna smiled.

"We'll also be bringing delicious dishes with us—it's what we do. That means you won't need to worry about burning the house down again because you'll have enough meals to last you for weeks."

Opening her mouth, to say what, she had no idea, Isadora was distracted when Primrose stepped through the curtain, her cheeks pink with pleasure as she showed off a simple calico dress that looked adorable on her.

The next thirty minutes were spent admiring the girls in all the dresses Susan found that fit them. Henry balked after showing them his second pair of trousers and a shirt, stating quite emphatically that all the trousers were the same, so what was the point of having to show everyone. Taking pity on the small boy, Isadora told him he could simply make sure everything else fit, and if it did, he could then wander around the store.

As Susan wrapped up all the purchases, although there was no need to wrap up the dolls the girls had selected or the slingshot that she didn't believe Henry was ever going to let go of again, she found her hand taken by Anna, who surprised her when she gave it a good squeeze.

"Now, don't you fret about all of us coming out tomorrow. It's not like you're shirking any of your duties. You'll just need to tell us what to do and keep us on task."

"I *am* good at organizing."

"Wonderful. Stanley just stopped by with your wagon. It's good as new, so allow me to encourage you to get on your way. I took the liberty of putting a casserole under the front seat, and I wouldn't want it to go bad before all of you get a chance to eat it."

After thanking Anna for her kindness and saying good-bye to the women, Isadora got the children loaded into the wagon and on their way. The ride home passed quickly, and before she knew it, Clyde was clomping down Glory Lane.

Smiling as the children scampered out of the wagon, running toward Uncle Amos, who was walking across the lawn, Isadora made her way to the front porch, finding Aunt Birdie sitting in a worn rocker there.

204

"I'm afraid I have some disappointing news" were the first words out of Aunt Birdie's mouth.

Isadora braced herself. "Disappointing how?"

"Hank quit." Aunt Birdie shook her head. "Told me Amos chased him out of the barn with an axe even though Amos doesn't recall doing that." She released a breath. "I tried to reason with Hank, told him Amos hadn't meant any harm, but Hank said he won't be returning, no matter that he needed the job."

"Please tell me the two men Ian recently hired are still here."

"They're in the barn, finishing up the afternoon milking."

"Then I suppose, given my position, I should go make certain they're not considering leaving as well."

After she marched her way to the barn, her concerns were soon put to rest when the two new hires assured her they had no intention of quitting their recently secured positions, and that they'd be back again the following morning to take care of the animals.

The rest of the evening was spent tidying up the yard, salvaging what she could of the laundry, serving up the meal Anna had provided, and then making sure the children washed up. After that, she began reading them a story they'd all agreed they wanted to hear: *The Princess and the Goblin* by George MacDonald, a book she'd found on one of the shelves in Ian's library.

When Daisy's eyes began to close, Isadora told the children they'd continue reading the story the next night, and after getting everyone tucked into their respective beds, she repaired to her own room, falling into bed a short time later and into a sound sleep.

That sleep came to an abrupt end when the sound of mooing woke her up. Sticking her head out the window, she found Buttercup standing directly beneath the window, mooing mournfully as she looked up at Isadora.

Not wanting the cow to wake everyone up, Isadora grabbed a wrapper and headed out of the house, following Buttercup as the cow led the way to the barn.

Apprehension stole through her when she reached the barn and saw that the door was wide open. When she stepped inside, that apprehension quickly turned to dismay as she realized there was not a single animal in sight, save Buttercup, all the other animals having gone . . . missing.

CHAPTER 22

THREE DAYS LATER

As soon as the train screeched to a stop at the Canonsburg station, Ian was the first passenger to step to the platform.

It had been a trying trip with little accomplished. All he wanted to do now was return to Glory Manor, and in all honesty, he wanted to see Izzie again.

Exactly when he'd begun thinking of her as Izzie instead of Mrs. Delmont, he couldn't say, but even with his almost every hour being consumed with business matters in Pittsburgh, his thoughts had returned again and again to the woman he'd left behind, a woman he couldn't stop thinking about, no matter that he knew it was foolish in the extreme to allow her to consume so many of his thoughts.

She was a woman in service and did not fulfill one of the main requirements he'd convinced himself he needed before he'd turn an interested eye in any lady's direction. But . . . she pulled at him in a way no woman ever had, disrupting his thoughts even when he'd been deep in negotiations with the union men.

Those negotiations were now at an impasse, a direct result of Mr. Andrew Carnegie's interference.

He'd long admired Andrew Carnegie—a self-made millionaire whom Ian had striven to emulate as he'd gone about the business of securing a fortune of his own, but his admiration for the man had dimmed significantly over the past few days. That dimming was a direct result of Andrew breezing into Ian's meeting and announcing to everyone assembled there that he'd been called from New York by his team of investors, who believed it would be for the best if *Andrew* stepped in to handle the trouble with the laborers at the iron mills. He'd then nodded pleasantly at Ian and told him he was more than welcome to stay to watch the proceedings, but that his job of negotiating new terms with the union men had come to an end.

Quite frankly, Ian's first impulse had been to stalk out of the room. But when Andrew made the announcement that he, along with other investors and most mill owners, had decided they were not receptive to *any* concessions, Ian had stayed put in the hope of talking a bit of sense into the man.

He'd been woefully unsuccessful with that, and by the time the meeting had come to an unpleasant end two full days later, the union men were threatening a strike.

Having missed the last train home to Canonsburg that day, he'd returned to his yet-to-be-finished mansion in Shadyside. Greeted at the door by his efficient secretary, Mr. Downing, he'd been handed a schedule filled with meetings for the following day, which ended any hopes he'd had about returning earlier than expected to Glory Manor.

"Ian, I was hoping you'd show up soon. Your horse has taken to sulking in the stable, refusing to allow anyone near him."

Glancing around the station, he found Jack Evans, owner of the Canonsburg Livery Stable, striding his way.

Ian shook Jack's hand and smiled. "I'm sure Rumor *is* put out with me. He's a difficult horse at the best of times and has never enjoyed being left behind. Unfortunately, I didn't have the time to make arrangements to have him transported back to Pittsburgh with me."

"He might be difficult, but he's a beauty." Jack fell into step beside Ian as they walked toward the livery. "You got him at Garrison Farms, didn't you?"

Ian nodded. "I've been considering making another trip to Garrison's to add a few additional horses to my stable. You're welcome to join me if you're in the market to increase yours as well."

Jack's smile turned rueful. "The Garrison horses are a little steep for my blood. But if you are looking to add to your stable, you should make the trip soon. I've heard Mr. Garrison is experiencing some financial difficulties and might not be in business much longer."

"Garrison Farms produces some of the best horseflesh in the country."

Walking into the stable, Jack shrugged as they moved to the stall Rumor was in. "From what I've heard, Mr. Garrison apparently took out a loan to expand his operation, wanting to move it from its current location to Kentucky, but the bank is calling in that loan earlier than expected. Sounds like a shady deal, but not something out of the ordinary around these parts."

"You think someone's trying to get his business away from him?"

"That's my guess." Jack opened the door to Rumor's stall, which had Ian's horse immediately presenting both men with his backside. "I would say Rumor is still in a bit of a snit."

"I'll have Hank give him extra attention. Rumor seems to like Hank more than he likes me at times."

"Hank's no longer at Glory Manor. He quit three days ago, something to do with Amos accusing him of letting the goats free and then chasing him off the farm with a pitchfork . . . or it might have been an axe, now that I think about it."

"I *knew* I should have come home sooner."

"There's no need to worry that Glory Manor is suffering," a voice said from behind him.

Turning, Ian found Stanley Huxman, owner of the local feed store, walking his way.

Ian stepped forward to shake the hand Stanley was already extending to him. "And why shouldn't I worry?"

"Because the good women of Canonsburg have taken a great interest, as well as a great liking, to the lovely Izzie. They've been out to the farm often, and from what I've heard, Glory Manor is running smoothly."

Ian blinked. "Is it really?"

"Indeed, so there's no reason to feel guilty about not being there." Stanley caught Ian's eye. "You heard Hank left?"

"Jack just told me."

Stanley nodded. "He was in a right state when he arrived back in town, claiming Amos had finally completely lost his wits. But there's no need for you to fret about your uncle. We menfolk have been taking turns riding out to check on Glory Manor, and Amos seemed perfectly fine to all of us."

Ian frowned. "Why did you feel the need to check up on Glory Manor?"

Stanley leaned against Rumor's stall. "It's a bit of a story, Ian, but I'll start it like this—Izzie and the children had an accident the other day when they drove into town to do some shopping. All of them were thrown out of the wagon, but by the grace of God, none of them were hurt." Stanley reached into his pocket and pulled out what looked to be a wheel pin. He handed it to Ian. "I've been carrying this around with me, hoping to catch you when you got back to town. I didn't want to worry Izzie with this, but if you look closely, it looks like someone sawed that pin."

Ian's hand closed around the pin. "You think someone deliberately sabotaged the wagon?"

"That's what it looks like to me." Stanley exchanged a look with Jack, then looked back to Ian. "When you add that in with Birdie's accident with the plow, I'm afraid Amos has the right measure of things and that someone is causing mischief at Glory Manor."

"I think I'd call it something a little more serious than mischief,"

Ian said as he moved over to where Rumor's saddle was hanging from a hook. "I have to get to the farm."

"There's also obeen curious things happening at a few farms surrounding Glory Manor," Jack said, taking a saddle blanket down from another hook and tossing it over Rumor. "Animals dying, crops ruined, irrigation ditches running dry, and lots of animals have gone missing, escaped from their barns or pens."

Ian frowned. "Sparky, Uncle Amos's dog, went missing about a month ago."

"Which reminds me, you'll want to stop by Guy Wilt's tavern after you get Rumor saddled. Guy was just visiting his sister down in Washington and saw a dog sitting on the train platform when he arrived. He thought the dog looked familiar, and when he returned to the station to come back here this morning, he realized it was Sparky."

"Sparky was in Washington, Pennsylvania?"

"He was," Jack said. "Strange thing, though. From what Guy found out from the stationmaster, Sparky showed up over a month ago but didn't look like he'd been living it rough. And what's even more peculiar was that he wouldn't leave the train station, just sat there all day. The stationmaster started feeding him when he decided Sparky seemed to be waiting for someone to come take him home."

Stanley cleared his throat. "Sounds like someone dumped him off in Washington and might have taken him on the train to do so."

"Why would someone steal an old man's dog and then not even bother to keep him?"

Jack stepped closer to Ian. "I think it might have something to do with whomever is trying to buy up vast amounts of land around here. Talk is, there's coal in these parts, and someone seems determined to begin mining that coal. That right there, along with the nasty suspicions we men in town have about that wheel falling off, is exactly why we've been taking it in turns to ride out and check on everyone at Glory Manor."

"And they've been fine? You haven't run into any trouble?"

211

"No trouble so far, and the house is still standing, something Izzie seems remarkably proud about." Jack released a breath. "Shame there's not more we can do about this, though, other than sending patrols out at night."

Ian threw the saddle on Rumor, cinched it, then turned back to Jack. "I'll be able to do something, Jack. It might take some time to track down the culprits behind this, but I have a lot of contacts in Pittsburgh, as well as contacts who have interests in coal mining. Someone will know something, and when I find out who is behind the trouble . . ."

"You'll take care of them?" Jack finished for him.

"Indeed."

With that, Ian swung into the saddle, thanked Jack and Stanley for their information, then headed out of the stable and down Main Street. He turned into an alley a short time later and reined Rumor to a halt in front of Wilt's Tavern.

Sure enough, sitting on the front porch was Sparky. The moment the dog caught sight of him, he let out a yip of excitement and raced off the porch, scampering around Rumor as Ian swung from the saddle.

"He's sure happy to see you, Ian."

Taking a moment to give Sparky some very enthusiastic pats and receiving some licks to the face in return, Ian straightened and nodded to Guy Wilt, who was walking down the steps of the porch.

"I can't thank you enough for bringing Sparky back," Ian said.

Guy reached down and ruffled Sparky's fur. "It was my pleasure. I know how Amos has been fretting about this dog. I was intending to take him to the farm later today, once my help showed up to take the next shift at the tavern. But I think Sparky is delighted you've shown up because he can go home sooner."

"He does love the farm, as well as Uncle Amos."

"I imagine he'll fall in love with that delightful Izzie as well," Guy said. "I only made her acquaintance yesterday when I brought a casserole Mrs. Wilt insisted I take out to Glory Manor before it grew cold." He smiled. "Izzie's a charming young lady, but I wouldn't wait too long to stake a claim, if you know what I mean. Women like that don't stay unattached for long."

Wondering if the entire town had gotten it into their collective head to try their hand at matchmaking, Ian settled for sending Guy a weak smile. Telling Sparky they were going home, and then thanking Guy again, Ian swung up into the saddle, pausing when Guy stepped forward.

"You tell Amos I sure am sorry about all his animals going missing."

Apprehension tickled the back of his neck. "Come again?"

"Did Jack forget to mention that?"

"I'm very much afraid he did."

CHAPTER 23

Thirty minutes later, after he'd heard the worst of it about the animals going missing from Guy, Ian allowed Rumor his head, hoping the breakneck speed would help him control the fury pounding through his veins.

Having lived with a father who'd unleashed his fury on Ian for the smallest infraction, Ian had made a point to always keep his temper in check, not wanting to turn into the father he'd feared every day of his life while he'd lived with the man.

His father had also, besides physically abusing his only son, wielded ridicule like a knife, the frequency of that ridicule convincing Ian he was nothing but a fool, until he'd been rescued by Uncle Amos and Aunt Birdie.

Consequently, appearing foolish was one of Ian's deepest fears, which was, no matter how he tried to deny it, one of the reasons he'd lost respect for Andrew Carnegie—a man who'd certainly made him feel like a fool, as well as incompetent, by forcing him out of the negotiations.

He was not incompetent when it came to matters of business, and he would prove it to the powerful men of Pittsburgh, although how he would . . .

Sparky suddenly dashed ahead, dragging Ian from his less-than-pleasant thoughts. Yipping madly, Sparky turned onto Glory Lane, Rumor pounding down the lane after him.

Feeling the last vestiges of the fury he'd been trying to control fade away, Ian reined Rumor in as the farmhouse sprang into view.

Gazing around the yard, Ian found it looking very tidy indeed, the grass short and no weeds to be found. Turning his head, he found goats munching their way through another part of the yard, kept in check by one of the new hired hands, Duncan Bowman.

Returning his attention to the house, Ian took in the sight of what seemed to be a fresh coat of paint. Who'd painted the house was anyone's guess, and someone had also attached flower boxes filled with bright pink and yellow flowers to the porch railing that ran along the entire front of the house, lending the porch a charming air. Two large pots of flowers were sitting on either side of the steps, alongside a ball, proof that the house was once again home to children.

Around the side of the house, he noticed laundry snapping in the breeze, his attention immediately pulled from that laundry when Uncle Amos walked into view, stopping in his tracks when he caught sight of Sparky racing his way.

Setting down the chicken he'd been holding, Uncle Amos knelt, held open his arms, and laughed when Sparky needed no other urging and jumped directly into them, licking Uncle Amos's face.

Ian swung from the saddle and strode his uncle's way. "Sparky's certainly happy to see you."

Uncle Amos placed a kiss on Sparky's head, then straightened, swiping a hand over eyes that were bright with tears. "Where'd you find him?"

"I didn't find him. Guy Wilt did when he was over in Washington. He recognized him and kindly brought him back to Canonsburg. He was going to bring him back to you later today."

Uncle Amos glanced at Sparky, now rolling around in the grass by his feet. "He ended up all the way over in Washington?"

"He did, through no fault of his own, I think. But before we discuss that, I owe you an apology." He caught Uncle Amos's eye.

"You've been saying over and over that there's skullduggery taking place at Glory Manor, and I, well . . ."

"Thought my suspicions were merely the rants of a man losing his wits?" Uncle Amos finished for him.

"I'm afraid so."

Uncle Amos surprised him by grinning. "I know my memory isn't what it used to be, and that I've been overly paranoid of late." He scratched his chin. "I just kept being told that plots were happening right underneath my nose, and what with my failing memory and all, I haven't been able to figure out what's true and what's merely my imagination." He shook his head. "I was even told that Izzie had arrived at Glory Manor to take away my chickens, which is why I scared the poor woman half to death by chasing her with my rifle."

The hair on the back of Ian's neck stood at attention. "Who told you Izzie came to take your chickens?"

"Hank. He's been telling me all sorts of rumors. But when I caught him letting the goats out of their pen a day or two ago, he called me a crazy old codger and quit on the spot." Uncle Amos's white brows drew together. "He apparently told everyone in town I'd chased him away with an axe, but I don't remember doing that. In fact, I'm surprisingly certain that never happened."

Ian touched his uncle's arm. "I don't want you to worry about any of that." He drew in a deep breath, hoping that would help control the fury that was once again racing through his veins. "I intend to take care of the matter, and believe me, someone—although I'm beginning to think there are numerous people involved—will be held accountable for the nasty business that's been happening on this farm."

"Then I'll leave the matter in your more-than-capable hands." Uncle Amos gestured toward the house. "And with that said, I think there's a few people over there who'd like to welcome you home."

Turning, Ian found what seemed to be half of Canonsburg spilling out of the house. Anna Gillespie was leading the charge toward him, followed by Maggie Rogers, her daughter, Susan, and right behind them, Aunt Birdie—walking spryly toward him and without her cane.

He strode over to his aunt, giving her cheek a kiss before he stepped back. "Where's your cane?"

Aunt Birdie beamed. "Doc McBride came to check on me yesterday and gave me an almost clean bill of health. I'm feeling a good ten years younger, and because of that, I've abandoned my cane almost entirely now."

Ian grinned. "Which is wonderful, but don't overdo it. You might feel ten years younger—which would make you, what, eighteen now?—but you still need to be careful." He nodded to the house even as Aunt Birdie rolled her eyes. "I see the farm has enjoyed some improvements while I've been away for all of *four* days."

"Improvements that are due to Izzie."

"*Izzie* painted the house?"

Anna stepped forward, exchanging a look with Maggie and Susan before all three women began looking at him quite as if he were a small child who had just said something amusing.

"Izzie's talents don't really extend to executing her grand ideas," Anna began, her eyes twinkling. "She's more proficient with organizing. She did try and help the men paint the house. She was relieved of that duty, though, when she began painting flowers along the window sashes, thinking it would add a touch of whimsy."

Aunt Birdie grinned. "They were rather unusual flowers, you see, and were taking her forever. The men finally fetched me because they didn't want to hurt her feelings. Surprisingly enough, she didn't seem to be bothered at all by being banished from that task, but that might have been because I told her she was welcome to paint flowers in my sitting room—after those rooms get their fresh coat of paint, of course."

Ian looked at the house again, finding the body of it still painted white, but that the trim had been changed to a bluish-gray, as had the railing around the porch. "Was it Izzie's idea to add the colored trim?"

"It was," Aunt Birdie said. "She consulted a book Susan brought from the store, a house painting guide." She smiled. "Izzie wanted to paint the entire house yellow with green trim, but I convinced her I might not be ready for that much change."

She gave his arm a pat. "You'll be pleased to learn that the fences have now been completely mended, the yard is almost free of weeds, and the ladies have fully stocked the kitchen. Why, we've been provided with so many tasty dishes that I fear my new dress Izzie brought me from the store is doomed to become a little snug on me before I get a chance to wear it to church."

For a second, Ian almost couldn't take in what she was telling him. While he'd been amassing his fortune in Pittsburgh, he'd forgotten what it meant to belong to a small community. People helped one another; it was simply what they did. But the people of Canonsburg had gone above and beyond what he would have ever expected.

Clearing his throat, Ian nodded to the crowd. "Your kindness to my aunt and uncle means so much to me. You've taken time out of your lives to help them, and I'd like to compensate you for your—"

"Don't be daft," Maggie interrupted, waving his offer straight aside. "We don't want to be compensated. Besides"—she smiled—"you're already going to compensate us because Glory Manor is hosting a picnic tomorrow after church."

Susan Rogers, Maggie's daughter and a woman he'd known since she'd been in short dresses and braids, broke away from the crowd, strolling over to join him. She sent him a cheeky grin. "And if the thought of compensating us is bothering you, rest assured there's no need for you to trouble yourself about that. You've made purchases from almost every shop owner in town, buying lovely cuts of beef to serve tomorrow, as well as purchasing buckets and buckets of paint to get the house looking grand again." She turned and nodded to a young woman Ian hadn't noticed before, who was standing with Violet and Primrose, holding their hands.

"You're also now responsible for the wage my cousin, Miss

Olive Perkins, is earning. Izzie hired her to look after the children while she's been busy seeing to other matters on the farm."

"Izzie hired Miss Perkins to look after the children?"

Susan nodded. "She did, but . . ." She moved closer and lowered her voice. "There's no need for that panic in your eyes. Contrary to your belief, there's not one eligible young lady in town who wants to take your name and all the social nastiness that will apparently come with it." She grinned. "That means you can stop fretting that all of us are out to attract your notice. We're not, although do take comfort in knowing we still find you charming—as well as handsome, of course."

Having no idea what to say to that, even as he felt a little unbalanced finding out that what he'd held to be true for so long seemed nothing of the sort, Ian managed to summon up a smile, right as Aunt Birdie gave his arm a squeeze.

"I should probably mention that you're now paying Olive a somewhat generous salary, although not as generous as what Izzie was originally going to offer her." Aunt Birdie's eyes began twinkling. "Bless her heart, Izzie thought offering Olive ten dollars a day might be taken as insulting until I stepped in and told her that most governesses expect a mere twenty-five dollars a month. I almost had to scrape Izzie off the floor, she was so taken aback. That's why I then decided you'd be fine with paying Olive thirty dollars a month, while having two full days off a week."

Not having the heart to tell his aunt that was a rather steep wage to pay Olive, Ian opened his mouth to ask where Izzie was, unable to deny that he was somewhat disappointed she'd not rushed out to welcome him home yet. His question got lost, though, when Daisy suddenly came barreling out of the house, Henry by her side. She stopped on the porch, caught sight of him, then was running as fast as her little legs would carry her, holding up her arms and then jumping right into his when she reached him.

She completely stole his heart again when she planted a wet kiss on his cheek, rearing back a second later to beam at him. "Missed you."

Placing a kiss on Daisy's cheek, he smiled. "I missed you too."

"Look, new frock," she said, pointing to the frock in question. "Daisies on it."

"It does have daisies on it, and you look quite beautiful in it, and . . ." He looked her over. "You're clean."

As Daisy nodded, Ian turned to Aunt Birdie. "I think Miss Perkins is going to be worth every bit of that thirty dollars since she seems to have achieved what I thought was going to be impossible—getting the children in the bath."

"Izzie got them into the bath," Aunt Birdie corrected. "She used the lure of shopping as a wonderful incentive. Amos then whittled the children some small boats to be used in the bath, and they've not given us a lick of trouble when bath time rolls around. In fact, they've been asking for a bath every night, even though Izzie told them bathing twice a week would suffice."

"It's a dog!" Henry suddenly yelled, racing past him with a "Hello, Ian," before he was greeted by Sparky. Sparky began yipping and wagging his tail, and if Ian wasn't mistaken, it was love at first sight for both of them.

"Boys do need a dog." Aunt Birdie sent a fond smile Henry's way before she looked back at Ian. "I'm anxious to learn how you found him, but that tale will need to wait for just a bit. We're currently in the process of cleaning out the sitting room so we can paint it."

"I'd be more than happy to help," Ian said, setting Daisy down. She immediately raced off to join her brother and Sparky.

"I assumed as much, dear, although we've been very fortunate to have the support of everyone in town since you've been gone." Her smile suddenly faded as her lips thinned. "But I suppose I should rephrase that and say *almost* everyone in town. Hank's apparently been telling some large fibs of late. He actually told everyone that I didn't want company out here at Glory Manor, which was ridiculous and has me questioning what his motive could have been for spreading such a lie."

Ian took Aunt Birdie's hand. "As I told Uncle Amos, after the mysterious disappearance of Sparky, I have some suspicions about what might be happening at Glory Manor too. But before I get into that . . ." He turned his attention to Mr. John Gillespie, Anna's husband, who was only now joining the crowd, wiping a paint-brush with an old rag. "I want to thank you, John, as well as all the other men who've been seeing after the farm."

John waved that aside. "You would have done the same for any of us. We didn't give coming out here a second thought after we learned all the animals had gone missing and then learned there'd been other suspicious happenings out here. There's no need for you to feel as if any of us have been doing something remarkable. You're a neighbor. Neighbors are simply helped when they're in need."

Just like that, everything Ian thought he knew about the world shifted. He'd been so determined to become accepted into the highest levels of Pittsburgh society and business that he'd neglected to realize what was truly important.

Family was important, as well as friends, and these people from Canonsburg had proven without a doubt that they were true friends to Glory Manor.

He highly doubted most of his friends in Pittsburgh would have gone out of their way to protect an elderly couple, four children, and an unusual housekeeper simply because there was an assumed threat to them. No, his friends in Pittsburgh would have needed clear proof that something was amiss, and then there was every chance they'd only go so far as to hire men to watch over the farm, unwilling to put themselves out and personally do the job.

He nodded to John. "You're right, of course, but that doesn't mean I can't thank you for your help."

John smiled. "It's been a pleasure, but don't think we're done helping just yet. The ladies have decided we're painting every room inside, which we're just getting around to today, now that we have more hands to help with the painting since most of the animals that went missing have been recovered."

With all the chaos his arrival had caused, Ian had forgotten all about the missing animals. "You say most of them have been recovered?"

"All but Mavis," Aunt Birdie said. "She's still out there somewhere, which is where Izzie is, if you've been wondering. She's been very successful with finding the missing animals. Seems to have a knack for locating them."

Ian frowned. "Is she out there on her own?"

"She's on Clyde, and she's got Buttercup, as well as Amos's rifle."

His eyes widened. "She's out there with nothing but a horse, a cow, and a rifle with no bullets?"

"Don't be silly." Aunt Birdie turned a fond smile on Uncle Amos, who was showing Henry and Daisy how Sparky liked to fetch sticks. "Amos knew exactly where I'd hidden the bullets."

"And you thought it wise to provide a woman who'd gotten herself stuck in the wringer of a washing machine with a rifle and bullets?"

Aunt Birdie waved that aside. "Since Izzie was more than forthcoming about her less-than-proficient housekeeping skills, I had no reason to doubt her when she told me she knew how to handle a rifle."

"But who taught her how to shoot?"

"That's something you'll need to ask Izzie, although I would suggest you ask her other questions as well, such as why she took a housekeeper position, or . . . well, I could go on and on. You're a bright boy. You'll figure out what needs to be asked."

"Is there something—or *somethings*—you're not telling me?"

"Of course, but since I'm not at liberty to disclose the conversations I've had with Izzie, it'll be up to you to discover more about her, including who taught her to shoot." She patted his cheek. "She told me she was going to head toward Glory Gully. Buttercup's been leading her in that direction over the past few days, which has Izzie convinced that's where Mavis will eventually be found."

"Buttercup's been leading the search for the animals?"

"Surprisingly enough, she's a very good tracker, but perhaps you should have Sparky go with you. I imagine he'll be able to find Buttercup and Clyde if you ask him to." With that, Aunt Birdie patted his cheek again, nudged him in the direction of his horse, and began walking for the house.

Whistling for Sparky, Ian swung into the saddle and turned Rumor toward Glory Gully, anticipation flowing through him at the thought of seeing Izzie, a woman he was quickly realizing was far more than she seemed.

CHAPTER 24

"I completely understand why you're in a bit of a snit, Mavis, having been undiscovered for the past few days," Isadora began, waving an apple chunk Mavis's way in a desperate attempt to get the cow moving. "But you've really no one to blame but yourself for that troubling situation. I've been scouring Glory Manor for what feels like months looking for you. How was I to know you'd be agile enough to get yourself down here?" She gestured to the gorge they were in.

Mavis turned and lowered her head, resuming what she'd been doing when Isadora had finally located the last missing cow— eating dandelions.

Isadora blew out a breath and stuck her hand into the pocket of the trousers she'd borrowed from Uncle Amos, finding them far more practical when searching for missing livestock than any of the ill-fitting skirts Mr. Godkin had packed for her. Fishing out the list of suggestions Uncle Amos had given her to coerce what he'd admitted was their most ornery cow, she looked it over, shaking her head when she got to the one suggestion she'd yet to put into play.

"Just remember, it is your fault that I have to resort to singing to get you to move."

Drawing in a deep breath, and relieved that at least there was only a horse and a cow watching her—well, two cows, since Buttercup stood at the top of the gorge—Isadora began belting out the first song that came to her: "A Rollicking Band of Pirates We" from *The Pirates of Penzance.*

A flock of birds suddenly burst out of a tree, causing her to jump. Her singing, or what she passed for singing, was evidently so horrible that they'd decided to abandon their cozy tree and find comfort elsewhere.

When her voice began to wobble over a particularly difficult note, she stopped singing, disappointment flowing through her when she realized the cow hadn't budged so much as a single inch.

"That's an interesting approach to get Mavis to cooperate."

Swinging around, Isadora found Ian making his way into the gorge, having nowhere near the difficulty she'd had with the steep incline. For a moment, she simply savored the sight of him.

He was dressed in business attire, complete with dark jacket, waistcoat, dark trousers, and a necktie, although the necktie was untied and merely dangling from either side of his neck. His hat was missing, which allowed her to appreciate the many burnished shades of his brown hair, and . . .

She shook herself when she realized she had no business savoring the sight of her *employer*, even if he was the most attractive and . . .

"What was that you were singing?" Ian asked, making it to the bottom of the gorge and striding her way, which reminded her that now was not exactly the moment to descend into a state of savoring.

"You weren't listening to me long, were you?"

Ian flashed a grin, that grin having immediate thoughts of savoring popping back to mind again.

"I think I heard you from the moment you began." His eyes crinkled at the corners. "Would have been difficult for me not to hear such dulcet tones or miss the birds flying rapidly out of the gully."

She frowned. "I thought this was a gorge."

"Gully, gorge, they're rather similar, but you're currently standing in Glory Gully, named by me when I was eight years old. I used to come here often as a boy, spending hours wading through that stream over there, looking for fish, turtles, and salamanders."

"I don't think I've ever seen a salamander."

"You haven't really lived until you've held a salamander, although they are somewhat slimy."

She arched a brow. "Do you think I'm the type to turn squeamish over a little matter of sliminess?"

"Before I left for Pittsburgh, I would have said yes. But now . . ." He considered her for a long moment. "I'm not so certain."

"What do you mean?"

Ian shrugged. "I was only expecting you to be capable of keeping Glory Manor *standing*, but you've evidently done so much more—and impressed me in the process."

Her cheeks began to heat, that situation not helped when Ian stepped closer to her.

"What are you wearing, and . . ." He gestured to her hair. "Who did your hair, and . . . where are your spectacles?"

Having completely forgotten that she'd abandoned her spectacles in her pocket after they'd begun annoying her and after she'd gotten far enough away from the farmhouse that she felt safe abandoning her disguise, Isadora retrieved her spectacles from her pocket. She winced when she noticed the frames were rather bent—probably because she'd sat on them at some point. Knowing they'd hardly fit properly until she could straighten them out again, she returned them to her pocket and summoned up a smile. "Did I ever mention to you that I don't always need glasses?"

"Because your eyesight occasionally improves on its own?"

"Exactly," she said, pretending she didn't see Ian send her an honest-to-goodness rolling of his eyes. "As for what I'm wearing," she continued, hoping she could successfully distract him from the questions he would most assuredly ask her about her eyesight, "these pants are a loan from Uncle Amos." She gave a flourish of a hand to the trousers. "We're of a like size, and I must say, there's something to this trouser business. They're far more comfortable than I imagined, and I now understand why my friend Beatrix enjoys donning them every now and again when she's . . . well, there's no need to bore you with the antics of my friend," Isadora hurried to finish, calling herself every sort of ridiculous for allowing herself to slip and mention Beatrix in front of Ian. "As for my hair, Miss Perkins is amazing when it comes to braiding, and she's been teaching Primrose different techniques. Primrose insisted on practicing on me this morning after breakfast." She gave the two braids hanging over her shoulders a tug. "What do you think?"

"It's becoming, although you look about fifteen years old," Ian said before he turned to Mavis. "Should I assume she wasn't moved enough by your spirited rendition of whatever that was you were singing to turn cooperative?"

"I'm afraid not, but just so you know, I was only singing because Uncle Amos wrote down that I might have to resort to singing if none of his other suggestions worked."

"I would have thought your serenading would have done the trick of getting her on her way, if only to put some distance between her and your . . ." Ian stopped talking and winced.

"Were you just about to say my *awful* singing?"

"Of course not. You have . . . a most unusual voice, but tell me this, what *were* you attempting to sing?"

"Are you familiar with *The Pirates of Penzance*?"

"I am, and should I assume you were singing one of the songs from that play?"

"You couldn't tell it was 'A Rollicking Band of Pirates We'?"

"Perhaps you should sing it again. I was quite a distance away, and I'm sure that's why I couldn't tell what song it was."

She didn't bother to correct her slumping shoulders. "You don't need to humor me. I know I'm a horrible singer."

"But you apparently know how to paint," Ian said, his words reminding her that he really was a charming sort. "Aunt Birdie told me about the flowers you wanted to paint on the outside of the house, and while she didn't want you to paint those there, she's offered you the walls in the sitting room. That must mean you're very good at painting flowers."

Her shoulders slumped another inch. "I'm rubbish at painting. Aunt Birdie was merely being kind."

Ian moved to stand beside Mavis, giving the cow a pat, one Mavis ignored as she continued eating dandelions. "Aunt Birdie told me you said you're good at shooting a rifle."

"I am, but that's not exactly a talent expected of a lady, and one I've never admitted to having, especially not within earshot of my mother."

"Who taught you how to shoot?"

Isadora wrinkled her nose. "By the overly innocent tone your voice has taken, may I assume you've been talking further with Aunt Birdie?"

He smiled. "I have, but she, being a loyal sort, didn't disclose much about you, other than to suggest I ask you some questions."

"That was certain to leave you curious about me and annoyingly shrewd on her part." A sigh escaped her. "What questions did she suggest you ask me?"

"Who taught you to shoot and why you need a housekeeping position. I have to admit, though, that the question I want to ask you most is this—was there ever a Mr. Delmont?"

She refused to allow her shoulders to slip so much as another inch. "As I told Aunt Birdie, I'm not good with subterfuge, nor am I comfortable lying to you since you were kind enough to allow me to stay at Glory Manor." She drew in a breath and forced the next words out of her mouth. "I've never been married. I simply assumed the title of *missus* so that I wouldn't immediately be shown the door while trying to secure a position of employment."

"Is the surname Delmont a bit of subterfuge as well?"

"This disclosure business would be far easier if you weren't proficient with cross-examining people."

"Ah, you've learned I'm an attorney?"

"I've gotten to know practically every woman in Canonsburg.

228

Do you actually think there's even a remote chance I wouldn't have discovered that?"

Ian suddenly looked rather wary. "Did you discover anything else?"

"Only that you're somewhat of a genius when it comes to investing, which does explain how you were able to afford to build a home in Shadyside, a place I've also learned seems to hold its own version of New York's Fifth Avenue, otherwise known as Millionaires' Row." She smiled. "And because I'm now apprised of the notion you seem to possess an impressive fortune, do know that I will expect you to remember that after you come to the conclusion that you're desperate for me to remain at Glory Manor and are only too willing to pay me a salary—and not a measly thirty dollars a month."

Ian leaned back against Mavis, who didn't even raise her head. "Duly noted, and because you're aware I'm an attorney, allow me to do what we attorneys do best—redirect the conversation back to the relevant topic we were discussing before you made your most recent disclosures. If I may remind you, we were speaking of your last name. What is it?"

She thought about the question for all of a second before she stuck her nose in the air. "I plead the Fifth."

"Of course you would," he muttered before he took to rubbing his chin. "Which means I'm either left with pulling out my most terrifying cross-examining skills, which, believe me, will have you spilling your secrets before you know it, or . . . we can agree to discontinue this line of questioning for now, but do know that I will expect some hard answers in the not-too-distant future."

Knowing there was going to come a time when she would have to disclose everything, but not wanting that time to be now because there was something delightful in not being Miss Isadora Delafield, grand American heiress, Isadora nodded.

To her relief, he sent her a nod in return, which had her spirits lifting. There was something liberating about Ian only believing her to be Izzie, his temporary housekeeper. That allowed her a refreshing bit of freedom in which she was able to enjoy an afternoon of easy banter with a charming and handsome man, with no worries that her every word was going to be judged, and . . . she didn't need to worry he was only being charming to her because he was interested in her fortune. As far as he knew, she was practically penniless.

Ian pushed away from Mavis, giving the cow a pat, which didn't have her moving at all. "Looks like Mavis hasn't changed her mind about being ornery."

"How's your singing voice?" Isadora asked.

"Worse than yours."

"That's bound to complicate the problem of getting her to move."

"I do have a solution," he said, releasing a sharp whistle a second later.

"I've always wanted to learn how to whistle," Isadora said, right as a dog scampered down the steep slope of the gully, loping over to join them, its tail wagging.

"I would be more than happy to teach you, but first, meet Sparky," Ian said as Sparky sat in front of Isadora and held out his paw.

Charmed, she bent down, shook the paw, then frowned as she straightened. "Didn't Uncle Amos used to have a dog named Sparky?"

"Same dog. He apparently had a bit of an adventure but was recently found in Washington, Pennsylvania."

"Is Washington close to here?"

"By train, yes. By dog legs, no." Ian whistled again. "Sparky, take Mavis home."

That was all it took for Sparky to surge into motion, and to Isadora's disbelief, the moment the dog began circling Mavis, letting out a few barks as he circled, Mavis abandoned her dandelions, let out a moo, and began moving, herded down the gully by Sparky.

"Should I walk beside them?" Isadora asked.

"Sparky will get Mavis back on his own. He's very good with cows." Ian stepped closer to her and took her arm. "Care to take a look at the stream before we leave? We might find a salamander, and I can teach you the basics of whistling while we look."

Having absolutely no reason to refuse him, nor did she want to, Isadora strolled with Ian toward the stream. As they stopped at the edge of the water, with the babble of the stream and the sound of birdsong in the air, Isadora found herself happier than she'd been in a very long time. Her life up until she'd left New York had been filled with the most lavish of frivolities, but now, when surrounded by the simple beauty of a stream and a handsome man by her side, she couldn't help but question whether her priorities in life had changed, and if they had, what that meant for her future.

CHAPTER 25

"Since you've admitted you're not Mrs. Delmont, dare I hope you're actually an Izzie?"

As she pulled her attention from a butterfly that had captured her interest, Isadora's lips curved. "My dearest friend in the world gave me that nickname years ago, so yes, I'm an Izzie."

Ian tilted his head. "A rather interesting response, but I'll leave further badgering about what your true name is for a later date. Tell me this, would you find it beyond the pale if I called you Izzie, especially since I get the uncanny feeling you occasionally forget you're supposed to be Mrs. Delmont?"

"Considering everyone in Canonsburg calls me Izzie, I find nothing untoward with you using my given name." She frowned. "I should probably continue addressing you as Mr. MacKenzie, though, because you are my employer."

"Ian will do just fine, but MacKenzie is my real surname, even if I'm not overly fond of the name because it reminds me of my father. He wasn't an honorable man, but when I told Aunt Birdie I wanted to change my name to her last name of Alderson, she would hear nothing of it, believing the name MacKenzie was my heritage. She was convinced I'd grow up to be an honorable man, which would restore honor to the MacKenzie name."

"Wise counsel indeed, since you've clearly managed to do that. Everyone in town speaks very highly of you, and even though I don't claim to know you well, you strike me as an honorable man."

Something interesting flashed through his eyes. He inclined his head to her, but then, before she could ask him any other questions, especially about his father, Ian walked over to the stream. Looking over his shoulder, he smiled. "We seem to be delving into some rather weighty topics, and it's too lovely of a day for that. Care to sit with me by the stream and dip your feet into the water?"

"I've never dipped my feet into a stream before."

"Then we must remedy that at once."

Less than three minutes later, Isadora had abandoned her shoes and stockings, rolled up her pant legs, and taken a seat on a boulder next to the stream. Lowering her feet into the bubbling water, she shivered as delicious cold swept over her toes.

"Have you really never gone wading before?" Ian asked, sticking his bare feet into the water next to hers.

"I'm afraid not, but this is delightful." She swished her feet through the water, shivering again when something tickled her toes.

"It's just the minnows." Ian smiled. "They won't hurt you, but they do occasionally like to nibble at the air bubbles that form around toes."

Forcing herself to keep her toes in the water, although having anything nibble at them was a little disconcerting, Isadora planted her hands behind her and leaned back.

"I think I finally understand exactly why Aunt Birdie named the farm Glory Manor," she said, watching a few puffy white clouds chase each other through the sky.

"She never told me how she came to choose the name."

"It's a lovely story, and one she shared with me after I admitted to her that I was convinced the advertisement I was answering would take me to a grand country estate. After finding that somewhat amusing, she told me she'd named the farm Glory Manor because she enjoys seeing God's glory every morning when she looks out over the land, never failing to appreciate the beauty she's been blessed to live with."

"Glory Manor *is* situated on some beautiful land."

"Indeed," Isadora said before she tilted her head back and simply allowed herself to enjoy the feel of the sun caressing her face, something she'd never been able to do with a pesky parasol overhead.

Just when she was beginning to feel as if her nose might be burning, Ian suddenly surged into motion. A second later, he swooped down, stuck his hands behind a rock, then straightened. "I've got one."

She was in the water a second later. "A salamander?"

"Yes, and he's a pretty big one."

Peeking into Ian's clasped hand, Isadora saw a little black face peering back at her. "He looks like a dragon."

"Except that he's only a few inches long, whereas I imagine a dragon would be a lot larger." Ian smiled. "Care to hold him?"

"He won't bite?"

"No, but you need to be very gentle with him. Salamanders have very delicate skin, and we don't want to damage it."

Telling her to cup her hands together, Ian passed over the salamander, nodding when she cradled the creature with a soft touch. It certainly was rather slimy, but that didn't bother her at all, especially not when she saw the bright yellow and red streaks running through the black skin, the sheer brilliance of the colors having her nervousness fading away.

Releasing the salamander a short time later, Isadora was surprised when Ian suddenly took her hand, lending her his support as they began wading up the stream, laughing every other minute as he tried to teach her how to whistle.

"Perhaps, like singing, you're not meant to be a whistler either," he finally said.

"Because I was always warned that whistling was inappropriate for young ladies, I'll have you know I do intend to learn how to whistle, even if I have to practice for hours."

Ian's brows drew together. "Who warned you about whistling?"

Realizing she was divulging too much, Isadora forced a shrug. "Surely you must know that ladies don't care to reveal all their secrets in one fell swoop, don't you? That hardly allows us to maintain an air of mystery, something we are encouraged to adopt from the time we're in short skirts."

"Ladies adopt an air of mystery on *purpose*?"

"Of course."

"Huh. Interesting." He began pulling her toward the boulder where they'd left their shoes and socks. "And here I've been of the belief that ladies refrain from spilling their deepest secrets because they've been told they're only supposed to talk about the weather."

"Or fashions," Isadora said with a grin, which faded a second later. "I was told that gentlemen prefer ladies with limited intelligence who aren't prone to speaking their minds."

Ian frowned. "Were you told that by a gentleman?"

"Perhaps." She gestured around her. "I've found that attitude different here, though. The women of Canonsburg have no hesitation with saying whatever they want while suffering no censure from the men in town." She smiled. "I must admit I find that attitude liberating."

Realizing she might have disclosed too much yet again because Ian was now watching her rather closely, she increased her pace, tugging him through the stream until they reached their abandoned footwear. "Even though this is more than enjoyable, now that Mavis has been found, I really should get back to help with the improvements taking place."

Taking the handkerchief he handed her to dry off her feet, she put on her stockings and shoes, then allowed him to help her to her feet, warmth flowing through her when he didn't let go of her hand as he helped her climb out of the gully.

Moving over to Clyde, Isadora accepted his hand up into the saddle, then took the reins as Ian swung onto his horse, sitting in the saddle like he'd been born to it.

"Where's Buttercup?" she asked, forcing her attention away

from Ian to look around for a cow she only then noticed was absent.

"She must have followed Mavis and Sparky. Probably wants to make sure Mavis doesn't give Sparky any problems."

"She's an unusual cow," Isadora said before she nodded to his horse. "But speaking of unusual, that's some horse you have there."

Ian smiled. "Rumor's a little temperamental at times, but I knew the moment I saw him running in a field at Garrison Farms that he was meant to be mine."

"He's a Garrison stallion?" Isadora asked, nudging Clyde closer so she could get a better look. "No wonder he's such a magnificent animal."

"You know about Garrison Farms?"

Seeing no reason to deny it, Isadora nodded, her gaze traveling over his horse. "Why did you name him Rumor?"

"Because rumor had it he was the fastest horse at Garrison's, and that, I'm pleased to say, turned out to be nothing but the truth." Ian cleared his throat. "But how are you familiar with Garrison Farms?"

"I see you're not ready to discontinue trying to get me to disclose a few of my mysteries just yet," she began before she smiled. "But because you did show me my very first salamander, as well as convince me to go wading for the very first time, I'm now feeling rather charitable toward you. I went to Garrison Farms a few years ago with my father and three brothers."

"And did you make any purchases there?"

"*I* did not," she admitted, ignoring the way his eyes suddenly sharpened on her. "I did, however, make the acquaintance of Miss Poppy Garrison, the daughter of Mr. Garrison. She's a delightful lady I hope to encounter again someday."

"Did your father make any purchases that day?" he pressed. "Perhaps for himself, his three sons, or his demanding daughter?"

"Your tenacity is very annoying, and I thought we'd come to an understanding about my demanding ways. In fact, I was under the impression you'd decided I was nothing like Katherina from *The Taming of the Shrew*."

He grinned. "My tenacity is what has allowed me to achieve the success I've enjoyed in business. As for the Katherina comparison, I suppose I *was* mistaken about that, especially because I highly doubt there will ever come a day when you profess yourself madly in love with me and begin catering to my every whim as Katherina did with her dear Petruchio."

She returned the grin, but then it slipped straight off her face when an unexpected truth sprang out of nowhere. It wasn't as if she was *madly* in love with Ian, but . . . she was drawn to him in a most concerning manner, and that could very well lead to her falling *slightly* in love with the man if she wasn't careful.

The problem with that, however, was that Ian MacKenzie was determined to marry a woman who would help him up the social ladder as well as help him cement his position as a prominent man of business.

She, unfortunately, was a great American heiress, and while that had never bothered her before, it bothered her now.

There was every chance Ian would certainly be interested in pursuing a courtship with her if she divulged who she was, but . . . she didn't want him to court her because she could improve his social standing.

What she wanted, if she was being honest with herself, was for Ian to want her—and only her—not her along with her social connections or the fortune she possessed.

She also wanted him to cherish the woman she was becoming—not the woman she'd been before she'd arrived at Glory Manor—and she wanted for him to kiss her . . . and really kiss her, not simply attach his lips to hers because he'd been trying to bring her back to—

"Is something the matter?"

Realizing she'd been lost in troubling thoughts for a rather long time, Isadora summoned up a smile. "Nothing's wrong, I was merely . . ." She looked around, desperately searching for a distraction, but only found a rather ordinary field spread out in front of her. "Ah, contemplating the beauty of that . . . ah . . . field."

Ian looked over the field in question. "It's rather barren because it wasn't planted this year."

"I suppose it is barren at that, but it has a very nice fence surrounding it."

Looking at her quite as if she'd lost her mind, Ian turned his attention to the very unremarkable fence she'd pointed out, turning back to her a second later. "I imagine that fence might become more interesting if we were to put some rocks on top of it."

"Why would we want to do that?"

"Because you obviously don't want to disclose what you were thinking about a moment ago. That means that I, being a charming gentleman, or so I've been told, will now graciously change the subject, and . . ."

"You've decided to change the subject to rocks?"

"Only because they'll make nice targets as you and I go about getting in some target practice." He tossed her a grin that had her heart kicking up a beat. "I've yet to be convinced you're proficient with that rifle you've got attached to your saddle. Shooting at rocks would be the perfect way for you to prove it."

She lifted her chin, willing her heart to stop galloping through her chest. A grinning Ian was downright irresistible, but she needed to resist him, at least until . . .

"Shall we make a game of it?"

Her lips curved into a grin. "But of course."

Ian nudged Rumor forward as she did the same with her horse. "What will be the prize for the winner?"

Her first thought was a kiss, but knowing that was hardly appropriate, she took a second to ponder the matter as Clyde galloped across the field, coming up with the perfect answer once she reached the fence. Swinging from the saddle, she nodded to Ian, who'd gotten down from his horse as well.

"The prizes will be this: if I win, you'll agree to pay me fifty dollars a month, as well as keep me on as your household manager."

238

"Is that different from a housekeeper?"

"It is, but we can discuss that further if I happen to win . . . and it will also allow me to figure out exactly what a household manager does."

He grinned. "And if I win?"

"I'll tell you my real name."

Ian's grin faded as he considered her for a long moment. "You really *are* proficient with a rifle, aren't you?"

Retrieving the rifle, she arched a brow his way. "I guess you'll just have to wait and see."

CHAPTER 26

While it was certainly true that Ian didn't particularly enjoy losing, finding himself now in possession of one household manager and paying her fifty dollars a month to take on that position wasn't bothering him in the least.

Glancing to his right, he smiled as his gaze traveled over everyone sitting in the pew they were occupying. Directly next to him was Henry, who'd put up a bit of a fuss when Izzie insisted he wear one of the jackets she'd chosen for him at the general store, proclaiming it was far too hot to have to sit through church in a jacket. But after Izzie pointed out he was going to be wearing short pants with that jacket, which would allow his legs to be sufficiently cool, unlike his sisters who were expected to wear hosiery with their new frocks, he'd settled right down.

Next to Henry was Uncle Amos, remarkably coherent today. He had hold of Henry's hand, which Henry didn't seem to mind at all. Sitting beside Uncle Amos was Aunt Birdie, looking lovely in the new dress Isadora had picked out for her.

He'd not neglected to notice Aunt Birdie glancing from him, to the children, and then to Izzie. But because he didn't want to encourage whatever new matchmaking scheme she was most assuredly thinking up, he was pretending not to notice the pointed looks she was sending him, even though she was becoming more and more obvious as the service wore on.

Sitting beside Aunt Birdie was Primrose, her hair braided in what she told him she was calling "the fishbone." She'd taken a great interest in styling hair over the past few days, practicing on anyone who'd let her. She'd set her sights on him that morning, but because he wasn't keen to attend church sporting braids, he'd encouraged her to let the other little girls she'd be introduced to at church know she was looking for victims. To his surprise, she'd done exactly that, having five little girls waiting in a line before the service, chatting with Primrose as she braided one head after another, as if they'd all been fast friends for years.

Next to Primrose was little Violet, wearing a cream frock with little dots of purple sprinkled throughout and clutching the doll that she rarely let out of her sight.

Daisy, dressed in a different frock than she'd been wearing the day before, but one that still had daisies scattered on it, was sitting on Izzie's lap, fast asleep, little snores erupting out of her mouth as Izzie absent-mindedly stroked Daisy's red hair. Izzie didn't seem to mind that Daisy's little hands were stained with icing from a cookie Anna had slipped her outside the church. That icing was smeared on the front of the rather plain gray dress Izzie was wearing, the plainness relieved by a pink scarf Aunt Birdie had insisted Izzie wear.

Izzie was once again wearing her spectacles, claiming her vision had been a little blurry after she'd gotten up. Ian was beginning to believe she was hiding behind her spectacles, although why she was doing so was evidently one of the mysteries she wasn't yet ready to disclose.

As the choir stood and began a hymn, which had everyone standing to join them, Ian shared his hymnal with Henry, who shot him a look of what could only be horror after Ian began to sing, whispering that Ian should think about mouthing the words instead of singing them.

After the hymn, everyone resumed their seats. Reverend Davis then walked to the pulpit, smiled, and launched into a sermon about retaining a sense of peace and a relationship with God while living in a world that was rapidly turning industrial.

Looking at Aunt Birdie, who was leaning forward, soaking in every word, Ian knew full well his aunt had suggested the topic to Reverend Davis, probably as a clear reminder for Ian to rethink his priorities.

In all frankness, he was beginning to believe that Reverend Davis might have the right measure of the world. Ian knew he'd been consumed with climbing out of the poverty he'd been born into, concentrating on the next investment opportunity, so much so that he'd forgotten what it felt like to simply enjoy a Sunday morning at church with family and friends.

After Reverend Davis completed his sermon, and after Aunt Birdie sent Ian a most telling look, they concluded the service with another hymn. This time he distinctly heard Izzie's less-than-dulcet tones, which had Henry shaking his head and grinning. When the last note from the organ sounded, everyone began exiting the church.

Ian stopped Henry in the aisle, bending closer to him. "You need to take Violet's arm and walk with her out of the church."

"Why would I want to do that?"

"Because it's what gentlemen do." He nodded to where Uncle Amos was already holding Aunt Birdie's arm, walking down the aisle.

Henry seemed to consider that for a second before he walked over to Violet, took her by the arm, and then took Primrose by the other. Together, and with Violet and Primrose grinning, the children made their way down the aisle.

Turning back to Izzie, Ian smiled. "I'll take Daisy."

"I cannot believe she slept through the entire service," Izzie said, carefully handing Daisy over to him.

"She's three. It's what they do at that age. Jumping in ponds to swim with the ducks one moment, and the next, they're snoring away, not a care in the world."

Izzie smiled. "At least she's stopped throwing herself in the pond. I think the bathing helped with that. She seems to enjoy clean water over murky."

Returning the smile, Ian shifted Daisy to his shoulder, extending Izzie an arm, which she promptly took. Strolling out of the church, he felt a sense of rightness, one he'd never felt before, and one he knew had something to do with the woman walking beside him.

That she had secrets was not in question, but oddly enough, he wasn't concerned about them. He was more interested in getting to know the woman of the present than the woman of her past.

That thought caused his pace to slow just the tiniest bit as the realization struck that somehow over the past day he'd begun to think of Izzie in a rather permanent manner.

She was his household manager, whatever that was, and he didn't even know her true name, but . . . that didn't seem to bother him, although he'd never—

"Shall I take Daisy so you can get the wagon?"

Realizing they'd left the church behind and were now standing in the crowded churchyard, Ian smiled, although he found it a tad concerning he'd been so lost in thought he didn't remember walking down the church steps. "She's not too heavy for you?"

Izzie wrinkled her nose. "Hardly, although she might have been too heavy for me a few days ago after I finished the laundry. I thought for certain my arms were going to fall right off after all the cranking, hauling, wringing, and then hanging out to dry I did." She tilted her head. "Did I tell you that Aunt Birdie banned me from using the iron?"

"Should I ask why?"

"I think that'll become evident after you put on a pair of trousers I attempted to iron for you." She grinned. "They've now got a lovely scorch mark on them. . . . Which is exactly why I wanted to broach the subject of a few other women I have in mind who'd love to come work at Glory Manor."

"Women I suggested to Izzie."

Turning to the woman who'd just joined them, Ian found Maggie Rogers, accompanied by her daughter, Susan, both women looking at him far too determinedly.

Shifting Daisy higher on his shoulder, Ian allowed his lips to curve. "How many women are we talking about?"

Maggie glanced to Susan. "What did we say, four?"

"Well, five, if we can convince Ian that Glory Manor is in desperate need of sheep." Susan sent him a nod. "Miss Lydia O'Dell has recently arrived from Scotland, and she's an expert on sheep. Knows all about how to shear them and what to do with the wool after the sheep have been sheared. I imagine that's a business you won't want to neglect getting into."

"Why would I want to bring sheep to Glory Manor? If you haven't noticed, we're having a bit of a difficult time of it as it is, and that's with only having limited animals on the farm. And"— Ian continued before Susan had an opportunity to start arguing— "what would I do with those four women you mentioned? I've already hired Miss Perkins to watch over the children and Izzie to manage the household."

Maggie's chin lifted. "I'm sure there must be a variety of jobs you could offer these women. You've not been home to Canonsburg often over the past few years, but work is hard to come by and there are many people in need of positions." Her chin lifted another inch. "You, everyone knows, have the funds available to assist these people."

"I was unaware there was that much of a need in Canonsburg," he said as something unpleasant settled in his stomach.

"Well, now you know," Susan said, stepping closer to give his arm a pat. "All that's left now is to see what you do with that knowledge." Taking her mother's arm, Susan nodded. "We can discuss this further today at the picnic you're hosting. I'll be more than happy to introduce you to the women I'm certain you're going to try your hardest to employ."

"They're such delightful ladies," Izzie exclaimed as Susan and Maggie strolled away.

"I don't know how delightful it is that they seem determined to part me from my money."

"From what I've been told, you have plenty of that. Besides, you might discover a way to make Glory Manor useful again—perhaps even profitable—*and* you'll be employing people in need in the process."

Taking Daisy from him, Izzie settled the child on her shoulder, sent Ian a smile, then moseyed her way over to a group of women who immediately began exclaiming over Daisy, who was waking up from her nap, rubbing her eyes, and then beaming her gap-toothed smile at the women now cooing over her.

Making his way to the wagon, even though he'd offered to bring out the carriage he'd purchased for Aunt Birdie years ago, one she rarely used, Ian found Uncle Amos and Henry inspecting the wheels.

"Now, you always want to be certain, my boy," Uncle Amos was saying to Henry, "that the bolts and pins are in fine order and that the wheels don't wobble. That'll lessen the chance of having a wheel come off during a journey."

"I checked the two front wheels, Uncle Amos," Henry said, puffing out his little chest. "They don't wobble at all."

"Good boy." Uncle Amos straightened and sent Ian a wink. "Henry's real quick with learning, and did I tell you how good he is with animals?" He ruffled Henry's hair. "I imagine you'll find yourself a good future on a farm someday, once you grow up."

"I'm gonna stay at Glory Manor forever, Uncle Amos," Henry said. "I love it there, and I'll be able to help you make sure no cows go missing, or chickens either."

Uncle Amos gave him another pat on the head. "You're already doing a fine job of keeping the chickens safe. We've not lost a single one since I gave you the job of looking after them."

Henry's cheeks flushed, and then he grinned when Ian lifted him up, set him on the driver's bench, then climbed up to join him.

"You will see to it that the boy has that future, won't you, son?" Uncle Amos asked quietly, stepping up beside the wagon.

The sense of peace he'd recently experienced faded away, replaced with remorse as an unpleasant truth about himself settled into his soul.

He'd been selfish.

His pursuit of success had consumed him over the years, and in that time he'd neglected to realize that people in this very community were in need, struggling to provide a living for themselves.

Clearly, there'd been something to Aunt Birdie remarking time and time again that God had a purpose for him, one she implied didn't revolve around increasing his fortune. All he needed to do now was discover that purpose, but he could start by relieving Uncle Amos's concerns.

He leaned down closer to his uncle. "You don't need to worry about the children. I promise I'll see after them."

"Good boy," Uncle Amos said with a smile, quite as he'd said to Henry only moments before. With that, and seemingly of the belief the matter was settled since Ian had given his promise, he walked away, telling Ian he was off to fetch the girls.

"Uncle Amos don't seem as confused these days," Henry said, drawing Ian's attention. "I bet that's 'cuz Hank isn't filling his ears with those fibs Aunt Birdie thinks he'd been tellin'."

"I believe you're right, Henry. But don't you worry about Hank. I'm planning on tracking him down and squaring matters with him. He's got a lot of explaining to do."

Flicking the reins, which set Clyde into motion, Ian drew the wagon to a stop in front of where Aunt Birdie, Uncle Amos, Izzie, and the girls were now assembled. Smiling as Izzie called out to Susan that she'd meet her at the farm, he climbed from the seat, helping everyone into the wagon.

"Is there room for me?" Olive Perkins asked, appearing by his side.

Ian frowned. "If memory serves correctly, Olive, Izzie arranged for you to have every Sunday off, as well as every Wednesday."

Olive sent him a cheeky grin. "Which is lovely for me, but I know perfectly well I'm off work today." She waved to Primrose.

"I'm merely hoping I can squeeze in because Prim told me she's got a new idea she wants to try out on my hair."

"Does she want to be called Prim now?"

"I think the nickname makes her feel accepted," Olive whispered back.

"Then Prim she'll be." Ian helped Olive into the wagon before he climbed back on the driver's seat. Setting the wagon into motion, he led the way back to Glory Manor, glancing over his shoulder every now and again to make certain everyone was still in the wagon, and that the wagons and buggies following them, which were many, were keeping up.

Before he knew it, they were back on the farm, the women immediately bustling into the house, carrying a variety of covered dishes, as the men took seats in the chairs Izzie had dug out of the barn. That she'd set up those chairs under the shade of large maple trees suggested she was a woman with an eye for detail, but before he could find a seat and relax, Henry was standing next to him, brandishing his slingshot.

Unable to resist the little boy, especially when he'd been joined by seven other little boys, all looking at him hopefully, Ian went about setting up an area for target practice, soon joined by a crowd of men, all of whom were more than vocal about the proper way to wield a slingshot.

Good-natured arguing ensued, along with rocks flying every which way, not many of them hitting the tin cans he'd set out as targets for the boys.

"Now, this looks like fun," Izzie said, coming up next to him, carrying a tray that was filled with glasses and a pitcher of lemonade.

He took the tray from her, following her around as she poured out glasses for everyone until her pitcher ran dry, which was then immediately replaced with one Susan brought over.

"Are the women allowed to try?" Susan asked, setting the now-empty pitcher on the tray he was still holding.

"You know how to use a slingshot?" Henry asked, stopping

in his tracks as he'd been racing by with more small rocks in his hands, his eyes filled with skepticism.

"Seems to me, Susan, that we need to show these boys and men how it's done," Izzie said, linking her arm with Susan's.

"Do not say that you know how to use a slingshot as well as a rifle?" Ian asked.

"I'm a little rusty with a slingshot, but I have used one before." She grinned. "Should we have another challenge?"

"I'm not increasing your salary."

"Spoilsport," she muttered before she brightened. "What if we play for what book we read to the children next?"

"You've been reading to the children?"

"Every night." She leaned closer to him, lowering her voice. "Prim was worried for no good reason about her reading abilities. She, along with Henry, and even Violet, are incredibly bright children. Prim has even taken it upon herself to do the majority of reading out loud at night, no matter what we're reading. So far we've read *The Princess and the Goblin*, and we just finished up *The Prince and the Pauper* last night." She smiled. "Considering Mr. Twain uses some very impressive words in that story, I'd say Prim is not as far behind other children her age as she thinks."

"What book do you want to read next?"

"I was thinking *Little Women*."

"That's a rather depressing tale."

"That's what Henry said, but I think it's good for him to understand the worth of girls, so . . . if I win our challenge, that's what we'll read. You'll also have to agree to join us and take your turn reading out loud."

"And if I win?"

"You get to choose the book."

Ian didn't hesitate. "*Treasure Island* by Robert Louis Stevenson."

"Oh, that's a good one. I have to admit I'm not going to be disappointed if I lose." With that, she pulled Susan forward, smiled charmingly at the men who were still assisting the boys, then held out her hand to little Thomas Crail, ruffling the boy's hair when he immediately handed her the slingshot.

Her first two attempts went wide, but then she seemed to find her confidence, and after knocking five tin cans over, she turned and gestured him forward.

Feeling more pressure than he'd felt even when he'd been in his last negotiation meeting with the laborers, Ian walked through the crowd, the pressure increasing as the men kept sending him expectant looks.

"Just so everyone knows," he said, taking the slingshot from Izzie, "Izzie did best me yesterday in a shooting challenge, so this might not conclude the way all of you think it will."

"You were always a fine shot in your youth," Uncle Amos called from the crowd. "But if you want to stay in Izzie's good graces, you might want to forget that."

"Don't you dare let me win," she said, sending him a wink. "It's either a fair challenge or you *will* find yourself reading *Little Women* to the children, and you're going to pretend you like it as you read."

When she sent him a smile that left his mouth turning dry, he found himself at a complete loss for words, but thankfully, he was spared any response at all when Henry gave him a nudge forward. Eyeing the cans, he took aim, relief flowing freely when the first can went skittering off the fencepost.

Two minutes later, it was over.

"*Treasure Island* it is," Izzie said cheerfully before she waltzed away, her arm linked once again with Susan's, a woman who'd certainly become, in a very short time, a dear friend to Izzie.

After the meal had been served, Ian finally settled into a chair underneath a maple tree, his gaze returning to Izzie time and time again. She appeared to be everywhere at once, directing the children as they helped clear the dishes, and then bringing out tray after tray of desserts, ranging from cookies to cakes and even fruit dipped in chocolate.

Her laughter was heard often, and when the sun began to dip

in the sky, she was still smiling as she stood in the lane watching the many carriages rumble away, a sleeping Daisy resting her head against Izzie's shoulder and Violet holding Izzie's hand. That the community had embraced her was clear, a belonging that Izzie certainly seemed to relish.

Having one more glass of lemonade underneath the tree with Izzie, Uncle Amos, and Aunt Birdie after the last guest had disappeared down the lane, Ian couldn't help but appreciate what had been a truly marvelous day.

He'd been accepted back into the fold with no hesitation, as if he'd not abandoned everyone for Pittsburgh over a decade ago. Granted, he'd come home whenever he could to check on Aunt Birdie and Uncle Amos, and he had stopped in different businesses in town to catch up briefly with the Canonsburg folk. But he'd not taken the time to inquire about their lives, something he was only now realizing he'd missed.

After the lemonade was gone, he went with Izzie to get the children ready for bed, and then he climbed up to the attic, retrieving his copy of *Treasure Island*.

Sitting on the edge of Henry's bed in the room the little boy was delighted to be given all to himself, Ian waited until everyone got settled on the bed and Izzie pulled in a chair from her room.

He began to read, then passed the book to Izzie, who then, a few pages later, passed the book to Prim. As he listened, the thought struck him that the enjoyment he was experiencing in the moment was a direct result of feeling he was a part of a family.

The children were certainly not his, nor was Izzie, but they'd all somehow managed to form a closeness with one another, something he was rather convinced he didn't want to let go or . . .

The sound of frantic barking pulled him from his thoughts before he rushed out of the room, Izzie at his heels, calling to the children to stay put as she ran.

The smell of smoke suddenly reached his nose, and with horror coursing through him, he ran through the back door, increasing his pace when he saw that the barn was on fire.

Three hours later, covered in soot and ash, and with the heat from the smoldering remains of what had been the barn laying heavy in the air, Ian stood with Izzie, who was drenched in soot as well, her plain gray dress covered in scorch marks and water from the many buckets she'd lugged from the pump to the barn.

The fire had been too intense to save the barn, but they'd been able to stop it from spreading over the lawn and to the farmhouse by dousing the area in front of the barn with water, which had kept the fire contained.

Through the grace of God, they'd saved every animal, all because some of the men who'd taken it upon themselves to do one last patrol around the farm had apparently stopped at some point to enjoy the night skies. That convenient circumstance had them close enough to provide invaluable help before the fire got out of control.

Most of the animals had been taken to the front of the farmhouse, the chickens corralled on the front porch, watched over by Henry, Prim, and Violet, Daisy having fallen asleep on Aunt Birdie's lap an hour before. The goats, pigs, and workhorses were roaming around the lawn, Uncle Amos keeping a sharp eye on them, aided by Buttercup and Sparky, who kept circling the lawn, mooing and barking respectively, if any animal seemed about to stray.

Uncle Amos was looking every one of his eighty years, his face drawn and his shoulders stooped as he shuffled among his animals, muttering time after time that he couldn't understand how the barn had caught fire, and also muttering that he was certain he'd not left a lamp or a candle behind after he'd checked the animals before repairing for the evening.

That his uncle was so distraught had temper boiling through Ian's veins, and as he looked at the charred remains of the barn, he vowed that no matter what it took, he would find out who was behind what was obviously arson, and they would be held responsible.

"I think we found the source, Ian," Stanley Huxman said, holding something gingerly in his hand with an old rag. He held it up. "It's a lantern." He caught Ian's eye. "You think Amos could have left it behind?"

"Uncle Amos was carrying a lantern when he came into the house after he'd checked the animals," Izzie said, speaking up as she dashed what was left of her pink scarf over her face, smearing the soot in the process. "It wasn't his fault, and if anyone doubts me, go look on the kitchen sink. I know you'll find the lantern he was using there."

Ian took hold of her hand. "I don't doubt you, Izzie. There've been too many mishaps to believe this was simply another case of Uncle Amos and his faltering memory. I'm convinced there's something else in play at Glory Manor."

As Stanley, Guy Wilt, Jack Evans, and Jonas Black, the owner of the farm directly adjacent to Glory Manor, took that moment to join them, Jonas shook his head.

"If that's true, someone's evidently turned desperate in their attempt to drive you from the farm."

"Which means they've also turned dangerous," Ian said, drawing in a breath in the hope of dispelling some of his temper. He caught Izzie's eye. "There's every reason to fear that there will be another attack, and I'm convinced that this next one could turn deadly. It's no longer safe at Glory Manor. We have no choice but to get everyone away, which means we're going to have to get everyone to my house in Shadyside, and . . . we're leaving first thing in the morning."

CHAPTER 27

Sitting on top of an old trunk Ian had fetched for her before the sun had even peeked over the horizon, Isadora bounced a time or two, snapping the latch into place when the lid finally closed all the way.

Nodding to Duncan Bowman, one of the two recent hires at Glory Manor, she slipped from the trunk, watching as Duncan, along with Earl Henderson, the other man recently hired, hefted the trunk from the nursery.

Smoothing back hair that had escaped from its pins hours before, Isadora made her way to the kitchen, nodding to the women bustling around and making breakfast for the men who'd arrived in droves at Glory Manor once word had gotten out there was trouble.

"Izzie, there you are, my dear," Aunt Birdie said from the kitchen table, her face drawn. "There's fresh coffee."

Accepting the cup Maggie handed her, Isadora looked out the window, spotting Ian standing off by himself, Sparky on one side of him, Buttercup on the other. "I imagine Ian needs this more than I do," she said, walking to the door.

Shivering ever so slightly in the cool morning air, she walked over to join him, unsurprised when she reached him and saw what amounted to nothing less than fury in his eyes.

It was easy to forget he was a dangerous man at times, given his usual charming nature, but seeing him now, with eyes narrowed and jaw clenched, there was no question that danger lurked beneath the charm, and that danger, she was all but convinced, was remarkably close to being unleashed.

Handing him the coffee, she turned to look at the remains of the barn.

"This could have been so much worse," Ian said, taking a sip of the coffee.

"You're right, especially if you consider all the supposed accidents that happened leading up to the fire." She turned back to him. "Do you have any idea who might be behind this besides Hank? He didn't strike me as the master manipulator type."

"I didn't get that impression of him either, which is why I don't believe Hank's the main culprit. He's been hired by someone, and believe me, I'll find that someone and there will be repercussions."

Isadora didn't doubt that for a second, but she couldn't pity whoever was responsible for the many accidents and other mysteries that had been happening on the farm. That person or persons, without a thought to the lives they'd put in jeopardy, had burned down a barn with innocent animals trapped inside, evidently not caring that the farmhouse could have caught fire too.

Ian raked a hand through his hair, blowing out a breath. "Is everyone packed and ready to go?"

"They are. The children are having breakfast with Miss Olive, as they've decided to call her, but their belongings are packed and they, being children, don't seem overly traumatized by being uprooted again. Henry believes it'll be a grand adventure, and they're all looking forward to riding on the train, which was the only thing they enjoyed, according to Henry, when they were first taken out of Pittsburgh."

"And Olive's agreed to travel with us to Pittsburgh to help out with the children?"

Isadora smiled. "She has, proclaiming it will be a grand adventure for her as well, and . . . I believe she's been given strict instructions from all the women in town to send back a detailed report of that house of yours in Shadyside."

Ian, surprisingly enough, returned the smile. "She's not going to have much to report. There's relatively little furniture in the house, and most of the rooms have yet to be painted."

"Which means I'll need to brush up on my flower-painting skills."

"Aunt Birdie told me you've been banned from painting flowers on the walls after you showed her an example of what you wanted to paint in her sitting room and she decided it was . . ."

"Awful," Isadora finished for him with a grin before she released a dramatic sigh. "It's amazing how many things I've been banned from doing lately." She held up a hand and began ticking the items off on her fingers. "I'm banned from painting flowers, operating the stove, using an iron, and, well, I could go on and on, but it's somewhat depressing now that I think of all my clear deficiencies."

"You're very good with organization," Ian said, reaching out to take hold of her hand, which immediately set her knees to wobbling. "I'm amazed you've been able to get us packed so quickly, and for that, I thank you." He leaned closer. "Seems I *might* have been wrong about *The Taming of the Shrew* business after all."

She rolled her eyes. "You weren't. I've accepted the unpleasant idea that I'm a somewhat demanding woman, but I do think I've changed since my stay at Glory Manor. However, we certainly don't have time to discuss that right now. The household, as I already mentioned, is packed and ready to go, so all that remains now is to get everyone to the train station."

"I still need to finish helping Jack Evans load up all the animals before we repair to the station. He certainly put Uncle Amos's mind to rest by insisting he take the animals to his livery stable. They'll be safe there because Jack employs those very large men he brought with him this morning. They don't take kindly to the fact that someone tried to harm the animals, so they'll keep a close watch on them and make certain their needs are met."

"But they're not takin' Buttercup with them, are they?"

Turning, Isadora found Henry and Violet hurrying to join them, Henry's eyes wide as he stepped beside Buttercup and placed his small hand on her neck.

"I don't think she wants to come with us," Ian said slowly, even as Buttercup let out a mournful moo, Henry's eyes filled with tears, and Violet's lip began to tremble.

Two hours later, Isadora found herself swallowing another laugh, the urge hitting her every time her gaze settled on Buttercup standing in the middle of the aisle and Sparky sitting directly in front of her. Both animals seemed absolutely delighted they'd not been left behind and were enjoying a ride on a train, in a private Pullman car no less, on their way to Pittsburgh.

The children were pressed up against the window, playing a game Miss Olive had suggested that involved finding particular items, such as birds or cows, which hadn't worked very well since they'd all turned and pointed out Buttercup, or telegram poles.

"I have no idea why I agreed to let Buttercup join us," Ian said, eyeing the cow in question.

"Henry and Violet brought out the tears." Isadora shook her head. "I'm afraid you're in for a rough time of it now. I have to imagine once the children discover our weaknesses, they'll exploit them often." She glanced toward the children again, frowning when she noticed that the bag Henry was holding on his lap seemed to be moving. "Excuse me." She stood up and walked to stand beside Henry. "What's that you have in your bag, darling?"

Guilt immediately flickered through Henry's eyes. "Nothin'."

She held out her hand. "Hand it over."

"Are you goin' to be cross with me if I tell you Elmer might be in the bag?"

Isadora narrowed her eyes. "More along the lines of horrified, but why in the world would you have brought Elmer with you?

She would have been fine going off with the rest of the chickens, enjoying a nice holiday in Canonsburg."

Henry shook his head. "I found her trying to sneak into the house. That means she didn't want to be left behind."

"Did you ever think she was sneaking into the house because she'd not finished pecking my legs to her satisfaction?"

Henry's lips began to tremble as he opened the bag, pulled out a very ruffled-looking Elmer, and hugged her to him. "Does that mean you're gonna make me send her back?"

Looking at the trembling lip, then to the chicken already snuggling up against Henry, Isadora threw up her hands. "Fine. She can stay." Turning, she marched back to her seat, ignoring the telling grin Ian sent her.

After the train pulled into the station and Isadora had herded the children, with the help of Miss Olive, into one of the carriages Ian hired, and then got everyone else settled into their respective rented carriages, a sense of anticipation began to brew.

"How far to your house, Ian?" Prim asked, scooting over on the seat when Ian climbed into their carriage, saying they could get on their way because he, along with Duncan and Earl, had finally gotten Buttercup into a wagon. Sparky had apparently chosen to ride in the wagon with Buttercup, lying down right beside the cow and refusing to budge.

"It won't be long, children," Ian said. "Shadyside is on the east side of Pittsburgh, well away from the industrial district." He gestured to the window. "Our progress might be a little delayed because the smog seems unusually thick today. But no need to worry our driver will lose his way. He probably has the streets memorized."

Peering out the window, Isadora frowned at the blanket of black swirling around the carriage and making it all but impossible to see the buildings surrounding the depot. "Is it always like this in Pittsburgh?"

"Sometimes it's worse," Prim said. "'Specially down by the factories where we used to live."

"It can seem like night all the time down there," Ian said, leaning back on the carriage seat. "There are so many mills operating twenty-four hours a day that smoke is constantly being pumped into the air, covering the city in ash." He smiled. "That's why I chose to build my house in Shadyside. We still get smog if the wind is blowing in our direction, but it doesn't completely block out the sun."

As the carriage rumbled down the streets, the children peppered Ian with questions about the city, pointing to buildings that would mysteriously appear out of the smog.

Thirty minutes later, they'd left the smog behind, rolling through well-tended neighborhoods, the houses becoming larger and larger.

"And this, children, is Fifth Avenue," Ian said, gesturing out the window. "We're almost there."

Taking in the sight of stately mansions as the carriage trundled down a well-maintained road, Isadora began to get the sense that Ian was a far more successful businessman than she'd been led to believe.

She'd gotten the distinct impression that he was a man of means, but she'd not been expecting to discover he truly had enough means to build a house that rivaled some of the houses built on her Fifth Avenue in New York City.

Pressing her nose against the window as the carriage turned and began rolling up a stone drive, she sucked in a sharp breath as she caught her first sight of Ian's massive home.

It was built in a Jacobean Revival style, mixed with a bit of Romanesque design, if she wasn't mistaken. Three stories tall, with a porch surrounded by an intricately carved railing, it all but screamed extravagance. She turned to Ian and narrowed her eyes.

"It's fortunate I was told by many of the Canonsburg ladies to expect something along the lines of impressive. However, I don't believe *impressive* does your house justice. It's more along the lines of *imposing grandeur*."

Ian blinked innocent eyes back at her. "I suppose it might be a bit imposing, but do you like it?"

She turned back to the window, smiling when she noticed that the children were pressed up against their window with their mouths agape. "It's lovely, and I must admit I'm now anxious to see what the inside holds."

"You're bound to be disappointed, then. It's so empty that voices tend to echo in almost every room."

"We get to live . . . here?" Prim suddenly asked, looking at Ian, who was now reaching for the door because the carriage had stopped directly in front of the house.

"Until the threat to Glory Manor is handled, yes."

"Oh, thank goodness," Prim said, exchanging a look with her siblings. "I was afraid you were gonna make us live here forever."

"You don't like the house?" Ian asked.

"Seems more along the lines of a . . . well, I don't know what it seems like," Prim admitted with a grin. "But I bet a person could get lost in there."

"I bet there's ghosts in there," Henry said, squeezing Elmer closer, which had the chicken letting out a squawk of protest.

"It's newly built," Ian pointed out. "That means it's not old enough to even warrant rumors of being haunted." He stepped out of the carriage, holding out his hand to Isadora.

After stepping to the cobbled path that led to the house, she turned and took Daisy from Ian, settling the child against her hip, her heart warming when Daisy immediately laid her head against Isadora's shoulder.

Even though Prim and Henry had seemed hesitant about the house, that didn't stop them from jumping from the carriage and racing to the front door. Henry had tucked Elmer into the crook of his arm, and by the squawks she was emitting, it was clear she didn't enjoy being carried at such a rapid rate of speed, or under his arm, for that matter.

Turning back to the carriage, Isadora found Violet holding fast to the doorframe with white knuckles. She, out of all the children, was the one who didn't seem to adapt well to change, and Isadora was beginning to notice that when she was frightened, Violet descended into silence and sought quiet places.

Unfortunately, there were no quiet places for her to run off and hide, at least none that she'd had a chance to find just yet. But right as Isadora was about to speak up and give Violet an encouraging word, Ian stepped forward.

"How about you let me carry you up the walk, Violet? That way, I can tell you things about the house. The bathtubs, for instance, are big enough for you to swim in." He held out his arms, and it only took a second for Violet to let go of the door and allow Ian to scoop her up. Settling her against him, Ian turned back to Izzie, a smile on his face but his eyes holding what seemed to be a trace of wariness. He nodded to the house. "What do you really think?"

"It's beautiful, although I'm not sure I understand why a bachelor would build such a house."

Ian began walking toward Aunt Birdie and Uncle Amos, who'd just gotten out of their carriage, Isadora falling into step beside him. "I'm not intending to remain a bachelor forever. And I built the house because it's expected that a successful gentleman will have an impressive residence, and there's not a more impressive street in Pittsburgh than Fifth Avenue."

Stopping when they reached Aunt Birdie, who was holding onto Uncle Amos's arm, he smiled. "What did you think about the ride through Pittsburgh?"

"Bit smoggy for my taste," Uncle Amos said before he gestured to the house. "But this is nice."

Isadora frowned. "You haven't seen Ian's house before?"

"Amos hasn't, but I have," Aunt Birdie said before she nodded at Ian. "It's come along nicely since I last here, and it certainly does the job of proving you've achieved that level of success you longed for as a child."

Before Ian could respond to that, a man walked out of the house, dressed in a dark jacket paired with dark trousers, his eyes filled with curiosity as he came to a stop in front of Ian.

"Mr. MacKenzie, I wasn't expecting you until tomorrow for the meeting with the union men."

Ian shifted Violet in his arms, extending his free hand a moment later. "We ran into some trouble at the farm, Jonathon. I felt it was no longer safe there, so here we are. Allow me to introduce you to everyone." He smiled. "Everyone, this is Mr. Jonathon Downing, my secretary, and . . ."

As Ian performed the introductions, Isadora couldn't help but notice the interest in Mr. Downing's eyes when he was presented to Miss Olive Perkins, who immediately flushed a delightful shade of pink before she hurriedly excused herself, mumbling something about tracking down Henry and Prim. Uncle Amos and Aunt Birdie followed her into the house, Violet and Daisy joining them, each little girl holding one of Uncle Amos's hands.

Left with only Ian and Mr. Downing, Isadora turned to the house. "Shall we go inside? I must admit I'm curious as to what the interior holds."

"It doesn't hold much," Mr. Downing admitted, leading the way into the house. "We've got beds for all of you, but that's about it." He looked to Ian. "Should I travel into Pittsburgh today to purchase some essentials?"

Whatever response Ian gave, Isadora didn't hear it because she'd stepped over the threshold and found herself greeted by a lovely curved staircase with an elaborately scrolled balustrade on either side of the stairs leading to the second floor. Halfway up that floor was a beautiful stained-glass window. After considering the space for a moment, she imagined a settee sitting in front of the plastered wall directly to the left of the stairs, with perhaps a large urn filled with brightly colored flowers next to it, and . . . there definitely needed to be a tapestry of some type spread at the foot of the stairs, along with . . .

"Mrs. Delmont is going to be taking on the role of household manager for now, Jonathon. I'm sure she's just about to suggest you call her Izzie, though, since she's once again looking rather confused about who Mrs. Delmont could possibly be."

Isadora pulled her attention away from the staircase. "I know who Mrs. Delmont is, but . . ." She ignored Ian's arched brow and smiled at Mr. Downing. "You may call me Izzie. Everyone does."

Mr. Downing inclined his head. "And you must call me Jonathon. But tell me, what does a household manager do?"

"I'm not exactly certain," Isadora admitted. "Although, I imagine my first order of business is to tour the house, starting with where the children are going to stay."

"That would be the nursery on the third floor," Jonathon told her, glancing up to the ceiling where the sound of little feet could be heard racing around. He tilted his head. "Should I assume Miss Olive Perkins will be residing in a room up there so she'll be close to the children?"

"I believe that would be the perfect spot for her."

Jonathon immediately strode for the stairs. "I shall assist her with choosing a room that will be well suited for her needs."

As Jonathon disappeared up the stairs, taking them two at a time, Aunt Birdie walked over to join them, releasing a chuckle. "I believe Mr. Downing has already realized what a delightful woman our Olive is." She ignored the sigh Ian released as she looked around. "Dare I hope there are any rooms on this floor that Amos and I may use? Those steps might prove a bit daunting for both of us, although we do have every hope we won't have to be away from Glory Manor long."

"I'll show you what's available on the first floor." Ian nodded to Isadora. "I'll be back directly."

As he led Aunt Birdie and Uncle Amos down a hallway that branched from the entranceway, Isadora walked back outside, immediately greeted by Sparky. Moving to watch Duncan and Earl unload a mooing Buttercup from the wagon, she fought a grin.

"What should we do with her?" Duncan asked right as Buttercup let out a mournful moo. She, unlike Sparky, apparently felt miffed she'd been forced to travel to the house in a wagon and not a carriage.

Isadora looked around, then began walking around the house,

Buttercup and Sparky following her, nodding when she spotted an unfinished flower garden, complete with white picket fence. "We can put her in there for now. I'm sure Buttercup would prefer the house, but that's not going to be an option, no matter how many tears or trembling lips the children may invoke to try to convince me otherwise."

Duncan and Earl exchanged grins before they tried to coerce Buttercup through the gate. She immediately turned stubborn and wouldn't move until Isadora ran to the kitchen, fetched an apple, and used it to tempt Buttercup into motion.

Swiping a hand over her now-perspiring brow, she told Buttercup to behave, having little hope that the cow wouldn't figure out how to escape her makeshift enclosure and find her way into the house.

After instructing Duncan and Earl where to take all the trunks they'd brought from Glory Manor, she finally headed back into the house, finding Ian waiting for her in the entranceway.

"Where've you been?" he asked.

"Buttercup was being difficult." She smoothed back a strand of hair that had gotten free from its pins. "Have Aunt Birdie and Uncle Amos found an appropriate room?"

"They're settling in as we speak. And since we don't seem to have any children or pets around—well, except for Sparky," Ian amended as Sparky scrabbled through the front door and ran to join them, "shall I take you on a quick tour?"

Sparky barked as Isadora smiled. "That would be nice."

Gesturing around him, Ian returned the smile. "Well, this is clearly the entranceway. A bit sparse right now, but I'm not sure what to do in here."

"I'd start by putting a few paintings on that wall over there." Isadora nodded to the wall in question. "That would warm up the space, especially if you added a green settee along with a large urn, perhaps Grecian and filled with colorful flowers that would complement the tapestry I'm sure you're going to want to put directly in front of the stairs."

Ian considered the wall beside the stairs before he turned back to her. "You've clearly got an eye for design, something I readily admit I don't have because I would have never thought to include a settee in that space." He was suddenly looking at her far too intently. "I imagine you'd do a marvelous job turning this house into a home, especially since Aunt Birdie mentioned to me you have a great proficiency for shopping."

"You want me to take on the task of turning your house into a home?"

"I know you'd be more than up for it."

Isadora frowned. "Well, yes, I do think I'd be capable of that. However . . . decorating a home is usually left to the discretion of a gentleman's wife. And while you currently have no wife, I'm sure you'll acquire one at some point. She, I'm afraid, might take exception to my decorating tastes."

Ian rubbed his chin for a moment. "An excellent point."

"Does that mean I should now assume from that less-than-clear statement that I should settle my attention on merely making the rooms we're temporarily using habitable, leaving the grand project of fully decorating and furnishing the house to your future bride?"

He tilted his head and considered her for so long she found herself fighting an unusual urge to fidget. "You shouldn't assume anything of the sort."

When he didn't expand on that, she crossed her arms over her chest. "You might need to be a little less cryptic."

"Cryptic is a hallmark of attorneys."

"Hardly helpful."

He grinned. "But amusing all the same." He nodded to the staircase. "Returning to that space, though, I do think you're spot on with your recommendations. That means you're going to want to pull out that pad of paper where you write down notes pertaining to matters of household business and begin making a list. Every room in this house could use your touch, and just to be clear, expense is no object."

"You truly want me to decorate your house, even knowing you could be annoying your future wife?"

"Perhaps she won't be as annoyed as you imagine" was all he said to that, but before she could respond to what was *certainly* a cryptic remark, Henry suddenly came bounding down the steps, Elmer still tucked under his arm, followed by Violet and Daisy, although Daisy was holding on to the railing and moving more slowly than Isadora had ever seen her move before, evidently never having had an opportunity to experience so many steps at one time.

Sending Isadora what seemed to be a wink, Ian hurried up the staircase and plucked Daisy into his arms. Then, with Henry and Violet speaking over each other as they told him all about the nursery, and how Miss Olive had remarked it was large enough to roller-skate in, Ian continued up the stairs, calling over the balustrade to her that she needed to add roller skates for the children at the very top of what she knew was going to be a very long list.

CHAPTER 28

FIVE DAYS LATER

Sticking his head in what Izzie had told him was going to be the reception room, Ian found not a single soul, which had him moving farther down the first-floor hallway. He stepped into the room slated to become the parlor, smiling when he spotted Izzie sitting on a battered chair, the spectacles she'd once again taken to wearing perched on the bridge of her nose as she squinted at something she'd just written down.

The sight of her left him feeling unsettled, especially since she'd done something different to her hair today. Instead of the braids Prim normally did for her or the severe bun she seemed to favor as well, she'd gathered her hair at the crown of her head, which allowed it to cascade over her shoulders and back, leaving her looking breathtakingly beautiful.

He'd never imagined he'd find a woman as beautiful as Izzie sitting in the house he'd dreamed of building since he was a child. And even though he'd decided straight out of school that he would only set his sights on a lady of high social standing, he'd begun to question that decision because of the woman sitting across the room from him.

He couldn't deny that she wasn't the high-society lady he'd

dreamed of marrying, but there was something compelling about Izzie Delmont, or whatever her last name truly was, something that drew him to her and had him rethinking everything he'd thought was set in stone as well. . . .

"Ian, ah, wonderful, I was just about to try and run you down to go over—" Izzie suddenly stopped talking as her gaze traveled from his combed hair all the way down to the tips of his recently polished shoes. "You neglected to tell me that I'd need to dress in style to visit the shops in Pittsburgh."

Walking across the room, he stopped beside her, noticing she was using an upturned crate as a desk. "You do have *desks* written on one of those lists of yours, don't you?" he asked, ignoring her statement.

"Don't be condescending, of course I do. But returning to your clothing, I have a more fashionable walking dress in the bottom of my trunk, but I didn't put it on today because you didn't bother to tell me that Pittsburgh inhabitants dress in their Sunday best to shop."

Ian leaned over her shoulder, peering at the list she was making. "Pittsburgh, quite like every other big city, sees a wide spectrum in how its shoppers dress," he said, leaning ever so slightly closer to her as he caught the distinct scent of her perfume. "What *is* that perfume you're wearing?" he asked, unfamiliar with the scent even though he'd had more than his share of young ladies present him with their wrists over the years for him to sample the newest perfumes found at the grand stores in Pittsburgh.

She seemed to give a bit of a shudder before she returned to her list. "It's an obscure perfume called The Gypsy Maid, one my friend Beatrix gave me on my last birthday." She turned her head just a touch, drew in a breath, then stilled. "What's the name of the cologne you're wearing? It's rather . . . refreshing."

Ian straightened as he realized it was hardly appropriate for him to remain so close to her, even if he had the most curious urge to dip his nose straight into the nape of her neck to discover if she'd dabbed a bit of The Gypsy Maid there.

"It's Florida Water," he finally remembered to say, his thoughts scrambled because the scent of her was still lingering in his nose.

"It smells like oranges."

"I think that's why I like it."

"You were wearing a different cologne the other day."

"You've noticed the colognes I've been wearing?" he asked as something that felt exactly like masculine satisfaction flowed through him.

Izzie cleared her throat, muttered something that sounded like "much to my concern," then cleared her throat again. "*Returning* to the way you're dressed, should I change to go shopping with you?"

"I'm afraid I'm not dressed this way because of the shopping. My meetings this week with the labor men have not gone well, so I'm off to attend yet another meeting, one that's to be moderated by Mr. Andrew Carnegie. I'm not holding out a great deal of hope the meeting will be successful. Mr. Carnegie has turned bullish in his stance with the negotiations, which probably means the mills could very well shut down since the union men, along with laborers who are not members in any specific union, feel they're being treated unfairly. Their only true power is their ability to go on strike."

Izzie consulted a dainty watch she'd attached to the sleeve of her gown. "It seems rather early for a meeting."

"The meeting isn't for a couple of hours. But by the time I take the horse car into the city, and then go over some notes I left at the office, the morning will be over, and it'll be time to face what is certainly going to be unpleasant."

"Should I go shopping without you?"

Ian nodded. "You should. I've already arranged for Jonathon to accompany you. He's a very competent sort, so he'll be of great assistance to you. He also grew up in one of the meaner neighborhoods down by the mills, so he's very adept at spotting danger. You'll not need to worry about your welfare, especially since Jonathon is also my sparring partner at the boxing gym."

He smiled. "While this pains me to admit, he's a better boxer than I am and has this air about him that suggests he's a dangerous man, which does seem to have people maintaining a certain distance from him."

Izzie returned the smile. "You have that very same air, although granted, you do a remarkable job of cloaking it underneath a layer of charm."

"You find me to be a dangerous man?"

She turned from her makeshift table and waved a hand from his head to his toes. "Indeed. You portray yourself as a successful man of business, but you can't always hide that you're dangerous, Ian. It occasionally seeps through the cheerful façade you display to the world, and when it does, well, let me simply say it leaves an impression."

"Does it frighten you, that danger?"

"Quite the opposite."

Male satisfaction flowed through him again, but before he could question Izzie further on exactly why she enjoyed what she apparently thought was his dangerous attitude, Jonathon gave a brisk knock on the door and stepped into the room.

"It's after eight, sir," Jonathon began. "You're running unusually late this morning, which is why I took the liberty of fetching your satchel, which I've left for you directly beside the front door."

Ian fished his pocket watch from his jacket, saw that Jonathon was right and it was well past eight, even though it certainly hadn't felt like he'd been talking with Izzie so long. "Thank you, Jonathon. I'm afraid time does seem to have gotten away from me."

"Distractions have a way of doing that to a person, sir," Jonathon said before he nodded to Izzie. "But speaking of time, you and I will be leaving this house in exactly forty-five minutes. That will allow us time to travel into Pittsburgh and be first in line when Joseph Horne Company opens its doors."

Izzie consulted her list. "And this Joseph Horne Company has furnishings, along with other much-needed items?"

"They do. We'll start on the sixth floor first. That's where furnishings are located."

Jonathon pulled out his pocket watch before he sent Ian a pointed look.

Knowing that Jonathon would soon take to escorting him to the door if he lingered any longer, one of his secretary's most important tasks being that of keeping Ian on schedule, Ian moved closer to Izzie, surprising himself when he suddenly reached out and took hold of her hand. Knowing there was nothing left to do with that hand except kiss it, since it was rather curious for a man to grab hold of a lady's hand and merely hold on to it, he brought her fingers to his lips, gave them a kiss, then frowned when she simply gazed back at him, clear bemusement in her eyes. Needing something to say to fill the silence that had settled over the room, he latched on to the first thing to spring to mind.

"The staff at Joseph Horne Company is very familiar with Jonathon. You'll have no difficulty charging any items you might find to purchase to my account."

Izzie tilted her head. "I'm not certain how much progress Jonathon and I'll make today, but if you're in agreement, I thought I'd concentrate on making the nursery more pleasant for the children, finding some furnishings, along with toys and a variety of books to cheer up that cavernous room."

"You should try to find some things for your room as well," he said, giving the fingers he was still holding a squeeze. "I've not neglected to notice it's sparsely furnished."

To his surprise, she waved that straight aside. "My room is fine. And until I get the nursery done, I won't have time to worry about the rest of the house."

The desire to pull her straight off the chair and into his arms took him by such surprise that he found himself at a loss for words. To distract from that pesky business, he kissed her fingers again, collecting his misplaced wits in the process. "Finishing the nursery sounds like an excellent plan, but do remember to purchase some roller skates if the store has some in stock. I promised Henry and Violet a pair, and I don't want to disappoint them."

Giving her fingers one last kiss as she nodded and told him roller skates were at the top of her list, he released her hand and strode for the door, feeling rather smug because he hadn't neglected to notice that Isadora's cheeks had turned rather pink while he'd been kissing her fingers.

Stopping once he reached the door, he turned. "My meeting shouldn't last the entire day, so I'll do my best to meet the two of you at Joseph Horne Company if I finish before the shops close for the day." Ignoring the raised brow Jonathon sent him, even knowing there was every reason to conclude his secretary found him to be behaving very curiously because he never left the office until the dinner hour, no matter if his meetings ended early, Ian strode down the hall.

Walking through the front door, he was pleased to discover it was merely a hazy sort of morning, one that had rays of sunlight peeking through, instead of the gloomy mornings he frequently encountered when the smog from the city settled over Shadyside during the night.

His pleasure in the morning, however, lasted only until he reached his office. After stepping from the horse car that was packed with men traveling into the city for work—men just like him who were unwilling to take the time to have a horse readied from the livery—he found three men waiting for him in front of his office, all looking grim.

He wasn't well acquainted with any of the men standing before him—Mr. John Gerber, Mr. Charles McClintock, or Mr. Louis Brown—only knowing them because they were engineers on the Eliza Blast Furnace and stopped in often at Norma's to catch a bite to eat. That the men had come to see him suggested an urgent matter of business.

"Ian," John Gerber said, stepping forward and holding out his hand, which Ian immediately took. "We were just about to leave. Miss Norma told us you could be found at your office by eight, but it's well past that now."

Ian inclined his head as he turned and shook Charles Mc-Clintock's hand, and then Louis Brown's. "I'm running a bit off schedule today," he said, gesturing to the front door. "But I'm here now, so come inside and tell me why you've paid me a call. I assume it's something to do with the labor talks being held later?"

Following him up the two steps that led to the front door of the office, John shook his head as Ian stuck his key into the lock and opened the door. "That's not why we're here. We heard you were asking about Roy Duffy, and we've got some news about him."

Something in John's tone suggested the news was not the type to be delivered outside on the stoop. Ushering the men inside, he led the way through the front receiving room and then into his main office, where he kept a desk on one side of the room and a large table with numerous chairs on the other, used when he met with men of business. Gesturing the men toward the chairs, he walked to the coffeepot Jonathon usually kept brewing for him. "May I interest anyone in coffee? It won't take long to make a fresh pot."

"Thank you, but no," John said, taking a seat. "We've a meeting scheduled later this morning with other engineers, so we don't have much time."

Ian moved to the table and sat down. "Dare I hope you've learned where Mr. Duffy is?"

John exchanged looks with Charles and Louis before he returned his attention to Ian. "There's no easy way to say this. Mr. Duffy suffered an accident at our mill over two months ago. He didn't survive."

It took a moment for that disturbing news to settle. He'd known there was a chance something unfortunate had happened to Roy Duffy, but he'd been hoping the man had merely gone on a drinking binge, as many of the men who worked in the mills seemed to do. It was a dangerous job, working in the mills, and many a man enjoyed escaping the thought of the danger they faced every day by dulling their senses at the numerous taverns located in and around Pittsburgh.

That Roy Duffy was dead was a circumstance he hadn't allowed himself to fully consider, but now, armed with that disturbing truth, he was going to have to tell the children.

They would be devastated to learn they'd been rendered orphans and would undoubtedly be worried about what the future would hold for them. The only consolation he could give was reassurance that he would be responsible for their welfare now, which meant he'd provide them with a home, see to their education, and make certain all their needs were met.

What meeting their needs entailed, he really had no idea, but he couldn't imagine turning the children over to anyone else, or never again being on the receiving end of Daisy's wet kisses, or . . .

"We have some details," Charles said, interrupting Ian's thoughts. "They're not pleasant."

Ian rubbed at a temple that was already beginning to ache. "Tell me the worst of it. I'd also like to understand why no one reached out to the Duffy family to let them know what had become of Roy."

Louis sat forward. "Roy hadn't been working at our mill long. A shear used to cut iron bars broke and landed on Roy, leaving him unrecognizable, which made it difficult to identify him. By the time a positive identification was made, a couple of weeks had gone by. And when the mill sent someone over to the address Roy had left on file, another family had already moved into his rooms and nobody knew where his family had gone."

An unpleasant memory took that moment to flash to mind. "This accident didn't happen to delay production all day at the Eliza Blast Furnace, did it?"

Louis nodded. "It did. The shear was so heavy we had to bring in equipment to pull it off the man buried underneath, a man we now know was Roy. Some of the investors were indignant that production suffered, and one of those investors was even heard to say—"

"'Just because a man got squished like a jelly isn't an excuse for production to grind to a halt,'" Ian finished for him, shaking his head as the temper he'd been feeling so often of late began to churn through him.

"You heard Nigel Flaherty say that?" Louis asked slowly.

"I did. Told him that was beyond inappropriate as well as insensitive since he was blithely talking about the death of a man." He caught John's eye. "You wouldn't happen to know where Roy Duffy is buried, would you?"

John nodded. "He's at the Homewood Cemetery. Management decided to step in and pay for a proper burial after they realized tensions about the dangerous atmosphere in the mill were reaching the boiling point. The men were furious about Nigel Flaherty's remarks, so management hoped that by picking up the cost for a burial they could defuse some of that fury." John frowned. "It's only a matter of time until that anger boils over though, especially when our wages keep getting cut while owners and investors still seem to be getting richer."

Ian's stomach clenched. "I'm sure you're right about the fury of the men, but getting back to Roy Duffy, do you know if he was buried beside his wife?"

"His wife is dead too?"

Ian leaned back in the chair. "Mrs. Duffy died a few years back, which is why Roy's children got sent to an orphanage when Roy didn't return home to pay the rent. That orphanage was full, so the children finally ended up at Glory Manor with my aunt and uncle."

"Orphanages do seem to be filling up fast these days," Charles said. "Too many men are dying in the mills, or else their wives die and they're forced to put up their children in the orphanages because they can't mind them with the long hours demanded in the mills." Charles narrowed his eyes on Ian. "Might be nice if *someone* could convince the owners that cutting the hours and giving the men a set wage instead of an hourly one would go far in boosting morale. That might very well see production increase once demand for our products begins to grow again."

"Demand will always increase with iron and steel," Ian said. "The country is still building at an unprecedented rate. Production is only currently suffering because the railroads are being unreasonable with what they're charging to transport raw materials to us. Because of that, we've been forced to increase our prices, which has builders holding off until more favorable prices are offered." Ian leaned back. "Negotiations are even now underway with the railroads, and once those are settled, demand will probably exceed what the mills are capable of producing."

"But will the owners of the mills take wages back to what they were before production slowed?" Louis asked. "That question is what has all of us worried, as well as contemplating a strike."

"A strike won't keep food on your table," Ian pointed out.

"True, but considering all of us are facing the same fate as Roy Duffy when we go to work every day, it only seems fair that we should know we're being sufficiently compensated. We also want to know that the owners and investors understand the risks we're taking and make their decisions accordingly."

"That might be asking too much," Ian said quietly. "But you've made some interesting points and given me much to ponder, especially about decreasing hours men are demanded to work. I've broached that idea before, but perhaps I need to investigate it more closely, see if I can find proof that productivity won't suffer if hours are cut. Roy Duffy's children might not have been left on their own so often if Roy hadn't been expected to work twelve-hour shifts."

John frowned. "How many children did Roy have?"

"Four, all under the age of ten." Ian drummed his fingers against the table. "It's going to be difficult to tell them about their father. I hope they'll find some small comfort in knowing I intend to make certain their parents are laid to rest together, although I have no idea where their mother is buried."

Charles pushed his chair back and rose to his feet. "You might want to ask Miss Norma her thoughts on the matter. She's always well informed about the happenings in the community." He nodded to John and Louis. "We should probably be on our way."

The three men rose to their feet as Ian did the same.

"I imagine I'll see you gentlemen at the meeting later."

A ghost of a smile flickered across John's face. "You will, although do know that none of us will take offense if you don't acknowledge us at the meeting. We're fully aware that owners and investors don't look highly on intermingling with the commoners."

Charles moved beside him and clapped Ian on the back. "I heard tell that you were once one of us, as was your father. It would be nice if we didn't have to leave the meeting today with no concessions won."

"You do have competent attorneys representing your interests, though, don't you?" Ian asked.

"Depends on what you consider competent. They're good, don't get me wrong, but . . ." Charles winced.

"They're no match for Andrew Carnegie?" Ian finished for him.

Louis stepped to his side and smiled ever so slightly. "It's not Andrew they're worried about. It's you. In case you're unaware, your reputation for winning negotiations precedes you, which does make it a little troublesome to find competent attorneys to go up against you. Attorneys, I'm beginning to realize, don't care to lose, which normally happens when they're dealing with you and contracts."

"I'm not certain you mean that as a compliment."

Louis smiled. "If you were working on our side, it would be." He shook Ian's hand again. "Just remember what Charles said. You were once one of us, and because of that, you understand the dangers all of us face every time we step foot in the mills." He gestured to John and Charles. "Any of us can be, as Nigel Flaherty so charmingly put it, 'squished like a jelly,' so keep that in mind as the negotiations start up again."

Walking with the men out of the office and through the reception room, Ian couldn't get the memory of the callous way Nigel had talked about Roy Duffy's death out of his head.

That callousness was embraced by far too many Pittsburgh industrialists, men who'd made a fortune through the backbreaking toil of laborers, engineers, and managers of the mills. Those industrialists did not care that thousands of men had died in the mills over the years. All they cared about was increasing their profits and their fortune.

He, to his chagrin, had obviously become one of those men.

The thought took him aback and left him realizing he did not want to be a man who blithely disregarded the death of a man as simply being the price of doing business. He also didn't want to be a man responsible for causing other men to suffer financial and family hardships because he was supposed to safeguard profitability for his contemporaries, along with himself, no matter the consequences.

"Gentlemen, a moment, if you please," he called to the men now walking down the sidewalk, striding to join them.

"You said your attorneys are hesitant to go up against me," he began. "But I should tell you that Andrew has taken me out of most of the negotiation process because he feels I'm too sympathetic to the laborers."

The three men exchanged looks before Charles stepped forward. "And you're telling us that because . . . you want us to tell our attorneys they don't have to worry they'll be going up against you?"

Ian shook his head. "No, I'm telling you because I'm not one to appreciate being banished to the sidelines. Because of that, I'm thinking I'll need to stand up and propose a contract that Andrew is not going to like, but one that will be fair to the laborers. I'm wondering if you believe I can find success with the unions if I push for a decrease in hours, although I know I won't be able to take the decrease in wages off the table."

Louis frowned. "The union men would probably be willing to consider that type of proposal. But you must know that Andrew Carnegie will be furious with you if he's taken you out of the negotiations and you defy him by stepping back in."

"You'll also be ostracized from Pittsburgh industrialists," John added, watching Ian closely.

"An excellent point," Ian said before he turned and began walking back to his office.

"Does that mean you've changed your mind about stepping forward?" Charles called after him.

Looking over his shoulder, Ian smiled. "Not at all. I'll definitely be proposing my idea, and if I get ostracized, so be it."

With that, and leaving the men smiling, he continued into his office, made his way to a wall filled with file cabinets, then began pulling out file after file, hoping he'd be able to collect enough case information from past negotiations to convince everyone involved he'd not lost his mind.

CHAPTER 29

"Is it me, or does it appear we've got almost every salesperson in the store assisting us now?"

Looking up from the navy velvet suit she'd found on a rack in the boys' department, Isadora glanced past Jonathon and discovered an entire swarm of salespeople gathered nearby, all of whom had pads of paper in their hands as they watched her expectantly.

"I do believe you're right." She smiled. "It's quite an improvement over my having to run down a clerk when I couldn't find the roller skates." She glanced down at her plain white blouse and black skirt. "I never realized I would be treated differently if I dressed in a manner I usually don't dress to shop in, especially when I'm off to . . ."

She swallowed the word *Paris* and returned her attention to the suit she was holding. "I must say, the salesclerks certainly changed their attitudes once you informed them I was here at Ian's request."

"Where do you normally shop?" Jonathon asked instead of addressing the service she'd first experienced at the store, proving her suspicions about his being far too astute for his own good were spot-on.

Giving an airy wave of her hand, she held up the jacket, inspecting the sleeve. "I shop in stores, same as everyone."

"Stores in New York?"

"Why would you assume that?"

"Because when you insisted I take you to a telegram office before we came here, I couldn't help but notice that the telegram you sent was going to New York, and to a Mr. Hatfield, if I'm not mistaken."

"You weren't anywhere near me when I composed that telegram."

"True" was his only response to that. "Is that where you're from, and is Mr. Hatfield the same Mr. Hatfield who Ian told me penned a reference letter for you?"

"Are you always this inquisitive?"

"Are you always so reluctant to answer a simple question? Questions regarding a person's home, I should point out, are considered acceptable to bring into conversation, at least according to the etiquette books Ian has lent me to read."

"You enjoy reading Ian's etiquette books?"

"Enjoy might be a bit of a stretch, but returning to Mr. Hatfield?"

Isadora blew out a breath. "Mr. Hatfield, who did provide me with a reference letter, is also acquainted with a dear friend of mine, one who wanted me to keep her apprised of any moves I might make. Since I've now moved from Glory Manor to Pittsburgh, I simply sent Mr. Hatfield a telegram telling him of my new location, which I know he'll pass on to my friend."

"Why does Ian believe you're confused about your last name?"

Unwilling to delve into that disturbing business, she held up the velvet suit and tilted her head. "What do you think about this?"

"I didn't know it was the fashion for little girls to wear trousers."

"It's not for the girls. It's for Henry."

The horror that immediately sprang into Jonathon's eyes was

all Isadora needed to replace the suit, looking around for other racks that might have clothing more suitable for a little boy who didn't seem to enjoy much fuss when it came to fashion.

"What may we assist you with now, Mrs. Delmont?" A saleswoman wearing a blouse similar to Isadora's asked as she joined them, her pad of paper and pencil at the ready.

"Boys' clothing, but nothing with frills, lace, or velvet." She glanced back to the suit she'd found darling and Jonathon had found anything but, releasing a sigh of longing, which Jonathon ignored, although he did roll his eyes.

"For the same little boy who's getting the red wagon?" The clerk consulted her notes. "Henry, age seven?"

"Yes, that's right."

The woman's eyes sparkled. "And is there a limit on how much you're going to spend on young Master Henry's clothing?"

"There's not," Jonathon answered for her. "Mr. MacKenzie would like the children to have a variety of choices to wear when they return to school, as well as for when they're at their leisure."

"How marvelous," the saleswoman exclaimed before she hurried off, her heels clicking against the wooden floor, telling them over her shoulder she'd be back in a trice with some selections.

Isadora consulted her list. "I must admit we've accomplished far more than I thought possible today. I do thank you for your advice as pertains to the furnishings in the receiving room. It never occurred to me that large men might not like the dainty chairs that are so popular these days."

"It's hard to get comfortable when you're forced to squeeze yourself into those types of dainty chairs."

"Again, something that never occurred to me. I certainly don't believe my mother ever sought my father's opinion about chairs, which"— she frowned—"might explain why he never spends much time at home."

"Home in New York?"

"You're very tenacious. And I'm not complimenting you, if that's in question."

Jonathon surprised her when he grinned, but that grin suddenly slid off his face. The next second, he had hold of her arm and was escorting her rapidly across the floor, telling the salesclerks who immediately fell into step behind them that they'd just realized they were parched and were going to repair to the tearoom. After assuring the clerks they would return after their tea, Jonathon tightened his grip and increased his pace, Isadora forced to break into a bit of a trot to keep up with him.

"Should I assume you've detected something of a dangerous nature?" she all but panted when they reached the elevator and he hustled her into it once the elevator operator opened the grated door.

"The only danger you're in is if I have a face-to-face encounter with Mr. Nigel Flaherty. He's a vile man who was responsible for getting me fired at the mills a few years back, although now that I think about it, because that firing led me to being employed by Ian, perhaps I should kiss the man instead of tearing him limb from limb."

Isadora bit back a smile when the elevator operator began edging as close as he could to his lever, and he seemed to get them to the street level in no time at all, a circumstance that had her stomach roiling. She turned to thank him after she'd stepped out of the elevator, but that thanks got caught in her throat when she realized the man had already shut the door and sent the elevator whizzing upward again.

"You do realize you just frightened that man half to death, don't you?" she asked, receiving a shrug from Jonathon in return.

"That was not my intention, but I've always wondered how rapidly those elevators can move, and now I know."

Shaking her head, she looked around for the tearoom, stilling when she caught sight of Ian moving their way. He saw them a second later and quickened his pace, stopping directly in front of her.

He was still dressed in his suit, but his tie had been loosened, and a shadow of stubble was just beginning to appear on his face.

"I was hoping I'd still find the two of you here," he said, nodding to Jonathon, and then sending tingles up her arm when he drew her gloved hand to his lips and placed a kiss on it, quite as if he'd become accustomed to kissing her hand and seemed to believe she now expected it.

Not willing to tell him those types of gestures weren't exactly what a housekeeper, or rather, household manager, expected since she did enjoy the gesture, she smiled at him as he released her hand. "We were about to get some tea."

"Then I've arrived just in time."

As Ian took her arm and Jonathon walked on the other side of her, Isadora soon found herself seated at the best table in the tearoom.

"So, tell me about the shopping," Ian said after they'd placed their orders, deciding to include some small cakes to go with the tea.

"There's much to tell." Isadora pulled out the sheaf of papers she'd been carrying all day, setting them on the table. "We managed to get furnishings for all the rooms in the nursery, including Miss Olive's room, as well as toys for the children, and yes, they'll have roller skates, and—"

"Izzie also bought you a pair," Jonathon said, amusement lurking in his eyes as he nodded to Ian.

"I haven't skated in years," Ian said.

"Well, you're going to skate with the children tonight, so . . ."

For some curious reason, his eyes clouded over at the mention of the children, but then he inclined his head as a ghost of a smile flickered over his face. "I'm sure I'll remember the basics of skating, even if I'm also certain I'll sport a bruised backside tomorrow."

Isadora nodded. "That is a distinct possibility, but returning to my list. We have saleswomen currently picking out new outfits for the children, and we have some salesmen up in furnishings who are putting together some samples of colors for the parlor, the receiving room, and the library."

"You *have* been busy."

"We have," Isadora agreed as the server returned and poured them all a cup of tea while another server placed a silver tray filled with small cakes on the table.

After thanking the men, she returned her attention to Ian. "But enough of the shopping. How did your meeting go today? Did Mr. Andrew Carnegie monopolize the floor, or were you able to have your say?"

"You remembered I was worried I wouldn't be allowed a say?"

"You told me that last night. It wasn't that long ago, so yes, I remembered."

Her cheeks began to heat when he considered her for an unusually long time. To distract from the fact that her face had to be bright red, she helped herself to a cake, almost choking on it a second later when a young lady glided over to their table, her flaxen hair arranged in a most attractive manner, wearing a dress Isadora was sure she'd seen in Paris when she'd been there last. That the young lady immediately began fluttering her lashes in an outrageously flirtatious fashion at Ian set Isadora's jaw to clenching, which turned out to be somewhat problematic since she'd taken such a large bite.

"Mr. MacKenzie," the young lady all but gushed. "What a delightful surprise. I wasn't aware you enjoy coming to this tearoom, or that you even enjoy tea."

Setting aside his napkin, Ian rose to his feet, as did Jonathon. As Ian took the hand the young lady immediately thrust his way, Isadora felt the most unusual feeling sweep over her when Ian gave the lady's fingers a kiss, but she took solace in the idea that the kiss couldn't be considered lingering by any stretch of the imagination.

The floor suddenly felt as if it had dropped out from under her, leaving her slightly light-headed as truth took that moment to rear its ugly head.

She was *jealous* of the lady now fluttering her lashes more rapidly than ever.

She'd never been jealous of anyone in her entire life, but that was exactly what was flowing through her—jealousy. The reason behind that jealousy could only mean one thing.

She, Miss Isadora Delafield, had fallen ever so slightly in love with the man who was currently her employer.

Granted, she'd come to the conclusion she was somewhat smitten with him, but . . . love?

It was an epiphany she was going to have to consider more closely, but not while in the middle of tea, or while Ian was being all but accosted by a—

"I don't believe I've had the pleasure of meeting this . . . delightful creature."

Forcing a smile, she turned her head to the lady who was apparently talking about her, although the snotty tone in which she'd said *delightful creature* suggested she found Isadora anything but.

Ian stepped forward to perform the expected introductions. "Miss Moore, allow me to present Mrs. Delmont. Mrs. Delmont, this is Miss Lillian Moore."

"Of the Richard Moore family here in Pittsburgh," Miss Moore added, frowning as she peered at Isadora. "You have icing, dear, smeared to the right of your lip."

Blotting her lips with her linen napkin, Isadora kept her smile firmly in place, not being able to recall a time she'd left icing on her face, but curiously enough, not being put out in the least that Miss Moore had pointed it out, nor that the young lady was now considering her in a most condescending fashion.

"I do so enjoy cakes," Miss Moore chirped before she smoothed a hand over her waist. "But since my parents are hosting a ball two days from now, I'm afraid I can't allow myself to indulge in such a treat, not if I want my delicious froth of a gown to fit to perfection."

Fighting the curious urge to release a snort over that blatant attempt to get Ian to remark on her figure, even though, to give the lady credit, she did have a lovely figure, Isadora blotted her lips again, grimacing when more icing showed up on the linen, something Miss Moore certainly hadn't bothered to point out to her again.

"But you must come to the ball," Miss Moore suddenly exclaimed, and for a second, Isadora thought she was talking to Ian. To her horror, she realized Miss Moore was directing her attention back to Isadora again.

"Ah, well," Isadora began. "Ah . . ."

Miss Moore waved Isadora's sputtering aside. "If you're worried about what to wear, you mustn't concern yourself over that. What you're wearing now is fine, dear." She smiled. "I especially adore your spectacles."

Knowing full well that the woman was lying through her teeth, Isadora frowned, spared a response when Ian suddenly cleared his throat.

"While it's very kind of you to extend Mrs. Delmont an invitation, Miss Moore, I've already asked her to join me as my guest at your ball."

Miss Moore's mouth dropped open even as Jonathon turned and began taking an absorbed interest in the tearoom, rubbing a hand over his mouth quite as if he were trying to hide a smile.

"My mother never mentioned that you were bringing a guest."

"My invitation did read *Mr. MacKenzie and guest.*"

"Well, certainly it did since that's proper etiquette, but . . ." Miss Moore shot a glare to Isadora before she summoned up a smile. "It'll be lovely to have you there, and do know . . ." Whatever else Miss Moore was going to say faded away when they were suddenly joined by another gentleman.

"I was wondering where you wandered off to," the man said, smiling at Miss Moore before he turned to Ian and stiffened.

For a second, Isadora thought the man might be Miss Moore's father, *Mr. Richard Moore of the Moore family*, until Ian gave a jerk of his head in the gentleman's direction and said, "Nigel."

"Ian," Nigel bit out before he turned to Jonathon and frowned. "Do I know you?"

Jonathon, Isadora was alarmed to see, was all but bristling

with animosity. "You do. I'm Jonathon Downing. You got me fired from my job at the mill because I punched you after you mocked a man recently arrived from Germany who didn't know much English."

"Which is exactly why I stepped in and hired him," Ian said with a smile, even though his eyes had begun to take on a rather dangerous look.

"Proving that what I've said about you being too sympathetic to the laborers is right on the nose," Nigel said, even as he took a few steps backward, putting distance between himself and Jonathon. "Interesting meeting we attended today, MacKenzie. Even though you won the union men over with your proposal, the investors and owners of the mills aren't thrilled you proposed such an unusual solution to the labor problems."

Ian shrugged. "It's a solid plan, Nigel. As I said when I got up to speak, Mr. Thomas Harrington of the Harrington Iron Mill was forced to cut wages a few years back. But because he also cut hours and made the men salary instead of hourly, production didn't slow. And after the demand for iron increased, he saw a substantial profit, all due to what I believe was an increase in morale among his employees."

"Time will tell if it works, but it's a risk many of us aren't excited to take, including Mr. Carnegie, even with you winning the day and getting everyone to agree to the concessions."

"I didn't win all of my points, Nigel, as you very well know. But reducing the twelve-hour shifts down to ten, even though I wanted them down to eight, and decreasing wages by eleven percent instead of twelve is a start. And my negotiations, whether you want to give me the credit or not, have taken the threat of a strike off the table."

Miss Moore let out a bit of a titter and reached out to touch Ian's arm, earning a frown she didn't see from Nigel in the process. "Not that I know much about business, Mr. MacKenzie, but you should use caution in how you handle those business matters." She sent a charming smile to Nigel. "Why, if you're not careful,

Mr. Flaherty might not include you in that new coal venture he was trying to explain to me a short time ago. From what I could understand of what he was saying, it's certain to prove a most lucrative investment."

For the briefest of seconds, Ian merely stood there, until his eyes narrowed and he took a single step toward Nigel. "I haven't heard any specifics about a new coal venture being planned. Where's it to be located?"

After sending a look of irritation toward Miss Moore, Nigel resettled his gaze on Ian and shrugged. "It's no secret that geologists have been scouring the southern part of this state, as well as Ohio, looking for coal reserves. They've been successful with their investigation, and I'm pleased to say that plans to mine the coalfields are well underway."

"Are they, now?"

Nigel nodded. "Indeed, but after your abysmal display today at the negotiations, I'm afraid this particular investment group won't be interested in having you onboard." Nigel turned from him and set his sights on Isadora. His eyes sharpened on her face right before they filled with male appreciation. "Forgive me," he began, taking a step toward her. "Ian has completely forgotten his manners and not introduced me to you. I'm Mr. Nigel Flaherty."

When Ian didn't step forward to perform the introductions, and even though Isadora was already all but convinced Nigel was not a man she wanted to know, she inclined her head. "I'm Mrs. Delmont . . . of the *Delmont* family," she added, sending a smile Miss Moore's way. Her smile widened when Miss Moore's eyes clouded with confusion, quite as if she couldn't quite figure out if Isadora was serious or not.

"How lovely to meet you, Mrs. Delmont," Nigel exclaimed, reaching out his hand as if to take her hand in his and place the expected kiss on it.

Not feeling in an accommodating state of mind, Isadora abandoned every etiquette rule that had been drummed into her head since birth and snatched up another cake, making it impossible for Nigel to take her hand. Blinking, he stopped his advance.

Rallying quickly, he smiled. "And how are you acquainted with Ian?"

Knowing Ian was certain to make up some story about her, and unwilling to find herself suddenly boasting an impressive pedigree, even though she actually had one, she caught Nigel's eye. "I'm his household manager."

Jonathon abruptly spun around as Ian sent her a scowl, that telling reaction missed by Miss Moore and Nigel, who were now looking at her as if she were some type of hideous creature who had wandered into their midst.

"What is a household manager?" Miss Moore asked, raising a hand to her throat.

"It's somewhat like a housekeeper," Isadora said cheerfully. "I'm simply not expected to cook or iron, but that might be because I've been known to catch the oven on fire, and I once burned an impressive iron print into a pair of Mr. MacKenzie's trousers."

As Miss Moore blinked in stunned disbelief, Isadora abandoned all the etiquette rules again by stuffing a very large piece of cake into her mouth, deliberately smearing the icing on her lips in the process. Swallowing a moment later, because speaking with her mouth full would have been taking matters entirely too far, she smacked her lips. "Delicious."

It took everything she had not to laugh as Miss Moore and Nigel simply stared at her in horror, until Nigel turned to Miss Moore, took her arm, and nodded. "While Mrs. Delmont is certainly charming, I've just noticed Mr. and Mrs. Bryce sitting over on the other side of the room. Shall we go greet them?"

Without bothering to say another word, Nigel and Miss Moore sauntered away, stopping as they reached a table where presumably Mr. and Mrs. Bryce were taking tea, along with a gentleman who had his back turned to Isadora.

"This isn't the time," she thought she heard Jonathon say before he resumed his seat, nodding to the chair Ian had abandoned.

Taking his seat, Ian drew in a deep breath, slowly released it, then drew in another as if he were having a difficult time controlling his temper.

"Have I missed something of importance?" Isadora asked, reaching for the teapot that had been left on the table and topping off Ian's and Jonathon's cups.

"It's nothing," Ian said as he picked up his cup, took a sip of tea, then sent her one of his charming smiles, the charm not as effective because his eyes were glittering with something disturbing.

"More cake?" Jonathon asked, setting another piece of cake on her plate before she could answer.

She lifted her chin. "I should tell both of you that I'm not a lady who appreciates being left in the dark. But since we are currently sitting in a lovely tearoom, where proper etiquette does demand that I don't start shrieking at both of you like a fishmonger, I won't press for explanations . . . for now."

Jonathon's lips twitched. "Not that I want to further aggravate you, but from the etiquette books I've read, aren't ladies expected to use utensils when they're enjoying cake?"

She grinned before she picked up her fork and stuck it into the cake. "Well, yes, but that was an extenuating circumstance, and besides, I couldn't seem to help myself." After polishing off her small cake, she looked at the piece of cake Jonathon had yet to touch. "Are you going to eat that? I've just realized I'm famished, and since *I* don't need to worry about fitting into a ball gown two days from now . . ." She glanced to the cake on Jonathon's plate again, smiling when he let out a bit of a sigh as he transferred the cake to her plate.

"You're rather annoying," he said, taking a sip of his tea.

"Izzie's soon to be annoyed as well after she realizes she *will* be wearing a ball gown in two days," Ian said, nodding to the cake on her plate. "That means you might want to go easy on that."

She narrowed her eyes. "I'm not going to that ball with you. If you've forgotten, I'm your household manager. You don't take your household manager to a ball where there will likely be influential men of business you need to impress."

Ian folded his arms over his chest. "But because you *are* my household manager and I am your employer, you really have no choice but to agree to accompany me to the ball since I've decided I want you there with me."

"I've never really done well with people trying to order me about, and—" She suddenly stopped talking when, for some unknown reason, the hair at the nape of her neck stood to attention.

Setting aside her fork, she lifted her head and looked around, freezing on the spot when she discovered the gentleman who'd been sitting at the table Nigel and Miss Moore had now joined, the one who'd had his back turned to her, was now looking her way, and . . . she knew him.

He was Mr. William Rives, a man heavily invested in the oil industry, and he was a friend of her father—and not just any friend, but one who'd often invited Isadora and her brothers on sailing expeditions with him on his yacht.

Calling herself every type of idiot because she'd let down her guard and gone out in public, mistakenly believing no one would recognize her, Isadora shoved her spectacles back into placee and all but jumped out of her seat, presenting her back to Mr. Rives.

Ian and Jonathon immediately stood, Ian's brows drawing together. "Is something amiss?"

Isadora fought to think of something to say, her gaze settling on the cake. "Forgive me, I believe I may have consumed the cake too quickly, and as such, well, this is indelicate of me to mention, but I must seek out the retiring room."

"Shall I go with you?" Ian asked.

She waved that away even as she took a step forward. "I'll be fine, but because I don't believe I'll care to be around food for the foreseeable future, do finish your tea and cake. You can join me after you're done. I'll be up in, ah, ladies' fashions—*not* looking for a ball gown, mind you—but merely seeing what, ah, new selections might be available."

With that, and leaving Ian and Jonathon looking rather bemused, she bolted out of the tearoom, forcing herself to not turn and see if Mr. Rives was still watching her and praying if he was, he wouldn't recognize the spectacle-wearing, drably dressed woman as Isadora Delafield, American heiress.

CHAPTER 30

"I should go after her," Ian said, watching as Izzie all but fled from the tearoom.

"She won't appreciate that. Women are sensitive about matters of digestion." Jonathon sat down and nodded to Ian's chair. "We'll finish our tea and, after giving Izzie sufficient time in the retiring room, you can join her in ladies' fashions. I have a clear view of the retiring room, so there's no need to worry about her safety. I'll know when she makes her exit."

Resuming his seat, even though he did so reluctantly, Ian glanced to where Nigel was now deep in conversation with the people he'd joined at the table across the room. Ian's temper immediately began to simmer.

"Are you of a like mind with me in believing it could very well be Nigel and his team of investors behind the accidents occurring at Glory Manor, what with how he said they're interested in land south of here?" he asked, earning a nod from Jonathon in response.

"I am, although I'm a bit puzzled why he would have admitted his involvement with that endeavor. Nigel's always taken an uncommon interest in your life. He must know you have family in that area."

Ian picked up his tea. "Nigel's consumed with adding to his fortune. He also knows that my main goal in life has been to increase my fortune as well. If I'm not mistaken, he can't understand putting family before profitability and probably believes I'm cut from the same cloth." Ian glanced to Nigel, who was now rising from the table, Miss Moore by his side. "I'm also sure he's distanced himself from whomever he's hired to do the dirty work of forcing folks from their farms. He wouldn't want to hear the nasty details of what's been needed to acquire the land, which will also allow him to plead ignorance if that person—probably Hank—gets apprehended." He looked back to Jonathon. "I'm going to need proof Nigel's involved before I can confront him."

"That might be difficult to come by since he is a slippery sort. It's unlikely he left a trail that can lead back to him, unless we can find Hank."

"Hank's not been seen since he claimed Uncle Amos chased him from Glory Manor. Although, if I'm right about him, he would be the one responsible for setting the barn on fire. Why he went to that extreme is anyone's guess."

Jonathon frowned. "I would think he did that out of frustration. Clearly he wasn't going to be successful with driving your aunt and uncle off the land, not with the new hires you kept bringing on and the way the entire town showed up to bring Glory Manor back to life."

"It was a cowardly act, setting fire to a barn with innocent animals trapped inside."

Jonathon smiled. "Cowardly as it may be, cowards are normally rather accommodating when they're caught. I wouldn't be surprised if he'd sell out everyone involved if we were able to track him down."

"The problem is finding him." Ian paused to gather his thoughts, narrowing his eyes when Nigel suddenly turned to him, inclined his head, then sent him a nasty smile before he began walking out of the tearoom with Miss Moore on his arm.

He looked back to Jonathon. "What if Hank's a Pittsburgh

resident? What if he returned here to lick his wounds because of the failure he'd experienced with Glory Manor?"

"That could be, which would make it easier to track him down since I have numerous contacts here I could prevail upon to keep an eye out for him." Jonathon leaned forward. "Tell me everything you know about Hank."

All that Ian knew was disclosed in minutes. Then, and because Izzie had yet to come out of the retiring room, he told Jonathon about Roy Duffy.

"Do you need me to go with you to begin the search for Hank?" Ian asked as he pulled out his wallet to settle the bill for the tea and cakes.

"I'll be fine on my own. The children need to be told about their father. You take care of that, and I'll take care of hunting Hank."

"I'm not sure how to go about telling the children their father's dead."

"Children are resilient, Ian, as you and I know firsthand," Jonathon said. "They'll certainly be sad and need to mourn their father, but if you ask me, they're going to be relieved to learn he didn't intentionally abandon them. That will go far in soothing the anguish of his death."

"I hope you're right." He glanced to the ladies' retiring room and frowned. "She's been in there a long time."

"Did you see how quickly she consumed those cakes?"

Ian grinned. "Did you see how she deliberately smeared the icing all over her mouth?"

"She's an interesting lady," Jonathon said, returning the grin. "And not that I'm about to try my hand at matchmaking, as so many people seem to do around you, but . . . she suits you."

"Sounds like an attempt at matchmaking to me" was all Ian could think to say, even though he was beginning to come to the same conclusion.

Instead of addressing that, Jonathon checked his pocket watch. "If I find Hank, do you want me to bring him to you or take him to the authorities and then fetch you?"

"Bring him to me."

Jonathon inclined his head and without another word strode from the tearoom.

After paying the bill, Ian walked to the retiring room and leaned against the wall as the minutes ticked away. Finally, the door began opening ever so slowly and Izzie peeked out, her gaze immediately returning to the tearoom before she let out what sounded like a breath of relief, then jumped when she caught sight of him.

"Ian, you just scared me half to death."

Frowning as he looked her over, Ian extended his arm, which she immediately took. "Why is your hat pulled so low over your face? I'm surprised you can see."

Izzie started forward, her pace unusually rapid as she steered him past the tearoom and toward the elevator. "I was having difficulty with the pins," she finally said, stopping in front of the elevator even as she glanced over her shoulder quite as if she were searching for someone.

"Is something amiss?"

She turned back around. "Just making certain that horrid Miss Moore isn't lurking around to ambush me with more of her snotty remarks or ridiculous invitations."

"It wasn't a ridiculous invitation. I want to take you to the ball."

"Then be prepared for disappointment because I won't be attending it with you."

"Because you believe it's unseemly for a household manager to attend a ball?"

The smile she sent him was entirely too innocent. "Indeed."

Before he could press her, though, the elevator door opened. He couldn't say he was surprised when Izzie asked the operator to take them to the children's department instead of ladies' fashions.

Thirty minutes later, and after Izzie had instructed the staff at Joseph Horne Company to deliver the goods she'd selected to his house on Fifth Avenue, and after he'd settled the details of the bill, they left the store.

Izzie kept glancing every which way, but when he asked her if she was still on the lookout for Miss Moore, she dismissed that with a smile and a shrug as she allowed him to assist her into the carriage his driver had already pulled up to the curb.

"Why don't you take this carriage to work in the morning instead of riding in the horse car?" she asked as the carriage rumbled into motion.

Even though he longed to press her on her peculiar behavior, Ian knew it would be a wasted effort since Izzie was once again putting to good use her proficiency for distraction. Sending her a frown, one she missed because her hat was now almost entirely obstructing her eyes and seemed to be pushing her dreadful spectacles down her nose, he settled back against the seat. "Calling for my carriage every morning is a bit of a bother. I don't have stables yet, so my horses, along with my carriages, are kept at a livery stable, which isn't close to the house."

"Are you going to build a stable?"

"Eventually, especially since I would like to have Rumor with me in Pittsburgh. I just haven't gotten around to finding the time to design a stable or hire on someone to design and build it for me."

"The children should be taught how to ride, and sooner rather than later at that. I could arrange to have a stable built if you don't have the time."

The mention of the children reminded him of the troubling business he needed to discuss with her. Abandoning his seat opposite her, he sat down directly next to her.

"Speaking of the children . . ." he began. "I'm afraid I have some troubling news."

"Does it have something to do with the exchange you had with that nasty Nigel—who I'm going to say is a most disagreeable man. Makes me glad I *didn't* change Elmer's name to Nigel, because Elmer, even with her propensity for pecking my legs, is nowhere near as odious as Nigel. I told you men named Nigel are shifty sorts, and here's the proof."

"No truer words have ever been said, but he's not involved with what I need to tell you." He paused for a second and then decided it would be for the best to simply spit out the whole awful disclosure. "I found out Roy Duffy, the children's father, died weeks ago in a mill accident."

Izzie drew in a sharp breath, her eyes widened in horror, and she suddenly grabbed hold of his hand. "How devastating for the children. You must tell me what happened, and don't spare me the details. I need to know everything so I'll be better prepared to answer the questions the children are bound to ask."

With her eyes sparkling with tears, she listened to his story unfold. When he finished, and because the tears were beginning to trail down her cheeks, he gathered her into his arms, holding her close.

"What will happen to them?" she whispered into his jacket.

"They'll stay with me."

She pushed herself from his chest. "You're going to raise them?"

He nodded. "I can't very well get rid of them, not when they've somehow stolen my heart." He wiped a tear from her cheek. "They could probably use a feminine influence in their lives."

She sent him a wobbly smile. "I'm sure Miss Lillian Moore would be more than happy to apply for that position."

"I'm not so certain about that after what happened at the tearoom." He smiled. "I have a feeling, what with how I went against Andrew Carnegie today, as well as the rest of the owners and investors in the mills, that I'm about to find myself not quite as sought after by the society set."

"Are you disappointed about that?"

Ian frowned. "I suppose I should be, because it's been my plan for years to be accepted into society. However, no . . . I'm not overly disappointed, although I can't explain why."

"Perhaps it's because, as Aunt Birdie often says, you've finally discovered the path God wants you to be on, and you now realize that what you thought you wanted isn't what you really wanted after all."

"You might be exactly right, but getting back to that feminine . . ."

Disappointment swept over him when the carriage pulled into the drive leading up to his house before he could finish the thought, which faded when the arrival of the carriage was greeted by children spilling out the front door, Sparky chasing after them, Elmer bringing up the rear.

"I get the oddest feeling Elmer's decided she's a dog," Izzie said, looking out the window before she returned her attention to him. "Would you like me with you when you tell the children?"

"Would that be too much to ask?"

"Not at all, and I say the sooner we tell them, the better."

Wishing she wasn't right but knowing she was, Ian stepped from the carriage when it pulled to a stop, helping Izzie out before he found himself surrounded by children. Giving Henry's hair a ruffle while picking up Violet, who immediately wrapped her thin arms around his neck, Ian turned to Izzie, who was already holding Daisy in her arms and smiling down at Prim, who was telling her all about the day they'd spent with Miss Olive.

Falling into step beside Izzie and heading for the house, he found himself praying that he'd have the right words to say to the children. If he didn't have the words, he prayed God would step in to assist him.

CHAPTER 31

Telling the children their father had died was one of the hardest situations Isadora had ever experienced.

Prim and Henry had taken it hard, retreating into tears and silence, while Violet had merely climbed into Isadora's lap, where she'd stayed for hours. Daisy, on the other hand, being all of three, had not been as affected. She'd snuggled against Ian as he'd sat in a chair, saying "Poor Papa" a few times before she'd scrambled off Ian's lap to play with Sparky when the dog came searching for her.

Ian had dealt remarkably well with the children. He'd hurried to assure them they'd have a permanent home with him, already having summoned a fellow attorney to draw up adoption papers so the children would know their futures were secure. Being an intuitive sort, and perhaps because he'd lost his parents at an early age as well, although she'd yet to hear the full story about his father, he'd told the children that although he was adopting them, he expected them to continue calling him Ian since he had no intention of trying to replace the father they'd obviously loved.

Realizing Ian was giving them a forever home, one that included Aunt Birdie and Uncle Amos, who'd already assumed the role of grandparents, the children seemed as if they'd had a great weight lifted off their small shoulders. What Isadora's role was to be in the family, she truly had no idea. But Ian had begun watching her with something interesting in his eyes, something that seemed to hold a bit of promise, although what . . .

"Ah, Izzie, there you are," Aunt Birdie said, walking into the drawing room, where Izzie was unpacking some curtains that had just been delivered from Joseph Horne Company. "Ian asked me to tell you that he, Amos, and the children are taking Buttercup, Elmer, and Sparky for a walk around the grounds. He didn't want you to worry." She took a seat in a chair that had also just been delivered and beamed a smile Isadora's way. "I must say, I'm pleased that Ian's made himself so readily available to the children. Why, he's only left the house that one time to fetch papers from his office concerning a pressing matter of business, but he's not spent much time with those business matters over the past two days. I have high hopes that means he's finally getting his priorities straight *and* learning that increasing his fortune isn't the most important thing in the world."

"He's certainly settled well into the role of guardian."

Aunt Birdie sent her a pointed look. "He makes a good father figure, which most ladies do find very appealing in a gentleman."

Isadora fought a smile. "You do know that you've been abandoning any semblance of delicacy lately pertaining to your matchmaking efforts, don't you?"

"Delicacy is overrated, in my humble opinion." Aunt Birdie's eyes began to twinkle. "And since that's out of the way, allow me to tell you yet again that I believe you really should reconsider attending the ball tonight with Ian. It would be a lovely evening for you and would also give you an opportunity to spend time with Ian without the children around."

"Delightful as that sounds, I can't attend the ball because I have nothing suitable to wear, no matter that the lovely Miss Moore proclaimed I'd be fine wearing a plain skirt and blouse."

"I would have thought you'd use the excuse of not believing you'd find yourself comfortable at a society ball instead of the tried-and-true excuse of not having something to wear."

Isadora refused to rise to that bait. "Ian said something similar earlier, although he was a little sneakier about it, using one of those catch-me-by-surprise tactics I'm certain he often puts to good use as an attorney."

"You'll have to disclose all your secrets to us eventually, dear. I'm beginning to wonder why you've held them so close to you this long. You and Ian clearly have a fondness for each other." She smiled. "You also share an easy camaraderie, and there's no denying how well both of you interact together with the children."

Since she'd not neglected to notice how easy it was being around Ian, but since he had yet to broach the topic of *them*, or what he thought might be possible between them, Isadora wasn't certain how to respond. She readily admitted, at least to herself, that her feelings for Ian were changing. She was no longer merely smitten with the man, but something decidedly more. But because she wasn't certain if he returned those feelings, and she was, for all intents and purposes, his employee, she felt uncertain of what to do next.

"I could always alter something you have in that trunk of yours so you'd feel suitably dressed to attend the ball."

Pulling herself from her thoughts, Isadora grinned. "I assure you, Aunt Birdie, even though everyone has remarked time and time again on how large my trunk is, there's nothing resembling a ball gown stuffed inside it. Besides, according to Ian, he's merely going to attend the ball for a short time, since he apparently promised his friend Victor he'd go. However, because we're at a riveting point in *Treasure Island*, he wants to be home to read with the children before they go to bed. That means it would hardly be worth my while to go through the fuss that's needed to prepare for a ball."

"You know how much fuss is needed to prepare for a ball?"

"Did you ever consider that I might have once worked as a lady's maid?"

"Have you seen what your hair looks like when Prim's not around to style it for you?"

"A fair point," Isadora conceded. "So allow me to simply say this—yes, I've attended balls."

"And when are you going to disclose that to Ian?"

"When the moment is right?"

Aunt Birdie considered her for a moment before she nodded to a chair next to her. "Sit."

Isadora abandoned the curtains, knowing there was nothing to do but take a seat because Aunt Birdie clearly had something she wanted to say and she seemed to think Isadora needed to sit down to hear it. Lowering herself into the chair, she folded her hands in her lap and smiled. "I'm sitting."

"So I see, and sitting with perfect posture, I must add, something you've frequently taken to abandoning since you've come to stay with us."

"Have I really?"

"You have, and good for you, I say." Aunt Birdie leaned forward. "It shows you've become comfortable around us, and it also suggests you're finally becoming comfortable with the Izzie you want to be, not the Izzie I fear you've been told you're supposed to be."

Before Isadora could think on that, Aunt Birdie settled back into her chair. "I'm sure you're aware that I was wary about you from the moment Ian carried you into the farmhouse, dripping wet and already beginning to break out in a spectacular rash. Even after you disclosed a few of your secrets to me, I still continued to keep a close eye on you."

"That's disconcerting."

Aunt Birdie waved that aside. "You were a woman of mystery, but more importantly, you'd captured Ian's interest, and because of that, and because he's dearer to me than anything, I was determined to figure you out."

"And have you?"

"Not quite, but I do know this—you're a woman who seems to be coming into your own, finally discovering what's important to you. That's a blessing right there, and something not everyone experiences." Aunt Birdie nodded. "I believe Ian is becoming important to you, and because of that, and because you're becoming important to him as well, he deserves to hear the truth. All of it."

Even knowing Aunt Birdie was right, and even though she'd been trying to compose a bit of a speech to use when she finally got up the nerve to disclose her true identity to Ian, Isadora simply hadn't found the courage to reveal all her secrets just yet.

"What if I tell Ian everything and the friendship that's developed between us changes?" she finally asked.

"To point out the obvious, dear, you and Ian have developed feelings for each other that go beyond mere friendship."

Isadora couldn't disagree with that, at least as it pertained to *her* feelings for the man.

She'd never been as attracted to a gentleman before. She'd also never enjoyed the sense of ease she felt whenever she was in Ian's presence. She'd laughed more while in his company than she'd ever laughed in her life. But she was afraid that if she told him she was a New York high-society lady, their relationship would turn more formal, no easy laughter to be found.

Aunt Birdie suddenly reached over and took hold of her hand, pulling Isadora from her thoughts. "You, my dear child, have been given the unusual blessing of landing in a world I believe is completely foreign to you. That blessing has allowed you to grow, putting you, or so I believe, on a new path. Ian's also been shown a new path for his life. God, I'm sure, is opening his eyes to the possibility of helping those in need rather than pursuing a future that was rather self-serving." Aunt Birdie gave Isadora's hand a pat. "God allows us to choose the direction those paths He shows us will take, so now it's up to you and Ian to decide if you want to forge a new path together, one I'm certain will exceed your wildest dreams. But to do that, you're going to have to tell him everything."

"I wish I had your confidence in believing God's hand has been in all I've experienced of late, but . . ."

The rest of her words got lost when Henry suddenly burst into the room, carrying Elmer under his arm while Buttercup ambled into the room behind him.

"Did you forget that Buttercup isn't allowed in the house, or that Elmer isn't allowed on the table?" Isadora asked as Henry immediately plucked Elmer off the table he'd just set her on and tucked her back underneath his arm.

"Sorry, Izzie, I forgot. Ian wanted me to come and tell you we got company. He also said that me and the girls had to come inside lickety-split with Uncle Amos." His eyes turned wide. "Jonathon's come back, and he's got Hank with him. But when I went up to the carriage to say howdy to Hank, he didn't say howdy back." Henry gave Elmer a squeeze, which she didn't seem to appreciate since she let out a squawk. "He don't seem like he wants to get out of the carriage, but that might be because Sparky's standing right outside the carriage, snarling up a storm."

Rising from the chair, Isadora headed for the door, pausing when Uncle Amos hurried into the room, holding Violet's and Daisy's hands while Prim followed behind them.

"Ian wants us to stay in the house," Uncle Amos said, sending a look to Aunt Birdie that she immediately seemed to understand because she was on her feet in no time.

"Children, what say we go into the kitchen? I've found a delightful recipe for a strawberry cake, and I could use some help baking it."

"I'll stay here with Buttercup," Uncle Amos said before he smiled at Henry. "And I'll watch over Elmer as well. I don't think that fancy chef Jonathon hired yesterday will appreciate having animals in his kitchen, although he might not be too keen on having all of you descend on him either."

Aunt Birdie's nose shot into the air. "Mr. Irvin may be a most sought-after chef, Amos, but given I know what Ian is paying him, I don't believe he'll give us a bit of trouble." With that, she ushered the children out of the drawing room, leaving Isadora and Uncle Amos behind.

"Perhaps I should take Buttercup back to the garden," Isadora suggested.

"You don't need an excuse to see what's happening with Hank, child. Ian asked me to tell you he'd like you to join them. I'll mind Buttercup and Elmer, make sure they don't get a hankering for any of the lovely flower arrangements you've put in this room."

Leaving Uncle Amos leading Buttercup toward the fireplace, although there was no fire in the grate, Isadora thought she saw him spread out a lovely blanket she'd been intending to use in the library right before encouraging Buttercup to lie down on it.

Fighting a smile, she strode down the hallway, stopping in the entranceway when the door opened and Ian stepped over the threshold, holding Hank's arm while Jonathon brought up the rear.

"What room should we use?" was all Ian said to Isadora.

"The pink receiving room has the most furniture."

To her surprise, Ian's lips twitched just the slightest bit. "I have a pink receiving room?"

"In all honesty, it's more along the lines of salmon, but that doesn't sound nearly as appealing as the pink room."

"To the pink room it is, then," Jonathon said, giving Hank a prod with what Isadora only then realized was a pistol.

"Is that necessary?" she whispered as they hurried toward the receiving room.

"He wouldn't cooperate or come with me until I pulled this out," Jonathon returned. "But I'm not going to use it on him, not unless he turns difficult."

Blinking when Jonathon sent her the tiniest of winks, Isadora followed everyone into the pink room, watching as Hank put up a bit of a struggle when Ian tried to get him into a chair, that struggle ending when Jonathon gave a wave of his pistol. Ian then got her settled on a pink fainting couch, taking a seat beside her while Jonathon remained standing, keeping the pistol trained on Hank.

When silence settled over the room as Ian merely sat and stared at Hank, Isadora cleared her throat.

"Would anyone care for me to fetch some tea?"

Ian turned her way and frowned. "You've clearly never been involved in an interrogation before. Normally, tea is not served, and normally, when the lead interrogator is staring the perpetrator down, no one interrupts with an offer to fetch tea."

"Is that what you were doing? Staring him down?"

"I was, but it's hardly likely to work now, since we've disclosed the tactic I was attempting to use."

"Maybe I really should fetch some tea and leave you and Jonathon to handle the matter without further disruptions from me."

"Or you could simply sit there. Perhaps quietly?"

"I could do that," Isadora muttered even as Jonathon seemed to press his lips together to contain a smile, an odd circumstance if there ever was one, considering the situation.

"I wouldn't mind some tea, and I also wouldn't mind if someone would explain to me why I've been abducted," Hank said as he glared all around. "It was hardly my fault Amos went after me with an axe, forcing me to quit my position. But even if I did leave you in the lurch, Mr. MacKenzie, I don't think that warrants this shabby treatment I'm suffering today."

As Ian leaned forward, Isadora suddenly saw the door open a few inches ever so carefully, revealing a face that certainly belonged to Henry.

She got to her feet. "Excuse me. I'll be right back." She lowered her voice and leaned toward Ian. "We've got a visitor, but I'll see to him. Don't feel as if you need to wait for me to return before you try out another one of your interrogation tactics."

"Those tactics aren't as effective if you give notice about them," Ian muttered while Jonathon might have released a snort.

"Right, sorry." With that, Isadora headed for the door, not surprised when Henry's face suddenly disappeared and the sound of scampering feet echoed down the hallway. Henry, on the other hand, certainly seemed surprised when she caught up with him and Sparky.

Taking hold of his arm, she pulled Henry to a stop. "Aren't you supposed to be helping in the kitchen right now?"

Henry swiped a hand over his nose. "The girls are still gettin' all the ingredients together. That's boring. 'Sides, Sparky wanted me to come with him to check on Hank." Henry reached into his back pocket and pulled out his slingshot. "I figured since Sparky was snarlin' at Hank, and 'cuz he wanted to lead me to him, that Hank ain't a nice man after all. That's why I was fixin' on givin' Ian my slingshot."

"No one is going to use a slingshot on Hank."

"They gonna use that pistol I saw Jonathon holding instead?"

"No. Now go back into the kitchen, take Sparky with you, and don't let me catch you outside the door to the pink room again. Understand?"

Henry sent her a scowl, grabbed hold of Sparky's collar, then stomped his way toward the kitchen, muttering something about no longer liking her. That, curiously, left her feeling as if she'd just passed some type of milestone—one where she'd gone from carefree society lady to a strict, almost matronly type who was obviously doing something right since Henry was so put out with her.

Waiting until she was certain Henry was heading for the kitchen and not trying to sneak back again, Isadora turned and walked toward the pink room.

She stepped inside and closed the door firmly behind her, lingering there so she wouldn't disrupt Ian, who seemed to be in the midst of another interrogation technique, one where he was speaking in an almost soothing fashion.

". . . and there's no use continuing to try and convince us everything that happened on the farm was Uncle Amos's fault, Hank. We know you were lying to him, lying to the folks in town, and causing mayhem in your wake. We also know that you were merely doing all those things at the bidding of someone else, and if you cooperate with us, I, as an attorney, can strike a deal with the judge who'll be hearing your case, a deal that might not see you behind bars for as many years as you're facing now."

"Telling lies isn't a crime."

"But arson is. I'm also fairly sure no judge is going to be lenient with you after they learn you were responsible for tampering with a plow that could have killed a seventy-nine-year-old woman or for tampering with a wheel that fell off a wagon carrying four young children."

"Birdie wasn't supposed to be on that plow, Amos was, and—" Hank suddenly stopped talking and pressed his lips together, as if he'd just realized what he'd revealed.

Ian smiled in satisfaction as he stood and nodded to Isadora. "Perhaps you should go and fetch us that tea, Izzie. I have a feeling it might take a while to get the full story out of Hank, but—" His smile turned deadly as his gaze settled on Hank. "I will get the full story out of you. Do know that I'll do whatever it takes to squeeze every last bit of confession from you, even if whatever it takes is somewhat . . . unpleasant."

That threat was all it took for Hank to start talking. By the time three pots of tea had been consumed, along with the cake Aunt Birdie and the children made, Isadora, along with Ian and Jonathon, knew the very worst of what Hank had done—as well as who'd hired him to do those things.

CHAPTER 32

"It's too bad you wouldn't agree to go to the ball with Ian, Izzie," Prim said, looking up from the copy of *Little Women* she was reading. "I just reached the part in the story where the March sisters are getting ready to attend a ball." She nodded to Isadora's head. "I bet I could have done something fancy with your hair."

"And she could've worn the necklace me and Daisy just made for her, which we're hopin' you think is real pretty, Izzie," Violet said, moving quietly into the room as she always did, Daisy dashing past her a second later to scramble up into Isadora's lap.

"Present!" Daisy bellowed even as Violet came to a stop in front of Isadora and shyly held out a necklace made of braided yarn with daisies, violets, and roses woven into the braid.

If she hadn't already lost her heart to the two little girls grinning back at her, as well as Prim, who'd abandoned her book to come take a look, their gift would have certainly done the trick.

"You made this for me?" she managed to ask as her vision turned blurry.

"It's got violets, daisies, and a rose for Prim," Violet told her. "We couldn't find a primrose, so that had to do." She wrinkled her nose. "We was going to add this little chicken that Uncle Amos helped Henry whittle, but we don't know where Henry's run off to right now."

"I'm right here," Henry said, stomping into the room and looking grumpy, Elmer tucked under his arm and Sparky walking by his side. He set Elmer on the floor and fished something out of his pocket. "This don't really look like Elmer, but that's what it's supposed to be. Uncle Amos helped me put a ring through it so you can put it on the thing the girls made you." He stomped his way to stand in front of her, thrusting out his offering a second later.

"Should I assume you're put out about something?" Isadora asked, taking the small whittled chicken from the little boy as she fought a grin.

"I've been banished from the first floor . . . again."

"What'd you do now?" Prim demanded, looking every inch the older sister as she plunked her hands on her slim hips.

"Nothin'. Some man dressed up fancy like Ian just arrived, and it weren't more than a minute after he arrived in the library, where me and Ian were getting down to a serious checker match, that I was sent packin'." He blew out a disgusted breath. "Not that I hate spendin' time with all of you, but you are *girls*."

"Indeed we are," Isadora said, setting Daisy to the ground before she rose from the chair. "And even though I'm sure you want to return to your checkers, I expect you to stay here with your sisters while I see who has come to call. I imagine it's probably Mr. Victor Laughlin, one of Ian's friends. Ian mentioned he might come visit soon to meet all of you."

"It's not that man. It's someone by the name of Nigel," Henry said. "And I don't know if you should be leaving this room either, Izzie. Ian had a funny look in his eye when Nigel walked into the room, and when he said that man's name, it wasn't in what I'd call a friendly voice."

Isadora was across the room in a flash, pausing by the door when Henry called after her.

"You might want to tell Buttercup I'm not gonna be coming

back anytime soon. She's waitin' for me at the bottom of the stairs, seein' as how she don't know how to climb them just yet."

She turned. "You let Buttercup into the house again? I thought we talked about that, Henry. She's supposed to stay outside in the garden."

"She don't like the garden, but I'm not sayin' I let her in the house. Maybe she done learned how to open the door."

She leveled what she hoped was a stern eye on the boy. "We'll be having a discussion about telling fibs when I return."

Leaving Henry looking remarkably guilty and Prim immediately launching into her own lecture on the subject of telling fibs, Isadora quit the room, feeling somewhat guilty as well since she'd been less than truthful of late.

She hurried down the two flights of stairs to reach the main floor, pulling the flower necklace the girls had made her over her head as she moved to where voices were sounding from the library. Hesitating in front of the open door, she glanced at Ian, who had his back turned to her, then stiffened when she realized Nigel had spotted her and was beaming far too brightly her way.

"*Mrs. Delmont*, I was hoping I'd get to see you," Nigel exclaimed as Ian spun around, a crystal decanter in his hand. "Do come and join us. Ian's pouring us both a brandy. Would you care for one?"

Walking into the room, Isadora shook her head. "I'm not really a brandy type, Mr. Flaherty."

"My apologies, Mrs. Delmont. Should I assume you're more of . . ." He paused and tilted his head. "What is that wine Mr. Ward McAllister always goes on about? Is it the 1871 Latour or the 1879 Brion?"

The hair on the nape of her neck stood to attention.

After seeing her father's very good friend Mr. William Rives in the tearoom, Isadora had been truly concerned that he'd recognized her. But when Mr. Rives hadn't bothered to seek her out or walk over to Ian after she'd left the table and inquire whether or not Ian was in the company of Miss Isadora Delafield, she had decided he'd not recognized her at all and had probably only been looking her way because Nigel had been telling tales of how a household manager was enjoying a cup of tea with an esteemed man of Pittsburgh business.

She might have been mistaken about that.

Forcing down the response that sprang to her lips—everyone knew Mr. Ward McAllister was infatuated with the 1871 Latour— Isadora gave an airy wave of her hand. "I'm sure I wouldn't know the answer to that, Mr. Flaherty."

"Please, call me Nigel, and may I say that's a lovely necklace you're wearing. It certainly dresses up the outfit you've apparently chosen to wear to the ball, taking Miss Moore's suggestion, of course. Do know that I *completely* understand why you'd make use of such a clever—"

"She's not going to the ball, Nigel," Ian interrupted, all but thrusting a glass of brandy at him. "But since the ball is starting soon, what say we forgo these banal pleasantries and delve into the reason you're here? Should I assume it's about Hank?"

"Who?"

Ian inclined his head. "Ah, so we're going to play games, are we? Very well, let me refresh your memory. Hank is the man you and your investors hired to muscle people off their farms when they wouldn't sell their land to you."

Nigel took a sip of his brandy, and then, surprisingly enough, he took a seat on a settee that had only just been delivered that day. He nodded to a chair beside him and ignored that Ian was glaring at him because he'd taken a seat before Isadora had taken hers. Isadora took the arm Ian held out to her, soon finding herself sitting in the chair farthest removed from Nigel. Ian, however, after he'd poured a glass of wine and handed it to her, took a seat directly beside his guest.

Taking a sip of his brandy, Ian smiled, although it was a rather terrifying sort of smile and didn't bode well for Nigel. "Now then, where were we?"

"You were prattling on about some man named Hank," Nigel said.

"I'm afraid I'm not the one prone to prattling, whereas Hank, well, when faced with a rather lengthy prison term unless he co-operated, was prattling for all of an hour right in this very house before he was taken off to jail."

Nigel's eyes narrowed. "Since I am unfamiliar with anyone by the name of Hank, I'm not certain what this man could have possibly said to make you believe I'm involved in any shenanigans."

"So that coal mining venture you're a part of isn't trying to acquire land in and outside of Canonsburg?"

A single bead of sweat ran down the side of Nigel's face, which he ignored. "There are many coal ventures being planned for that area."

"Yes, but unfortunately, the venture I know you're involved with is simply not going to happen."

Nigel's gaze sharpened on Ian's face. "What do you mean?"

Ian swirled the brandy around in his glass before he lifted his head and smiled. "I think *not going to happen* is self-explanatory. But if you need clarification . . ." His smile turned deadly. "I've only just purchased, as in an hour ago, every single one of those farms you had your sights on down by Canonsburg. It's really quite remarkable how quickly word can reach a town through the telegram. But since a very good friend of my Uncle Amos runs the telegraph station, he very kindly saw to it that the telegrams I sent out were immediately delivered, and that the responses to those telegrams reached me in a timely fashion. Clearly, the good folks of Canonsburg are far more receptive to selling me their land than you."

For a long moment, Nigel didn't say anything, but then he rose to his feet. "There are other powerful men involved in this deal, MacKenzie. They'll not take kindly to you ruining everything."

Ian's smile turned deadlier than ever. "That's where I think you're mistaken, Flaherty. You see, as an attorney, I realize what happens when the law needs to deal with powerful men. Yes, I've gotten Hank to confess that it was you who hired him, but you and I know that your attorney, a man I've often gone up against, and a

314

man who possesses formidable skill, will convince a judge or a jury that you were completely ignorant of the means Hank was going to use to get the land you wanted. Why, I even imagine your attorney will go about the unpleasant business of paying people off, which means you'll never see so much as a day in jail over crimes you and I know you were responsible for ordering. However, I'm a powerful man as well—not as powerful as you, of course—but I'm respected. I have to believe the other investors will not want to get into the mud with us if I threaten to press charges against you, even if those charges won't amount to much."

Ian got to his feet and faced Nigel. "While it is true that most people turn a blind eye to some of the questionable tactics men of business use to get what they want, I'm afraid I can't do that in this instance since you went after my family. It's not possible for me to allow you to blithely walk away without some type of punishment. That is exactly why I decided the best punishment I could give was taking something from you that would affect your bottom line."

For a second, Isadora feared Nigel was going to punch Ian, but then, concerningly enough, he turned and leveled cold eyes on her, looking her over for an uncomfortable minute before he returned his attention to Ian.

"You should remember I'm not a man to be crossed, Mac-Kenzie. I'll ruin you, but before I get to that, as luck would have it, I currently have the means to take something from you as well—your self-respect and pride."

"Do tell," Ian all but drawled.

"Oh, I shall, and I'll enjoy every second of it." Nigel nodded to Isadora. "It just so happens that what I have to say involves your household manager, *Mrs. Delmont*."

The hair on the nape of her neck stood to attention again as all the breath got stuck in her throat.

"You'll leave Izzie out of this, Nigel, and that's not up for debate."

"Ah yes, dear *Izzie*. What a delightful name, and even though

I'd love to leave the lovely lady *out of this*, I'm afraid I can't because, you see . . ."

Isadora braced herself, knowing without a doubt that what Nigel was going to say next was not going to be pleasant.

"That lady sitting over there is no Mrs. Delmont. She's Miss Isadora Delafield, esteemed member of the New York Four Hundred, and one of the great American heiresses of today."

CHAPTER 33

As the seconds ticked away and Isadora didn't dispute Nigel's outlandish claims, Ian suddenly realized, given the starkness of her face and the panic in her eyes, that she *wasn't* going to dispute the claims because they were nothing less than the truth.

The affection he'd held for her began to shrivel in that moment as unpleasant reality settled.

She'd played him for a fool.

How she must have laughed at him as she'd offered her deal of working without pay, one he'd thought spoke highly of her work ethic, but a deal he now understood must have been nothing but a lark, given the fortune she clearly commanded.

"Oh dear . . . Do not tell me you were foolish enough to form an attachment with Miss Delafield, MacKenzie. But given the anguish in your eyes as you wait for her to say I'm lying is certain proof that you have."

Ian set aside his glass of brandy so that he wouldn't shatter the glass as his hand clenched around it. "It's time for you to leave, Nigel."

"But the fun's just starting. Don't you want to know how I discovered her identity—or better yet, why I believe she left New York?"

The emotional part of him wanted nothing of the sort, but the lawyer in him craved answers, which had him inclining his head. "Very well. Go on."

Nigel puffed out his chest. "From what I learned, it appears as if Miss Delafield was going on one of those—how do you call it?—ah yes, 'flights of fancy' that are popular with so many impetuous young ladies. She obviously thought it would be a dramatic adventure to assume an identity that was so far removed from who she truly is, and it was a most brilliant plan." He inclined his head to Izzie. "Brilliant until you let your guard down and allowed yourself to be seen in public at Joseph Horne Company."

Izzie didn't say a single word to that, although her lips thinned and something interesting flashed through her eyes.

"Imagine my surprise," Nigel continued, "when after I was introduced to Mr. William Rives, a wealthy industrialist who was visiting from New York City, I was then presented with a prime opportunity to see you laid low, MacKenzie. Not that I realized that while I was enjoying tea with him and the Bryces."

"I don't know Mr. and Mrs. Bryce, nor do I know a Mr. William Rives."

"That's precisely why I was pointing you out to them," Nigel returned with a nasty smile. "As I was doing that, after having mentioned that you were the negotiator who probably lost Mr. Bryce a whole lot of money since his family is invested in the mills, Mr. Rives made a most shocking statement." Nigel returned his attention to Izzie. "He, for the briefest of moments, thought he recognized you as being the daughter of one of his very good friends, a Mr. Frederick Delafield. I did get a chuckle out of that and immediately explained to the man that you were merely MacKenzie's household manager, a woman bereft of any of the social graces."

Nigel's smile turned smug. "Now, I normally wouldn't have given Mr. Rives's remark further consideration, but you annoy me, MacKenzie, what with your propensity for getting up on your soapbox to promote better working conditions for the laborers. I followed up on Mr. Rives's observation because of that, and because I did think there was something odd about your household manager, since it's rare indeed to witness a woman—even of the servant class—eating cake with her fingers and not making use of her napkin." Nigel stopped speaking and sent a pleasant smile Isadora's way. "That was a lovely bit of acting on your part, Miss Delafield, although I'm not certain that mother of yours would care to entertain the thought of her only daughter taking to the stage."

"You've spoken with my mother?" Isadora whispered.

"I've not had the pleasure . . . yet." Nigel looked back at Ian. "But to continue my story, after I did a bit of sleuthing and discovered that Mrs. Delmont was going by the name of Izzie, which is remarkably similar to Isadora if you think about it, just as Delmont is remarkably similar to Delafield, it got me thinking. Because I'm a man with unlimited funds, I happen to have an honest-to-goodness personal telephone in my house, and even though it cost me a small fortune to have lines set up between here and New York, I've found the luxury of having a telephone to be well worth the cost. I was able to place a call to a very savvy contact I have in my pocket in New York City, and then he, very quickly, was able to phone me back with some astonishing information regarding your Mrs. Delmont."

Ian fought to keep his expression carefully schooled, even though he wanted nothing more than to scowl at Isadora, who was now paler than ever but looking rather resolved.

Nigel chuckled. "What I discovered about her was this: Rumors are rampant about Miss Isadora Delafield. She's apparently gone missing, although her mother is claiming she's merely off on a flight of fancy before she makes a most advantageous marriage— and to a duke, no less."

"That's not true," Isadora said, rising to her feet. She set aside her glass of wine with a hand that Ian couldn't help but notice was trembling. "I am not a lady to go off on flights of fancy. And I have no intention of marrying the Duke of Montrose."

"That's not what my source told me," Nigel contradicted. "He told me that you're known to be a somewhat snobbish sort, spoiled as well. Because of that, and because the duke is most sought after by many New York socialites, you left the city to pique the duke's interest and to ensure he'd choose you to wed at the end of the season."

Nigel turned back to Ian. "It's a shame you allowed yourself to become involved with Miss Delafield, although I'm sure you wouldn't have allowed that to happen if you'd truly known who she was. No grand heiress will settle for a man who grew up in abject poverty with a drunk for a father, but you won't have to tolerate her being under your roof for long. I took it upon myself to send one of those telegrams you so enjoy to the Delafield house, not wanting to impart such delicate information over telephone lines, which are occasionally unsecure."

He presented Izzie with a bow. "I'm sure your family will be here within the next day or two. I sent that telegram yesterday and included your current address for their convenience. Why, I imagine they're even now on a train, anxious to fetch their missing and, let me add, *troublesome* daughter home."

Nigel sent Ian another smile. "Now, if you'll excuse me, I'm off to the ball. Do feel free to still attend, MacKenzie. You might be in for an embarrassing time of it, though, because I intend to spread the tale of Miss Delafield's duplicity far and wide—a bit of retaliation, if you will, for costing me the loss of those potential coalfields. I must say, I'm relishing the thought of disclosing to Pittsburgh society that you're nothing but a fool."

With that, Nigel turned and sauntered from the room, laughter drifting after him.

Silence settled in his wake, and knowing there was nothing to do but hear the worst of it, Ian turned to Izzie. "It's true, then?"

"I can explain."

His heart wanted to believe her, but his head, the part that had allowed him to amass an enormous fortune by using the wits God had given him, balked. "And will it be a factual explanation or more of the lies you're obviously proficient at spinning?"

Additional color leached from her face as she raised a hand to her throat. "I understand you're angry. I would be too, but—"

"*Angry* doesn't do justice to what I currently feel toward you. You've made a fool of me, Izzie—" He caught himself. "I mean, Isadora. And for that, I'm afraid I'll never be able to forgive you."

Unshed tears sparkled in her eyes, eyes that were no longer covered by the spectacles she'd taken to abandoning whenever she was in the house—spectacles that had certainly only been a clever prop to disguise her true identity.

"It was never my intention to hurt you or make a fool of you. I was merely trying to avoid the attentions of a most repulsive man."

"You would have me believe you're not interested in a duke?"

"I'm not. He's lecherous, won't take no for an answer, and after I gave him the cut direct in the middle of a Newport ball, I apparently became a challenge to him—and one he wasn't willing to lose."

"You attended a ball in Newport?"

"Well, yes, but if I'd known the Duke of Montrose was going to take such an interest in me, I would have pleaded a headache and not attended."

"Does your family own one of those grand cottages I've heard about in Newport?"

"Are you going to become even more furious with me if I admit that we do?"

"That's a strong possibility."

Isadora blew out a breath. "We do own a cottage in Newport, as well as numerous other homes throughout the country . . . and a small house in Scotland."

Ian raked a hand through his hair. "What could have possibly possessed you to come up with a plan to disguise yourself as a housekeeper and seek out employment?"

"No one ever notices the help, and no one in their right mind would have considered that I might go off on my own and take up a position." She took a step closer to him, freezing when he took a step back. "I only did so after I was convinced by a man who used to work for the duke that my very life was in danger."

"In danger because you'd have to move to England, where the weather is frequently far chillier than it is in New York and you might catch a cold?"

Her chin lifted, and her eyes turned chilly, lending clear credence to the fact that she was, indeed, a high-society lady. "Don't be insulting."

"My apologies, but I find it a little difficult to summon up any sympathies for you when you've cast me in the part of fool. My father, besides being an abusive man, enjoyed ridiculing me. He'd mock my efforts to try and please him in front of his cronies, and I swore after Aunt Birdie and Uncle Amos took me away from him that I would never allow anyone to play me for a fool again. I also vowed I'd never place myself in a situation where I'd feel abandoned, because that's one of the most helpless feelings in the world—waiting for someone you hold in affection to return to you. I finally accepted that my father had abandoned me and was never going to return to apologize, but I allowed you into my heart, Izzie, and yet, clearly, you had plans to abandon me all along."

"That's not true."

Ian arched a brow. "You would have me believe that you were considering staying in Pennsylvania with me when you evidently have unlimited access to a great fortune and are a member of the New York Four Hundred?"

"When you put it like that, it does sound unbelievable, but I *did* want to stay here with you and the children. And I was going to tell you everything. Nigel simply beat me to it."

"I don't believe you. You can say you meant to tell me, but you've had plenty of time."

She dashed a tear from her cheek. "Did you ever consider that perhaps I didn't tell you everything because I wanted you to continue treating me as a normal woman? Not as an heiress who would immediately send you to the very top of every societal ladder in the country if it became known you and I were forming an . . . attachment?"

"As you said earlier, don't be insulting. Do I strike you as a man who'd be comfortable using your social status to improve my lot in life?"

"You're the one who told everyone that your goal in life, besides amassing a fortune, was to marry well."

Ian blinked as he realized that was certainly nothing less than the truth. He frowned. "I concede that point, but do know that I've changed my mind about only marrying a woman of a certain social standing. That goal seems ridiculous to me now."

"And how was I supposed to know that?"

"How was I supposed to know that you were the type of lady to show no qualms about embracing such duplicity, especially since you've allowed the children to become attached to you, as well as Aunt Birdie and Uncle Amos?" he countered.

"I was in fear for my life."

"Right. From a duke."

"Rumor has it he's done away with his previous three wives. Should I have allowed this man to continue pursuing me, knowing he could very well do away with me if I didn't produce that 'heir and a spare' he told everyone he so desperately needed?"

Ian frowned. "I'm sure those rumors are exaggerated, just as I'm sure you could have avoided this duke's attention without assuming a new identity or insinuating yourself into my household. The children, who I should remind you are still recovering from the shock of their father's death, have come to love you, as have—" he paused, drawing in a deep breath before he continued—"as have Aunt Birdie and Uncle Amos, and that, my dear, is a most grievous offense."

"I love the children, as well as Aunt Birdie and Uncle Amos. I did not deliberately set out to—"

"I'm afraid I don't have the patience to listen to more of your lies and excuses. You're welcome to stay here until your family comes to fetch you, if that occurs within the next two days. If they don't arrive in a timely fashion, though, I'll arrange to have Jonathon escort you back to New York, and to . . . Fifth Avenue, I assume?"

Izzie's eyes flashed with a bit of temper. "What will you do if the Duke of Montrose shows up in my parents' stead? Hand me over to him and wash your hands of me once and for all?"

"You're being insulting again. If this duke shows up here, and if you want nothing to do with him, he'll not get near you. You have my word on that." He ignored the fresh sheen of tears in her eyes. "Now, if you'll excuse me, I have a ball to attend."

"But Nigel said he was going to tell everyone about me tricking you."

"That is precisely why I'm going." Ian smiled. "You may have made a fool of me, Isadora, but I'm more than capable of reclaiming my pride and my reputation. I would suggest you spend the evening packing your belongings. I don't want you to have an excuse to linger under my roof after your family arrives." With that, he inclined his head, turned on his heel, and strode from the room, calling himself every sort of a fool because he'd been tempted to take back his hurtful words after he'd noticed that the tears that had been brimming in her eyes had begun to trail down her far-too-beautiful face.

CHAPTER 34

Slipping out the front door the next afternoon, Isadora drew the hood of the cloak she'd found at the bottom of her trunk over her head, protecting her hair from the drizzle of a gloomy day that mirrored her thoughts.

She'd not followed Ian's instructions to gather all her belongings and have them packed and ready to go when her family came to fetch her. That blatant bit of mutiny was a direct result of her making a most monumental decision—she wasn't going to leave Pittsburgh, not unless Ian personally put her on a train, because . . .

She'd fallen in love with the life she'd been living of late, fallen in love with the children, Aunt Birdie, Uncle Amos, Buttercup, Sparky, even Elmer, and . . .

She was in love, and not merely a little bit, with Ian. In all honesty, she was completely and utterly in love with that exasperating man, but she'd hurt him, undeniably so.

That hurt was one of the biggest regrets of her life, but she wasn't willing to merely do as he asked and depart from his life, not until she was given an opportunity to tell him she loved him and to beg his forgiveness.

In order to do that, though, she needed some space to gather

her thoughts and compose a compelling argument that would convince him she was worthy of another chance and worthy of his love.

Nodding to a well-dressed lady pushing a pram that she'd almost barreled into as she'd been lost in thought, Isadora ignored the sharp glance the lady sent her, wondering if the lady was trying to decide if she was the notorious Isadora Delafield, whose secret had evidently been exposed the night before at Miss Moore's ball.

Ian had, indeed, gone to the ball, and from what she'd learned as she'd been eavesdropping on a conversation he'd had with Aunt Birdie earlier that morning, Nigel had been as good as his word, telling everyone gathered at the ball about Isadora's true identity. Ian, however, instead of allowing himself to become the focus of Pittsburgh gossip, had apparently turned Nigel's story around. Undoubtedly using charm to great effect, he'd spun a tale that convinced the guests he'd known Isadora's secret all along, and that he'd been the one to offer her a place of refuge to recover from a social season in Newport that had turned overly demanding.

Instead of being annoyed with Ian for painting her as an emotional sort, needing respite from the frivolities of a season, Isadora had found herself impressed by his explanation, as well as the fact that he'd apparently also managed to reveal Nigel's underhanded methods in attempting to acquire land from Uncle Amos and Aunt Birdie.

Pittsburgh society had not been amused, and even though Nigel, as so many men of fortune before him, would eventually find himself welcomed back into the folds of society, for now he'd been cast out. Not even Miss Moore was interested in continuing her association with him.

Turning from Fifth Avenue when she spotted a large tree that would shelter her from drizzle that was rapidly turning into large raindrops, Isadora stepped to the right to allow two gentlemen walking her way room enough to pass. Confusion was her first response when she felt one of those gentlemen take hold of her arm.

That confusion turned to horror a mere second later when she felt what was clearly a pistol poke into her side right as a closed carriage pulled up next to her.

A scream began bubbling up her throat, but before it could erupt through her lips, the carriage door opened and she was thrown inside, landing on the hard floor right as the door slammed shut and the carriage bolted into motion.

As she pushed herself up from the floor, the horror she'd been feeling turned to outrage when her attention settled on a gentleman sitting on the carriage seat. That gentleman was beaming a yellow-toothed smile and was, unfortunately, none other than the Duke of Montrose.

"Do know that it does pain me to see you gagged, my dear, but if you'll promise to refrain from taking me to task, I'll be more than happy to remove the gag. We'll then be free to discuss pleasant matters, such as poetry, my many estates in England, or how I intend to use that lovely dowry your delightful mother told me will be mine after you and I are married."

Sending the duke a glare as they bounced along a road that couldn't be considered well traveled, given its many holes and ruts, Isadora pondered his offer.

They'd been riding in the carriage for hours and had yet to discuss anything of importance, probably because she'd not been able to refrain from lecturing the man who'd had the audacity to abduct her. That lecturing finally earned her a gag after the duke proclaimed she was giving him a dreadful headache.

His headache had apparently only increased after she'd made three attempts to escape, each attempt unsuccessful and leaving her with numerous bruises incurred when she'd thrown herself from the moving carriage and tumbled to the ground.

The first time she'd tried to escape, the duke was taken by such surprise that he actually seemed to convince himself she'd tumbled from the carriage by accident, blaming a door that must not have been soundly latched.

However, by her second attempt, he'd begun keeping a closer eye on her, and by her third, well, after he'd jumped after her and pulled her from the mud puddle she'd landed in, he'd stuck his pistol into her side. Realizing he wouldn't be opposed to using that pistol on her, she'd climbed yet again into the carriage. The duke had then resorted to securing her leg with one end of a rope and tying the other end to his leg.

She'd been considering a fourth attempt, hoping to pull the man right out of the carriage with her. But when she'd tried to move her leg the slightest bit to test if her attempt would work, she'd not been able to move much at all, that trying circumstance a direct result of the duke being so portly.

Now, hours after her last attempt to escape, she was forced to sit in filthy clothing that was still wet, gagged as well as tethered, rapidly losing hope that she'd ever figure out a way to escape.

"Ah, I do believe we might be approaching our destination," the duke suddenly said as the carriage began to slow and he drew aside the curtain that covered the window. He smiled as the carriage came to a complete stop, returning his attention to her.

"I'm sure, like me, you'll be relieved to know that the carriage part of our trip is now at an end. We'll be taking a train from here." He leaned toward her. "I thought it prudent to travel by carriage until we were far removed from Pittsburgh. No sense in drawing someone's attention in that disgraceful and dirty city. That might very well have disrupted the plans I have for you, my dear."

Glancing to the window, Isadora would have smiled if not for the gag stuffed in her mouth. The station they'd stopped at was bustling with people. There was little likelihood that someone wouldn't take note of a woman with a rope around her leg and a gag in her mouth. All she needed to do was . . .

"A word of warning before we depart the carriage," the duke said, almost as if he had the ability to read her mind. "You should understand that even though I've decided you'll make a more-than-suitable wife for me, what with the fortune you have attached to your name and your beautiful face and figure, I'm not a man tolerant of shenanigans. And while I would be *most* disappointed to not return with you as my wife to England, there've been many ladies who've allowed me to know they're more than amenable to part with their fortunes to acquire that all-too-coveted title of duchess."

She tried to talk through the gag, wincing when he suddenly sat forward and pulled it from her mouth.

Stretching lips that had turned numb, Isadora cleared her throat. "Are you suggesting that if I pursue shenanigans, you're going to lose interest in me and set me free?"

"Lose interest in you, yes. Set you free, not a chance."

The implied threat behind those words was evident, but before Isadora could think of a response, the duke leveled a dangerous gaze at her.

"To ensure you don't do anything foolish, my dear, or anything that will draw undue attention while we board the special Pullman car my men have arranged for us, I should tell you that I left a man behind in Pittsburgh. If that man receives word from me—and I think you'll soon understand what type of word that will be—he'll then travel back to that lovely home you were staying in and . . . well, those were adorable children I saw you walking with around the grounds. It would be unfortunate if something of an unpleasant nature were to happen to them."

Any thought she had of trying to escape disappeared as fury licked its way through her veins. That the duke seemed to have no qualms about harming innocents was almost too much to take, but it meant she truly had no choice but to cooperate.

"Fine," she ground out through gritted teeth. "I'll behave."

"Now, that wasn't so hard, was it?" he countered as he bent to untie her leg before he did the same to his own. He then bundled her into her muddy cloak, tucking her hair under the hood, his hand lingering on her cheek and leaving her skin crawling.

Warning her to keep her head down as they quit the carriage, he led her to a private Pullman car at a station she learned was quite some miles east of Pittsburgh. The duke's men joined them to make certain the duke didn't want them to travel in the Pullman car with him since Isadora had tried to escape so many times before, but after assuring his men he had the situation well in hand and instructing them where to set two large bags they were carrying, the men left to take their seats in a different car, leaving her alone with the duke again.

Apprehension swept through her when the door to the Pullman car closed with a bang and the duke locked that door and turned.

"Ah, now isn't this cozy?" he asked, moving to a round table that was covered with dinnerware, two silver-domed dishes already waiting for them.

"I'm sure you're longing to freshen up," the duke began, nodding to the small retiring room included in the Pullman car. "I've taken the liberty of purchasing you a few essentials—corsets, stockings, petticoats, shoes, and, of course, a few delightful frocks." He nodded to one of the large satchels his men had left behind. "You'll find everything in there."

Thankful for an excuse to get out of the duke's presence, Isadora snatched up the satchel and hauled it to the small retiring room, breathing out a breath she hadn't realized she'd been holding. Stripping herself from her soiled clothing, she splashed water from the small sink over her face, finding a cloth beside the sink that she used to scrub the dirt from her hands, arms, and even legs. It took several minutes to get into the corset the duke had chosen for her, her skin crawling again when she imagined him picking it out and knowing he'd been picturing her in that corset as he'd selected it.

Twisting her hair into a simple knot at the back of her head, she secured it with pins she found in the satchel. Then, and not bothering to glance at her reflection in the mirror, she drew in a deep breath, preparing herself for the unknown. As she released the breath, she said a small prayer for courage, not knowing if God would answer her prayer or not since she'd been remiss over the years in her relationship with Him.

It had been only after she'd gone to the service in Canonsburg that she'd realized a relationship with God wasn't the formal affair she'd always believed, not with how easily the people of Canonsburg seemed to embrace their faith. More importantly, though, they lived out that faith through kindness, which they'd extended to her without hesitation. That had shown her that even though she, along with many of her societal contemporaries, attended church every Sunday, the true spirit of faith had been woefully neglected. In fact, in all frankness, she'd often left all thought of God behind after those services, returning to her life of frivolity and certainly not striving to make anyone's life easier or . . .

"I'm losing patience."

Pulling herself back to the dreadful situation at hand, Isadora opened the door and walked across the train car, refusing a shudder when the duke's gaze all but devoured her.

"You'll be pleased to learn the terrapin is delicious, as is the lamb."

Having no choice but to take a seat and dine with the man, not when he was once again waving his pistol her way, Isadora settled into a chair. But then, in a blatant act of defiance, she reached across the table and snatched up the salt shaker she didn't wait for him to pass her. Then, after salting the lamb, she picked it up with her fingers, took a large bite, and proceeded to chew with her mouth open.

Disgust immediately flickered through the duke's eyes. "I won't tolerate your theatrics, Isadora, and you're putting me off my supper by showing me the contents of your mouth. You will cease immediately or you'll spend the rest of our journey hungry."

Setting down the lamb, she picked up a wineglass filled to the brim with Burgundy wine and took a large gulp but immediately spit the wine back into the glass when she recalled the duke had an unfortunate habit of poisoning people.

A second later, she watched as her plate was taken away from her, as was her wine glass, the duke resuming his seat as he sent her a look of annoyance. "I told you—no more theatrics."

"Spitting my wine out wasn't theatrics. It was more an attempt to make it more difficult for you to poison me."

He stuffed a piece of terrapin in his mouth, chewed it, swallowed, then let out a very unrefined belch. "Someone's been listening to unfounded rumors and accusations."

"I don't know how the rumors could be considered unfounded when all three of your wives have ended up dead."

Blotting his lips with a linen napkin, he smiled. "An excellent point, but I don't care to discuss my previous wives—or poison, for that matter. Aren't you curious as to how I was able to track you down?"

"I would imagine that boiled down to luck."

"Or my tenacity to never accept defeat when it comes to something I want, and, my dear, I do want you."

As the train began to pull out of the station, Isadora realized any chance of escape was now impossible, not that she would purposely try to escape unless she could render the duke incapable of sending that message to his man. Settling back into her chair, she forced a belch of her own, ignored the narrowing of the duke's eyes, then propped her feet on top of the table, realizing she'd gone too far when he threw a potato at her.

Thankfully his aim was less than accurate, but because she didn't want him to toss what seemed to be creamed spinach her way next, she took her feet off the table, sat up in her chair, then immediately slouched back down after he sent her an approving smile.

"You're beginning to annoy me."

"I'm surprised you didn't discover that I have a few annoying tendencies when you were questioning everyone in Newport about me."

"You've apparently kept those tendencies well hidden because members of Newport society had only the most glowing things to say about you."

"That's because most of us in society don't know each other all that well, no matter how often we attend the same social events."

"Do you want to know how I ran you to ground or not?"

"Since you're probably going to tell me no matter my answer, by all means, divulge away."

He slurped a spoonful of creamed spinach, then met her gaze. "It was a brilliant strategy on my part. Because, you see, after I learned you'd fled New York, I realized you were a lady prone to games."

"I wasn't playing a game."

He ignored that. "I'm very good at games—I always win—so I decided the best strategy I could invoke would be that of waiting you out. I then sent my men to watch over your house. They were instructed to intercept any mail, messages, or telegrams that might be delivered there." He spooned another bit of creamed spinach into his mouth. "You would not believe how many disappointments I suffered, what with the messages I had to plow through regarding fish deliveries, invitations, and letters from distant relatives complaining about their many illnesses." He smiled. "I do hope your mother won't be too put out with me if she learns I'm behind why she wasn't invited to some of the mundane frivolities New York offers in the summer. Do tell her, though, that I enjoyed the play she'd been invited to attend, one she wouldn't have known was taking place after I absconded with her invitation."

"My mother is back in New York?"

"Of course. What type of mother would she be if she neglected to return after she was notified that you'd taken flight?"

"What of my father?"

"He, thankfully, has not returned." A bead of sweat appeared on the duke's forehead, but he immediately wiped it away. "Fathers have been known to be somewhat reluctant to marry their daughters off to me in the past, so it's a fortuitous circumstance that your father seems to have a great liking for making himself scarce in New York."

"He's expected home any day."

"'Any day' is a day too late for you, my dear. But getting back to my story. My patience finally paid off when a telegram was delivered to your home, sent by a Mr. Nigel Flaherty, who'd apparently become aware of your whereabouts. He very kindly included an address of where to find you, and after intercepting that telegram, I, along with a few of my most trusted men, made haste to Pittsburgh."

"When did you arrive?"

"A few hours before you and I were finally reunited. I was forced to have my rented carriage travel up and down that street, waiting for you to finally step out of the house without one of those pesky children with you, or that elderly couple." He took another slurp of creamed spinach. "My efforts clearly paid off because here you are, and we can now move forward with our lives."

"And are we to move forward with our lives on the first ship bound for England?"

"Don't be ridiculous. I'm remarkably short on funds now, what with how much I had to dole out to find you. I need your dowry."

"And you think because we've now been alone together that I'm sufficiently ruined enough to where my parents won't hesitate to turn over that dowry to you in order to save my reputation?"

"I don't want anyone to believe I'm marrying soiled goods," the duke countered. "Although . . . you didn't allow that MacKenzie to take liberties with your person, did you?"

It would have been so easy to say that she had allowed Ian liberties, which might have disgusted the duke so much he'd abandon his plan to wed her. But then, realizing the duke would see that as a challenge and knowing she could never put Ian in that type of danger, even though he was most likely capable of handling it, she shook her head.

"Mr. MacKenzie is too much of a gentleman to take liberties with the help."

"I'm a gentleman, and yet I've often . . ." The duke stopped talking, narrowed his eyes at her, then returned to his spinach, not lifting his head until he consumed the entire bowl. Releasing another belch, he leaned back in his chair. "As I was saying, I won't tolerate gossip being spread about my duchess, which is why no one will learn of our time alone together, not even your parents."

"What?"

"Information like that is far too easily overheard by members of the staff, so all your parents will know is that you were trying to whet my appetite for you, which had you so foolishly running away. Then you sent me a personal message, telling me where to come fetch you, and I, being a magnanimous sort, gave in to your demands and married you."

"And that marriage is to take place . . . ?"

"Tomorrow afternoon. We're even now heading back to New York City, where we'll then take a carriage to the harbor. I, through the proficiency of my men, have found an accommodating captain of a most derelict ship named *The Tempest*. That captain, I'm pleased to report, has agreed to marry us."

"And then we'll repair to my parents' home and inform them of our marriage?"

"Indeed, which will then see your lovely dowry being turned over to me, which will then provide me with the funds I need to purchase passage for us back to London."

Isadora frowned. "But what if I refuse to go through with this marriage ceremony with you?"

"That, my dear, would be a grave error on your part. If you've forgotten, my man is still in Pittsburgh, awaiting further instruction. You wouldn't want me to instruct him to . . . seek out those adorable children, would you?"

Bile rose in Isadora's throat as she shook her head.

"Wonderful," the duke exclaimed as he lifted his glass of wine to her. "And with that settled, allow me to toast my lovely bride-to-be."

CHAPTER 35

"You should at least send a telegram to make certain Izzie made it back to New York City."

Dragging his attention from a copy of *The Taming of the Shrew* he'd picked up in Pittsburgh only that morning, Ian met Aunt Birdie's gaze and shook his head.

"She left without telling any of us good-bye. That is clear proof Izzie, or rather Isadora, wants nothing more to do with us. She probably wouldn't even respond to a telegram from me."

"That's your pride talking, son," Uncle Amos said, looking up from the newspaper he'd been reading. "And while I know you were deeply hurt by Izzie withholding the truth about her identity, in my humble opinion, you overreacted."

"She made a fool of me—a fool of us all."

"She didn't. She merely neglected to tell us about her unfortunate upbringing."

Ian arched a brow his uncle's way. "How could growing up in the lap of luxury be an unfortunate upbringing?"

Uncle Amos arched a brow of his own. "Because Izzie isn't a woman meant to be stifled. She's a woman who needs her freedom. I doubt she found much freedom in the confines of high society, but she found that freedom with us."

"Again, she left without saying good-bye. And while I think she did that to lessen the pain of saying good-bye to the children, she's left them feeling abandoned, a devastating feeling I know from personal experience."

"As I've said before," Aunt Birdie countered, "her leaving in such an unexpected manner was quite out of character. That, to me, proves she was overly distraught and not thinking clearly." She nodded. "Frankly, I think we should do more than merely send her a telegram. I think we should go and see her in person."

"I have far too much work to do to travel to New York."

"You only have that tremendous amount of work pouring into your office because you listened to my counsel regarding how I've always believed God had a better plan for you all along—one that sees you working with the common men over the wealthy ones. Because it *was* my counsel that helped you find your true purpose in life, I would think you'd listen to my counsel now and realize I'm right."

For a moment, Ian didn't respond because what his aunt had said was nothing less than the truth. After he'd decided to throw in his lot with the laborers instead of the investors and owners of the mills, he felt as if a great weight had been lifted from his shoulders.

There was always a line of union men and laborers waiting for him at his Pittsburgh office, and he couldn't refute Aunt Birdie's claim that God had different plans for him than those he'd imagined, those plans using the education he'd been fortunate enough to obtain for a greater purpose than merely building up a personal fortune.

Knowing he could no longer ignore the needs of the working man, he'd turned his back on the many requests he'd had to continue representing the owners and investors. He decided he was only going to put his skills as an attorney and negotiator to use by seeking justice for those without a voice.

Even with that decision, though, he still felt as if a part of him was missing, and he knew that part was Izzie.

He'd confessed to her that he held her in affection, but it wasn't mere affection he held for the woman . . . it was love.

Unfortunately, he was well aware he'd left her convinced that his affection for her was dead, so even if he took his aunt's advice and inquired about her welfare, he couldn't very well expect her to—

Henry took that moment to race into the room, Elmer, unsurprisingly, tucked under his arm. He skidded to a stop in front of Ian, looking determined. "I need to ask a favor."

"You want to teach Buttercup how to climb stairs so she won't continue standing at the bottom of those stairs, mooing in a pathetic fashion and making everyone feel sorry for her?" he asked.

Henry's eyes widened. "That's a great idea, but that's not the favor I want to ask."

"What's the favor, then?"

"I want you to take me and the girls to New York to see Izzie."

Of anything Ian had been expecting, that hadn't been it. "I don't think that's a good idea."

"Do you have a better idea that would have Prim, Violet, and Daisy happy again—one that wouldn't see them cryin' so much?"

"They've been crying?"

"All the time, but they hide it from you so you won't feel bad since we know you must be missin' Izzie as much as we are." Henry stepped closer and dropped his voice to a whisper. "Maybe you could tell her you was sorry about yellin' at her, and then for not talkin' to her, and for whatever that was about some society ladder."

"How did you hear about a society ladder?"

"Izzie used to talk to herself a lot. She said somethin' about it was just as well you were so mad at her 'cuz she'd never know for certain if you wanted her around for herself or for a society ladder, but I don't know what that means."

A sliver of regret slid through him. He'd been so indignant about what he'd felt were her blatant lies that he'd not actually allowed himself to consider the reasoning behind why she'd withheld the truth from him for so long.

She'd told him she just wanted him to continue treating her like a normal woman, and she'd evidently convinced herself that he would begin treating her differently because of his well-known goal of wanting to marry a lady of high society.

The only problem with that, though, was that he no longer cared about society. He'd felt emptier somehow after leaving Miss Moore's ball, even though his reputation was still intact. What he cared about instead was the welfare of the children he had made officially his, Aunt Birdie and Uncle Amos, the people of Canonsburg, the men who needed him to represent them, and . . . Izzie.

Izzie was important to him.

He lifted his head right as Prim, Violet, and Daisy walked slowly into the room, their little faces pale and their expressions solemn.

"See, I told you," Henry whispered as Ian got up from his chair and motioned for the girls to join him.

"Henry has just asked me for a favor," he began.

"He wants permission to teach Buttercup how to walk up the stairs?" Prim asked.

"No, it's far more important than that, but just to be clear, Buttercup really is going to have to stop being allowed in the house."

"She's lonely without her friends from the farm," Violet said as her little lip began to tremble. "Just like we're lonely 'cuz we're missin' Izzie."

Lifting Violet up into his arms, Ian placed a kiss on her forehead and smiled at Prim and Daisy, who'd joined Henry and were watching him somewhat warily.

"I'm missing Izzie too," he admitted. "Which is why I'm going to grant Henry's request. We're going on a trip, one to see if we can convince Izzie to come home, but—" he caught Henry's eye— "Buttercup is going to have to stay behind."

CHAPTER 36

By the time Ian arranged to have a Pullman car attached to a train that was headed directly to New York City, and managed to get the children, Aunt Birdie, Uncle Amos, Miss Olive, and Jonathon packed, entire hours had disappeared. It had also taken hours to get to New York, even with the train making no stops as it trundled through the night. Finally, though, with his pocket watch displaying the time as being close to noon, they'd reached their destination.

Turning to the children, who were sitting in the rented carriage outside of Izzie's impressive Fifth Avenue home, he smiled. "We're here. And I know this is a lot to ask of you, but I think it would be best if I go in alone. Pave the way, so to speak."

That idea was quickly dismissed when Henry, Violet, and Daisy declared they had an urgent need to use a retiring room, and Prim proclaimed she had an urgent need to see Izzie.

Thankful, at least, that Aunt Birdie and Uncle Amos, along with Miss Olive and Jonathon, were content to wait in the other carriage he'd rented, Ian picked up Daisy, took hold of Violet's hand, and headed for the imposing front door with Henry and Prim by his side, and with Henry wriggling in a way that lent credence to the idea he really needed a retiring room.

A dignified-looking gentleman sporting a formal dark coat and matching trousers opened the door before they reached it. The man took one look at Ian and the children and seemed ready to close the door on them.

"We're here to see Miss Isadora Delafield," Ian hurried to say, his words having the man pause as his gaze sharpened on Ian.

"And you would be?"

"I'm Mr. Ian MacKenzie, and . . ."

"We're the children who love Izzie, and we've come to bring her back home with us," Prim said, surprising Ian by speaking so directly to a man who was almost as imposing as the house. "Are you Izzie's father?"

"I'm Mr. Godkin, the butler, but perhaps all of you should come inside. Miss Isadora's father has only just arrived home from a trip, and he and Mrs. Delafield are currently having a . . . discussion in the library."

"Beggin' your pardon, sir," Henry said, jumping from one foot to the other. "But do you have a retiring room? Me and my sisters need one powerful bad."

With his lips curving just a touch at the corners, Mr. Godkin ushered everyone inside and then took Henry by the hand, leading him and Violet down a long hallway, Daisy scampering to catch up after Ian set her down. "I'll be back directly," Mr. Godkin said over his shoulder. "Feel free to seek out the library on your own. It's down that hallway to your right. You'll know which one since you'll be able to hear . . . the voices."

"I'll go watch over the girls," Prim said, rushing after Mr. Godkin.

Not wanting to dawdle in the entranceway, and finding it somewhat curious that Mr. Godkin hadn't told him he'd tell Izzie she had guests, Ian strode down the hallway opposite the one the children had taken, raised voices guiding his way.

". . . completely beyond the pale for you to have encouraged a man Isadora evidently didn't want to marry . . ."

"He's a duke. How could I not encourage her, Frederick? It's every mother's dream to have her daughter married well."

"You're not the one having to marry a man I have to believe is completely unsuitable, especially given his age, for my Isadora, and . . ."

Knocking on the partially closed door because he certainly didn't want to allow Isadora's parents to believe he was the type to skulk around eavesdropping, Ian braced himself when his knock caused the argument to come to an abrupt end. Footsteps sounded a second later, and then the door swung open, revealing a very large, very angry-looking gentleman and a very petite, albeit furious-looking woman who resembled Izzie standing behind him.

"Forgive me for interrupting," Ian began. "I'm Mr. Ian Mac-Kenzie, and I'm a friend of your daughter, Miss Isadora Delafield."

The woman's dark brows drew together. "My daughter does not know anyone by the name of MacKenzie."

"Begging your pardon, Mrs. Delafield, but I believe she does. She's been staying with my family in Pennsylvania ever since she left New York."

"But . . . that's preposterous," Mrs. Delafield all but sputtered as Isadora's father's gaze suddenly sharpened on Ian's face, holding a touch of anticipation.

"I'm Frederick Delafield, Mr. MacKenzie, and I'm hoping you're now going to tell me that you've brought our Isadora home."

The floor seemed to lurch underneath Ian's feet. "I thought she'd be here."

"She's not with you?"

"She left yesterday after we . . . well, no need to get into that because we've got bigger problems. She should have been back to New York by now."

"She was traveling by herself?"

"That's what I assumed, although she didn't bother to say good-bye or take her trunk with her."

"And you didn't believe that was peculiar?"

"I did, but you see, we'd had a bit of a disagreement, and I told her I really didn't want to have anything to do with her after . . ."

Ian frowned. "Wait a minute, did you not receive a telegram from Mr. Nigel Flaherty, telling you where to find Izzie in Pittsburgh?"

"Who is Nigel Flaherty? And no, we've received no telegrams or messages of late, which has been somewhat perplexing," Mrs. Delafield said before she raised a hand to her throat. "But what if Isadora's been harmed, and how are we to find her without knowing where she could be?"

Frederick moved to Mrs. Delafield's side and drew her close to him. "We'll find her, Hester, but I'm going to need you to remain strong while I set a plan into action." He looked to Ian. "Are you sure she was intending to make her way back to New York?"

"I assumed so, but . . ." His words trailed off when what could only be described as a whirlwind entered the room. At first, he thought he was looking at a young man, but upon closer reflection, he realized that standing before him was a young woman dressed in riding pants that one would expect to see a gentleman wearing at a horse park, complete with top hat and riding crop.

"I do apologize for interrupting, but Mr. Hatfield and I were just down by the harbor and saw your yacht anchored there, Mr. Delafield. We've been waiting for you to . . ." The young lady's voice trailed off as she settled her sights on Ian right as the children came rushing into the library, Daisy bellowing "Izzie, Izzie" at the top of her lungs.

A second later, silence descended as the children stopped in their tracks, turning their heads this way and that as they evidently tried to locate Izzie.

"Where's Izzie, Ian?" Prim demanded.

"On my word, are you Ian MacKenzie?" the young lady dressed as a man asked, striding across the room to stand directly in front of him. "Izzie sent me a telegram telling me she was staying with you, but . . . where is she?"

"I don't know," Ian said quietly before he nodded to the children. "But I don't think we should continue this conversation with them in the room."

Something flashed through the young lady's eyes before she

turned to the children and smiled. "Children, I'm Miss Beatrix Waterbury, Izzie's very best friend. And while she's not presently here, a few of us are about to go and bring her home—and no, you can't come with us," she said to Henry, who was already heading for the door. He stopped and turned, looking mutinous.

"But Izzie will want to see us. We're her best children."

"I'm sure you are, but you can't come with us." Beatrix turned and nodded to Mrs. Delafield. "Instead, Izzie's mother, Mrs. Delafield, is going to take you up to the nursery and show you where Izzie lived when she was a little girl. I know Izzie still has all sorts of toys up there she'd want you to play with until she gets home."

"We don't want to play," Violet said, her lip trembling. "We want Izzie."

Beatrix crouched down next to the little girl. "I know you do, darling, but you need to go with Mrs. Delafield right now. That will let the rest of us get on with bringing Izzie back."

Prim, having proven herself an intuitive sort, stepped forward. "We'd love to see Izzie's nursery. Violet, Henry, Daisy, come with me." She nodded to Mrs. Delafield. "I'm Prim, ma'am, and I'll introduce my brother and sisters while we go up to the nursery. After that, I bet you'll want to hear about the adventures we've had with Izzie so far, especially the ones with Elmer."

"I left Elmer in the carriage," Henry said, panic in his voice.

"Where she's fine since she's safely enclosed in a basket," Ian pointed out.

Even though their departure was marked with muttering, the children did follow Mrs. Delafield, who was looking somewhat overwhelmed at being tasked with watching over four children. After they disappeared from sight, Ian turned back to Beatrix.

"What is it? What do you know? And don't tell me nothing because I could tell by the look in your eye moments ago that something important sprang to mind."

"Clearly, Izzie's been telling tales about me, but . . ." Beatrix looked to Frederick. "I've known all along where Izzie was, sir, but she had reason to be hiding, as we were concerned that the Duke of Montrose might try to force her into marriage with him. There's no time to explain more, other than to say that Izzie wanted me to come here just as soon as you got home and tell you where she was, knowing you would be able to help."

"Why do I get the impression this 'we' you just mentioned involves more people than you and Isadora?" Frederick asked slowly.

"That's because the plan to get Izzie spirited out of the city was all due to the brilliant strategic abilities of Mr. Godkin and Mr. Hatfield, two men I'm going to say right now should be commended and not disciplined. But we'll delve into that later. Izzie recently sent me a telegram telling me she was with Mr. MacKenzie and that she was fine, but . . ." She blew out a breath. "She's apparently not fine because if she'd left Pittsburgh on her own accord, she would have sent another telegram to let me know when to expect her back in the city."

"Do you think you have an idea where she might be now?" Frederick asked.

"Perhaps. Mr. Hatfield and I were just down by the harbor, and after we noticed your yacht there, we thought we caught a glimpse of the duke making his way down a dock. In all honesty, I was relieved because I thought that meant Izzie was still safe from him, but . . . what if he has her? What if he's already set sail for London?"

"Can you show me where you saw this duke?" Ian demanded, and after Beatrix nodded, he strode beside her toward the door, Frederick following a mere step behind.

"You can take Mr. Hatfield's horse," Beatrix said to Ian, moving through the door Mr. Godkin was already holding open for them. Another man Ian assumed was Mr. Hatfield called out to him to be careful since his horse tended to be on the temperamental side.

"I'll take my phaeton. It's right outside," Frederick said, turning to the right and heading for a horse and phaeton that were parked a short distance away.

"Take Jonathon with you," Ian called to Frederick as Jonathon jumped from the carriage he'd been waiting in. "Izzie's in trouble. We need to get to her quickly."

Jonathon needed no other urging. Running, he leapt into Frederick's phaeton. After calling to Uncle Amos and Aunt Birdie to wait for them in the house, Ian swung up on the horse next to Beatrix's, galloping beside Beatrix down the well-paved road a second later.

Thankful that Beatrix obviously knew the city well, he concentrated on dodging the traffic that was clogging the streets, as well as fighting to keep the horse he was on going in the right direction. Bile began to rise in his throat as he raced through the streets and couldn't stop considering every terrible thing that could have happened to Izzie if the duke had indeed found her.

Reining his horse to a halt what seemed like days later when they reached the docks, he looked around the harbor, having no idea where to start his search.

"He was over there," Beatrix said, swinging down from her horse and pointing to a dock filled with boats. "We'll have to ask around, see if anyone saw the duke."

With Jonathon and Frederick soon joining them, they rushed to the dock, questioning everyone they encountered on whether they'd seen a rather large man in the company of a beautiful woman.

"I don't know if that woman was beautiful or not since she was wearing a cloak," a ragged-looking sailor finally told Ian. "But the man with her was certainly large, and the men he had with him weren't any I'd want to meet in a dark alley. They got on that boat named *The Tempest*. It's right over there. Still docked."

Barely remembering to thank the man, Ian ran for *The Tempest*, finding his way onto that ship blocked by three men who looked intimidating but who weren't blocking his way for long.

Leaving the men moaning on the deck, Ian picked up his pace, running down the first companionway he encountered, drawn to someone speaking what sounded like words of a wedding ceremony.

Slipping through the door from which the voice was coming, fury ignited in his veins at the sight that met his eyes.

Izzie was standing face-to-face with a portly gentleman, her lips pressed tightly together, but there was a large man behind her, pushing her head up and down in a nodding motion.

The man Ian assumed was the Duke of Montrose suddenly spoke up. "She's clearly nodding, which means yes, she will take me to be her . . ."

Ian didn't wait to hear anything else. With his long legs eating up the space that separated him from Izzie, he was soon standing directly before her, but he didn't do anything more than catch her eye before he turned to the duke, planting his fist squarely against the man's jaw.

That was all that was needed to have the man crumpling to the ground, but then the rest of the duke's men let out yells of rage, rushing toward Ian. Pushing Isadora out of the way, Ian, for the first time in what felt like forever, allowed the fury to burst out of him, and with the help of Frederick, Jonathon, and even Beatrix, who was wielding a dripping mop she'd apparently plucked from a bucket somewhere, they quickly had the situation well in hand. Soon, all the duke's men were on the ground, not moving so much as a single muscle, probably because Frederick and Jonathan were training pistols on them.

"You're all fools."

Glancing toward the Duke of Montrose, who was still on the ground, Ian arched a brow right as the man released a laugh that was anything but pleasant.

"You can't stop me from marrying Isadora. We've been alone together since we left Pittsburgh. She's a ruined woman now, unless she marries me, of course."

Ian looked up and found Izzie watching him with wide eyes that seemed to be filled with apprehension. "She doesn't look ruined to me," Ian said simply. "In fact, she looks like the most beautiful woman I've ever seen in my life."

His feet were suddenly in motion, and then he was standing before the woman he knew he loved with all his heart. Reaching out, he pulled her close, and when she leaned into him, he took that as a sign she was happy to see him, which was exactly why he kissed her.

CHAPTER 37

The second Ian's lips touched hers, Isadora felt the terror she'd been trying to hold at bay disappear because . . . she was safe.

And because Ian's lips were now firmly pressed against her own, she had a feeling she'd be safe for many, many years to come.

"You'll be made to look the fool if you declare yourself now, my boy. She's ruined goods, she is, and no man wants to saddle himself with ruined goods."

Ian pulled his lips from hers, and she braced herself for rejection because the duke had spoken nothing but the truth—she *was* considered ruined in the eyes of society because she had spent time alone with the dastardly duke, not that he'd touched her except to shove a pistol in her ribs when she was misbehaving, but society would think the worst. Ian might not believe the duke, but he'd made it perfectly clear how he felt about being made to look foolish, and . . .

"If people want to call me a fool for being with Izzie, so be it," Ian surprised her by saying as he took her hand and brought it to his lips, catching her eye. "Truth be told, I call *myself* a fool because I almost allowed you to slip away from me."

The simple act of drawing breath became difficult to accomplish, but before she could get a single word out of her mouth, Ian was turning back to the duke, a surprisingly pleasant smile on his face, but a hint of fury still in his eyes.

"Just to be clear, though, there won't be any mention of Izzie being alone with you. You'll keep your mouth shut, even after you and your men find yourselves behind bars."

"You can't very well have me arrested if you want to keep it quiet about Isadora having a bit of an adventure with me."

"It wasn't an adventure, it was an abduction," Ian countered.

"And after the police hear about what happened to your previous three wives, you'll never be able to abduct another unwilling heiress again," said Beatrix, whom Isadora just then realized she had yet to even greet. "And before you plead ignorance to doing away with your previous wives, do know that Mr. Hatfield, a man you once dismissed from service, is all too willing to tell the authorities about the suspicious circumstances surrounding their deaths."

"And even though I'm grateful everyone seems to want to protect my reputation," Isadora added, "I want to file a report about what he put me through. I certainly don't want to take the chance of him perpetrating such a crime again if he's allowed to go free."

The duke chuckled as he propped himself up on his elbows. "And who do you honestly think the authorities are going to believe—a woman or a duke?"

"I would imagine they'll believe my daughter, since I am known as one of the most influential and, need I add, wealthy industrialists in the country—if not the world," Frederick said, stepping forward.

The next moment, Isadora found herself pulled into her father's embrace, Frederick rubbing her back with a large hand.

"You've given me quite the fright."

"I'm sure I have, and I am sorry about that, Father."

"You ran away."

Isadora glanced to the duke, then back to her father. "Can you blame me?"

Frederick smiled. "Not at all, and do know that I'll be having a long chat with that mother of yours about the circumstances leading up to your flight."

"She is *your* wife, if you've forgotten, not merely my mother."

"I might have forgotten, but further conversation about that needs to wait." Frederick nodded to Jonathon. "You mind helping me get this man and his cohorts to a police station?"

Jonathon smiled. "It would be my pleasure, and along the way, allow me to tell you all about your daughter's role as a household manager."

"What is a household manager?" Frederick asked.

"Well, you see, sir, no one actually knows. Especially your daughter." Sending her a grin along with a wink, Jonathon began moving toward the men on the ground, stopping when an entire swarm of policemen suddenly entered the room. With one word from Frederick, with whom all of them were familiar, they didn't hesitate to begin securing the duke and his men, ignoring the threats the duke was now spewing with rapid intensity.

Frederick looked to Ian. "I'm still going to go down to the station to ascertain no one allows the duke to escape. You'll see my girl home, as well as Beatrix?"

"Of course."

When Ian took hold of her hand, she didn't protest, grinning at Beatrix, who was looking at their entwined hands with a raised brow. Holding out her other hand to her dearest friend, Isadora turned her back on the duke and strode away from a man she never wanted to see again. She felt Ian squeeze her hand, and with Beatrix on her other side, she made her way off the boat, down the dock, and toward what she was remarkably certain was now going to be a most splendid future.

⁂

Two hours later, sitting with Daisy on her lap and Violet and Prim pressed up against either side of her, with Henry at her feet, Isadora gazed around the drawing room, not quite certain how it had happened that she'd been snatched from a most dreadful fate and reunited with the ones she loved.

The children had been ecstatic to see her, not allowing her to get a single apology out about leaving without a proper good-bye as they'd hugged her tightly with their little arms, Henry informing her that he was never letting her out of his sight again.

"Elmer!" Daisy suddenly yelled, lifting her head from where she'd been leaning it against Isadora's shoulder as she pointed toward the door.

Sure enough, Elmer was running through the doorway, looking remarkably ruffled as Uncle Amos suddenly strode into the room, holding a basket and looking somewhat sheepish. "We forgot her in the carriage."

"Should I ask what a chicken is doing in my drawing room?" Hester said to no one in particular.

"It's clearly a pet," Frederick said. "And no, you're not going to demand it's taken outside."

Hester drew herself up, but then she suddenly seemed to deflate right before Isadora's eyes. "You always wanted a pet, and I never let you have one." And then, to Isadora's amazement, her mother released a sob and fled from the room.

"I'll be right back," she said, setting Daisy on her feet and heading after Hester.

"Mother, wait," she called, having to break into a bit of a trot when Hester seemed to increase her pace.

She finally caught up with her in the green room, her mother's favorite room in the house and the place Hester always retreated to whenever she was upset.

"What's wrong?" she asked, moving to stand next to her mother by the floor-to-ceiling window.

"My foolishness could have seen you married to a man who might have murdered you someday."

"True, but it's not as if you were acting any differently from all the other societal mothers. I will say, though, that I do hope you'll abandon your lofty goals for me because I, no matter how much you may desire it, won't be marrying a man with a title."

"Of course your mother will abandon those goals," Frederick said, striding into the room and drawing Isadora's attention.

"She's not going to have much choice in the matter since I've decided she won't be participating in the New York high season this year and may not participate in the season for years to come."

Hester dashed a tear from her face and lifted her chin. "I most assuredly will be participating in the season, and I don't like you telling me what to do."

"You'll listen to what I have to say, Hester, if you want any chance of making our marriage work. I'm willing to give us that chance, which is why I'm going to suggest that you, instead of enjoying the coming season, travel with me to Europe to visit our sons, and then bring them home."

"But I don't like to sail."

"You used to love to sail, back in the days when we actually liked each other, before I became consumed with business and you became consumed with society. That's why I want us to bring our boys home. It's time for them to take over the family business, something I've been reluctant to give up until now. But that, my dear, will allow us time to rediscover each other and hopefully reclaim the love we did, at one time, have for each other."

When her mother got a rather sappy look on her face, one Isadora had never seen in her life, she quickly excused herself and, if she wasn't much mistaken, the moment she quit the room she thought her father might have drawn her mother into his arms and kissed her.

Smiling at that odd turn of events, Isadora walked back to the drawing room, arching a brow when everyone in that room—Ian, Aunt Birdie, Uncle Amos, Beatrix, Miss Olive, Jonathon, Prim, Henry, Violet, Daisy, and even Elmer—turned her way.

"Should I ask?" was all she could think to say.

Henry stepped forward and puffed out his little chest. "We've got things to tell you, Izzie, so you might want to sit down and get comfortable."

Not quite able to hide a grin, Isadora sat down on a settee next to Beatrix, turning her attention back to Henry. "I'm listening."

"We've come to bring you home," he began. "And we're not taking no for an answer."

"How delightful."

"Oh." Henry grinned. "I thought you might make it trickier, seeing as how this is your home and it's pretty nice, 'specially the nursery your mother showed us."

"My mother showed you the nursery?"

"She did," Prim said. "And she's having some of your dolls packed up to go home with me, Violet, and Daisy, as long as that's all right with you."

"I'd love for you to have my dolls."

"We're not here to talk dolls," Henry said, rolling his eyes. "I wasn't done tellin' you why we want to take you home."

Isadora fought another grin. "Go on."

Henry looked to Aunt Birdie, who sent him a nod before he looked back to Isadora. "Aunt Birdie says home is where your heart is, and we think your heart is with us. So we want you to come home. But that's all I'm supposed to say, and now it's Ian's turn." Henry waved Ian forward, and Ian moved to stand in front of Isadora, giving Henry's hair a ruffle.

"We made him practice on the train ride here what he's supposed to say," Prim said before Ian could speak, earning a wink from him in return.

"They were quite the critics," he said as her parents walked into the drawing room, Hester's cheeks a lovely shade of pink.

Isadora couldn't help but notice that her father was holding her mother's hand, but before she could think more on that encouraging sign, Ian cleared his throat.

"If the two of you would find a seat, I'll get on with matters before Henry ends up taking over and saying everything to your daughter I'm supposed to say."

Hester and Frederick were sitting down in a blink of an eye, watching Ian a little warily, but smiling at him at the same time. "You may continue," Hester said with a regal nod.

Ian returned the nod and moved to stand closer to Isadora.

Blowing out a breath, he smiled. "Before I begin with what the children and I decided I should say, I do have a few matters of business to discuss."

Isadora frowned. "You want to discuss business *now*?"

"Indeed, because there are things I've decided to change, and you need to be apprised of those changes and agree to them before I move on to what the children believe is the good stuff."

Isadora found herself intrigued, as well as knowing she had to let him say his piece before he got on with the *good stuff*, which was something she was beginning to think might very well change her life forever. "I'm listening."

"I've decided I'm no longer going to represent the mill owners and investors, instead offering my legal services and ability to negotiate fair contracts for the men who actually work in the mills."

"I would expect nothing less."

Ian blinked. "Ah, well, that was easy, but offering my legal services to those men will mean living in Shadyside, since it's close to Pittsburgh."

"I love your house in Shadyside, and I've got some wonderful ideas about how to finish furnishing and decorating it."

"I didn't know you liked decorating," Hester said, retreating into silence when little Violet put a finger to her lips.

"Also," Ian continued after he sent Violet a grin, "as you might recall, I'm in the process of purchasing quite a few farms that surround Glory Manor."

"I remember."

"Well, some of those farmers still want to work their land, which I told them they're more than welcome to do. But a few of the farmers want to move to a warmer climate, so . . . I'm buying sheep to graze on one of the farms."

Isadora nodded. "Because Maggie has a woman in mind who enjoys raising sheep, and that woman needs a job."

Ian's brows drew together. "Well, yes, but I don't want you to believe I'm buying sheep simply because I'm an overly generous sort. There's much profit to be made with sheep, and . . ."

"Having a flock of sheep will also create a need for additional workers, and Maggie did say there are many people anxious for work in Canonsburg," Isadora finished for him.

Ian frowned. "I'm trying to paint you a picture of the man I truly am so that you'll not experience any surprises in the future."

"I'm of the belief Izzie already knows the man you truly are, so you might want to move things along," Beatrix spoke up.

Isadora sent her friend a grin. "My sentiments exactly."

Ian shook his head and grinned as well. "I'm beginning to understand why the two of you are such fast friends. But I will try and wrap up the rest of what I need to disclose quickly."

Accepting the round of applause those words evoked, Ian presented everyone with a bow, then returned his attention to Isadora. "Because it seems the matter of the sheep has been put to rest, allow me to address the other plans I have for one of the farms I bought. Miss Norma, a woman you're going to adore, brought it to my attention that the orphanages in Pittsburgh are overcrowded. That's why I've decided to build an orphanage on one of the larger farms, which will allow the orphanages in Pittsburgh to have a place to send children when they run out of room." His gaze seemed to sharpen on her. "I've been thinking you're the woman to organize the planning of the orphanage for me."

Isadora felt a flash of disappointment sweep through her. "You came all this way to ask me to organize plans for an orphanage?"

"Of course not, but I'm not getting to that until I finish all of my disclosures."

Her disappointment faded straightaway, and she waved him on. "Fine, disclose away."

Ian took a single step toward her. "I don't want your money."

"Goodness," Hester breathed, raising a hand to her throat.

"That might be crossing the line," Isadora began, having a hard time keeping a smile off her face. "I suppose I can agree to that, but you'll need to understand that my father made arrangements for my fortune to be put into a trust with my name on it years ago. The money is mine, and don't think for a minute I'm going to hand it over to my brothers." She smiled. "I'm sure I'll be able to think of some purpose to put my fortune toward. And since that's now settled, what else?"

"I don't know how that can be considered settled because it seems to me as if you've still got quite a fortune," Ian said.

"It's settled in my mind because you don't want my money."

Ian glanced to Uncle Amos. "Do women ever get easier to understand?"

"Nope."

"How reassuring," he said with a sigh. "Where was I?"

"Disclosures," Beatrix provided helpfully.

"Right." He suddenly began looking rather nervous. "You might find this next disclosure to be one that really does cross the line."

"Go on."

"I don't want to travel in society."

A lovely warmth began spreading from her toes all the way through her body. She'd all but convinced herself that she'd never know for certain whether Ian appreciated her for herself or whether a part of him had appreciated her social status more. But now, what with his declaration about not wanting to travel in society, she knew she'd been worrying for nothing.

She cleared a throat that had turned constricted. "How delightful because I don't want to travel in society either."

He took another single step closer to her. "Are you certain about that? If I need remind you, your life up to this point has centered around New York high society. You'd be giving up a lot if you return with us to Pittsburgh."

"I won't be giving up anything, Ian." She rose from the chair. "I've discovered that I don't want to spend my life attending one ball after another, my only concerns being what I'm going to wear or what new dance steps I'll need to learn. I have a purpose in Pittsburgh, and I feel useful. I'll never regret leaving society, not if I have . . ." She stopped talking, not wanting to reveal too much until he finished whatever it was he needed to say.

"Well, good. That's good" was all he had to say to that, which wasn't exactly what she'd been expecting, but since he was looking remarkably pleased, she didn't have the heart to point out that he was an attorney, and *good* wasn't exactly the best word an attorney had at his disposal.

"So," he continued, "I've covered my job, the orphanage, the house in Pittsburgh, society, and . . ."

"Remember to tell her about Glory Manor and the children," Aunt Birdie called out.

"Ah, right." He nodded. "Aunt Birdie and Uncle Amos are going to help with the orphanage, inviting the children over often so they can fish with Uncle Amos and Aunt Birdie can teach them to cook."

"And Ian said me and my sisters get to visit Glory Manor all the time," Henry added. "But just so you know, Uncle Amos says we can keep Buttercup and Elmer with us at the house in Pittsburgh."

"And there you have it," Ian said. "I think we've covered everything."

"You didn't tell her that we decided we'd attend school in Pittsburgh so we wouldn't miss seeing you during the week when you're at work," Prim said.

"Right." He smiled at Isadora. "It was their idea to live in Pittsburgh but spend as many weekends as we can at Glory Manor."

"And we're going to spend time with you in Pittsburgh as well," Aunt Birdie added. "Amos and I don't want to miss out on seeing the children grow, so you can expect us to be frequent guests." She exchanged a smile with her husband. "We've decided that the big city isn't as bad as we thought, and we're perfectly content to divide our time between the farm and Ian's home in Shadyside. Although"—she caught Isadora's eye—"we might not be keen to travel to New York all that often." She gestured around. "This is a little too big."

"It can be overwhelming," Isadora agreed.

"And that, I believe, is everything," Ian said, glancing around with a look that almost dared anyone else to speak up, his brows drawing together when Beatrix suddenly raised her hand. "You wanted to add something?"

"I just want to say that I think you're a lovely man, but do know that Izzie is my closest friend, and if you hurt her, I think it should be noted that I'm a better shot than she is."

Ian inclined his head. "Yes, thank you for that, Beatrix. And now . . . to continue."

Isadora's knees began to wobble as he took her hand, kissed it, and smiled.

"The children want me to tell you that they love you."

Her vision immediately blurred from the tears that were now flooding her eyes. Directing her attention to the children, she summoned up what she knew had to be a wobbly smile. "I love all of you too."

She turned back to Ian, who reached out and brushed tears from her cheek.

"Should I continue, or do you need a moment?"

"I'm fine, but if you drag this out much longer, the children might stage a revolt."

The next second, she found him down on one knee, holding a ring up to her.

"I don't have much else to say except that I love you, Izzie Delafield. When you left, I found that my life didn't feel whole. If you'd be so kind as to agree to marry me, I promise to love you forever, and I'll do whatever is in my power to keep you happy, well loved, and safe."

She raised a hand to her lips, then smiled. "Do you remember when you told me I'd only truly be like Katherina from *The Taming of the Shrew* if I proclaimed myself madly in love with you, willing to abandon my demanding ways?"

"I thought you were going to punch me after I said that, so yes, I remember."

Her smile turned into a grin. "I might have been considering punching you, but . . . I do love you madly, although I really can't promise I'll never be demanding again."

Ian was on his feet so fast she barely had a moment to blink.

Slipping the ring he'd been holding onto her finger, he stilled. "You didn't say yes."

"I did, in my own way, but *yes*, it would be beyond my wildest dreams to become your wife."

Ian smiled as everyone broke into applause, and then he was kissing her.

She felt a tickle on her leg, then realized Elmer had snuck under her skirt. But since the chicken didn't peck her even one time, instead settling down on her foot and leaning against her leg, quite as if that was Elmer's way of letting Isadora know she'd missed her, Isadora pulled Ian closer. As she enjoyed the feel of that closeness, she knew she'd finally found the life she was meant to live. She'd been put on a path to a fulfilling life by a loving God, who'd known all along that Isadora was capable of living a life of purpose. She simply hadn't known how to find that purpose on her own.

Epilogue

October 1885

Sitting in the back of the wagon, her elaborate white wedding dress pooled around her, Isadora found the *clip-clop* of Clyde's hooves soothing as the wagon rumbled ever closer to the church in Canonsburg where she would be met at the end of the aisle by Ian, the man she couldn't wait another day to marry.

He'd recently presented her with a spectacular mare he'd purchased from Garrison Farms. But Ivy, named by the children, who'd thought it was appropriate to pay homage to a plant that had originally kept Izzie at Glory Manor, was rather spirited, so Isadora had chosen Clyde to pull the wagon, not willing to put the children sitting beside her in any harm.

She and Ian had decided to return to Garrison Farms in the near future to purchase additional ponies for the children because there were no finer ponies to be found than the ones Mr. Garrison and his family bred. That Ian had told her Mr. Garrison's troubling financial issues had been resolved, although he wasn't certain about the details, had been good news indeed. And she was looking forward to reacquainting herself with Miss Poppy Garrison, a lady she didn't know well, but one she thought could become a good friend.

Isadora smiled as she looked down at Daisy, who was sitting on her lap and playing with the heart-shaped locket Isadora had filled with the dried petals of the flowers the children had used when they'd made her the flower necklace. "It's pretty, isn't it?"

"Henry's chicken's pretty too." Daisy smiled her gap-toothed smile, touching the wooden chicken that was hooked at the top of the locket.

Elmer, the real chicken, released a squawk from where she was nestled on Henry's lap, earning a grin from Henry in return. That grin was at complete odds with the trembling lip he'd brought out earlier when Isadora had made the suggestion Elmer might want to stay at home instead of attending the church service.

"I see the church," her father said, turning his head to smile at her, holding the reins in a practiced hand as he steered Clyde down the main street in Canonsburg. "Looks like the entire town has turned out to watch you and Ian get married."

Leaning forward, Isadora saw buggies and wagons lining the street leading to the church, but there were no signs of any people. The good folks of Canonsburg obviously had already taken their seats, waiting for her to arrive.

Accepting her father's hand after he pulled the wagon to a stop in front of the church, she stepped to the ground, joined by the children. Hester and Aunt Birdie arrived a moment later, driven to the church in an open buggy with Beatrix at the reins, all three ladies looking windblown but not seeming overly concerned about that.

"She's a bit of a free spirit, your Beatrix," Aunt Birdie proclaimed as she looked Isadora over, her eyes suddenly turning bright with tears. "You do look beautiful, my dear, although I do miss those spectacles you used to wear all the time."

"I can't say I miss those," Isadora said, taking the hand Aunt Birdie held out to her and giving it a squeeze.

"Amos and I are simply delighted for you and Ian," Aunt Birdie said, dashing a handkerchief over her eyes. "I told you what seems like months ago that you'd arrived at Glory Manor to find your path, and . . ." She looked to the sky. "I can only thank God that you discovered that path and will now be a part of our lives forever."

Patting her on the cheek, Aunt Birdie turned and smiled when Henry offered her his arm. Telling everyone she'd see them inside, where she was going to check on Amos, who'd been given the honor of standing up with Ian as his best man, she walked away.

"Jonathon's sitting with Miss Olive," Henry all but shouted as he raced back to join his sisters a moment later. "I think we'll be seeing another weddin' soon."

Isadora kissed her mother on the cheek before taking the arm her father held out to her, drawing in a deep breath.

"You don't have to go through with this if you're having second thoughts," her father said, his lips curving into a grin.

She immediately began tugging him toward the door.

As Anna Gillespie applied herself to the organ with enthusiasm, Isadora watched as the children marched their way into the church, Daisy dressed in bright yellow, Violet dressed in purple, and Prim dressed in pink. Henry looked dashing in a blue suit, but not the velvet one Isadora had first thought to have him wear.

A collective sigh drifted through the now-open door of the church, and after Isadora allowed the children enough time to make it down the aisle, she took her place with her father, and then they walked into the church, pausing directly over the threshold.

It was filled to capacity with everyone from the community, as well as some of Ian's friends, her brothers, and even Miss Norma, who'd been helping with the orphanage that was well underway.

There was no need to worry that the dastardly Duke of Montrose would show up unexpectedly and ruin her day. After he'd been arrested what seemed like years ago, he had made the monumental mistake of descending into a bit of a tirade, screaming as he was held behind bars that he knew how to wield poison with great effect, especially since he had three dead wives to prove it. That tirade was directly responsible for the police charging him with murder.

Bertie, as many society ladies thought of him, although everyone else considered him the Prince of Wales, had stepped in and asked for the duke to be extradited to England, where Bertie promised to deal with him most severely.

True to his word, the Prince of Wales stripped the duke of his titles and his lands, and then had him committed to an asylum, where he was to spend the rest of his days guarded by the queen's men. By having the duke, whose name, amusingly enough, turned out to be Percival, committed to an asylum, England was spared the embarrassment of having a duke put on trial for murder, something Bertie wanted to avoid at all costs.

Feeling her father give her arm a bit of a squeeze, Isadora began walking with him down the aisle, beaming at everyone beaming back at her. She finally turned her full attention to the man waiting for her, her vision turning misty when Ian sent her a smile, one that was filled with love.

After placing her hand in Ian's, Frederick lifted aside the veil that was barely covering her face, kissed her cheek, and reminded Ian that Beatrix was an expert shot. As Ian grinned, Frederick stepped back, leaving her holding Ian's hand.

As Reverend Davis welcomed everyone and began the service, Isadora felt a sense of peace sweep through her, mixed with a great deal of anticipation.

Her future, she knew, was going to be something she'd never imagined, and she couldn't help but believe that God had thrown up the obstacles she'd had to overcome in order to get her where He wanted her to be.

After Reverend Davis proclaimed them man and wife, Ian took her face in his hands and kissed her, a kiss that was filled with promise and love, and a kiss that had her knees going wobbly.

Keeping a firm grip on her hand after he drew away, Ian turned them as one to face the congregation now on their feet and applauding the new husband and wife.

As the sun shone through a stained-glass window shaped in the form of a cross, Isadora felt her lips curve into a grin as she caught sight of Buttercup moseying through the door, Sparky by her side, although how they'd gotten to town was a bit of a mystery. Buttercup and Sparky were soon met by Elmer, who'd escaped from Henry and was clucking up a storm as she raced to join her friends.

"That's a sure sign our life is certain to never turn dull," Ian said, shaking his head and grinning as the children suddenly raced after Elmer, Violet and Daisy giving Buttercup and Sparky hugs as soon as they reached them, quite as if they'd been parted for years instead of a few hours.

"I wouldn't have it any other way," Isadora whispered, and then, with the man she could now call her husband by her side, she began walking down the aisle and into what was certainly going to be a most unusual, yet completely wonderful, life filled with love, laughter, and purpose.

Jen Turano, a *USA Today* bestselling author, is a graduate of the University of Akron with a degree in clothing and textiles. She is a member of ACFW and RWA. She lives in a suburb of Denver, Colorado. Visit her website at www.jenturano.com.